Bello:

hidden talent rediscovered

Bello is a digital only imprint of Pan Macmillan,
established to breathe new life into previously published,
classic books.

At Bello we believe in the timeless power of the imagination,
of good story, narrative and entertainment and we want to use
digital technology to ensure that many more readers
can enjoy these books into the future.

We publish in ebook and Print on Demand formats
to bring these wonderful books to new audiences.

www.panmacmillan.co.uk/bello

Winston Graham

Winston Mawdsley Graham OBE was an English novelist, best known for the series of historical novels about the Poldarks. Graham was born in Manchester in 1908, but moved to Perranporth, Cornwall when he was seventeen. His first novel, *The House with the Stained Glass Windows* was published in 1933. His first 'Poldark' novel, *Ross Poldark*, was published in 1945, and was followed by eleven further titles, the last of which, *Bella Poldark*, came out in 2002. The novels were set in Cornwall, especially in and around Perranporth, where Graham spent much of his life, and were made into a BBC television series in the 1970s. It was so successful that vicars moved or cancelled church services rather than try to hold them when Poldark was showing.

Aside from the Poldark series, Graham's most successful work was *Marnie*, a thriller which was filmed by Alfred Hitchcock in 1964. Hitchcock had originally hoped that Grace Kelly would return to films to play the lead and she had agreed in principle, but the plan failed when the principality of Monaco realised that the heroine was a thief and sexually repressed. The leads were eventually taken by Tippi Hedren and Sean Connery. Five of Graham's other books were filmed, including *The Walking Stick*, *Night Without Stars* and *Take My Life*. Graham wrote a history of the Spanish Armadas and an historical novel, *The Grove of Eagles*, based in that period. He was also an accomplished writer of suspense novels. His autobiography, *Memoirs of a Private Man*, was published by Macmillan in 2003. He had completed work on it just weeks before he died. Graham was a Fellow of the Royal Society of Literature, and in 1983 was honoured with the OBE.

Winston Graham

THE TUMBLED
HOUSE

BELL

First published in 1959 by Hodder & Stoughton

This edition published 2013 by Bello
an imprint of Pan Macmillan, a division of Macmillan Publishers Limited
Pan Macmillan, 20 New Wharf Road, London N1 9RR
Basingstoke and Oxford
Associated companies throughout the world

www.panmacmillan.co.uk/bello

ISBN 978-1-4472-5535-2 EPUB
ISBN 978-1-4472-5534-5 POD

For
DENIS *and* KAY HOCKING

Chapter One

You could have said that Joanna was potentially unfaithful to her husband from the moment she met Roger Shorn that Sunday in February. She had been at Brighton for a week-end with the Colcutts, and Roger came to lunch. He asked her if he might beg a lift home on the Sunday afternoon, and although she had thought of staying for dinner she at once said yes. She always hated driving. That was all it amounted to at first.

Though not particularly notable in this rather grand company, he stood out in it just the same because of the odd way he had of looking and being distinguished anywhere. She saw it clearly. She also saw clearly that the minute she came into a room she was still the only woman in it so far as he was concerned. Perhaps that should have made a red light flicker somewhere; a different reflex in her own feelings certainly should, if she had been alert to it. But just at this time she badly needed someone to like her, someone to admire her, someone to be sympathetic. She needed warmth like a vitamin-hungry child. He gave it her.

For the first few miles on the way home they talked about the house-party. Roger was at his best; light and amusing, he always knew the right anecdote about people, slightly malicious but disarmingly funny. The Colcutts, they agreed, were flying high. Roger told her of a house-party he had been to at Christmas to which the host had invited only couples who had been divorced during the past year.

"How did you qualify?" she asked.

"I got in as a season-ticket holder. How is Don, by the way? Setting the West Coast on fire?"

"It's a terrific success. He's about his furthest distant now. Vancouver last week."

"People in Canada like young conductors as they like youth of every kind. Here you have to face a more sophisticated culture. But it'll be the same in the end."

"So long as the end doesn't take thirty years to arrive."

"Why should it?"

"Well, among other things he has to overcome the handicap of an English name."

"Is it a handicap in his case? I should have thought it an advantage to have had a famous father!"

"I'm sure not. Far better to have been called Volkonski."

The wind was collecting the dust and the old leaves and blowing them in surly spirals about the road, but the heater kept the car warm and cosy.

Roger said: "How did Don take his father's death?"

"He cabled asking if he should come home, but naturally I said not. There was nothing he could do."

"What's happened to Sir John's cottage?"

"It'll be sold when Don gets back, but there's such a pile of personal papers there that we felt we had to leave them to Don to sort out."

Roger lit a cigarette. "I was a great admirer of John Marlowe. Don ought to write a book about him."

"Sir John's book says all the important things."

"None of the personal things that people like to know. 'John Marlowe, Barrister and Philosopher. A revealing portrait! By his Son.'"

"You know all the angles," she said.

"I love you when you're slightly contemptuous," he said. "I first saw you like that coming down the stairs after that first party. Like a Raeburn portrait, but with greater subtlety of tone. The only thought in my head then was: that portrait's going to be mine."

"And it was."

"Too briefly. Why did you throw me up, Joanna?"

"It happened. Need we bother?"

2

"You don't know how often I've regretted introducing Don to you. Without that complication. . . . ."

"When did you first meet Don?"

"I knew John Marlowe first—oh, eight or nine years ago. Then Don a year later—just before he went in the army—very young then, very explosive, very single-minded."

"He still is."

"Don't you think—if it hadn't been for him you might sometime have come back to me?"

After a second's hesitation she said: "Is this the way home?"

"Not the most direct."

"I thought that signpost said Arundel."

"It did."

"Am I being kidnapped?"

"Far from it. But I thought we might go home through Midhurst. The Old Millhouse is empty, I suppose?"

"Apart from John Marlowe's ghost."

"Well, I thought we might stop on the way through, pay our respects."

"I didn't know you admired him so much."

Roger Shorn changed gear and slid past a group of hardy cyclists. "As a journalist I'm interested in all manifestations. John Marlowe had the courage to do the unfashionable thing. The pursuit of money is the religious creed of today. Anyone who challenges contemporary thought is interesting."

She glanced at him. His clever full lips were slightly pursed, his eyes narrowed, his long fingers held the wheel easily. He turned suddenly and smiled at her. "Believe me?"

"Of course."

"I even watched TV on Friday evening," he said.

"Oh, God! That was a challenge to no one."

"They'd used the wrong technique. Television is the medium of the close-up."

"I was so angry with myself, because it wasn't a bad part."

"It wasn't your part. They should never have asked you to do it; but that being said——"

3

"That being said, it's all there is to say."

He was silent for a moment. "All art is a conflict between self-expression and self-criticism. Sometimes, darling, it's a disadvantage to see things too clearly too soon. I warned you years ago."

"Meaning?"

"Meaning that you may be like me—too intelligent either to create or to interpret satisfactorily. It's an obvious danger."

"It may be obvious but——"

"But what?"

"What does one do about it?" she said.

"One comes to terms."

"I'm not sure I should be prepared to accept the only terms I can see offered."

They got to Midhurst about six. The cottage was out of the village on the Petersfield road. Set in an acre of garden, it was the conventional two cottages knocked into one, with the remains of the old mill at the end and a wheel with water still trickling over the edge. Roger Shorn stopped outside to open the gate, then drove in as far as the garage at the side.

"Have you been down since he died?" he asked.

"For the funeral, of course. And the week after. Not since."

"You don't mind my stopping and looking round?"

"I have the key. We might as well go inside, now we're here."

He glanced at her and then got out and opened her door. She was almost as tall as he was, slim built but strong.

By now dusk was not far off, but the day, already as grey as an etching, had no colour to lose. She led the way along the flag-paved path between the waving shrivelled heads of michaelmas daisies to the front door. The Yale key slipped into the lock easily enough, but the tumblers were hard to turn as if disuse had rusted them over. They went into the low square hall and from there into the main living-room, where her father-in-law had worked and spent most of his time. It was half dark and Roger clicked the light switch but there was no result.

Joanna went to the window. "It's dry enough after all that rain. . . . Everything's thick with dust."

"The last time I came here," said Roger, "in fact the only time, was just after Sir John Marlowe had published his book. I came down to talk over some aspects of it for a notice in my column in *The Sentinel*. I remember it rained most of the time and we spent it in here, except for an hour when we went out to the pub for a meal. But that was eighteen months ago. . . . Where's the main switch?"

"In the kitchen."

While he was gone she sank down on the window seat unbuttoning her coat, pulling off her gloves. In this room nothing had moved since its owner's death. Even the air had last been breathed, one felt, by John Marlowe himself. His pipe still lay on the eighteenth-century Dutch marquetry writing-desk. Behind it was the Orpen portrait of his wife, and on the console table were the Guillermin and Leonhard Kern ivories collected by her. Books were piled on a wing chair.

She had not moved when Roger came back. He switched on the light and said: "That's better. How lovely you look with your coppery hair and your Irish eyes. . . . Joanna, there's quite a variety of tinned foods in the kitchen. Let's have dinner here."

She ran her finger fastidiously along the edge of the window-sill. "It's oppressive."

"It won't be when we get a fire going. I'll fix the meal. It will be like the old days."

"Why d'you suppose I want to remember them?"

"Were they so distasteful?"

"Not—distasteful. But people are like snakes, Roger, growing skins and discarding them. What happened four years ago is just something left behind—an old skin, best forgotten on all counts."

He inclined his head. "On principle I'm all against the backward glance. Forward with the People, in fact. Or forward without them. But I think dinner here would be much more fun than in some dreary roadhouse, even on the most contemporary terms."

She said slowly: "I suppose there are some things I could do here. The solicitor last week was asking. . . ." She got up and went to the desk, picked up a photo in a frame, put it back. "I wish Don were here. I loathe picking over dead things."

"Let me do it for you—if you'll tell me what you want."

She shook her head decisively, opened a drawer and turned over some of the papers. He had come over to her, picked up a book lying on the desk, tapped the dust off it and looked at the title. She took out an empty cheque-book, opened it to see the date on the stub.

"*Flecker's Poems*. Odd choice. Cigarette?"

She smiled and nodded and took one. He lit it for her. His closeness was something she was very much aware of. She said. "I wish I didn't always feel so much at home with you, Roger——"

"It's a community of temperament. I told you all along."

"There are quite a lot of things——" She stopped: "Who's that?"

Her eyes had gone past him. He turned. "What?"

"There was someone looking in the window! A woman."

He went to the window and peered out. Dusk had fallen. "I can't see anyone. Wait." He went into the hall. She heard him open the front door and go out into the garden. He was gone about five minutes. When he came back he said: "There's no one about at all. Are you sure you saw someone?"

She blew out a thin smoky breath. "A woman with a scarf round her head."

"There's certainly no one about. I went right to the gate."

Joanna shrugged. "Maybe it was a banshee warning me."

"Warning you?"

"To keep away from dark men."

"I should have thought it was the last thing your Irish ancestry would have told you to do."

She went to the window herself now, staring into the darkened garden. An owl cried from the branches of a cherry tree and flew across the dying evening sky. Roger watched her, his handsome sallow face shadowed with a hesitation he didn't often feel. Joanna Marlowe was one of the few women he could never be sure of two steps ahead.

He said: "Well?"

She raised an eyebrow. "I almost never keep away from dark men."

They had a successful meal with a bottle of good claret, and once it was settled she was glad she had stayed. Something that mattered was happening to her, for the first time for months. Life had an edge, on which one moved insubstantially but alert. Roger was at his most charming, with that subtle sophisticated attractiveness of manner given to a few men in their early forties. While he talked his hair ruffled over his forehead, his face came alive.

"Coffee without milk. But you don't take it, do you? I've been handicapped tonight. Thank God for olive oil and a tin of butter."

"I'd nearly forgotten how well you could work these things. A delicious talent."

"Tell me what your next play is."

She looked at her coffee. Her lashes were the same colour as her hair, that very dark auburn that comes without freckles. He studied her; there was a hint of wildness in eyebrow and nostril that he liked to see.

"I've about struck an all-time low," she said.

"What makes you say that?"

She shrugged. "It comes down to what we were talking of in the car, doesn't it? I used to think I was going places on the stage. It's uncomfortable waking from that sort of dream."

"Darling, you're exaggerating."

"Oh, maybe. I can get by. I've a face and a figure. I needn't ever be short of jobs, of a sort. But I had ambitions to be something more than one of the crowd."

"Why not go back to the legitimate stage for a change? One doesn't stop developing, you know, even at the great age of twenty-six."

"My dear, Don earns very little, as you know. We need the money."

"Perhaps living with Don makes everything more difficult."

"Living with Don, who obviously *is* going to amount to something, who already does, makes thoughts about oneself harder to take. That's all."

"Did you ever tell him about us?"

"I told him before we married that I'd had an affair. I named no names."

There was silence. She said suddenly: "And what about yourself? You've said absolutely nothing. What happened to the girl you were going with last year?"

He blinked, his face half amused, half clouded by the question. "Fran? It didn't work. I can never make anything of hard women. We broke up in the autumn."

"I see."

"Since you gave me up," he said, "it's never been quite the same. You don't find easy substitutes for the one good thing."

Her eyes glinted restlessly. "What is the one good thing? I haven't noticed you depriving yourself of the second best."

He said: "We must have more meals together like this. And soon."

"The town would talk, darling."

"Let us have clandestine pleasures, then. Sybaritic meals in lonely cottages with nobody to look on. I'll be an uncle to you."

"That's quite the most conventional lie I've ever heard you tell."

"Joanna, I'm the father of a grown man."

"Yes, how is Michael?"

"Overgrown. But will you?"

Her gaze slightly unfocused from his, as if she was taking her physical body out of his arms. Her smile faded, lingered at the corners of her mouth. "We'll see."

Neither spoke then for a time in the silence. Her mind was going round and round within a small circle of assembled facts, never straying outside them to glimpse the remoter issues, picking a heady and reckless and slightly sensual way round a central position of loneliness.

The hall was shadowy when they went out, the stairs in darkness. She said: "I'll get you brandy. I think I know where there should be some." She went into the kitchen and unlocked a cupboard.

He waited for her. He said: "You know it's true what I said —however much you may scorn."

"What?"

"There hasn't been anyone like you."

She came back with the bottle but he did not move aside. She smiled into his eyes.

He said: "A thing like that doesn't happen very often, a fusion, a unity, call it any name. When it does happen it can't happen to one only. I know it happened to me."

"So?"

"It's simple reasoning from there on. I can't claim that you haven't found it since. I don't know. All I know is that it couldn't have been unimportant in your life."

"So?"

"You should be honest with me."

She said: "Darling, you know you couldn't bear it. Would you like your brandy here?"

He put his hand on her shoulder, tentatively but firmly. She moved a trifle bur did not withdraw. In her mind at that moment there was no inner position to withdraw to. He kissed her. She put her hands down defencelessly, deliberately.

He drew her to him, kissed her again on the mouth and neck. She said with a hint of detached mockery: "This is very good brandy."

"Maybe."

"Fine Liqueur Cognac, vintage 1893."

"Don't drop it," he said. "Put it very carefully on the floor."

Chapter Two

It was nearly two months later that they all met, two of them for the first time, and all together for the last time; in the penthouse of the Dorchester where Wolseley Dorrit the Canadian pianist was giving a supper-party. An, old friend of the Marlowes, he had flown to England in the same plane as Don for a concert at the Festival Hall, and, being the only nephew of a man with a big stake in Canadian Pacific, he could afford to spend twice his concert fee on entertaining his friends afterwards.

There amid the Third Empire Messel, with the long windows looking out over the moonlit trees of the park and with the susurration of the late night traffic carried upwards by the breeze, they talked over drinks for half an hour and then went into the glittering dining-room for supper.

Dorrit took one end of the table and Don Marlowe the other. Don was a strongly-built fair-haired young man with candid eyes and a breadth of shoulder. Explosive was a word Roger had used, and it fitted. Generous, quixotic, with a streak of wry humour, alternately self-doubting and self-confident, at twenty-nine he stood professionally on the threshold between obscurity and eminence, and the frown on his face tonight showed he had not yet made up his mind whether the last three hours had pushed him any distance one way or the other. He was in any case tired after his tour and would have been happier to have gone off somewhere for a quiet supper with his wife, instead of coming to this gilded affair.

Joanna. Joanna was talking to Dorrit at the other end of the table. Don's eyes travelled over her composed, beautiful, rather esoteric face to her bare shoulders, her elbow-length green gloves pulled off at the wrists, the swell of her breasts under the silver-grey frock, the narrowing curve of her waist. In this empty mood following the expenditure of spirit of the last few hours, his thoughts kept without impulsion to the main lines of love and desire and friendship.

Friendship. His eyes moved on and met those of Roger Shorn, who was sipping his wine assessingly. Don grinned at him and Roger smiled back. Further down the table his young sister Bennie was talking to Roger Shorn's boy, Michael. Odd they had never met before, considering his long friendship with Roger.

"You are Sir John Marlowe's son, aren't you?" said the wife of the Canadian High Commissioner over the fish course.

"Yes," said Don.

"If I were his son I should be very, very proud of his memory. It must have been a shock to hear of his death."

"It was. He seemed well when I left. He was just beginning another book."

"I read his *Crossroads* when it first came out. I think it's done more for the disillusioned young than anything else written in this generation."

Don murmured something polite.

"And it's good, I think," she added, "to be the distinguished son of a distinguished father. I enjoyed the concert tonight just as much as I can say. May I mention just one thing?"

"Of course."

"You're—quite different to meet from what I expected. I mean after seeing you conduct." She continued in some confusion: "To meet, you seem so much younger, more unassuming. Less commanding. I do hope I'm not offending you by saying this."

"I'm due for the psychiatrist any day," Don said. "Then it'll all be winkled out."

She looked at him seriously and then suddenly smiled. "But you're joking! ... But that's exactly what I mean."

At the top of the table Wolseley Dorrit said to Joanna: "Don is looking good after his trip. I guess you must have missed him quite a lot."

"I did," said Joanna.

"Next time you must go with him. I can't tell you how much I appreciate him taking this concert. It made such a difference."

In a pause in the general talk the hiss and bubble of the fountain in the courtyard outside could be heard. Hock was poured into Roger Shorn's glass, and Roger twisted it round once or twice in his long slim fingers before putting it to his lips. A moderate wine, a Reisling Spatlese, he thought, but not a good year, probably '54. One couldn't expect too much on these occasions.

Both his partners were occupied, so he was free to look round. He glanced at his host, who was still talking to Joanna Marlowe, and then quickly back at her husband, Don, poor fellow ... But lucky fellow. The only one here of *real* innate gifts, but showing them and growing them too young. The time to achieve success was when it was too late to enjoy it. That way struck an equilibrium in life and so pleased the gods.

Nearby Roger's son was talking animatedly to Don's sister, Bennie Marlowe.

Michael Shorn was saying: "I can't understand why we haven't met before. Dad's known your brother and your father for years."

Bennie Marlowe looked at him with her wide dark eyes. "Is it so surprising? You are at Cambridge——"

"Was."

"And I am away half my life. You didn't come to Don's wedding?"

"When was that? Two years ago? No. Anyway, it doesn't so much matter not meeting you until now so long as we make up for lost time."

She raised her eyebrows and smiled but did not speak.

He said: "Don't you find it an awful bore flying, for a living?"

"No. I like it."

"Well, will you come out with me sometime?"

"Thank you. I'd love to."

"What about Monday?"

"Monday night I shall be in Istanbul."

"What a life! Tuesday?"

"Tuesday should be all right. But I hate promising when I'm actually on a flight. If I get stuck in Rome it's expensive to telephone."

"Aren't you afraid of being kidnapped by a Turk?"

"Not more than by a Greek. And less than by an Italian. Have you met Don often before?"

"Only when Roger has brought him home."

"Your father's very good looking, isn't he?"

"Women usually think so. Can we say Tuesday night then? Eight o'clock?"

"I live in Pond Mews, near the South Kensington Tube. Will you——"

"Alone?"

"No, with another girl."

"I'll call for you then. Mind an old and smelly car?"

"No, I like them."

"We'll do a round of the town. D'you know the Eleuthera? Or the Middle Pocket? I'm practically uncrowned king of night clubs."

"I thought you'd just come down from Cambridge?"

"I was sent down. We disagreed on certain principles."

She looked at him again, her expression one of smiling doubt. "Michael, perhaps I should warn you. I love dancing but I hardly ever. I do so many other things that I haven't time. And I'm not uncrowned queen of anything."

"You are now," he said quietly.

The waiters, ankle deep in carpet, served the last course. Great rococo mirrors multiplied their activities down interminable but diminishing *salons*.

Dorrit said to Joanna Marlowe: "Tell me, who is that talking to Don now? I kind of know his face."

Joanna plunged her fork into the foam-covered sweet, but then let the fork lie. "Roger Shorn, the columnist. I thought, as host. . . ."

"Oh yes, we were introduced. But when it came to fixing this party I know only eight or ten people in the country so I left it to Don and to my agent to make up the numbers."

"It would be Don who invited him. They are old friends."

"I guess as a columnist he's a pretty powerful man."

Joanna shrugged. "I don't think they get as powerful on this side of the Atlantic, Wolseley. But of course a man like Roger has influence in all sorts of ways. As it happens, he got me my first part in television."

"Is that so? Before you married Don?"

"Oh, yes, a couple of years. That's his son talking to Bennie."

"You don't say. I shouldn't have thought he was old enough to have a grown-up son. Tell me, is that sweet not to your liking? Maybe you'd rather have cheese?"

"Thank you, Wolseley, no. I can't eat a thing more."

Roger and Michael took a taxi back to Roger's flat in Belgrave Street.

They were silent for a time while the cab circled Hyde Park Corner and turned into Grosvenor Place. Then Michael said: "Enjoy the evening, Dad?"

"I bore with it all right. One reaches a stage when experiences which should be exciting are only freshened up if something gives them a new cutting edge."

"And that means what?"

"Applied to tonight it means that the Brahms No. 4 and that dreary Schumann A Minor could only have been really enjoyable if conducted and played superlatively well."

"And you didn't think they were?"

"I didn't think they were. Don, for once, lacked finesse, and, as for that little draper or whatever he is in private life. . . ."

Michael hunched his shoulders. "You should put that in your column."

"Music criticism isn't my job. . . . Did you like Bennie Marlowe?"

"Very much. I got quite a new cutting edge."

Roger smiled. "All right, all right. Michael, keep Thursday free. I have Sir Percy Laycock and his daughter coming to dinner. Laycock's a millionaire, self-made but unassuming and agreeable. It could be rather important."

"What is she like?"

"I haven't met her but I believe she's about twenty-two and quite pretty."

"Are you trying to marry me off?"

"There's no conscription. But she'd certainly be a match if you fancied her."

Michael looked at his father's pale distinguished face as it was lit by a passing car. He looked like a poet, like Day Lewis or a shaven Tennyson, successful but sad.

"What have you against Bennie Marlowe?"

"Nothing at all, Michael."

"I detected something in your voice."

Roger smiled. "Go on with you. Think again."

The taxi stopped and they got out and went upstairs to a Georgian apartment on two floors. The living-room had dark green panelled walls, with heavy curtains in a striking green and white flowered design flanking the white venetian blinds. Lamps with black drum shades cast light down on polished eighteenth-century surfaces. Not disfiguring the walls were two Italian triptych pieces, a Delacroix pencil drawing, a Dufy sketch. Roger poured himself a whisky and said: "Take a beer if you want one. I have to phone a paragraph through to the office tonight."

"Dad," said Michael.

"Yes?" Roger paused with his hand on the door of the study.

"I hope you won't think it rude of me if I say, now that it looks as if I shall be in London more or less for good, I should very much like a couple of rooms on my own."

"You've a room of your own here."

Michael shook back his black hair. "It isn't quite the same. You know how it is. You must have felt the same in your own life."

"Well, let's talk of it when you've got a job. It would be expensive, you know."

Michael picked up a bottle of beer and opened a drawer in the Sheraton writing-desk. "As it happened I saw a place today that would just suit me. That's why I mentioned it. And not too expensive. But it would have to be snapped up."

"Where?"

"Roland Gardens. Just the two rooms."

Roger said: "You'll find the opener in the other drawer. . . . How much?"

"Ten a week."

"Furnished?"

"No, but I could borrow enough to make do from friends."

Michael opened the beer. He clinked the bottle against the glass and some froth escaped on his fingers. He licked them and put the bottle down.

"I thought if you could advance me the rest of my allowance for this year. . . . I'll get a job soon enough, but I just want a month or so to breathe, to look round. I'd still like to get into engineering."

Roger went across and lowered the blinds. The action drew his thoughts away to Joanna for a moment or two.

"I like you living here, Michael. You've only been back two weeks."

"I know. It's—awkward. Of course I'd look on this as discharging any obligation. . . ."

"It isn't a question of discharging an obligation. One doesn't treat one's son like a bad debt. And of course I can get you work."

"My sort of work?"

"Maybe. It's really a question of being able to wait for the suitable thing."

"We'll keep in close touch, of course."

Roger considered his son. "I think you're putting the cart before the horse, Michael. However, let's not talk about it now. Lunch with me tomorrow. We'll consider it then."

After the door had closed Michael finished the last of the beer and dabbed his lips. Over the years a *rapport* had developed between father and son. The various women in the older man's life had never really come between them, and their liking for each other went deeper than the usual relationship because from the first it was as if the usual relationship had nor existed. There was not often a conflict of wills between them: when it came Roger usually got his way while appearing to concede everything. But in the matter of the flat Michael suspected that his father's was a token resistance which would give ground under pressure.

Chapter Three

The newspapers were delivered at nine on a Sunday. Although it was Don's turn, Joanna slipped out and made tea, and he did not wake until she tapped the tea-cup with a spoon and slid the bundle of papers under his pillow. He stretched and yawned and smiled his thanks at her, while she pulled back the black-and-white-striped curtains and slid into the other bed.

"A lovely day." She arched her back, stretching. "Pour me a cup of tea."

He did so. "It's good to be back. What did you do with your Sundays while I was away?"

"I told you. Don't you ever read my letters?"

"Did you go down to the Old Millhouse much?"

"... Just for the funeral, and then a couple of times since. I'm afraid you'll find it a mess. We didn't touch more of his papers than we needed."

"Did Bennie go with you?"

"For the funeral, of course. The other times I rang her but she was away."

Don sipped his tea meditatively. "Though we didn't see a lot of him, something important is missing since I came back."

"I know."

"You feel it too? I can't quite get used to the idea of his not being there. Last night I nearly rang him."

"I saw him twice just before Christmas. He seemed much the same as always—self-contained, cheerful, as usual more interested in what I was doing than in talking about himself. I asked if he'd like to spend Christmas with me here, but he said he wanted to work. Bennie went down for Christmas Day, and that was the last time she saw him."

There was silence for a tune.

Don said: "What days are you working next week?"

"Monday, Tuesday and Friday."

"I'd like to get out of London for a bit. I have to see Henry de Courville on Thursday."

"Henry? Why?"

"I gather that George Bratt is quite seriously ill." Bratt was assistant conductor at Govern Garden.

"Does that mean they may have something to offer you?"

"It might. It's an ill wind. ... Of course it would only be temporary; but still. ... Perhaps we could go down to Midhurst next week-end."

He looked at her, but some trick of the light shadowed the expression in her eyes. "What does Roger say about last night?" she asked.

Don fished the papers from under his pillow and passed them to her. She opened *The Sentinel* and turned to page three. "Half a paragraph. The usual thing."

"Let me see."

While she poured more tea he read it for himself. "Youth had its fling," she said. "Why be so patronising? And it's not young for a pianist. If he were eighteen it might be worth remarking."

Don laughed. "Roger's paragraphs never do satisfy you. ... Did you see much of him while I was away?"

She didn't look up but weighed his casual question in the micro-scales of her own mind. "I saw him once in February. Then I had a meal with him a couple of times last month."

A distant dog was barking in the quiet square. She picked up a picture paper.

Presently Don said: "D'you know, last night I was trying to think of the word that precisely described my feelings for you then—vaguely Old Testament and distinctly old-fashioned in these disillusioned days."

She looked at him and past him, then at him again.

"Uxorious," he said. "That was the word."

"I don't think you needed the word."

"Last night you were—different, Joanna. High strung—almost as if there'd never been anything between us before."

Disconcerted at his perception, she put down her paper. "Do you mind?"

"It's not for me to mind, darling. I like you all ways."

"Dangerous indulgence."

He smiled and began to turn over *The Sunday Times*. She picked up a brush and tidied her copper hair. She suddenly said: "Don, don't ever *expect* consistency, will you? If I'm in any way ... different from when you went away, don't expect me to explain the difference, and I don't want you to try. Love's a part of personality: it doesn't go back, it goes on, it's organic. If I'm different, be patient."

He frowned at the paper. "Since we married you've been all women to me. If that's indulgence, then it's indulgence. I recognise a dicey score and *ad lib* as I go along. I like, and want, the good and the non-good, virtues and faults, the lot. The one thing you must never change is being changeable."

She said: "Next time you go away——"

The telephone began to ring.

He said: "Brompton 4040. Yes. Oh, hullo, Wolseley. Good morning to you. ... Very well, thanks, I hope you did. ... I hope you're not coming round to lunch yet; we're still in bed. ... Well, you know how it is. What? What paper? *The Gazette*? We do take it, but I don't think we've looked at it yet. A what? My father?. ... What on earth for? Oh, Moonraker. I don't often read him, it's pretty lousy stuff. ..."

"What is it, Don?" Joanna said.

". . . Well, if it's as offensive as that. . . . Well, yes, I'm glad you did. . . . Thanks, yes. No, not a bit. . . . Joking aside, we're expecting you in a couple of hours. Any time after twelve, in fact. Right. See you then. Good-bye."

Joanna had opened the newspaper, but when Don put back the receiver she didn't go on looking but handed the paper to him.

Don said: "Some sort of gossip about us. I expect it's nothing important."

He found the page and began to read. Joanna sat at the kidney-shaped dressing-table watching him through the mirror.

It wasn't usually hard to tell what he was thinking; but he went through the article with scarcely a change of expression. Then she saw his eyes move to begin it again. She stopped brushing her hair.

"Well?"

He got out of bed and passed it to her and began to dress.

Moonraker's weekly feature on the centre page had amused her when she first bought *The Sunday Gazette*. There was a knowing, forthright malice in it that tickled the palate before staling it.

The article was headed "The Great Marlowe Imposture".

"Arrival back in England this week of Don Marlowe twenty-nine-year-old British conductor and darling of the high-brow teen-agers, has caused this writer to examine afresh the Great Marlowe Legend which has sprung up around his father, the late Sir John Marlowe—remember *Crossroads*?— and is still growing.

"Don Marlowe we all know. A Beecham touch on the platform; boundless go (and, let it be whispered, boundless go with an e in front of it); youth on his side. When to these you add a famous name, can you wonder that he is on the up-and-up, stepping briskly over rivals ten and twenty years his senior? What we are inquiring into is how the name became famous? Do any of us really know?

"Let us examine the legend. John Marlowe, Queen's Counsel, Recorder of Cheltenham, legal big name of the late forties and middle fifties, knighted for his war services, resigns his career in mid-stream. A future Lord Chief Justice hurries off to his country cottage at the age of fifty.

"He has been called, he explains, to Higher Things. So he retires to his cottage and writes a book called *Crossroads*.

"We have all read it. (Or if we haven't we pretend we have.) It is practical philosophy for the man in the street, all neatly signposted to tell the individual what he should do, and society what it should not do, in the moral dilemmas of today. It's clever. You can't fault it on that score. The trained legal brain knows just how to put over knotty problems with the knots untied.

"It is an instant best seller. Twenty editions in England alone, his publishers told me yesterday. Fourteen translations.

"In January of this year Sir John died, laden with honour and royalties. Sadly mourned by all, not least by his handsome son and pretty air-hostess daughter.

"Well, well, speak no ill of the dead, say I.

"But Sir John lives on, through his book and through the legend which his retirement created. And sometimes legends blow themselves up into great over-inflated balloons. Then it is the duty of the journalist to harden his heart and investigate the facts. Recently I have been doing just this, and I am sorry to have to tell you that the balloon has burst.

"Why did Sir John resign? Could he no longer stand the strain of expensively rewarded advocacy? Not at all. He was quietly elbowed out to avoid a scandal.

"Perhaps no one will ever know the full facts—or no one will tell them. But it is whispered in the shadowy corridors of the Law Courts that Sir John was partial to pretty women clients. He dined and wined them expensively when the solicitors concerned were far away. He even made offers of marriage to them—which were gratefully accepted—and then withdrew. What simple, gullible creatures women are!

"Also the Powers-that-Be were not happy about his behaviour as a Recorder. Sir John knew how to turn a blind eye in court if it helped a lady friend.

"Now the English Bar has a reputation unequalled in the world. It is quick to protect itself. To save a scandal, Sir John was given the opportunity of leaving by the back door. Wisely he took it. Can you blame him?

"Of course it was all done very quietly. On the records he has a clean slate. But records don't tell everything. And truth will out.

"But the book? The famous book which is still making its impression on the thinkers of three continents. Could such a man have written such a book?

"The answer is simple. In the West Country town of Blakiston there lived an elderly and infirm clergyman named Chislehurst. Mr Chislehurst had a German mother and a degree of Philosophy in the University of Leipzig. Mr Chislehurst published in 1951 a booklet entitled 'Man and the Future'.

"It was published privately and very few people saw it. But Sir John Marlowe saw it. Sir John read it, marked it, learned it and inwardly digested it. He went to see the Reverend George Chislehurst. Sir John was jovial and kindly. He helped George to clear off one or two trifling debts. A friendship sprang up between John and George. They became buddies.

"In 1954 George consented to part with all the rights in his material for £100, on the understanding that John made due acknowledgement of his debt to the old man when the book was published. In June 1957 John published his *magnum opus* without any acknowledgement to George at all.

"George blew his top. He showered letters of protest upon Sir John, who bore his burden as he bore his new-found fame with becoming modesty. The Rev. George fell ill, stricken with anger and grief. He had a stroke and lost his speech and the use of his right hand. His friend went down to visit him but was refused admittance. In October of that year the Reverend I George Chislehurst died and was buried unhonoured and unsung.

"Sir John went to the funeral, deeply distressed at his loss. After it was over he hurried home to Midhurst to put the finishing touches on the eighth and amended edition of *Crossroads*.

"The last part of his book is sub-titled 'Man in the Dock'. We wonder why. Was he thinking of the elderly clergyman whose grave is now untended in the churchyard of St Anne's, Blakiston? Or was he thinking of himself?"

Wolseley Dorrit said: "Well, I'm real sorry I was the one to pass on the poison, as you might say; but I thought if I didn't tell you someone else would, and sometimes it's better to be forearmed."

Don said: "Wait a minute, I think that's Bennie now. I wonder if she will have seen it."

"I'll let her in," said Joanna.

Bennie, accustomed to restricting her personality most days of the week, bloomed today in a wide-skirted frock of flowered grosgrain, and came into the room a young, light and amiable presence, her colour freshened by her walk. She saw at once that something was wrong and thought at first that her brother and Joanna had been having words. When the situation was explained to her she read the article in silence, and from various points in the room they watched her reaction.

She said: "What a foul and stinking piece of. . . . I—I don't know what to say!"

"We've all said it," murmured Don, picking some music off the piano stool and sitting down.

Joanna carried a sherry to her. Bennie smiled her thanks, then looked at her brother. "What are you going to do?"

"At the moment I'm too hopping mad to think straight."

Bennie sipped her drink and went across to the writing-table on which was her favourite photograph of her father. "Do you know who Moonraker is?"

"No. Sometimes these columns are farmed out. But I don't think this one is. The venom is too consistent from month to month. Anyway I shall find out."

"And when you do?"

"I shall kick him twice round St Paul's Cathedral."

"Warn me to be there," said Bennie.

"There is a law of libel in England?" said Wolseley.

"I'll go into that tomorrow. But a little personal violence would help too."

Joanna was Stan ding by the window. The light fell without comment on her tawny hair, her elegant complex beauty.

"Who is this man they mention—the Reverend George Chislehurst? Have you heard of him before?"

Don threw the music he held on to the top of the Blüthner grand. "I've a vague idea. But probably you remember better, Bennie?"

"Oh yes, I knew him. He was there during a couple of the holidays—not all the time, but visiting." She frowned at her drink.

"They used to talk on and on into the night. Nothing I can tell you about him will help to unscramble this mess."

Joanna excused herself to see to the lunch but refused Bennie's offer of help. She seemed glad to be able to go.

Bennie picked up the paper again. "It's like a dirty anonymous letter, isn't it? You want to put it in the fire but must read it again first."

"You can't burn this," said Don. "There are three million copies of it."

"I'm awfully ignorant," said Wolseley Dorrit "but what exactly is a Recorder? We don't have them in Canada."

"Certain cities and towns in England have the right to hold separate courts of quarter sessions and the Recorder is the legal officer who sits as the judge there. It's usually, given to a distinguished barrister who hasn't yet become a full judge. There's very little money in it, unless you're Recorder of London, but it's usually accepted for the honour and prestige. Dad used to say that in principle it shouldn't work: a barrister in the hurly burly of the courts who four times a year becomes a judge and then afterwards goes back to his own job again—but in fact it seems to work pretty well."

"The charge about his resigning from practice . . ." said Dorrit.

"That's where I think we can catch this louse. But oddly it doesn't rile me as much as the second charge. It won't be so easy to disprove plagiarism as it will the other, with Chislehurst dead. I wonder if the old boy's sister is still alive."

"Moonraker may have been down to see her," said Bennie.

"I thought of that. These old women get queer ideas. If *she* thinks Father pinched the stuff from her brother's book. . . . I suppose Chislehurst did write a pamphlet; if so we must get hold of it."

Wolseley took off his glasses to polish them. "Usually newspapers do things only if they have a purpose. At least that's the way back home. What I can't see is any purpose in this."

"A man like Moonraker," said Don, "probably has two spurs and sits permanently on them both. One is to keep his own name in front of the public, the other is to get rid of his poison by spitting it anywhere he can. A man like that, deep in his guts hates himself and the whole world."

Joanna had come back and was standing in the doorway listening to this last sentence. There was a hint of tautness about her. For a second or two it was as if a stranger was among them, to whom they could turn for a new and detached and subtler opinion of the case. Then her eyes moved to her husband.

"Let's go down now before the potatoes burn to cinders, darling. And let's talk about something else while we eat, otherwise no one will appreciate my casserole."

Chapter Four

Mr Vincent Doutelle, Q.C., took up the clipping from *The Sunday Gazette* and folded it carefully once or twice.

He was a tall shiny man who looked as if he had just come from a facial. His fair greying hair was slicked back, his jaws moved slightly. Don sat with his elbows on the arms of the chair so that his head seemed sunken into his shoulders. Paul Whitehouse, of Tranter, Page and Whitehouse the solicitors, who had brought him for counsel's opinion, was tapping a pencil into the palm of his other hand.

"My advice, Mr Marlowe," said the barrister, selecting his words, picking them over delicately like crumbs, "is that you have no remedy at law."

Don turned his head to look at him with a long considering stare, but he didn't speak. Mr Doutelle went on:

"It's an infamous article. I didn't have the privilege of knowing your father, but I know his repute. I've no doubt that there's not a word of truth in any of this; but the law takes the view that a dead man can suffer no material damage. I'm bound to tell you that you have no case."

"Go on."

"Well, briefly the position is this. Let's deal first with civil libel. A civil action for libel on a dead man may be brought by his posterity if the libel can be shown to injure *their* reputation—in this case yours and Miss Marlowe's. The most obvious example would be to say that your father was never legally married. This would imply that his children were illegitimate, and you could no doubt still sue on that. There can also be an action of a rather

27

different kind if a publication can be shown to have injured a dead man's estate. This article *might* eventually affect the sales of Sir John's book; but in that case the action would have to be brought by the charitable organisations which benefit. I very much question whether they could be persuaded to embark on a costly lawsuit whose outcome to say the least would be in doubt." Mr Doutelle unfolded the cutting and tried folding it another way. "In *principle*, of course, any man may issue a writ against another; but I am bound to tell you that in the circumstances of this case your writ would be dismissed in interlocutory proceedings on the grounds that it disclosed no cause of action."

Don moved only to cross his legs. Mr Doutelle said: "Now as to criminal libel. The writer of an article on a dead man can be charged with criminal libel if the article is written with intent to vilify a dead man's family so as probably to cause a breach of the peace—for instance an assault by the son of the injured man on the writer of the libel. That exists as a *possibility* in law. But again I have to tell you that it is to say the least a doubtful proposition today. No prosecution for criminal libel on a dead man has been successful for upwards of a hundred and twenty years. A case that comes to my mind as most narrowly approaching this occurred in about 1887 when a most scurrilous article was written about a dead man when a statue was about to be erected to his memory. A breach of the peace did in fact occur when the writer of the article was assaulted by the dead man's sons; yet the judge—and a very distinguished one—directed his acquittal in the trial which followed. I will quote you part of his judgement if you would like me to, but the substance is that to libel the dead is not *in itself* an offence known to our law."

"As a matter of interest," Don said, "I have every intention of assaulting the writer of this article."

Mr Doutelle coughed and looked at Mr Whitehouse. "Well, that is not a proposition I can discuss with you, except to say that if it were undertaken for the purpose of creating a situation in which an indictment could be preferred, you would fail."

"Tell me why," said Don.

"I've tried to tell you, Mr Marlowe. It would be an impossible task in this case to prove an intent to vilify you or Miss Marlowe. ... The most probable circumstances I can conceive in which the present criminal law might operate would be if I were to write an article about, say, the late Earl Lloyd George so scurrilous that it created riots in the Rhondda Valley; then there would be a considerable chance of my finding myself committed for trial. In other words, it must to some extent be a public issue. A brawl in a street between two or three persons would hardly be sufficient."

Don looked round at the leaded-paned bookcases with their pale brown Law Reports. He uncrossed his legs.

"So that means that according to the law twenty men may write twenty articles saying that my father was a thief and my mother brought home men at ten shillings a time and died in an inebriates' home. Correct?"

Mr Doutelle tried precise corner to corner folding of his news-cutting. "No, not exactly," he said after some hesitation. "But the strongest force against any such occurrence in England today is public opinion. I am surprised that even *The Gazette* permitted this to appear unless there were some strong supposition of proof."

Paul Whitehouse said: "I've suggested to Mr Marlowe that he would be best advised to write a reply—for *The Times* or one of the influential weeklies—answering these calumnies. He's in a strong position so far as most of the charges are concerned. I would be glad to vet it for him to see he doesn't overstep the mark."

"Moonraker being alive, eh," said Don, "and liable to cut up rough if insulted?"

"Well, editors have to live according to the law. But it seems to me you could write a thoroughly well-reasoned and convincing reply proving to the satisfaction of every sensible person that this article is a complete fabrication."

"I can't prove it as easily as all that. This gutter crawler has spent some time collecting his sweepings. It would take time to get chapter and verse for a full reply, especially for this stuff about the book. Perhaps I could do it, but why should the onus of proof be on me when it should be on him!"

Mr Doutelle said: "I see exactly how you feel. But I agree with Mr Whitehouse that a retaliation through the Press is by far your best defence. And of course, you may not be alone. Your father's reputation stood high. There will be other reactions besides yours."

The Hanover Club was full of men when Don got there. Obviously *The Gazette* article was a topic of conversation, but he didn't encourage it by going into the bar. Instead he went straight up to lunch and sat at one of the round tables between a Professor of Biology and an elderly literary critic. At a small table in a corner Don saw Roger Shorn lunching with his son and a well-known publisher called Bartlett.

After a few minutes of desultory talk the professor said. "I see the Muckraker has been at it again."

"You get *The Gazette*?"

"No, I was told about it this morning. Very distressing for you."

"You don't know who he is?"

"Moonraker? No. You should be able to find out. This club knows everything. I suppose you don't know, Casey?"

"Moonraker?" said the literary critic. "It was Bryan Hooker until he was killed in that airplane crash eighteen months ago. I don't know now. I've lost touch with the cesspools."

After a pause the professor said: "I knew your father well when he was chairman of this club. In this decadent society in which we live, integrity is a hard thing to equate: given the wrong accent it quickly excites ridicule and suspicion of cant. The best thing I can say about your father is that with him the accent was never wrong. He was my idea of an honourable man."

"Not Brutus's."

"Not Brutus's. I was on the committee with him for four years. I played bridge with him. We often talked together." The professor peered at his young companion. "How much does this mean to you, Marlowe? I have no sons, but if I had, I suspect they would not esteem me highly."

"That's fair to no one."

"But isn't it broadly true?"

Don ate for a moment or two before he answered. "No, I don't think so."

"I'm glad you don't think so—and rather relieved."

"Why?"

"I'm never quite sure with the younger generation——and you seem very representative, if I may say so. Or perhaps you hide your seriousness under an agreeable flippancy, and the unperceptive mistake it for the whole man."

Don was pursuing his own thoughts. "I must say it wouldn't shatter me—though I'd be surprised of course—if it turned out he'd had a mistress in Balham and another in Tooting. He was a widower; he had his own life to live. What I *am* very sure of is that he was moral in the more important sense of being scrupulous and unmean. I'm absolutely sure he wouldn't have allowed anything to touch his integrity in a court of law. And it wasn't in his *nature* to steal someone else's work and pass it off as his own."

"Quite so."

"One surely resents lies about the most unlikable character. But that doesn't arise here. I liked him and I thought most other people did." Don contracted his brows. "Of course I saw too little of him, but we were both busy; you know what sort of life a successful silk leads. And then when he retired I was just in the process of getting married. The personal tie was never compulsive, but it was always there. . . . In an odd contradictory way it has got closer in the last few months, since he died."

"That too happens sometimes," said the professor, peering back into his own distant past.

The interview with the publisher had gone pretty well and Roger Shorn had just bought coffee and brandies in the bar. The publisher thought he could find room for Michael in two or three weeks' time. Interpreting the things unsaid, Roger realised that what at present was being offered his son was employment as a junior clerk. It wouldn't do as a permanency but it would be a beginning. A junior partnership was the thing Roger had in mind, but mention of a sum of six thousand pounds had somehow got itself intruded into the discussion, and Roger knew he had no hope whatever of raising this.

Presently the publisher excused himself, the other two resumed their seats and Roger ordered two more brandies. When they came he said: "Well, I think that's fixed. We'll settle the details next week. But of course don't expect too much to begin."

Michael sipped his brandy. "I suppose there's a technique in stamp-licking. I wonder if one should go to a night school for a course."

Roger stared at his handsome son, at the jet-black hair worn long, at the sensitive eyes, at the brooding mouth which suddenly could flash its white and lovely smile. His love for his son was in a sense a serious modification of his own sophisticated beliefs; it was a weakness but an amiable one, and one that he indulged quite consciously, with a half-raised eyebrow of irony at his own irrationality. Michael could go a long way. In spite of his occasional quirks of temperament, people liked him, fell quickly under his spell. Perhaps he would make an influential marriage. What fools men were when they were young, not realising the importance of that.

"Let me buy you another brandy," said Michael. "Just as a celebration."

"You can't. You're not yet a member of this club."

"From what I shall earn at Bartlett and Leak it doesn't look as if I shall ever be able to afford to become one."

"It's a beginning. It's better than nothing." For once Roger spoke sharply. "Don't imagine I'm a millionaire, Michael. I'll do everything I can to make your life tolerable during the next year or so—including paying three months' rent of the flat we saw this morning—but don't imagine I can subsidise you any further."

Michael said thoughtfully: "I don't at all want to seem ungrateful. I think it's really that I wanted a different sort of job. You know I'm not interested in the literary world."

"You soon will be. I can do a lot for you as time goes on."

"In publishing, you mean?"

"Yes, my dear boy, or something like it." Roger stubbed out his cigar. "I have to go now. D'you want to stay on here?"

"No, I'll come with you."

As they moved out of the bar they met Don Marlowe coming in. Don said: "Can you stop a minute, Roger?"

Michael said: "I'll meet you at the door, Dad," and walked on.

Roger's pale eyes went with interest over his friend's face. "Have you been reading *The Gazette*?"

"In Philadelphia nearly *everybody* reads *The Bulletin*," said Don. "Do you know who Moonraker is?"

"No. *The Gazette*, as I needn't tell you, isn't one of *The Sentinel* group. Personally, I'm very sorry about this."

"How can I find out?"

"About Moonraker? I don't know. The editor might tell you but I doubt it."

"Who is the editor?"

"A man called Warner Robinson."

"Do you know him?"

"Scarcely by sight." Roger hesitated and then patted Don's arm. "Look, this isn't the place to exchange confidences. I wish I could come back with you; I looked for you in the bar before lunch. But as a friend I would advise that this is a case in which one should proceed carefully."

"For any special reason?"

"Well, it looks to me very much like an editorial job. That is to say the editor has approved and accepted responsibility. So there's a good deal of weight behind it. The whole thing is probably exaggerated, but I should think they must feel they have something fairly substantial to go on."

"I think they've got nothing substantial to go on."

Roger shrugged. "Try to see this in its perspective, Don. Debunking is a disease of civilisation. Modern man likes to think: 'I'm no good, but neither is my neighbour'. Every eminent personality has it coming to him sooner or later. The trouble with this, of course, is that it is not sooner, when he could defend himself, or later, when no one would care."

"Do you know the editor well enough to fix a meeting between us?"

"It wouldn't be any use. *Ride* the storm, don't fight it out. You'll certainly do no good by beginning a vendetta against a six-million-pound combine; it's heads they win, tails you lose. Write them a letter if you want to, though they probably won't publish it."

Don telephoned his friend Alan Rice. "Alan, d'you know the editor of *The Sunday Gazette*?"

"Robinson? He's not a buddy of mine but I know him, yes. Why?"

"Do you think you could arrange it that I meet him?"

"You mean casually? Over a drink or something?"

"I'd prefer it that way."

"It is to do with this article about your father?"

"Yes."

There was a pause at the other end. "Why not just phone him and ask to see him in his office?"

"I don't think he'd play. He'd probably trunk I'd be bringing a horsewhip."

"And wouldn't you?"

"Not the first time."

There was another pause. "Don, I might be able to fix something, but it won't help me with my own editor if he learns I've been arranging a rough-house for Warner Robinson. Dog doesn't eat dog."

"There won't be a rough-house."

"Also, my dear fellow, as a word of advice, you're just starting your own career. *The Gazette* has long fingers if you get at cross with them."

"It seems I already have."

"Not necessarily you. Your father I suspect was on their White List."

"What d'you mean?"

"Don't you remember the references in his book to sections of the Press? And once or twice he was outspoken in court before he retired. I'm only guessing, but *The Daily Gazette* was pretty sneering in its obituary."

"I didn't see that."

"But you never know with newspapers like *The Gazette*. All for sensation. They can be quixotically generous as well as vilely vindictive. In a month, having got this off their chest, they may bring out some terrific boost for Don Marlowe the young conductor."

"When we meet I'll tell them what they can do with their boosts."

"That's what I'm afraid of."

Don considered the scrawls and scribbles on the printed telephone instructions. "Give me an idea where I might find Robinson. He can't travel to and from his office in a sealed container."

"He doesn't. . . ." There was another pause. "Do you know the Red Boar Club in Fleet Street? He usually lunches there."

"Are you a member?"

"Yes. I tell you what I'll do. I'll take you in and then after a few minutes I'll leave you there. That's the best I can promise."

"Don't worry, I'm not going to create a riot. Tomorrow?"

"It's as good as any other day, I suppose."

"Thank you very much, Alan. You're a real friend."

"I'm not at all sure about that."

Chapter Five

The Red Boar Club was nearly opposite the Law Courts, but its clientele was almost exclusively of the Press. The bar and the main dining-room were down sixteen steps in a converted cellar. Here the temperature was a uniform seventy-eight winter and summer, and tobacco-smoke hung in cirrhus clouds about the room. You broke through them going down the steps like a plane coming in to land.

Alan Rice led the way to the bar and elbowed enough room to order a couple of Martinis.

Don said: "Do you often come here?"

"Well, a couple of times a week. Hullo, Charlie, back safe, I see. ... One doesn't come for the quietude or the air-conditioning."

"What does one come for?"

"Best steaks in London. Company. We journalists are a gregarious lot. And we thrive on noise. Not like you musicians. Cheers."

"What do you suppose musicians thrive on?"

"Well, noise of a different sort. He's here."

"Which one?"

"At the table at the end. Talking to Joseph Halliday. You know, the chief reviewer of *The News*."

Don stared under the smoke and between the jostling waiters at two heavy, well-groomed middle-aged men not dissimilar in looks who were talking over their food.

"Which is which?"

"The bloke in the blue suit is your prey. We've picked a bad day."

"Why?"

"Well, he often sits in isolation. Fred, I thought that was a good spiel of yours last night. I bet the paper sold like bread."

While Rice involved himself in discussion Don watched the table in the corner. Behind him two men were talking about a coup which had cleaned up the news last week. It sounded a pretty underhand piece of work but they spoke of the writer with bated breath, as if he had achieved something not noticeably inferior to the Choral Symphony. Twenty minutes passed and then Joseph Halliday got up and nodded to Warner Robinson and left his table.

Don tapped his friend on the shoulder. "Thanks, Alan. This lets you out."

Alan glanced swiftly at Don and then across the room. "O.K. O.K. You don't mind if I don't wait for you, do you?"

Warner Robinson was scooping out some Blue Stilton when Don reached his table. He had a square rather distinguished face on which the skin hung loosely as if it had a slow puncture. But there was nothing deflated about the way he looked at Don as he moved to take the other chair.

"This is a reserved table."

"I'll not occupy it more than a minute or two. You are Mr Robinson, aren't you?" Don was speaking as quietly as the noise allowed.

Robinson stared at him with ferro-concrete eyes and then went back to digging out the Stilton. "What do you want?"

"My name is Marlowe. Don Marlowe."

Robinson put the spoon back in the cheese. A waiter infiltrated through to take it away. "That doesn't mean much to me."

"I'm a musician. My father was Sir John Marlowe. He died in January."

Robinson looked behind his visitor and snapped his fingers. "No butter."

"Oh, sorry, sir."

Don said: "On Sunday your paper carried an article by Moonraker. You must know about it. It attacked my father. As he isn't here to defend himself, it's up to me to do something about it. But I can do very little while I don't know Moonraker's real name. Will you give it to me?"

The butter came and Robinson spread it on a biscuit. Then he cut a piece of the cheese and put them both into his mouth. In silence Don watched the efficient jaws until everything was gone. So an unsatisfactory sub-editor would be disposed of.

"Moonraker is just a name."

"You probably know who wrote it on Sunday."

"I do. But as editor I take responsibility for my staff."

"Do you mean you wrote it yourself?"

"No, I do not."

Don waited while Robinson finished his cheese. His teeth clicked once or twice but he made no attempt to continue the conversation.

Don said: "I never quite understand what basic fuel a man uses who writes an article like that under a *nom de plume* and stays skulking behind his editor afterwards."

"Lack of schoolboy honour, eh?"

"No, I should have thought just plain lack of guts."

"Well, it's a matter of opinion."

"Can I ask you as a particular favour to tell me who wrote that article?"

"Certainly not."

"I'm bound to find out sooner or later."

"I don't think you are bound to do anything of the sort. Nobody knows it outside my office. It will do you no good to learn it."

Don breathed out to cool his anger. "I wonder if you'll publish a letter from me answering the statements Moonraker has made."

"Send it in if you wish. It will receive consideration."

"But nothing more?"

"It depends what you say."

"Coffee, sir?"

"Please."

"I don't understand you," Don said. "You profess to your readers a high standard of fair play. A 'clean' outlook on sex, stand by the little man, down with bureaucracy, show the flag. That right?"

"In your present mood, Mr Marlowe, you couldn't be wrong."

"But columns like Moonraker's ooze with slimy pus. Under the 'healthy' outlook there's a sort of gangrene. What do you get out of it, you and your staff and your readers?"

Robinson looked up at Don with his wet cement glance. "Are you a member here?"

"No."

"Then I must ask you to leave. But before you go, since you ask, I'll tell you that my policy and the policy of my paper is determined by a board of directors who don't view their responsibilities lightly. Their policy, if you are interested, is to give the maximum freedom of expression, and the maximum salaries, to a few top-rank journalists, who are allowed to pick and choose their subjects without dictation from me and under the general aegis of the newspaper. That complete protection could not be given them if they all wrote under their own names. They would be subject to the interference and boycott of every little pettifogging Tom, Dick and Harry who happened to read some offence into their articles. If you ask what I and my staff and my readers 'get' out of such a policy, I can only tell you that we get the satisfaction of knowing we speak without fear or favour, deflating a reputation if we think it over-blown, or, *equally* I would point out, drawing the attention of the world to a man who in our opinion has been overlooked. Our three and a half million readers rely on our honesty; they know we are not influenced by friends at court or intimidated by big names. They know where they are with *The Sunday Gazette* and more and more of them buy the paper every week. Now, good day to you, Mr Marlowe."

Don pushed his chair back. "I'm sorry. This obviously hasn't got us anywhere. I thought there might have been some sort of civilised meeting ground. I made a mistake in supposing that the man at the top of the dunghill would do anything but crow."

He turned and pushed his way through the noise and smoke towards the stairs.

Chapter Six

The British Ambassador to Greece had been recalled for consultations, so the B.E.A. flight from Istanbul was held up forty minutes at Hellenikon waiting for him. It was six-fifteen before the Viscount touched down and seven-fifteen before Bennie was free. When she reached Pond Mews an enormous and very old and battered Delage was already parked outside her door. She ran up the stairs and found Michael Shorn talking to Pat Wilenski, the half-Polish girl with whom she shared her flat.

"So sorry I'm late. We were held up. I hope Pat's been entertaining you."

Michael smiled. "She's been doing fine. Bennie, I'm impressed by your uniform."

"Don't be," she said, warmed by his eyes. "I'll be out of it in five minutes."

"No hurry. We've all night."

"Give him another drink, Pat. Do we run to it?"

"Just."

Bennie fled into her room and began to change to the accompanying murmur of his deep voice and Pat's laughter.

"I haven't drunk your last drink," said Michael, getting up again when she came back. "I saved it for you."

As they left and Michael went round to open the car door for Bennie, Pat whispered to her: "Uh-huh. Dynamite. But dynamite."

"Think so?"

"I am sure so."

"He's a friend of the family."

"Don't let that deceive you."

Michael said: "I've put a rug over your seat so you won't dirty your frock. All set? This door has to slam. Right." He went round and slid in beside her. "Can you pull that thing out with the ring on it? Further. Till it dangles. That's it." He pressed the starter and the car suddenly began to quiver all over like an angry donkey. They backed round and shuddered off.

He took her to Manettas for dinner. "These lights are really for ageing actresses. A pity bringing a girl here who's got nothing to hide. How was the flight?"

"Like a train. One woman felt faint."

"What do you do then?"

"Oh, give her smelling salts and be generally kind and attentive."

He said: "I'm thinking of taking a ticket to Istanbul and feeling faint. Can I book a stewardess as well as a flight?"

"No, but there's plenty of choice."

"Have I told you, by the way, how you look in your uniform? That wonderful tight skirt. I'm still suffering from the flash-burn."

"Well, I'll give you no treatment for it."

He insisted on ordering champagne and they chatted amiably. She found herself enjoying his light sophisticated humour, but sometimes in repose the animation left his face and he looked sad. She wondered why. When the dinner was over he wanted to order brandy or a liqueur but she wouldn't have either.

"Have you come into a fortune?" she asked.

"No, but this is a celebration."

"Of what?"

"Our first meal together. And I've got myself a job and a new home. Isn't that something to celebrate?"

"Of course. I didn't know. What is it, Michael?"

"I'm taken on as a junior partner in a publishing firm."

She sipped the last of her champagne. "I'll drink to that!"

"Trouble is there's nobody junior to me! But on the strength of that I signed the lease of a two-roomed flat yesterday."

"Can I come to the house-warming?"

"You'll be the first guest."

She lowered her eyes. "Where is it?"

"Practically round the corner from you. Roger is paying the rent, and I'm going to beg, borrow or steal the furnishings."

"He's certainly very good to you."

"Within certain limits he's extraordinarily good. Let's go on somewhere, shall we? I want to show you the town."

Bennie climbed again into the huge old car and pulled out the ring while he started the engine.

"It's a nineteen thirty-one four-litre straight-eight. I've an extra thirty-gallon petrol tank on the back."

"How far do you get on that—thirty miles?"

"Naughty. Once you get three tons moving it practically goes under its own steam."

They roared down Piccadilly, stopped snorting and palpitating at traffic lights, then were off again with a great backfire that made people turn their heads all the way along the street. They turned up towards Soho, and after a bit of edging and squeezing got the car parked in a side street.

She said: "How do you know London so well, when you've spent all your time at Cambridge?"

"Not all my time. That's what the Master objected to."

He led the way to a door which looked like the back entrance to seedy offices, but music could be heard somewhere. They climbed stone stairs and came to a door marked Council For European Affiliation. He turned the handle and went in, and they were in a night club, where an ash blonde was taking coats, and the proprietor, a tall dark Sicilian with hair like fine fur, bowed from the waist and flashed a cash-register smile of welcome.

You went down a plywood passage which at the end debouched on to a small room with painted bamboo tables; to the right was a room with a bar built to give the impression of being a billiard-table on its side; to the left was the dance floor in which a Negro in a salmon-coloured dinner-jacket sat playing Cross-Hands Boogie on an overstrung Bechstein. Here and there giant umbrella poles sprang from the floor and flowered to form a gaudy roof decoration. Over the bar was the illuminated name of the club, the Middle Pocket.

"This is quite a place," said Bennie.

The room wasn't crowded, but the lighting was very subdued and it was hard to see faces at any distance. Then the pianist finished and a girl came up and put on records. As the coloured man went to the bar Michael called him and he came over.

"Meet Miss Bennie Marlowe, Dick. This is Dick Ballance, an old friend of mine."

"How d'you do, Miss Marlowe. Any friend of Michael's has a big welcome here. What are you drinking, man?"

"No, this is on me. Your usual?"

"What else?" Dick unbuttoned his coat to show a flowered purple cummerbund and spread his large plump hands. "I get worn out thumping that broken-down old virginal." When Michael had gone to the bar he said: "What lovely hair you've got, Miss Marlowe. I guess I should know something about it, if you'll excuse me mentioning it, because I run a hair-dressing barber-shop in Hammersmith. This is my spare time job, like. I sure do appreciate pretty hair, see. Oh, thank you, Michael, thank you, man."

After they had talked for a few minutes Michael said to Bennie: "Dance?" and they put their drinks on the table, and Ballance grinned his blessing and they took the floor.

"This *is* an odd place," she said.

"You think so? I'm glad. But why?"

"The night clubs I've been to before have always been so respectable. You feel anything could happen here."

After a few more times round Michael said: "Heavens, there's Peter Waldo. I must say hullo to him at the end of this."

The music stopped, and the Negro was returning to the piano. Bennie tucked in a bit of hair and Michael watched the lift of her arms appreciatively.

"Are you and Don very angry about that piece in *The Sunday Gazette*?"

"Yes. Wouldn't you be?"

"I didn't read it, but Roger was talking about it. Oh, Peter!"

A tall young man at the bar turned as they came up to him.

"My darling boy, I thought you were at Cambridge."

"I've applied for the Chiltern Hundreds. This is Peter. This is Bennie Marlowe."

"Bennie? Short for Benzedrine? I can see it should be. One's pepped up at the sight of you, my dear."

Peter Waldo was in his middle twenties, with a long neck and long slender fingers and china-blue eyes which took time to focus.

He said to Michael: "This place isn't really awake yet. Are you staying on?"

"No, I'm showing Bennie the town." Michael fetched their drinks from the table.

Peter Waldo said to her: "Did you leave your angel's wings in the cloakroom? You're quite the nicest thing I've seen for a very long time."

"Bennie comes from Istanbul," said Michael, handing her her beer. "You were out there this morning, weren't you?"

"Yes," she agreed, her eyes clear and unembarrassed. "I left at ten."

Peter made a little face and swallowed his drink, not quite sure what to make of it all. "Tell me, did this delinquent bring you here in a traction engine held together with glue and cheap string?"

"Now, now," said Michael. "A joke's a joke."

"Why don't you leave it on a gentle slope by a river? One push and you could buy yourself a car."

"What with?"

"Oh, that." Peter Waldo waved a hand that nearly knocked a man's drink out of his hand. "Seriously, Michael, I know a man who has a just-pre-war Lagonda. He only wants three hundred and I swear you could beat him down on that. The engine's as smooth as silk. . . ."

They talked cars for a few minutes, and then Michael said: "I'm neglecting you, Bennie. Whenever I meet Peter I get bogged down." He led her to the dance floor. To Peter he said: "I've got a flat. Come to my house-warming next week."

Peter had followed them a few steps. "D'you *want* to go on with this fellow?" he asked Bennie. "I know far more about London than he does."

She smiled: "Thank you. I think I'd better stay with him. I promised his father."

"Oh, that explains everything."

"You beast," said Michael, smiling at her as they began to dance.

They went on to what was called a "political" night club, recently opened by a psychiatrist. It seemed to differ very little from any other except that some of the clients looked as if they had recently been patients. To get in you made your way between two enormous white hands of plaster of paris, and the first notice said "I Hate Yellow Cats", which according to Michael meant that the hostess had a thing against blondes.

They ordered a drink and watched a rather indifferent floor show.

Bennie said: "You're not like Roger at all, are you? In features, I mean. Are you like your mother?"

"As a young man Roger made a habit of marrying. My mother was the First of the Few."

"What happened?"

"She left him. She's still going strong somewhere. Roger bumped into her a few years ago. I gather she'd grown fat and blowsy."

"Did he tell you that?"

"Not in so many words. In any case it's better to know the truth, isn't it?"

"I'm not sure. In that case I should have thought not."

Michael turned, and his rather sombre lonely face was illumined by the wonderful smile. "Don't start feeling sorry for me. That would be silly. I admire Roger for always being straight with me. He's always told me what I wanted to know. A lot of people get half-way through life before they work out the answers for themselves. Roger's told me the answers before I begin the sums. It makes a difference, that."

"I'm sure it makes a difference," she agreed.

"You're not drinking your beer."

"Sorry. I'm awash."

"But not drunk."

"Not drunk."

"Seriously, Bennie, I want this to be the beginning of a lot of times together. Maybe not always chasing the neon lights—that's not important—but together."

She smiled at him. "Thank you, Michael. I think I'd like it better that way."

"Are you not enjoying yourself?"

"Enormously."

"Let's go somewhere else. This place bores me."

They went back to Soho to a French club, where a number of odd women sat on high stools drinking pernod, and a trio played nostalgic tunes from the Left Bank. From there Michael drove her a quarter of a mile to a bombed site, to a Negro club, where in a low cellar barely lit at all, real jive was going on to a first-class Negro band. By the time they got out of there Bennie was feeling muzzy in spite of herself, and although she knew the next and last place they called was well north of the rest she couldn't be sure how far. All she knew was that the carpets were too thick and she didn't like the proprietor.

"What time is it?"

"Something after three. Tired?"

"No. But slightly drunk now."

He laughed. "Have a coffee. There's practically no heroin in it."

After a while she said: "Do you often do this?"

"Do what?"

"Make a round of the night life."

"Not often like this. I'm showing off, Bennie, to you."

"I'm tremendously impressed. I can't imagine how you've discovered all these places."

"It's all part of the service."

"There's one place I might take you sometime," she said reflectively. "It's full of Teddy Boys, and sometimes they beat each other up. It's all rather entertaining."

"Where's this, in Istanbul?"

"No. Paddington."

He watched her to see if she were serious. "And how do you come to know it?"

"It's close to a hostel where I work."

"No," he said. "Let's get this straight. You told me you work for B.E.A."

"So I do. But I have time off. I haven't *much* spare time, but I do some voluntary work in a hostel in Paddington. I like the sister in charge. I've known her for years. I usually manage to put in a day a week."

"What makes you do that? Isn't it hard work?"

She smiled back at him with wide, sleepy eyes. "No harder than enjoying yourself any other way."

"Like this, eh? Come on. You're tired. I'll take you home."

They were let silently out; and she did her stuff with the choke, and he got the car to start; and they went thundering off, the uncertain roar of the exhaust beating against the sleeping quiet of the night. She dosed her eyes and must have dozed for some minutes, because when she opened them the car had stopped. She looked sleepily round, but could not recognise the high wall of Pond Mews. There was a lot too much sky.

"Where are we?"

"Hampstead Heath," he said. "I thought we'd watch the sunrise."

She stared out at the star-lit sky. It was completely dark. "What time is it?"

"About twenty to four."

"The sun doesn't rise till after five."

"How do you know?"

"Disadvantage of working for B.E.A."

"I suppose I must have forgotten about summer time."

"I suppose you must."

"Do you mind?"

"Well, I think an hour and a half to wait. . . ."

"We can occupy it."

He bent over her, smoothed her hair back with his hand and kissed her.

When she could get her mouth free she said: "By now it must be quite a quarter to four."

"Yes, quite a quarter to four."

47

She put up her own hand to her hair, loosening the grip of his arms. "Like me to tell you about the stars?"

"Later."

She sighed. "It's one of the great drawbacks of working for B.E.A. One becomes informative."

He began to kiss her again. Breaking a little away after a minute or so, she said, trying to withdraw behind her own brand of humour: "Sirius is the brightest, but in fact it's quite small compared with one like Arcturus."

"Bennie," he said. "Be quiet. You're so beautiful you destroy me."

"That's bad."

"Go to sleep, darling. Go to sleep."

His hand came up to her face and began to stroke it. He had soft and gentle fingers. She decided she could take this.

"You think you're cool and calm and collected," he said. "But it isn't true. That lovely sensuous mouth isn't for nothing. You think too much. Let your brain go to sleep."

Beyond his arm she could see the half-dimmed glow of London. A turning car flooded its lights across the budding trees. His hand slid down and inside her frock to close over her shoulder. It was still gentle but it was firm, compelling.

"Michael," she said.

"Yes?"

"There are other nights."

"What's wrong with this one?"

"Nothing. . . ."

"Your heart's beating fast," he said. "I can feel the pulse in your neck."

"It's the altitude," she said. "This cabin isn't pressurised."

"Bennie, you're so very beautiful. I've never met anyone like you. Truly, truly I haven't. I believe your heart——"

His hand slid downward. She made a quick movement to stop him. But he didn't stop. She wrenched herself violently away, and her frock tore. For a second there was a pause while they took breaths in the dark.

With an icy, sick feeling behind her eyes she swallowed and tried to say lightly: "Sorry, darling; it's a restricted area."

There was a tremendous communication of tension between them that went far beyond what had been done and said.

He sat stroking the steering wheel with trembling fingers. Sometimes—though rarely—impulses gripped him that led him into wild blunders. He made moves that he half knew to be ill-judged before they were made; yet even after, while the mood still gripped him, he couldn't go back. So now. He knew the one way out was to pass the thing off lightly, as she was trying to do, to say sorry, my mistake, to make a joke of it. But two waves had collided in his heart and in his mind. Common sense, judgement, were still out of focus.

"I suppose I've bitterly offended you."

"No. Of course not."

"Have you hated this evening?"

"You know I haven't, Michael."

"D'you hate me?"

"Of course not."

"You must feel I've let you down."

She said: "It's I who've let you down ... if that was what you wanted."

He said with a tremendous effort: "It was your own fault. You're too lovely. Why were you afraid?"

"Being afraid or not afraid doesn't enter into it."

"I'm a boor and a fool, that's it, isn't it? But this sort of ending is the usual thing."

She said breathlessly: "Michael, you must have spent twenty pounds on me. For that, what do you usually get? I suppose you class me now with the blonde who gets a headache on her doorstep. I'm not playing fair. You think because I won't let you paw me about. ... Is that the way I should have paid back?. ... All right, I'm sorry, but that's not my way. I'm sorry, I'm sorry. I don't know whether you are right or I am, but as you say, there are dozens of girls who agree with you. There must be a lot even who would let you go to bed with them in a nice cosy flat, not stuck on Hampstead

Heath, and for half the price. . . ." She stopped, dry-eyed, choking with tears that had gone the wrong way.

"All right, *I'm* sorry," he said, cooling slightly. "It's all my fault. I *know*. I'll drive you home in a moment or two. I'm only trying now to explain, to put my point of view. You know it's not any other girl I want, I only want you. But I think you take it all too *seriously*. This sort of thing is fun if you let it be fun and don't tie it up with all sorts of other things."

"Such as?"

"Love and marriage come later. They're more important, but they're not *harmed* if you've enjoyed yourself first. There's so little time. We must live life while we're young. Ask men and women of forty about their youth and ninety-nine per cent, if they're being honest, will tell you it's the things they didn't do that they regret—not the things they did!"

A meteor flickered across the sky, but by now she couldn't even pretend an interest in it. "Michael, there's nothing I can say to you now that won't make me sound like a frozen spinster. But if it were true that some people say that—even if I say it when I'm older, it won't alter what I feel *now*. Perhaps people change when they get older. Perhaps they forget how they felt when they were young. To me sex without love is—is just not in the book at all. All right, I don't understand, you say. That may be. But, until I love you, I'm not willing to let you prove me wrong."

There was silence. "And when will that be?" he said.

"I—don't know."

He said: "Will you try to answer me one thing quite honestly?"

"I'll try."

"Don't you in your heart want to be made love to? Hasn't that been a part of your thoughts ever since you grew up?—as making love has been a part of mine?"

"I don't think this is going to get anywhere, Michael. Don't ask me anything more now, please. Let's go home."

Chapter Seven

"No," said Dame Maria, "we've got to go through that again. It's lifeless, without character; look *pleased*, angelic, not with those fixed grins. As soon as we get on the big stage you behave like circus ponies. Louis, from the beginning again!"

Six black-clad girls described multiple *fouettees* as they entered again from the wings and whirled past the two chairs in the middle of the stage, while the staff pianist played the tune. Air bearing female warmth and scent of talcum powder wafted past Don, and his chair vibrated with the thud of their feet.

"Well, it's better. Now, Karena, *please*. . . ."

Presently Dame Maria grudgingly admitted it would do, and at once the whole stage disintegrated into chattering murmuring figures strangely humanised and foreshortened as they came down upon their heels and threaded their way off. Soon there were only the two chairs in the middle of the stage and Henry de Courville sauntering on from the wings.

"So you see," Dame Maria said, patting Don's arm, "we've our hands full. A new ballet and two revivals, and we are two ballerinas short. I have ten like that one, coming along, but not yet really ready for the exacting role. That, my dear boy, is even more important than extra woodwind for the new ballet."

Don let out a thoughtful breath. Ballet, even in the raw, wove odd spells about him. "Could I possibly disagree?"

Somewhere carpenters began to hammer. "No, well, there it is. Last season, I admit, it's true. . . ."

"Last season," said de Courville, "we were playing half the time with a crowd of deputies. The main orchestra was in Australia."

"So long as I get time enough on the new things," Don said.

"Don't worry," said Dame Maria. "You've the four necessities: musicianship, the right psychology, a sense of theatre, and you understand the importance of the stick."

"Like a Victorian father," said Don.

"Well, there are points of similarity. But you'd be surprised how many we've had here with such poor stick technique; they double with the left hand and make geographical gestures of no importance. But perhaps you wouldn't be surprised. You know far more about it than I do."

"I'm coming to doubt that."

Henry de Courville said: "The Administrator hasn't gone yet. If you'd like to come to his office we can sign the thing now."

"Thank you."

Dame Maria was accosted by the choreographer, who as usual was worried about something, so Don said good-bye to her and the two men went off together.

"She doesn't often pay compliments," Henry said. "But have a care; a specially high standard is set for the favourites. . . . By the way, did you see today's *Times?*"

"No, I came straight here."

"There's a letter about your father. I have it on my desk, so we can pick it up on the way."

"When they came to Henry's office he took up the newspaper and handed it to Don. The second letter on the editorial page was headed: "Sir John Marlowe". Don's eyes went to the signatures. Lord Queenswood and three others, all Q.C.s.

To the Editor of *The Times.*

Sir,

In a recent issue of *The Sunday Gazette*, in a column contributed under the pseudonym of Moonraker, grave and highly damaging insinuations were made about the late Sir John Marlowe. These must be wounding not only to his family but to his many personal friends, not to speak of the thousands who came to know him through his book and through his other writings.

The signatories of this letter all knew John Marlowe for upwards of twenty years. Two were fellow benchers of the Upper Temple and all knew him intimately both in and out of court. Since they are in a position to do so, they therefore consider it their duty publicly to refute the statements made in this Sunday newspaper in so far as these statements referred to John Marlowe's professional activities as a Queen's Counsel and as Recorder of Cheltenham.

No charge of unprofessional conduct was ever levelled against him, by his fellow benchers, by the Bar Council, or by any other legal or municipal body. It is false and tendentious to imply that if there had been any irregularities these could have been hushed up without resort to a full and formal inquiry. John Marlowe did not resign from the Upper Temple; he could have returned at any time. His decision to *cease to practise* was received with the greatest regret by everyone in the legal profession. He was an ornament to the Bar, a candidate for high judicial office in the not distant future, and a man whom any aspiring barrister could well use as a model.

But this article, we would suggest, raises wider issues than the reputation of one man. Attacks upon the living are a common part of daily journalism; but irresponsibility and malice are curbed by threat of legal sanction. Attacks upon the dead are a relatively rare and very unsavoury development, and the law offers too little redress. This is a case surely on which the Press Council should act.

Yours faithfully,
Queenswood,
Arthur Morrissey,
John Lambton,
P. J. Greer.

Don handed the paper back. "I shall write to Queenswood and

the others. I wish someone could ditch the charge about his book as effectively."

"Did you ever know the Rev. George Chislehurst?"

"No. Did you?"

"I met him at your father's house in the country, before he retired, one Sunday. I'd got to know your father the year before, and when he heard I'd been ill he invited me down for the week-end. It was queer—he could never bear to be ill himself, it hurt his pride—but he was always sympathetic when other people were. Chislehurst turned up while I was there. Except for his clerical collar he looked like everyone's idea of a radical reformer of the nineteenth century." They walked out of the office and along the corridor. "By the way, I met Knott of *The Observer* today. He says on Tuesday they dug up a second-hand copy of Chislehurst's book and sent it along with your father's book to Professor Lehmann of London University for an opinion as to whether there are any resemblances. Lehmann is going to write an article that will be published in *The Observer* on Sunday."

"I suppose Knott doesn't know who Moonraker is?"

"No. But he did say he's certain the same man has been writing the column since Bryan Hooker was killed."

"The trouble is," said Don, "even if I get to know, there's apparently nothing I can do about it, at least so far as the law is concerned."

"You certainly can't do a thing while he stays anonymous. That's probably what he's counting on. But if you do find out his name I wouldn't be absolutely sure there's *nothing* you can do. You remember I read law for a year. There are more ways of killing a cat than choking it with cream."

"I don't follow you."

"Well, follow me now." Henry knocked at the door of the Administrator's office and they went in.

Joanna had only been in a few minutes when Roger rang. She nearly didn't answer it. Twice on the way home she had been stopped by reporters, once coming out of the studio at Lime Grove and once at the door of the house. But in the end she went to the telephone.

When she heard Roger's voice she looked quickly at the door of the bedroom and pushed it to with her foot, even though she knew there was no one in the house.

"Joanna, I didn't see you on Tuesday."

"No. I didn't go out."

"But you said you'd come for an hour. I waited."

"I never said that. . . ."

"You said you'd try——"

"Roger. . . . Don't ring me like this. It's risky and it's unfair."

"To whom?"

"To me. I have to work this out. I can't if you keep . . . intruding yourself."

"Doesn't Don? He's in a bolt position."

She said: "It isn't that sort of a war."

"What sort, then?"

"I tried to explain how it was before Don came home."

"All you said was——"

"All I said was that there are some things I still draw the line at."

"Self flagellation isn't in season, my dear. . . ."

"Listen, please."

He stopped. "All right. I'm listening."

After a minute she said: "There's no black or white to this. I'm not pretending so. The truth isn't one thing; it isn't even a number of things I can take apart and look at. It's something very complex and deep inside, that I want to unravel—alone. You can't help—you can only complicate."

"Yes, but——"

"I want the chance to see this straight. In the next few weeks either I leave Don or I don't."

"As simple as that?"

"As difficult as that."

He said: "Forgive me, I'm not trying to be cynical at Don's expense, but don't catch your moods from him, Joanna. Don't be too intense. Your detachment has always been one of the things I've admired most in you. It takes a pretty intelligent person to see their own lives in perspective. Do that, my dear."

"Meaning what?"

"D'you remember what Sir Toby said? 'Dost thou think, because thou art virtuous, there shall be no more cakes and ale?'"

"Perhaps Sir Toby didn't have to live with himself afterwards."

"There isn't an afterwards in love; only a continuing present."

"Darling, I'm grown up. Remember?"

"Sorry. You provoke me. I can't bear to be slick—to you of all people. But what I said would be true."

"I don't even think I wish I could believe it."

"Where is Don now?"

"At Covent Garden. I'll ring you if I get the opportunity early next week."

"I shall wait for it."

"Good-bye," she said, hearing the front door; and then Don whistled as he ran up the stairs.

Roger had rung Joanna in an interval of his preparations for receiving Sir Percy Laycock and his daughter. Here all his peculiar flair for cooking came out, and by the time Mrs Smith, his "help", returned he had been in the kitchen two hours and everything for the evening was under way, the wine decanted, the saddle of lamb cooking in bay leaves. Even the potatoes were ready mashed with butter and eggs and cut into shape; it would only be for her at the last moment to roll them in almonds and drop them in deep fat.

At seven he went into the living-room for a quick drink before he changed. He was irritated when a few minutes later Michael came down.

"What have you done to your suit? It looks as if you've slept in it. And that shirt isn't clean."

Michael said: "I forgot to hang it up when I came in last night. And this seems to be the only shirt."

"Then go and take one of mine, for heaven's sake. I don't want you looking like an out-of-work waiter."

They went up the stairs together, Roger with his hand proprietorially on Michael's shoulder. While they were picking through the shirts he said:

"I think you'll find Sir Percy Laycock interesting. He has quite, strong religious beliefs—and as I told you he's a self-made man. His father left him three clothing stores, and in twenty years he opened a chain of sixty. They all prospered, and since then he's bought up other rival concerns until he has become a very rich man indeed. They say he has a million pounds uncommitted."

"That would make anyone interesting."

"But he's agreeable too. And rather ingenuous. He's never been in touch with the literary world at all—and he looks on it with awe and with interest. He's a man to know—very few people do. He's not a diner out. I've tried to get him here before. One can't appear to press."

"What about this pique silk?" said Michael.

After a spasm of hesitation Roger agreed. "But treat it with care. They cost me ten pounds each."

"And the daughter?" said Michael.

"I haven't met her; you must judge for yourself. But don't forget what liking her might lead to."

"I've never been in doubt about that since I was twelve," said Michael.

Roger gave a little nervous irritable shrug of the shoulders. For once he was not in the mood for that sort of joke.

Since Tuesday night Michael had been going through a species of private hell that was unlike anything he had ever imagined existed before. He didn't know what had hit him. Up to now taking girls out had for him been one of the best games in the world—a delightful amusing ever-changing past-time. Women—there were millions of them. More than half the population of the world was female, and at least one per cent of it highly attractive, bent, as he was bent, on enjoying themselves. This blunt instrument that had struck him on Tuesday night, this crab that had clutched his stomach, this sickness which had robbed him of his sleep and of his food,

57

it could hardly be connected with sex, one hesitated even to call it love. All he understood was that it was acute misery beyond his worst imagining.

Last night he had been out with Peter Waldo—which was as near as one could attain to the certainty of forgetting. Ashes, it was all ashes; drink tasted like paraffin, food choked him. He had stumbled home to his own bed about four, to sleep for two hours and then wake with the worst and least deserved hangover of his career. Today he had crawled about, going through the motions of cleaning his new flat, but with the feeling of utter disaster so much upon him that he could hardly move.

When Sir Percy Laycock arrived he came in on two sticks, plump, small, not old, smiling, apologetic for being late. He was not expensively dressed and his Cockney accent still clung to him like a home-knitted pullover. Marion was tall and brown-haired—not at all pretty, rather heavy in a young way. Her Molyneux frock was the wrong colour and she had no small talk.

Michael wondered what Bennie was doing, and thought of the tiny mole by her mouth and the feel of her naked shoulder and the look in her long dark eyes. While the rest of the party was drinking one cocktail he contrived to down three, and since he had eaten nothing all day they went to his head.

With a half-cynical detachment he watched his father turning on all the familiar charm: the easy conversation, the dignified but modest smile, the instant courteous deferment to one of his guests when they chose to reply. He was like a great man entertaining two of his followers, condescending to them without the smallest trace of condescension, making them feel at home, flattering them by developing some casual comment of theirs into a profound or clever thought and making it appear that it had originated with them.

Usually Michael was proud of the way his father managed these occasions. It was a well-oiled model of the way things should be done. But tonight it jarred and jarred. He felt trapped in an environment that didn't interest him, and trapped by Roger, who as usual got all his own way in the major things while giving ground on the less important. What Michael was fundamentally interested in was *machines* ... bridges, blue-prints, problems of power and structural stress. More than ever in the last few days he had realised his father's inflexible persuasiveness. For all his kindness and generosity, you were given the illusion of freedom but not the reality. You were moved about like a flag on a map.

Michael found himself tonight also resenting the way Roger so quickly and so easily thawed Marion Laycock's shyness and got her on his side. It was done so gently that it was like sleight of hand. And for some reason he resented it more because he saw it was a man-woman relationship regardless of the difference in their ages.

He considered how his father would have approached Bennie if he felt as *he* did. Not by trailing her round half a dozen night clubs and then making clumsy lap-dog passes at her on Hampstead Heath. That was the unforgiveable blunder. Any moron could have told him that Bennie was not that sort of girl. The point was he knew himself. But something had got into him and carried him on.

The avocado pear stuffed with crab came and went with the Puligny Montrachet. Michael left most of his food but drank the wine.

"Michael feels that too," said Roger, passing the ball, and the girl, neatly back to him.

"I'm sorry," Michael said. "I wasn't listening."

"I was only pointing out. ..."

What humiliation he had come to! A hundred times since Tuesday night he had gone through the sequence of events, the conversation, the tone of her voice, the feel of her lips, the brief firm clutch of her hand when she said good night. He had never been so angry, so anxious to undo what he had done. But when you are angry with yourself there is no scapegoat.

Perhaps it was already too late to recover lost ground. She'd no wish to see him again. Pat Wilenski had answered the phone every time he had rung. He was certain Bennie had been there the first time.

He suddenly heard Marion speaking to him and turned a half-tortured face to her.

She said. "I only asked if you liked being at Cambridge."

None of the smiling look in her eye that she had for Roger. "I'm not at Cambridge," he said. "I was sent down three weeks ago."

"Oh," she said, not blinking at that. "Bad luck."

"Not really. Mainly bad management."

Roger said with a smile: "Michael's been following in distinguished footsteps."

"It is practically the only distinction worth gaining there nowadays," said Michael.

Sir Percy looked at him, and there was a moment's uncomfortable silence before Roger came in with: "I was never lucky enough—or if Michael prefers it unlucky enough—to get near any university. I began teaching at a private school when I was eighteen, though looking back I can't think what I can possibly have known myself."

"What were you sent down for?" Marion asked Michael directly, when the conversation had broken up again.

"I disagreed with the Master."

"I thought wild oats had gone out of season."

"Oh, we still contrive to have our simple boyish fun."

She flushed but didn't say anything more.

The young lamb disappeared with the Mouton Rothschild '49. When the sweet came Sir Percy congratulated Roger on his cook, and Roger had to confess modestly that he was responsible for most of it. Laycock, a widower for six years, was full of admiration for Roger's surprising talent, and the talk waxed ever friendlier. Only at Michael's end had the blight settled.

Michael had again left the succulent food congealing like an insult on his plate, but he had again drunk the wine, and gradually he began to come round and feel more at ease; there was after all an E.P.N.S. lining to life.

He heard Roger say: "I'm more than ever interested in this project of yours about a newspaper or a magazine, Laycock. Being a journalist myself, I know some of the pitfalls and I envy you the financial power."

"Yes, well it hasn't got very far yet," said Sir Percy, dabbing his napkin to his mouth. "One thing I wanted to ask you tonight—what is your opinion of *The Daily Globe*?"

Roger hesitated for the first time. "As you probably know, it's been losing ground for two years."

"I know the directors slightly," Sir Percy said. "They're all wealthy men but they obviously won't want to go on dropping money indefinitely."

"I think they're willing to, to some extent, because they believe in their policy."

"Which is a quality newspaper with a popular appeal. Yes ... if the loss doesn't become too great. What would your solution be?"

"I think every editor in Fleet Street would give you the same answer. They'd say that *The Globe* is trying to pursue two contradictory objectives, and to become a real success it would have to choose which of the two it really wants most. If it's to aim at a mass circulation it cannot have quality; if it is to have quality it cannot get a mass circulation."

"That's a very cynical outlook."

"Most editors are cynical, I'm afraid."

Sir Percy savoured the last of his wine. "*The Daily Telegraph* seems to get away with a compromise policy all right."

"Well, I think *The Globe* could succeed on its present lines if the problem were tackled in a different way."

"How?"

"I don't believe any newspaper can carry on on an even keel for any length of time. It must go up or down. And the essence of any upward movement must lie in the vigour of the editorial policy. Not directly by its editorials but by what it *makes* of the news. . . ."

"What are you going to do now?" Marion said, trying not to bring hostility in her voice but blunt through embarrassment with this silent young man. "Are you going to be a journalist too?"

"No," said Michael. "I'm going to be a publisher and issue salacious memoirs at extravagant prices."

He did not mean this as an off-putting remark: he tried to be lightly amusing but for some reason everything he said tonight sounded heavily sarcastic, even to himself. She flushed again. Once more Roger stepped in. "Michael's now with Bartlett and Leak. They're a good imprint, one of the old-fashioned houses that still take their job seriously."

"What do you do?" Laycock asked pleasantly.

"I haven't started yet, sir," Michael said. "But I think for the first ten years my job will be making the tea."

"The directors of *The Globe*," said Percy Laycock reflectively, "have repeatedly refused offers to buy the paper, made by one of the big combines. But they would welcome fresh capital if it comes from the right source. In their view I imagine I would be the right source, because we have much the same beliefs. With a substantial investment, say a quarter of a million, I could find myself in virtual control of a London daily paper." He glanced at Roger self-consciously to see how he was taking it. "Perhaps you think that ambition rather naive. After all, it's a long way from chain stores to the newspaper world."

"I don't look on it as naive in the least," Roger said. "In such a position one can be one of the most powerful influences for good or ill in the world today. But you'd need the most expert advice before taking such a step. If you're serious I'd be glad to see that you got it."

"Ah." Sir Percy laughed. "You encourage me. I might even *be* serious. It's a curious thing, I reckon I'm ready to run far more risks now than I did when I was a young man."

"After all, sir," said Michael, "you have nothing to lose but your chains."

There was a dead silence. It was more than a silence, it was a vacuum. In those few seconds Percy Laycock's face altered its shape from the rounded contours of middle-aged success to the angular lines that had once driven him on his way.

"Young man," he said. "There are various ways of making one's living in this world. I am not ashamed of the way I've made mine——"

"Michael's a young fool," said Roger, for once interrupting his guest and trying to speak lightly. "He's come back this year with a kind of undergraduate humour which I find infinitely trying." Speaking as if Michael wasn't there he added: "A couple of years in the city will cure him. I'm sure he didn't mean any offence."

"Naturally I didn't wish to take it," said Laycock. There was a pause while he waited for Michael to speak and while Michael struggled with an insane sense of laughter. Then he went on: "In actual fact there's no reason why I should, since I agree with him. In a good cause, if I find a good cause, I'm quite willing to risk losing some of my chains."

The Laycocks stayed till eleven. Then Sir Percy telephoned for his car, and in a few minutes picked up his sticks and limped out escorted by his daughter. The evening had not been a success. After dinner Sir Percy went out of his way to be pleasant to his host, but there was about him that slightly strained air which shows when agreeableness is imposed by the will.

To Roger with his almost feminine perceptions the evening was a constant rearguard action. For the first time for years he knew that he himself was talking too much. He had become known as a conversationalist not only because of the intelligence of his own talk but because of the intelligence with which he listened to other people: but tonight the silences could not be used; they had to be filled, and often they were filled to excess. So he did not press Sir Percy to stay for a last whisky. He went with them to the door. Sir Percy thanked him for a delightful dinner and a most pleasant evening, and they went out to their waiting car.

While they were going Michael stayed in the drawing-room lighting a cigarette. He still felt fuddled and light-headed. He knew he had behaved rather badly tonight but he was certainly unprepared for the livid face with which Roger returned.

"You *damned* ignorant ill-mannered young fool!"

Michael put his lighter away and looked at his cigarette to try to hide his surprise. He had never been spoken to by his father like that before. "Oh, come off it, Dad. Don't blow the thing up into—into something more than it was."

"Listen," said Roger, coming to him. "On this evening I have spent three carefully arranged preparatory meetings, fifteen pounds on wine and food, several hours of cooking, forethought, for my own future and for yours, a great deal of personal and nervous energy. I bring to this house a man worth a million pounds, uncommitted, friendly, receptive to intellectual company, and with an only daughter. And because of you, because of your ignorant, lumpish, loutish manners, because you got out of bed the wrong side this morning or your nanny forgot to change you, the whole evening is *thrown* on the dust heap. But what do you care, you conceited, bumptious, ignorant, overgrown schoolboy! Nothing, so long as you can sulk and try out your shoddy sarcasms."

"Good God," said Michael, frightened now and resenting his fright. "I wasn't feeling too fit, that's all. Everything I said they took the wrong way——"

"You weren't feeling too fit because you've been on the tiles three nights running. You weren't feeling too fit because for one solitary evening you had to please someone else and not yourself!"

"I'm sorry if you see it that way." Michael pushed his hair back, his own temper rising. "I didn't expect him to get on his dignity. And the girl was so dull——"

"The girl was dull because you frightened her or offended her every time you opened your clumsy mouth. D'you realise where you could have been in two years if you'd married her? Head of your own publishing firm or head of practically any other undertaking you chose to take up——"

"Well," said Michael, "you can buy some things at too high a price."

"Listen, Michael. One can well marry for policy and not for a pretty face. You can have your mistresses after if you want to. But a chance like that won't often come your way."

"She seemed awfully receptive to you," said Michael, suddenly flaring up. "If you feel that way about it, why don't you marry her yourself?"

64

He thought his father was going to hit him and dropped his cigarette. Then, annoyed again at his own fear and angry at the damage that fear had done to his self-eseem, he bent to pick the cigarette off the carpet.

"It will be a good thing," said Roger, "when you're in your own flat. A taste of poverty will make you realise that life isn't all bed and Bennie Marlowe."

That touched the rawest spot in all the world. "You can leave Bennie out of this!"

"Can I? You love-sick fool! You've done everything since last Sunday except weep! But you won't do any good with her, my boy. Better to stick to your cheap tarts——"

"Shut up!" shouted Michael, to drown not only his father's voice but the voice within himself. He swung away, pushed past Roger to the door, hesitated there trying to think of the right reply, his face twitching. There'd never been anything like this between them before; their friendship had been a sheet anchor; the worst disagreement a few cool-tempered words.

"I'll see that the rent of your flat is paid," said Roger.

"I wouldn't *have* your money," said Michael. "I'll fend for myself on twelve-ten a week. Many an overgrown schoolboy has done that before."

He went out.

Chapter Eight

Wolseley Dorrit was flying back to Montreal on the Friday evening, so Don drove him to London Airport. When they got there the plane from Istanbul was due, so he waited for Bennie, to drive her home.

"Don, how nice! And how convenient. Couldn't you do this oftener?" She slung her shoulder bag on the back seat and settled into the one beside him.

"It's all part of the Marlowe Car Hire Service. What was the flying like?"

"All right. The corn is ripe already round Ciampino. I'd adore to live in Italy."

"You don't look as if you'd had much sun recently. All this hoisting up in one country and down in another three or four times a week must get pretty jangling on the nerves. I should loathe it."

"Well, you hate flying anyway."

"Only modern man could devise an occupation that at the same time is both boring and dangerous. I hope Wolseley will be all right."

"Wolseley is a great deal safer up there than I am on the road with you."

"Thanks." Don braked sharply at a traffic light and his tyres squealed on the road. "I suppose I was born out of my time. On the whole I should like to have been the pet musician of some fat Hanoverian prince. One lived at least at the whim of a music-lover."

"What's this I hear about your being taken on at Covent Garden?"

"Six months only, but it's a gift from heaven. Nine hundred pounds will keep the wolf a bit further from the door."

"It's odd," Bennie said. "Anyone not knowing would think you were wealthy: a well-known young conductor, and Joanna a TV star."

"Which just shows how wrong anyone can get. It's being 'casual labour' that does it. Even for this job I get paid probably less than a Smithfield porter."

Bennie knew how much he disliked discussing his lack of earning power, how much he disliked seeing Joanna do the occasional advertising programme; yet sometimes the very fact of avoiding discussion led them into difficulties.

"I gather that Daddy's estate won't amount to much."

"Practically nil, according to Whitehouse. Anyway, he kept us handsomely and educated us. One shouldn't expect much more than that. Oddly enough, I don't think he'd made provision for the year's lag in surtax when he retired. When you've been earning £20,000 a year and suddenly drop to nothing . . . I know last year when he was down he said rather wryly that if he'd known his book was going to make so much money and that he was going to be so poor, he would have kept some of the royalties for his own use."

"Don, when did he tell you he was going to retire?"

"It was a few weeks after I got engaged to Joanna. I must say I was surprised; I'd always thought his interest in philosophy was a side-line and that his life was wrapped up in the law. But I didn't *query* his decision. If that was what he wanted to do, then obviously he should do it."

Bennie took off her cap and shook out her hair. "D'you think we were a peculiar family, didn't hold together enough?"

"Why?"

"I've wondered. I suppose when Mummy was killed that broke the linch-pin."

"How else could it be? A busy man left with a daughter of seven and a son of fifteen. Maybe he got more busy afterwards, to try to forget. . . . I don't think we were much different from what any other family would have been."

Yet he thought as he spoke that if it hadn't been for Moonraker probably they wouldn't have had this conversation. Life moved in a series of superficial moments strung together painlessly so that the days and the years slipped away, and only afterwards sometimes you paused and looked back and wondered if banality had been enough. Bennie was right; his moments of real contact with her and with his father had been painfully few; a mountain of trivial content disguised the fact, so that one didn't know it had been like that until too late. But could it have been any different? Once they had swung apart, once they were not together in everyday contact, didn't the weight of events personal only to each one spring the hinges too wide?

Bennie said: "Did you see *The Sketch* today? They smoked out Miss Chislehurst and tried to persuade her to give them an interview. She obviously wasn't having any, but what little she did say showed she was on Moonraker's side."

"My feeling is that the rest of the Press don't quite know which way to take this attack at present. They suspect that *The Gazette* has brought off a first-class scoop, but on the whole they're a bit uncertain about the repercussions, and so for the time being they're standing on the sidelines. *The Globe* commented yesterday on Dad's high reputation and said that the present law of libel as it applied to dead persons was chaotic and highly unsatisfactory."

"Good."

"As comment, good, yes. I met a man called Smith at the club as I was coming out to pick up Wolseley. He asked me if it was true, what Moonraker said."

"Enchanting person."

"No . . . only tactless. Many people must be thinking the same."

They joined the Great West Road. Traffic was heavy both ways, the overcharged artery of a sclerotic city.

"Bennie, Joanna and I are going down to the Old Millhouse tomorrow. It may be we shall work some of this out there. Why don't you come?"

"Your first week-end off with Joanna? No, there'll be another time."

"Do you still do that voluntary hostel work?"

"I try to. I don't put in a lot of time."

"I admire your social conscience."

"Maybe it's not such an asset."

He glanced at her, surprised at her tone. "I think I'm a bar or two behind. D'you mind bringing me up with you?"

"There's nothing much to bring you up with. Don, d'you think I'm a prig?"

"My dear girl!"

"Well, do you?"

"Don't be a fool."

"You see," she said, trying to explain as if to a stranger; "living to me is a sort of give and take. I take what I want from it and try to give something back—not because I ought to but because I want to. It makes sense that way. It doesn't make sense any other way. I've no profound convictions; I just go on instruments, as it were. But lately. . . ."

"What?"

"Oh, never mind." She had been frowning at the back of the car ahead. "Forget it."

He drove on for a while in silence. She thought he was not going to make any comment but at length he said: "It's odd how much on the defensive one is these days if one does anything which is not entirely in step with jungle ethics. If you're now going to say you're ashamed of yourself because you help some down-and-outs in North London——"

"Calm down, darling. I was only wondering if I might become a more fully integrated personality if I went on the streets for a bit."

"Fully integrated personality—hell!"

"That's what chiefly shocks you?—not the suggestion?"

"I'm as shocked as a maiden aunt to hear you using dog-eared phrases out of Psychiatry for Beginners."

"It would give Moonraker a new angle to work on," she said.

"Incidentally d'you think it was an isolated broadside last Sunday or do you imagine he'll come back with something more this week?"

"I don't know," said Don. Until then the possibility hadn't occurred to him.

Chapter Nine

When Don and Joanna got to Midhurst on the following evening the sun had just set, and the afterglow silhouetted the tall trees in which a great many birds were making a great deal of noise. "They keep on tuning up," Don said, "but their conductor never comes."

He went into the kitchen to find the main switch and then came back putting on the lights as he came. He found Joanna still at the front door.

"What's the matter?"

"Nothing."

"Are you cold?"

"No."

"We'll get a fire going. It'll be different then."

Joanna followed him into the living-room, glanced round it as if expecting to recognise the ghosts of a different mood. It was all there, utterly and precisely untouched. Don's mother looked at her with the unchanging half-smile of a church madonna. He bent at the fire and tried to persuade the paper to catch.

She said: "I'll bring the sheets in from the car."

When she got back the fire was flickering and Don was standing thoughtfully by the desk. "His pipe," he said, holding it up.

"You understand why I haven't been much on my own."

"Perhaps you were right in not wanting to come here for our week-end."

She hesitated. "It will be better soon."

They had brought food down with them and Don got a bottle of wine out of the cupboard. When she saw it Joanna said: "D'you think we could have something else tonight, a Burgundy or a white wine?"

"There's nothing as good as this claret. I thought it was your favourite drink."

She half smiled. "I'm temperamental."

He made a gesture disclaiming responsibility and changed the bottle for a Chablis. After supper he played through one of the ballets he was to take; presently she joined him.

"Don't stop. I think I missed the sound of the piano almost as much as anything while you were away."

There seemed to be music scores all round him, as thick as telephone books. He got up. "It's years since I saw a 'Daphnis and Chloe'; I can't even remember who did it."

"How long have you had this house, Don?"

"Dad bought it after the Munich scare, partly as a place for Mother to come if there was a war. Queer after that that she should refuse to budge from London and be killed by a bomb."

"Did your father never think of marrying again?"

"I think he did once, not very long ago. He was friendly with a Mrs Delaney. I never met her, but Bennie did and liked her. For some reason it never came to anything, and I think she left England. I've found the Chislehurst booklet, by the way."

He handed her a thin book bound in yellow boards. "*Man and the Future. A Christian Affirmation*. By George Ludwig Chislehurst." Fifty-six pages of close type. No publisher's name, but the printer was Frederick Moore of Dorchester.

It seemed to be a justification of the Christian ethic on philosophical grounds. There were chapters on St Augustine, Aquinas, Berkeley, Fechner. She went to one of the bookshelves and took down a copy of *Crossroads* by John Marlowe. Don watched her tall shadow move jagged-edged along the books. She said: "If there's any similarity at all you'll obviously have to have some sort of expert opinion."

"*The Observer* is apparently getting one for tomorrow."

She opened *Crossroads* and turned a page or two. Chapter One was headed "The Problem Stated". "We are living in the most exciting and significant time since the beginning of man as a thinking creature. It needs an effort of disciplined imagination to understand all that that means, but once the effort has been made, then there is an end to despair and the poverty of self-pity." Her eyes, strayed further on. "The one real purpose of life is to intensify life and so to enlarge it. The one real hope of man is that he should recognise that there are two meanings to the phrase 'a higher standard of living'. ... The one essential for all our rationalism is that we should refuse to be intimidated by it. For it must be constantly seen, and kept, in historical perspective, along with all the other means and ways by which men have tried to apprehend the truth."

She said: "Is it really an epoch-making book? I can't judge at all."

"Neither can I. I was too close to him. Of course some people shoot it down and say it isn't all that original; but the majority of men whose opinions count rate it high."

She glanced at a page or two more and then closed it. "If they were friends—I mean Chislehurst and your father—if they talked together for hours on end, as Bennie says they did, there might very well be an unconscious resemblance in the books."

"Chislehurst's book was published five years before the other. Dad had too good a memory to use things out of a friend's work which he had read recently—without permission and acknowledgement, that is."

"I wish I could see into Moonraker's mind. It isn't clever to suggest something that can easily be disproved."

Don said: "I was thinking the same."

Next morning he woke at nine. Joanna was still asleep, one arm flung across the counterpane, her hair ruffled in the way he liked to see it ruffled. Outside the window starlings were quarrelling and a finch was providing the counterpoint. He slid out of bed and dressed quietly, watching Joanna to see that she did not wake.

He went downstairs. When he opened the door the sunlight crowded in as if it had been queuing there. A thrush carrying a snail hopped across the path as he went down it. He walked towards the village. Tomorrow he started work with Henry de Courville, who had done the choreography and Simon Bellegarde, who had written the music, on the new ballet, *Les Ambassadeurs*. So far he had only read through the music a couple of times, but, in spite of everything else, that filled his mind now. It was an unfamiliar terrain, to be occupied and lived in and interpreted alone.

The man was just sorting out his morning orders.

"A *Times*, a *Gazette*, an *Observer* and a *Sentinel*, please."

"There you are, sir. Lovely morning. Forecast wasn't too good for later in the day. One and six, two shillings. Thanks."

Fold the papers under your arm. Don't concede anything by opening them now. Country gentleman out for a stroll before breakfast. Disconcerting to be the victim of this anonymous spite. For if one faced it, the likelihood was that much of the ill-will was directed against him. What was the purpose of attacking the reputation of a dead man unless there was someone still alive to care?

As he walked back to the cottage he passed the local policeman. "Good morning, sir, nice to see you down again after all this time."

"Oh, thanks. I've been away since my father died."

"Yes, sir, I heard. We've missed him a lot, you know. Always used to see him out in the garden and taking his morning stroll. Always made you feel you'd got his personal interest, like. He was a great man."

Don smiled. "I'm afraid the house will have to be sold."

"Ah, that's a pity. That's a pity. Sorry Midhurst is going to lose touch with you, sir. Matter of fact, I thought perhaps it had been sold that night in February when I was coming past on my late beat and saw a car in the drive. But I shone my light on it an' saw 'twas yours."

"When would that be?"

"Oh, 'twould be about one o'clock in the morning, one Sunday in February. I expect Mrs Marlowe was down for the week-end."

"Yes, she did come once or twice while I was away."

Don walked on. The cool spring breeze blew on his face and

flipped at the corners of the papers he carried. Japanese cherry and almond trees were in blossom in an overgrown cottage garden. A dog barked and thrust its muzzle through the gate at him.

When he reached the Old Millhouse he went into the kitchen and filled the kettle and switched it on. He put a teapot and two cups on a tray. Then he sat down and opened *The Sunday Gazette*.

This week the article was in two parts, the first being an attack on the Home Secretary. The second part ran:

"There has been a fine tizzy in the dovecotes since our article last week on John Marlowe, Knight of the British Empire, ex-barrister, ex-philosopher (Remember *Crossroads*?).

"Some amiable folk have rushed to his defence. A few, less amiable, have tried to bring pressure on this newspaper to take back what it said.

"They should have known better.

"Among the latter come tripping four elderly legal big-wigs under the leadership of Lord Queenswood. In a reproving governessy letter to *The Times*—'Master Ernest, where are your manners!'—they contradict some of the statements I made last week, deplore the standards of modern journalism, and commend our ways to the attention of the Press Council.

"Leaving the Press Council to its slumbers for the moment, let us see who these four gentlemen are and how they are qualified to deny our charges. Lord Queenswood is, as we all know, a distinguished if elderly Lord of Appeal. We do not deny his sincerity in this matter but we deny his competence. He was serving on the Cartwright Commission at the Hague during the events leading up to John Marlowe's retirement. A judge does not sum up in a case he has not presided over.

"As for the barristers. First among them is Mr Arthur Morrissey, Q.C. *Who's Who* gives his age as fifty-three and says he was educated at Westminster and Magdalen. Where was John Marlowe educated? I give you one guess——"

The kettle was boiling. Don rose and switched it off. When he came back his eyes skipped on.

"So some rush in where angels fear to tread.

"But statements are not made in these columns without evidence to support them. We don't wantonly blacken the names of men who can no longer defend themselves. All we seek is that, where the public interest demands it, the truth shall be proclaimed.

"All that I said about Sir John Marlowe last week was based on evidence in my possession.

"There is an eminent witness, who will testify that John Marlowe confessed to him that he was a fraud, that his retirement was not voluntary. We have letters in our possession from women clients whom John Marlowe defended in the courts, addressed to him and beginning, 'Darling Johnny'. Remember the notorious Narissa Delaney? Remember her divorce? Remember the trickster Stanley Salem?

"What about the books? We don't ask you to take our word. Just compare them.

"Convinced? You will be.

"We sincerely sympathise with his relatives. We wish them all well.

"But we will not be prevented from speaking the truth."

Don made the tea and carried it upstairs. Joanna was still asleep. She lay with her body slightly twisted. In the curtained morning light her forehead looked damp under the tawny hair.

Don bent and kissed it.

She stirred and sighed. He began to pull the curtains back, making no noise. She suddenly opened her eyes and half sat up. Recognition was slow, and before it came he saw a brilliant hostility that broke up only as she fought her way out of sleep.

"Ten o'clock and all's well. You don't usually moan so hideously when I kiss you."

"Oh, God," she said, and shook her head. "I was dreaming."

"Were you being pursued by wolves or only Moonraker?"

She glanced quickly round the room. "You've been out?"

"Yes. Drink your tea."

"What has he got to say?"

"It's very much the mixture as before."

"Let me see."

"Drink this first. Fill up with Supercarburant for greater pep on the road."

While she read the column he opened *The Observer*. The article was on the middle page. "In view of the widespread interest which has been aroused by *The Gazette* article of last week in which it was alleged. ... The Reverend George Chislehurst ... the two books were therefore sent to Professor Lehmann. ... In the following article he has made an attempt to. ... Don's eyes skipped down the column. Lehmann began with an estimate of John Marlowe's book.

"*Crossroads*, a work which appears to have come near to achieving the impossible by appealing both to the man in the street and the man in the ivory tower. ... Sodermann, whose views are not to be ignored, has described it as 'a book whose exact scholarship and lucidity of mind has laid bare the bones of twentieth-century behaviour in such a way that the moral dilemma of the West seems a little less intractable since its publication'. A big claim. There are those who will deny it, and I confess I am one of the sceptics. Yet we are all too close to see what its lasting contribution will be. Already there are signs of a Marlowe 'school'; Deepdale and Ross-Parker would be unlikely to deny their attribution. ... And the play now running at the Gate by Colin McGee has obvious affiliations of thought. ...." Lehmann then went on to question some of the conclusions in the book; and it wasn't until he had got through all this that Don found what he had been looking for.

"However, a detailed comparison of Chapters 6 and 9 in George Chislehurst's books with Chapter 2 and 5 in Marlowe's work shows fundamental resemblances of thought which could hardly be the outcome of coincidence. Although the treatment is quite different the reasoning is the same, and it is hard to escape the conclusion that one mind has been at work on both, however that may have come about." There followed some details; then Lehmann went on: "There is, of course, no comparison in the status of the two books as a whole. Marlowe's brilliant analysis of today's malaise, whether one accepts it *in toto* or not, can stand well enough without the two chapters referred to, good though they are. There cannot be any over-all measuring up between *Crossroads* and this turgidly written treatise which appeared five years earlier. Even the conclusions are quite different. Nevertheless there would appear to be some basis for the accusations levelled by *The Gazette* so far as these particular chapters are concerned."

Don looked up and saw Joanna watering him. He said "Instalment Two," and passed her the paper. She read it carefully.

He looked out at the sunshine. "Tennis this morning?"

She said: "Odd you mentioned Mrs Delaney."

"Who's Stanley Salem? I know the name."

"He was in a financial swindle a few years ago. I read more of the gossip papers than you."

"Perhaps you've some idea, then, why Narissa Delaney is 'notorious'?"

"I remember her divorce but not anything particular about it. But the name suggests racing to me. Wasn't there a Bob Delaney who had racing stables and got into trouble with the stewards?"

Don put a finger inside the neck of his polo sweater, as if it chafed him. "None of this sounds exactly Dad's style to me—but you may be right."

Joanna slid out of bed and put on a house coat. She said: "I hope the water's hot. We switched on last night, didn't we?"

"Yes. Oh, that reminds me. Did you spend a night here during February?"

She had gone to the suitcase they had brought and was rummaging about in it. After a moment she said: "Why do you ask?"

"I met the local policeman when I went for the papers. He said he saw our car here on this late beat one night in February."

She had found what she wanted, a bath cap, and for a moment or two she concentrated on pushing her hair inside. It kept escaping in wiry auburn folds.

"Yes I did."

"On your own? Weren't you frightened?"

"What was there to be afraid of?"

"I don't know. But usually you're so fey."

"I'd been down to spend the week-end with Doreen and Bryan Colcutt at Brighton. It was rather a grand party. On the way home on the Sunday evening, I thought I'd drive round this way to see if everything was all right. I didn't intend staying long. But when I got in I began to dislike the thought of driving the rest of the way in the dark. You know how I hate meeting oncoming lights, in a car. So I camped out until the morning."

"I haven't seen the Colcutts for ages. When I get a bit more time we ought to fix a date."

She had managed to confine her hair at last. Her face thus laid bare had a rather wild look, with narrowing temples, fine jaw and delicate fastidious nose.

She said: "Yes, we'll do that sometime."

Chapter Ten

When Bennie left her flat on the Monday morning Michael was waiting for her.

"Hullo," he said. "Remember me?"

She smiled. "Pat does."

"That's only because you've refused to speak to me."

"I haven't—refused to speak to you. I've been away."

She moved slowly past him and he fell into step beside her. "I came this morning to ask you to my flat-warming tomorrow evening."

"I doubt if I can, Michael. I'm on stand-by part of the time."

"Look." He stopped again and she stopped. "I'm sorry about what happened last Tuesday."

"It was nothing."

"Then why won't you come tomorrow evening?"

She said: "Aren't you supposed to be starting your new job this morning?"

"I'm due at Chancery Lane in ten minutes——"

"You'll be late——"

"We're having a few drinks; there'll be a dozen people there; bring Pat too. You can't come to any harm with a chaperon."

Bennie said; "I'm not afraid of *that*. . . . If I don't go now I shall be late myself."

"Good. I hope they ground you for a week."

She said: "All right. All right, I'll come, thank you very much."

"Thank *you*." His sudden relieved smile almost embraced her; she was touched by his obvious sincerity. "I'll put out the flags."

"Now go to work quickly or you may be grounded for more than a week."

"It's a permanent grounding for me," said Michael. "I wish I were your pilot."

"It sounds like a comic song?"

"Not a comic song; a love song."

She looked past him towards the end of the mews. "We'd soon get off course, don't you think?"

"We'd leave a vapour trail, Bennie. Nothing more."

During the following afternoon a young woman went into the Agnew Galleries in Bond Street. There were very few other people in, but almost at once a man came across and spoke to her.

"Well, Miss Laycock, I didn't know you were a picture fancier."

The colour came rather quickly to her cheeks. "I'm not really, Mr Shorn, but I'd an hour to spare, so I thought. . . ."

"Exactly what I do," agreed Roger. "It's a good way of filling a few spare minutes. . . . I called on your father on Saturday. Did he tell you?"

"No."

"It was to apologise for Michael the other evening. I just don't know what got into him."

"Oh, I think my father is a little touchy sometimes. We really didn't think anything more about it."

"You're both very kind—and very forgiving. . . . There's a pleasant small Rowlandson over here; I love his church scenes." They went across together. "Michael said afterwards he'd been feeling ill all day. I think sometime he would like to apologise personally."

"Thank you, but it really wouldn't be a bit necessary. We both enjoyed our evening enormously."

Roger said: "Your father seems interested in entering the newspaper world. On Saturday he did me the honour of inviting me to become his official adviser."

"I'm delighted to hear it. I'm sure you'll be able to help him, Mr Shorn."

Roger's glance idly assessed the people in the next room, and then dismissed them. "Well, though it may seem immodest, I have to agree. I have been in journalism twenty years, and I know almost everyone in Fleet Street. I also know the pitfalls. To come into this world as a stranger, as your father would, would be asking for trouble, however highly one may esteem him as a businessman."

She laughed. They had stopped opposite a painting of a horse.

"Do you like it?" he asked.

"No."

"You're a woman of discernment."

"Well, not really. It's just that I would never buy a horse like that."

"Or a painting like that."

"Or a painting like that—incidentally."

He eyed her. "If you're a judge of horses you'll have seen the Stubbs exhibition at the Whitechapel Gallery."

"No. I'm afraid I never know about these things until too late."

"It shows him as a very good artist by any standards. I do implore you to see it before it closes."

They went on round the room. He talked interestingly but never for the sake of showing his knowledge. He got her to talk too. Presently he looked at his watch, and she thought he was going to excuse himself and go; instead he said:

"Have you still an hour or so?"

"To spare? I——"

"Before you answer, I was going to suggest you went to see the Stubbs pictures now. I'd like to see them again myself. Once is not enough."

She looked startled. "You mean you would come?"

"If I might. I haven't to be back at the office till six."

She looked at her watch, not to see what time it was but to give herself a second to think.

"But I expect that would take too much of your time," he said.

"I haven't actually anything else on but——"

"But you would rather go another day."

"No. But I don't want to put you to the trouble of making another journey. . . ."

82

Roger smiled into her eyes. "I was going in any case sometime this week. To take you would add a great deal to the pleasure." Before she could look embarrassed he turned away. "Let's have another five minutes here and then go. I think there's only that small room to look into now."

Half an hour before Michael's party was due to start his father called.

"I was passing," said Roger, "so I thought I'd look in to see how you were going on."

Michael hesitated, his eyes slightly masked but not with resentment. Roger had spoken as if nothing had happened.

"Oh. . . . I'm fine thanks."

"You haven't collected many of your things from the flat."

"No. . . . There's no hurry."

"How are you managing about furniture?"

"It'll take time, of course."

Roger looked his son over with his polite cultured glance. "Mind if I come in?"

". . . No." Michael drew aside.

Roger went into the narrow hall and then into the big ground-floor living-room. Since he first saw it it had been scrubbed out and furnished with some second-hand pieces. A Victorian dining-table was covered with an Irish linen tablecloth, and on it were bottles of drink and cocktail glasses. There were striped rush and sisal rugs on the floor, and bright cushions made the best of two leather armchairs.

Roger whistled. "You seem to be getting on pretty well. Expecting friends?"

"Yes. A few people are coming to a sort of house-warming."

Roger fingered the curtain material. "I hope you're not going to run up a lot of debts."

"No. I cashed my Savings Certificates. They'll see me through."

"Cigarette."

Michael half hesitated. "Thanks."

There was a pause while they lit up. Softening in spite of himself, Michael said: "I made a pig's ear of it the other night, didn't I?"

"It wasn't as disastrous as I thought."

Michael frowned through the cigarette smoke. "I suppose having a difficult son is worse than having a difficult wife . . ."

"Much worse. There's no divorce in fatherhood. But the fault was partly mine. I'm too much of a planner, Michael. A born schemer. Perhaps you've noticed."

"I've noticed."

"It's bad psychology to expect other people always to fit in. . . . How have your first days gone?"

"With Bartlett and Leak? Oh, they've been all right, thanks. They put me on reading manuscripts today. They were all pretty terrible."

"As you grow older," said Roger, "you'll come to realise the dreadful mediocrity of nearly all talent. That's what turns the average critic after a few years either into a harmless babbler or a sneering misanthrope. I suppose you want me to go now?"

"No. I'm not expecting anybody for a few minutes."

"I'm glad we've had this talk. Last Thursday I got pretty hot, and it's not a thing one ever has reason to be proud of."

"I gave you good excuse."

"Yes, I know, but personally I'd like to forget the evening. Agreed?"

Michael looked at his cigarette. "Yes, certainly agreed. And thanks for coming."

Roger's visit to the art galleries had put him in a good mood; but he had needed this reconciliation too. All was well now with the Laycocks, but his recollections of Thursday still held a residue of discomfort. Priding himself on a clear-sighted view of things, in which illusion and passion had their place but no more than their place, he didn't like even the smallest slip that suggested his authority over himself had gone off duty for an hour or two. It was too reminiscent of earlier times. He had come today not so much to put things right with Michael as to put things right with himself.

As he left the house a taxi was just drawing up at the door, and Peter Waldo got down from the driver's seat. There was another man sitting beside him in an additional seat which had been fitted where the luggage usually went. Roger had been going to hail the cab, but when he saw there was no meter on it he walked on.

Peter came up the steps. "Who was that? President of the World Bank?"

"No, my father."

"Now I know where you get your looks. Oh, this is Boy Kenny. I met him at the Middle Pocket last night. D'you mind? I thought he might be helpful."

"Pleased to meet you," said Boy.

You could never tell what sort of friend Peter Waldo would pick up. Kenny was a big man of about twenty-eight, with narrow eyes and narrow lapels and narrow trousers and black curly hair shimmering like cellophane. He would have been handsome but for his nose, which looked as if it had suffered like the maid's in the song of sixpence.

"Boy's quite a find," said Peter Waldo. "His experiences have been legion. Borstal and Brixton from the inside. I've promised him you'll publish his life story."

"You write it and we might," said Michael, leading them in.

"My dear," said Peter, looking round the room with his unfocusing blue eyes. "Why do you want more furniture? The place is as lush as a seraglio."

"It lacks the concubines."

"Never fear; they'll come. By the way, I've invited a few people on my own. You said you didn't know many folk in London."

"That's all right. Not too many, I hope."

"No. Probably about thirty."

Michael shouted. "What? That's twice as many as I've asked, you fool!"

"It'll be all right. Half of them won't come."

"If they do we're sunk. I haven't half enough drink."

"I thought of that," said Peter, fumbling in his pocket. "But then I think of everything." He took out a pill box and opened it to show a number of capsules.

"What on earth are those?"

"Phenobarbitone. You break them and sprinkle them on the gin."

"Don't be a fool——"

"My dear, all the old ladies of Kensington do it now. It's perfectly harmless and it saves——"

"And have everybody go to sleep on me! Take them away!"

"That's what you might think in your innocence, child. I swear to you the only effect will be that everyone will get drunk on a third of the liquor and save you a lot of money."

Bennie and Pat were late, so when they arrived the party was already at its height. Michael saw them at once and fought his way over, smiling a welcoming but rather anxious smile. "How lovely and cool you both look! Sorry for this crowd; Peter invited most of them. What will you drink? It's got to be gin and something."

He led the way back, elbowing and smiling among the noise. Peter's friends were a mixed lot. Some sat on the floor like inelegant sea-lions. Everybody was already very gay. At the table Michael thrust drinks into their hands.

"You remember Bennie, don't you, Peter? And this is her friend, Pat."

"Why, it's my little friend from Istanbul," said Peter, turning his full look of innocence on her. "Do you come here by magic carpet or is there a lamp to rub?"

"Of course she comes by magic carpet," said Michael. "She works on an air-liner."

"Oh. . . . Oh, I *see*. . . . You're one of those beautiful dedicated images. I always thought air-hostesses were kept in dust-proof containers between flights."

"Shut up, Peter," said Michael. "I wonder when these friends of yours are going to start moving on——"

"When the drink dries up."

"Which will be soon. I wish when they've gone we could get a dance going with a few selected friends. Bennie, it's such a relief to see you again. Have you *really* forgiven me?"

She smiled at him. "There's absolutely nothing to forgive. *Please* forget about it."

"Drink your drink. You're four laps behind the leaders."

Talk surged around them. Babel and smoke and laughter. Peter Waldo was talking to Pat, and under his kindly eyes she was suddenly vivacious in a way she seldom was at borne. Bennie said: "So this is where you live."

"It's where I'm going to live. Just now I'm camping out."

"I like your curtains."

"I dashed around. It *would* be a good idea if we could dance. Peter, have you a gramophone at your flat?"

"No, darling boy."

"I left one at Dad's place," said Michael. "It's a big old thing. But we could get it, I suppose."

With the second drink Bennie began to feel peculiar. It was not an unpleasant sensation, but it was as if she'd had three neat gins on an empty stomach. The normal restrains were not quite functioning.

Two elderly men near her were arguing about poetry. One, a little grey-haired gnome, said: "But Arthur, when one is *confined* within the corset of the ballad. . . . Restriction can be so stultifying. . . ." She wanted to join in. It was all very odd.

"Let me top that up," said Peter.

She let him, but decided not to drink it just yet. Everybody seemed extremely happy.

"He had an appointment to see me," said the other elderly man, brushing the dandruff off his velvet jacket. "But I made an excuse and cancelled it. The sheer social *nausea* of meeting one's friends' friends. . . ."

She heard Pat laughing at something Peter Waldo had said. She looked at Peter, at his long slender neck, at his slender bony hands, at his clean boyish face with its dazed inattentive eyes, and she had a strange illusion for a moment that his neck was like a snake's and that his eyes were hooded when he looked down. They seemed to know neither good nor evil. Then she glanced at Michael and feared for him. That too was a part of the strangeness, for Michael looked much the stronger of the two young men.

Bennie began talking to a dark girl called Kathie, who was

wearing purple corduroy slacks and had hair like parted curtains. Later she saw Michael whispering to Peter and Peter nodding and gazing from his eminence over the sea of heads. Then Michael came up to Bennie and put his mouth against her ear.

"Bennie, we think it would be rather fun to slip out of here without anyone noticing. We'll go round to my father's place and pick up my old radiogram. By that time we think most of the others will have drifted away."

"Shall we wait for you here?"

"No, come with us. We can put the radiogram in the boot. You and Pat slide out first. We'll join you in a couple of minutes."

"All right."

Bennie passed on the information to Pat, who giggled and nodded her head. They eased and manœuvred their way to the door. As they left, Bennie saw the dark girl Kathie following them and also a tall man with curly brilliantined hair and a peculiar nose.

The six of them met at the gate. Bennie sat in the front of the Delage with Michael while the other four piled in the back. She did her stuff with the choke ring without being asked. Michael said: "You clever girl," and they started off with a jerk and a roar.

She hoped he was clearer in the head than she was. The sudden change of atmosphere had made her feel dizzy and sick. But she was quite happy enough to enjoy his method of driving which seemed to be to use all his gears all the time. They stormed through London, screeching up to traffic lights, racing across the yellows and lurching in and out of traffic. They swung round the last few corners and snorted to a violent stop in Belgrave Street, so that the four in the back were flung into a laughing heap.

By the time they had sorted themselves out Michael was up the steps with Bennie pressing Roger's bell.

"Quiet!" said Michael. "No giggling. I have a stern parent to deal with."

"Leave him to me," said Boy. "I'll sink him front or stern."

They were in the mood to laugh at that while they waited. After the second ring Michael said: "I think he must be out. Bad luck. But I've got a key."

"Then why didn't you use it in the first place?" asked Kathie.

"My dear, one observes the courtesies. Anyway, I think he's forgotten I've got it."

Michael let himself in, and they followed him up the stairs whispering now like conspirators. When Michael saw there were no lights anywhere he said: "It's all right. There's nobody here."

"Decorations need not be worn," said Peter.

They switched on lights in the living-room, then the three men went up the next flight to Michael's bedroom. After a minute or two Kathie followed them, and then Pat; but Bennie sat in a chair in the living-room trying to steady her head.

It was not so much that she couldn't talk or walk properly as that she was on the verge of not being able to and couldn't understand why. If she'd drunk a lot she would have understood it. But there wasn't any such excuse, and she didn't know whether she was going to feel worse or better in the next five minutes.

There was plenty of laughter from upstairs and she heard Michael calling "Bennie!" She answered and got up, but walked slowly about the room, trying to feel her feet again. She peered at the Delacroix drawing on the wall.

A lovely room. She had never been here before, but everything about it spoke of good taste. There was no point in going up; they were already coming down again. She walked to the window and lifted the blind to look out at the waiting car, then went to peer at a tiny Italian painting on wood above the desk. She admired it for a moment or two, glad to fix her eyes on something stable, glad that some of her dizziness was passing. As she turned away to go to the door to meet the others with the radiogram she caught sight of a newspaper cutting lying attached to the top of some letters on the desk. She had no difficulty in recognising it because Don had showed it to her: it was the letter to *The Times* from the judge and the three barristers in defence of her father.

Pleased that Roger too had cut it out, she was again going to turn away when she saw that the letter underneath, to which the cutting was clipped, was signed Warner Robinson, Editor.

Last Friday Don had told her of an interview he had had earlier in the week.

A tremendous crash behind: she swung guiltily towards the door. There were cries and shouts and she heard Michael's voice: "You damned idiot, Kenny, what made you let go?"

"I didn't let go. The end slipped out of me fingers——"

"Good job you got out of the way, darling boy; it would have crushed your ribs. Get hold of this end——"

"My dear man, it's completely *wrecked*!"

"Don't take on so. The man couldn't help it. I'll buy you a new one."

Bennie picked up the letter. The heading was "*Sunday Gazette. Editorial*", and was dated the previous Thursday. It ran:

Dear Shorn,

I think you can take space to reply to this on Sunday. We don't want a long spiel, just enough to scare the pants off them. You might for once be rather dignified, not treading on the toes of the Aunt Ednas more than you need. A lot of letters from Marlowe fans, and some of them have already become ex-Marlowe. It's a healthy sign.

Yours, Warner Robinson (Editor).

Chapter Eleven

They were asleep when the telephone rang. Don woke more slowly than usual and fumbled the receiver to his ear.

"Don, this is B-Bennie. Could I come round and see you?"

"What *time* is it? What's the matter?"

"It's only about half past two. I've been out and I wanted to see you rather urgently."

"What is it?" said Joanna.

"It's Bennie. Yes, you can come if you want to, my dear. Where are you?"

"Back at my flat. We've b-been out and I felt I couldn't sleep till I'd seen you."

"Of course come over. D'you want me to fetch you?"

"No. I'll ring for a taxi."

Joanna was sitting up when Don put the receiver back. "What's the matter, Don?"

He switched on the bedside light and pushed his fingers through his hair. "Heaven only knows! She sounded upset. I couldn't cross-examine her over the phone." After two days of concentrated work with de Courville and Bellegarde he had been in a very deep sleep, and he could still hardly think straight.

"Is she coming round now?"

"Apparently. I expect that little Polish girl's been getting into trouble."

"No," said Joanna. "Bennie wouldn't worry us over that."

He put on his dressing-gown and offered her a cigarette. They smoked in silence until there was the sound of a taxi outside. Don went down and let Bennie in.

"Hullo." Obeying an unusual impulse, he bent and kissed her. "Nice of you to call round. We're nearly always in at this time."

Her cheek was very cold and she shivered at his touch. She turned into the drawing-room but he said: "Joanna's upstairs."

He followed her up. In the bedroom Bennie slipped out of her coat, her short dark frock rippling as she sat on the edge of Don's bed. He noticed that her fingers were unsteady.

"Let me get you something to drink," he said gently.

Bennie shuddered. "Nothing for me, darling. I've only had three drinks since eight-thirty, but they've made me feel drunker than I've ever felt before."

She began to tell her story. While she told it her mind roamed in an unattached way over the evening, moving far from what she was speaking about, as if it did not need to direct the narrative. The letter, first in her bag, then, on her return to the remnants of the cocktail party, taken out and folded small in the cross-over of her brassiere. The broken gramophone, the attempts to mend it, Peter Waldo's promise of a new one tomorrow or the next day; the end of the party, her longing to get away, but she could not leave without deserting Pat and Pat wouldn't go. The cocktails had suited Pat and had made her sublimely happy. It was a lovely party and she wanted it to go on for *ever*.

Bennie stopped in her story and put her hand down her frock and took out the cutting and the letter. She said: "It's lucky it's a paper-clip and not a pin; otherwise I should be tattooed for life."

Afterwards they had gone on to the Middle Pocket. Michael had been thoughtful, not pressing her to drink when he saw she didn't want to. Boy Kenny had met some of his own kind who frequented the club, and he went off with them and wasn't seen again. At last something Pat drank caught up with her and she went very white and threatened to pass out on them. From then on it had been easy. "No, don't come, Michael, please. I'll get a taxi, thank you for a *lovely* time. Yes, ring me, I shall be home all day Friday. She'll be all right when she gets to bed. No, I *have* to go with her. Thank you, darling, thank you. Good-bye. Good-bye."

Don handed the letter to Joanna, who had been watching him

with sleepy green eyes. She took it and stared at it and didn't seem to see it.

"Cigarette?" Don said to Bennie.

"No, thanks. I'm smoked out."

He lit another himself.

When she finished reading it Joanna didn't speak. She put a hand up to her cheek, rubbing it as if it hurt.

Don said: "I just can't believe it."

Bennie said: "I didn't know what to do. I felt I had to let you know."

"Perhaps this is still part of a nightmare," Don said wryly. "If so I shall be glad to be wakened up."

Joanna said: "*I* can't believe it either. There must be some mistake."

"I suppose the mistake has been ours."

But Bennie was watching Joanna.

It being mid-week the Hanover Club was crowded for lunch next day. When Don went up to the dining-room he chose a place between two strangers so that he should not have to talk.

Roger was usually in on a Wednesday, but of course one could never be sure. In spite of everything Don was not looking forward to this meeting. His angers when they came were impulsive ones, quick to grow and quick to spend themselves. A deliberate anger was to him a contradiction in terms.

Also, in between waves of resentment, he was hurt and upset—and genuinely curious and puzzled. A man devoid of malice himself, he could not understand it working in others. At the back of his mind, contrary to reason, was still a feeling that somehow there had been a terrific misunderstanding—that somehow it could all be explained away.

"Will you pass me the pepper, please?" said the man next to him as Roger came into the room.

Odd that presence. So much in command of himself, so well turned-out, handsome, amusing, cultured, so much more like a diplomat than a diplomat; where was the flaw?

Roger saw him and raised a friendly hand. Don nodded back.

Roger went across the room and sat at a small table where a distinguished surgeon and an American First Secretary were lunching.

"The pepper, sir, please."

"I beg your pardon."

Don went slowly on with his meal. Men came and went at his table. He dallied over cheese and then ordered another beer. The American got up and paid his bill and went out. Roger was talking to the surgeon, who had finished his meal. A noisy quartet of late-comers blocked Don's view for a minute or two while they decided where to sit; when they finally moved the surgeon was just leaving.

Don rose with his half empty glass and went across to the table where Roger was eating alone. "Mind if I sit down?"

Roger looked up and smiled. "Just the man I wanted to see. Throw that malt stuff away and have a glass of my wine."

"You wanted to see me? I wanted to see you. Who starts first?"

By the tone of voice Roger had gathered there was something wrong. He raised his eyebrows. "You, by all means."

Don said: "Bennie was in your flat last night."

This remark was open to an obvious misconstruction. Roger said: "My dear Don, you must be crazy. I haven't seen Bennie since the night of your concert."

"Michael took her. They went to fetch a gramophone of his. She found this on your desk."

He opened his pocket-book, fingered among the papers there, took out the clipping and the letter. Then he put it on the table in front of Roger.

Roger took up a piece of toast and while he ate it he lifted the Press-cutting and read the letter underneath as carefully as if he had never seen it before. Two or three men went past towards the pay desk. One spoke to Don, but Don didn't raise his head.

Roger said: "Well, thanks for letting me have it back. I missed it this morning."

His face hadn't changed much; there was a darker look to the sallow line of his jaw. When he raised his head his eyes were narrowed with the lower lids slightly wrinkled. He looked Don full in the face and picked up the letter and put it in his pocket.

"It makes it a bit awkward for you, doesn't it?" Don said quietly.

"Life's full of awkward situations. One doesn't seek them out but ... when they come along. ..."

"I think this one has come along."

"What d'you propose to do about it?"

Don looked down at his hands and carefully put them under the table. "I thought you might answer a few questions."

"It depends what they are."

"You are Moonraker?"

"Would you believe me if I denied it?"

"We've been—pretty close for a good many years. Was there some reason for—picking on the Marlowe family?"

Roger pushed his plate away. He looked at Don again as if he was meeting unexpected hostility from a stranger. "Reason? Not of that sort. I'm afraid one doesn't always have reasons in journalism."

"Also I suppose one doesn't have friendships."

Roger frowned. "Of course one has friendships—and one tries to preserve them. But sometimes, however unfortunate it may be, it's just not possible to allow them to stand in the way of obvious duties. If I——"

"This was an obvious duty?"

"Don, the Marlowe legend was obviously a subject for study. I studied it, as I would any other. It was my job. I came—regretfully—to certain conclusions. One really can't say more than that. I'm sorry."

There was a pause. Roger had stopped eating but he sipped his wine. "If you'd ever worked on a paper you'd realise that no one is entirely a free agent, from top to bottom. Everyone moves at the dictation of the man next above him. One makes a living, one survives——"

"So does the louse," said Don.

Roger's face darkened and flushed, then he shrugged. "Well ... that's true. I have nothing against the louse. We belong to the same planet. Our systems may differ in complexity but not fundamentally in design."

"Except that he lives off dirt but doesn't spread it."

"That could be."

Don waited. Roger finished his wine. The room was now only half full. Don said: "That's all you have to say? You don't want to add or subtract anything—make any other explanations?"

"What is there to say? If there was anything I could say that would help now, I would say it. Obviously I didn't intend you should ever find out——"

"I can believe that."

"Not entirely for the reason you suppose. But now that you have, it's pointless and gutless to make excuses. And they wouldn't really *alter* your feelings, would they? I shall be genuinely sorry to lose your friendship if that has to be. This thing came up, as I've told you. Your father was no great favourite with *The Gazette*, and one or two incidents arose which gave them cause to suspect his reputation. When that happens, is it a newspaper's job to go on or draw back? At least it isn't a journalist's job to question the choice. Making an enemy of you is part of the price one pays. That's why I wrote under the other name—unless one is anonymous one can't *move* for fear of treading on someone's toes. Well, I've trodden on yours, and I'm very sorry it had to be you. But there it is."

Don said: "And we can do nothing about it?"

"Well, no . . . frankly, what is there you can do? My advice to you is to forget the whole thing, Don. No one will think the worse of you because they think less well of your father. In fact, it could be looked on as a good advertisement for you. All publicity is advertisement. If I mentioned your name adversely in my column for a year, at the end it would have done you more good than harm."

Don said: "Disregarding the ethics of the attack as such, are you telling me that if you'd said to Robinson, the Marlowes are friends of mine, put someone else on it, he wouldn't have agreed?"

Roger lit a cigarette. "You don't understand how newspapers work."

Don said: "Gutter journalism stinks pretty badly in spite of all efforts to deodorise it. It's interesting that you who want and appreciate the best of everything, music, books, wine, painting, should make the money to get these things by being a sort of anonymous Paul Pry. Incidentally, I always thought you had private money: I knew *The Sentinel* couldn't pay you enough."

"My dear Don, I hadn't your advantage of a famous father."

"Is that it? At least that reason makes sense. Otherwise there's no sense at all but only petty and useless venom. John Marlowe never did you any harm—in fact according to you he befriended you. . . ."

"Utter nonsense!" said Roger with a sudden spurt of anger. "We have a right to question whether something has any title to exist. This overblown silly reputation that's accumulated round your father's name had no justification in fact whatever. It's right and just that it should be shown up for what it is."

"With lies?"

"With the truth."

"You believe it's the truth?"

"Of course it's the truth. If you were not blind with ancestor worship you'd see it yourself."

Don said slowly: "I think you know you're lying."

"I'm sorry. I've an appointment at three in Fleet Street."

"Tell Robinson I'll see this through to the end."

Roger looked at him. "With what?"

"With anything to hand."

"Give it up. Use your common sense."

Don said: "Listen, man. I promised myself that when I found out who Moonraker was I'd kick him round the block. That may be unsophisticated by your standards—but nothing you've said today has led me to change my mind."

Roger dabbed out his cigarette. "Don't be silly, Don. You didn't endear yourself to Robinson by the way you broke in on his luncheon the other day. You're not just up against me; you're up against a combine. Don't provoke them further."

Don said: "Go down to Fleet Street and stay there, Roger. For everybody's sake I suggest you don't come here again."

Chapter Twelve

Don spent most of the afternoon writing letters. He wrote three, the first being to the Editor of *The Times*. In it he stated Moonraker's identity and invited Roger Shorn, if he had proofs of what he had said in *The Gazette*, to publish them in a letter of reply. (On Thursday *The Times* telephoned Don; following this they rang Roger; on Friday they published the letter.)

Don's second letter was to the secretary of the Hanover Club. He again pointed out Moonraker's identity and suggested that if Roger could not produce the proofs of his statements he should be invited to resign. His third letter was to *The Gazette*.

Roger seldom went to *The Gazette* offices and he seldom met Warner Robinson. Neither of them had ever considered this as being done specifically to conceal Moonraker's identity, but that was the end result. However, on Friday, Roger called in on his way back from the offices of *The Sentinel* and was shown straight up.

Warner Robinson was sitting back in a swivel chair which put him in a good position for having a tooth out, and he continued to stare at the ceiling for a few seconds before raising his head and nodding Roger towards a chair.

"Hullo. How are you? I see our friend Marlowe has succeeded in smoking you out. Does it matter?"

Roger propped his umbrella beside the unlighted gas fire before taking a seat in the rexine chair on the other side of the acre of littered desk.

"It's bound to be inconvenient sometimes in the future, apart from any immediate problem."

"How did he find out?"

"I was careless. My son is friendly with Marlowe's sister."

"Too bad."

There was silence for a few moments. Robinson pushed across a box of cigarettes, but Roger shook his head.

"Here's the letter I got from him," the editor said. "Of course he's spoiling for a fight."

Roger read the letter. "Yes. This is why I thought I'd call in. I presume we have to concert some sort of policy in the changed circumstances."

Robinson lit a cigarette himself. "Have you done that stuff on the Leader of the Opposition for this week?"

"Yes, but if necessary it can wait."

"For what?"

"Marlowe wants his medicine in greater detail."

Robinson flicked out his lighter, and his large loose-skinned face was temporarily without expression. "Why bother?"

"Why not?"

"I can tell you why not. A nine days' wonder in this competitive age is lucky if it lasts three. We've done our best for Mr Marlowe by sketching him over two Sundays, but that's the limit. I don't like him and his arrogant ways any more than you do, but we've achieved our object, and that's all that counts."

Roger patted his shirt cuff where some raindrops had fallen. "Is it?"

"Well, it's the main thing. We're a national newspaper, and we've taken a little time and trouble to debunk a national figure. O.K. But going on bickering now would reduce it all to a parochial squabble that only about one per cent of our three million readers would be interested in. It was a good scoop while it lasted. Now it's on the spike. Pass on."

"You saw his letter in *The Times* today?"

"Yes. It doesn't cut any ice. Any more than this does." Robinson flipped the letter in front of him. "We're not in a court of law. Nobody's compelled to do anything about it."

Roger said: "There may be a certain amount of pressure brought on me—now that I'm known."

"What sort? Moral pressure? A box of squibs. In another ten days everyone will have forgotten all about it."

"I shouldn't necessarily want them to do that," Roger said quietly.

"I mean forgotten the pettifogging details. You're more likely to be regarded as a journalist who at the risk of unpopularity has performed a public duty."

"I thought that's what we agreed it was."

"Yes, well . . . let's be modest about our angel's wings. We both thought John Marlowe's reputation due for a little sweating down. I was given to the idea because of those remarks he made about *The Gazette* in the Foster-Rugby action. Maybe *you* were because you envied the son or didn't like his success or wanted his wife or something. Motives don't matter. The result has been satisfactory. We found more than enough grapeshot lying around, and however Don Marlowe squeals his father's reputation has gone out of the gun. What more do you want?"

"Personally nothing."

"Good."

Roger frowned thoughtfully out at the rain. "I take it *The Gazette* isn't pulling out of this quarrel irrespective of what happens next?"

Robinson leaned back again and drew in smoke. "*The Gazette* stands where it always does, behind its staff and behind its contributors. Particularly so where it doesn't like the people on the other side. It would give me pleasure to sit on young Marlowe's head and listen to him squeal. But I think—no I'm damned sure—the way to make him squeal loudest here and now is to ignore all his protests and maintain a lofty silence. And that goes even more for you personally than for *The Gazette*. The fact that you've got yourself known isn't my pigeon. But you can still ignore him and move on."

Roger was silent a moment, "If I need it, will you give me space?"

"If you need it, come to me and we'll see," said Robinson. "But I think you'd be insane to start in-fighting over details. That's playing him at his own game. You'd get bogged down with proofs and counter proofs. You lose all the advantage that can be gained from John Marlowe being dead."

Roger looked mildly amused. "Maybe you're right."

"Of course I'm right. You'll let me have Sunday's column by six or seven this evening, won't you?"

"It's written. I'll phone it through to Stamp."

"Good. Good. Lunch with me sometime. One day next week."

Roger looked at the editor and their exchanged glances were an unspoken cognisance of a changed situation, just as the original one had never found its way into words.

"Thanks," Roger said briefly. "We'll do that."

So *The Gazette* on Sunday carried no reference to John Marlowe or Don Marlowe or the feuds of last week. One paper rather disingenuously carried an article by a barrister on the procedure and enforcement of discipline within the Bar by the Inns of Court and by the Professional Conduct Committee of the Bar Council. Atticus in *The Sunday Times* had a paragraph on the dispute and made a comment on the ethics which should govern "gossip columns by pseudonym".

Don did not go to the Hanover Club for several days. Work on the new ballet had started in earnest, and he was to conduct three times in the following week. He worked hard but felt his creative concentration in short supply.

Almost the first person he saw in the club when he went in was the honorary secretary, Laurence Heath, who at once came across and invited him to the bar for a drink. "We had a meeting of the committee on Monday, Marlowe, especially to consider your letter. I thought of writing you about it, and then it seemed better if we could talk it over."

Don sipped his Martini and looked at Laurence Heath.

Heath said: "Perhaps I ought to make it clear at once that there was no division of opinion whatever as to our sympathy for you, and our dislike of this attack on your father."

Don nodded his acknowledgement.

"On Monday, Marlowe, while the committee was meeting, I telephoned Roger Shorn and gave him the general trend of your letter. He said to me that he did not feel it necessary at present to go into further details about the charges he had put down. His view was that the detail was sufficient and that no further onus of proof lay on him. Naturally that isn't my view and it isn't one that the committee held."

"I'm glad."

"I hope you won't misunderstand me, though, when I say that, in spite of this, we concluded we were not justified in taking official action. We can't expel or censure a member for his behaviour *outside* the club. The only way it really affects us is that John Marlowe was chairman and we resent this slur on his good name. But we can't be judges of the private lives of our members. . . . Last year, as you may know, one of our members was cited as co-respondent in a divorce case by another. A lot of ill-feeling existed between the two men at the time, but we were not entitled to pass judgement on the one at fault." Heath finished his drink and pressed the bell on the bar for the waiter. "On the other hand the member who got drunk so often that he used to go to sleep at the dinner table we had to ask to resign. Another of the same?"

"Thanks."

"It's against that background that we have had to assess this case."

"And your crockery?" said Don.

"Crockery?"

"There will be danger to your furniture and fittings if I meet him here."

Heath blinked. "I think it would be a great mistake, Marlowe, to prejudice your case by any action of that sort. What happens here we *have* to take notice of."

"So I gather."

"If you'll take my advice you'll allow the thing to rest so far as this club is concerned. I firmly believe"; Heath lowered his voice as other drinkers came up and moved around him: "I firmly believe that members here will show their feelings towards Shorn in their own way when they meet him. I know I shall."

Don spent a long time over lunch. He half-regretted having written to the club in the way he had. It would have been better to have up-ended the table over Roger that first day. Now that he had half-threatened the committee it made the fracas when it came deliberate and not spontaneous. It wouldn't do. And yet he was not prepared to sit down and be a good boy under Laurence Heath's veto. Henry de Courville's suggestion was the only answer.

After lunch he ordered three double whiskies in separate glasses and carried them on a tray up to the library, which was as usual deserted at this time of the day. Then he got paper and took out his pen and clicked his teeth together on the end. At school and in the army he had gained a reputation for mildly bawdy verse about the particular abuse or grumble of the moment. They had amused his companions a lot; but he had done nothing like it for six years. Now he sipped his first whisky and began to scribble a few lines at random.

After half an hour he stopped and read what he had written. It was rubbish and went into the waste-paper basket. Stop or go on? In reaction he was tempted to give it up altogether. He knew, although she didn't say so, that Joanna wanted him to let the calumny alone. Already the second article was ten days old. People would quickly forget. Who was to care? The recognisable person of John Marlowe was already unrecognisable in Midhurst churchyard. If his shade still existed, then surely it had passed beyond emotions of anger or resentment. There was only himself and Bennie.

But what of the book? The thing was there, the impact was there, the impression it had made on people; he had come on it again and again during his Canadian tour. *Crossroads*, whether one liked it or not, had made itself felt, was something to be reckoned with. And was not the fate of the book concerned here? An artist of course was judged by his art, not by his life. It didn't matter twopence if Rembrandt was a rogue or Beethoven a bore. But in *Crossroads* among other things was a code of behaviour and a reason presumably for following that code. If a man was a thief and a cheat, by all means write him off, and his book with him. If he was not, should the thing he created be wilfully destroyed by lies that were allowed to go by default?

Don went to the shelves and took down a copy of the book, which had been given to the club by his father. It was a third edition, and some notices were included on the back. "*In this witty and profound book John Marlowe has written the most vital restatement of moral truths produced in our time.*" "*It is quite impossible within the limits of this review to do any kind of justice to a book which will certainly become a classic of its kind.*" "*Brilliant and challenging.*"

Don opened a page at random and glanced down it. "The atom is composed of positive and negative electrical charges achieving an equipoise by opposition. So men achieve an equipoise by the striking of a balance of the opposing sides within themselves. Division and stress within the human mind is not a disease, it is a necessity of growth. But humanity can exist in all stages and states from the fissionable condition of the psychopath, through normality, to the apathy and disillusion which scientists in another sense might call heat death. It is with these last that we are dealing now, and I would suggest that they present the biggest problem. For there is not safety in numbers but danger . . ."

Don put the book back and finished his second whisky. Then he began to write again. It was a pretty reflection, he thought, that the son of a man who could write about that sort of thing had to descend to abusive doggerel to gain his point. An hour later he left three empty glasses in a row on the desk and a few crumpled papers behind him and quitted the club with a rather mixed feeling in his mind but with the sense of a duty discharged. He took the Bond Street tube to the house of his friend Derek Mackie, and they spent a couple of hours playing sonatas together. Afterwards Mackie confided to his wife that Don had thumped all afternoon and that his Canadian trip had not improved him.

Roger had had a surprisingly irritating few days. On Monday several newspapers had called him asking why his column in *The Gazette* had had no reference to John Marlowe and offering him space to state his case in detail. Then on Tuesday he had met the editor of *The Sentinel* at the Press Club. John Alexander was a sober young man who liked to feel that he represented the intellectual, uncommitted Middle Classes, the rather timorous *avant garde* of suburbia and the commutors. They had been standing at the bar together, and Roger had made a jocular remark that he hoped Alexander was not too upset at having discovered there was a Mr Hyde on his staff. He had expected an amused disclaimer; instead Alexander had turned rather stiffly to someone else, and an hour later Roger had got a note saying that while he, Alexander, after a very full consideration did not propose to take the matter further, he could not pretend to anything but extreme distaste and disappointment on finding that an important contributor to his paper should be writing anonymously etc., etc., and in such a way.

Roger had restricted his visits to the Hanover Club to the evenings, knowing Don was seldom there then; but he found the story was all over the club. Some of the older members obviously didn't like it, a few chaffed him heavy-handedly and asked for the latest details of the Marlowe feud, some were clearly impressed, a half-dozen went out of their way to congratulate him, but these were men of no account who had been waiting the opportunity to ingratiate themselves.

Much of this reaction could be treated with his usual amused detachment. The has-beens, the arthritics, the distinguished but retired, cut no ice anyway. But two men who were still influential went out of their way to avoid him. Roger persuaded himself that all this would pass over in a couple of weeks. But he had made a study of being liked among those whose liking he wanted, so he was a sensitive plant when the wind blew chill.

On the Wednesday he was due to dine with Sir Percy Laycock and Marion.

Roger had seen Marion again last week, when he had taken her to the theatre. He had made the excuse that it was a play he had to see and write on and had explained subtly that he had a second seat if by any chance she was free to come.

He found Sir Percy in an unpredictable mood. Marion greeted him shyly, but there was just a suggestion of a look in her eyes that hadn't been there before.

"We've been learning a lot about you this week," said Sir Percy over cocktails. "I'd no idea in the world that you were Moonraker. Dangerous man!"

"One hides one's light," said Roger. "Not merely for reasons of modesty. If people know they're in the presence of a columnist they guard their tongue too closely."

"Well, it certainly surprised me," said Laycock. "Must say it rather shocked me too."

"Shocked you?"

"Well, yes. Not a very savoury job, is it?"

Roger flushed. "In one sense it's not a column I relish doing. In another sense it's a challenge."

"Yes. Knowing you, I can see that. Have you been doing it long?"

"Not long."

Marion said something and the subject was changed; but later in the evening Sir Percy returned to it.

"I don't often read *The Gazette*, you know. It's not quite my sort of paper. But Moonraker's a name one hears about, and I got my secretary to get some back-numbers yesterday so I could read your column."

"I'm complimented."

"Well. . . . it's important to me."

"How do you mean, important to you?" asked Marion.

"Mr Shorn knows."

"I'm not sure that I altogether do," Roger said, smiling.

Sir Percy took off his eyeglasses and polished them. "Well among other things, you're advising me on my first contact with the directors of *The Globe*."

"I hope you don't think my writing this column makes me any less likely to give you good advice!"

"No ... certainly not." Laycock put his eyeglasses back and re-focused through them. "But I had thought that my contacts with you might not have stopped at the exchange of advice."

"I'm flattered to hear it."

"I'm sure you're not—or you shouldn't be. However, that's all very much in the air as yet, isn't it? Let me recommend this port. I think it's a bit of good stuff."

When Marion left them Sir Percy began to talk about *The Daily Globe*. It was plain that the idea of gaining a controlling interest in it had got under his skin.

"You don't think I'm a fool, considering breaking into the newspaper world—with my background?"

"My dear Sir Percy," Roger said, "if you look at the history of journalism you'll find that almost all the great newspaper families have sprung from roughly your background—Liberal and Nonconformist, that is. Whatever happened to them later, that is where they came from: the Berrys, Beaverbrook, the Harmsworths, the Cadburys. It's much the same in America. You have every precedent in your favour."

"That's very heartening."

"But it doesn't mean you must rush into anything. You've indicated your interest; now let the idea sink in. In a month or so have the Mander brothers to dinner. I'll be glad to be present. Then, if anything can be provisionally worked out with them that night, it will be time to call in a really first-class lawyer."

Sir Percy puffed at his cigar in silence. "You can read between the lines as well as anybody, Shorn. I don't need to say what the prospects might be in this for you. That's why I was put a bit off balance by discovering that you wrote the Moonraker column. And still more so by this particular Marlowe affair. What was behind it?"

"Nothing more than you read. The editor of *The Gazette* had collected some information which suggested Sir John Marlowe was a humbug. He asked me to do the rest."

"You're sure of your facts?"

"Oh, absolutely."

"That's good," said Laycock. "In a sense of course it was a fine journalistic scoop; only I could wish it hadn't been written the way it was. I wouldn't like that said about my father after his death, however much he might have deserved it. What are you going to do now?"

"In what way?"

"Well young Marlowe wants his proofs. I imagine he's entitled to them. You didn't have anything in *The Gazette* on Sunday."

"The editor clamped down on it. He said the public was losing interest. One of the disadvantages of not being one's own master."

"Quite," Sir Percy agreed dryly. "But what are you going to do personally? Other papers would probably be willing to publish."

"D'you think it's in anybody's interest if I did? Would it help Don Marlowe to have letters from his father put in print, all the sordid story dragged out in detail?"

"But hasn't it already been dragged out in your two articles? Anyway I wasn't thinking so much of the Marlowes in this as of you. You have your reputation as a journalist to consider. It's particularly important now."

Roger tapped off an inch of white ash. "It isn't quite as straightforward as it looks. Once one gets down into the arena, as it were, proofs are met with counter proofs, and so on. Did you see the article by Professor Lehmann in *The Observer* of last Sunday week? Does one need more proof than that?"

"Of the plagiarism charge? Perhaps not. I wouldn't be really certain. But it doesn't prove the other things, does it? In fact, all the evidence there has been, which isn't much certainly, has been to say that Marlowe was above suspicion so far as his professional life went."

"I've definite proof to the contrary."

"Then why not put it in black and white?"

"Because some of it isn't *in* black and white. Some of it was simply gained by interviewing people. People who wouldn't necessarily be willing to be quoted."

"If it was a law case they'd have to speak."

"Yes, but it isn't a law case."

"You know," Sir Percy said slowly, "I think I'd be in favour of amending the law of libel to let it cover men recently dead. Then young Marlowe could challenge you in court, and you could clear yourself of the charge of slinging mud for the sake of cheap sensationalism."

"It might well be a good thing," said Roger.

He came away from his dinner feeling exhilarated but edgy. Laycock needed no urging on the way Roger wanted him to go, and there was plenty for Roger at the end of it. But it would be no easy job preserving a balance above the various pitfalls. The Marlowe case added only one larger and more dangerous than the rest.

And Marion? Did one go on? There were pitfalls here too.

The Laycocks' house was in New Cavendish Street, so Roger walked across to the Hanover Club, for a last drink before going home. He found there some half-dozen indefatigables talking in the bar. One of them, when he went in, said:

"Here comes the Moongazer. Sit down and have a drink. Whose grave have you been rifling today?"

He was a bearded artist called Knowles, a fairly close friend of Roger's, and the jibe had been spoken without animus. All the same it was unwelcome.

Roger said: "When I see you, Charles, I realise why this is becoming known as the Hangover club." He sat down and accepted a drink. Most of the others in the group he would normally have avoided, but tonight he was in need of company.

"Think of the trembling that will be going on in Golders Green," said Knowles. "Who is safe when there's Moonraking among the ashes? Think of the dismay among the late Empire builders of British West Hampstead. Who were the cads among the cadavers? Why——"

"Shut up," said Roger. "You're drunk."

But Knowles went irrepressibly on. When the whisky was in him this sort of talk bubbled from him like a spring.

"Soon we shall be selling not the first rights in our articles but the last rites. Think of the untapped circulation. Don't miss our splendid new cut-out pattern in grave clothes! All your mortuary questions answered. What shall I *wear*? Knells for the Nellies. . . ."

Two men came in and went to the bar, a tall barrister called Rowe and another man. Roger knew them by sight but had hardly ever spoken to them, so he was surprised when after a few moments Rowe came over.

"Shorn, have you seen the Suggestions Book?"

"Not recently. Why?"

Conversation stopped. Even Knowles stopped.

"I think you ought to see it. I've just been along to make a comment about the condition of the card tables, and there's a recent entry that I think might interest you."

The Suggestions Book, as in most clubs, existed in the library for members to put in any complaints they might have or suggestions for improving the running of the club. In the silence Roger said:

"You think so?"

"Yes, I think so."

"I'll take a look on my way out."

"Who put the entry in?" asked Knowles.

"Marlowe."

"Oh, I'll go and fetch it. This might be interesting."

Roger regretted now that he had not gone to see for himself, but he would not seem to argue with Knowles. He sat quietly with his drink appearing not to care until Knowles came back.

Knowles said: "It's not only in the Suggestions Book; the damn' thing is pinned on the notice board!"

"I didn't see that," said Rowe.

"I asked the porter. He said Marlowe left at four, but he didn't notice he'd pinned anything up. Anyway, it's there and signed, just the same as in the Suggestions Book."

Knowles was going to hand the book to Roger but somebody said: "No, read it out. If it's in the book it's a club matter."

Knowles hesitated and glanced at Roger inquiringly. But Roger gave no sign. Knowles cleared his throat and said: "It's signed D. J. Marlowe and it's in verse.

"'Suggest in the interests of hygiene
That the rules of this club be amended
To exclude from among us
The louse and the fungus;

That indulgence of such be suspended.

"'Suggest that the wolf in sheep's clothing,
When the mask from his visage is torn,
Should no longer be feared
If he's thoroughly sheared
For we see that he's thoroughly Shorn.

"'Suggest that the joy of the jackal
Is to savage and worry the dead,
For he's not in the mood
To fight for his food
And would rather eat carrion instead.

"'Suggest that a man who transgresses
Humanity's betterment claim
Should be classed with the skunk
And the liar and the funk
And expected to live with the same.'"

Chapter Thirteen

Before leaving that night Roger Shorn left a note for the Committee of the Hanover Club drawing their attention to the entry in the Suggestions Book, pointing out that it was libellous and asking for its removal. Next morning the permanent secretary read the letter and the lampoon, hastily phoned Laurence Heath, and then removed the Suggestions Book to his private office. The copy on the notice board had been torn down by Roger before he left. When he came in that evening nothing was to be seen.

The following morning, however, a typewritten copy of the verses was pinned on the notice board and several carbons were found under members' plates at the luncheon table. This was not Don Marlowe's doing for he had not been in the club. The verses on the notice board stayed there until Laurence Heath arrived for dinner and took them down.

That night Heath wrote to Don Marlowe complaining of the improper use to which he had put the Suggestions Book. A reply was received from Don by return offering his apologies but pointing out that he was only trying to draw the attention of the club to the fact that Roger Shorn was a disgrace to his profession, a fact of which the club in general seemed as yet to be unaware. He also said he intended to send a copy of the verses and the letter to each London newspaper.

That evening Don gave an interview to the *Daily Mail*, who published it in Tanfield's Diary. "Royal Ballet Conductor Don Marlowe told me last night that he intends to turn the heat on his father's accuser in much the same way as was done by Gladstone's sons in the big row of the twenties, when Peter Wright, an old

Harrovian and ex-secretary of the War Council, made a violent attack on the morals of the dead Prime Minister. . . ."

Roger didn't see Robinson again, preferring to excuse himself from the luncheon date; nor for a few days did he go to the Hanover Club. A few other newspapers had made minor comments on Don's latest move, including a note in the *The Globe*: "Speak Up—or Apologise?" Roger was also receiving a number of letters from strangers. About seventy per cent protested at his attack on Marlowe; a few were anonymous and abusive; but a minority supported his line: "Well done; there's too much whitewashing of hypocrites and liars."

In any case he knew that in a short while the interest would die down. Nothing in this age survived long; a world crisis was sure to threaten, a film-star would decide to tell all, or girls would be murdered in a wood. Don would grow tired of being abusive and the letters would slow to a trickle and dry up.

An event he seldom missed, since it kept him in contact with people, was Private View Day at the Royal Academy, and this year he had invited Laycock and his daughter to be his guests. He called for them at three, but before they were far on their way Sir Percy brought up the inevitable subject.

"What's young Marlowe like, Shorn?"

"Very good at his job. But rather obsessed with his own importance."

"It's clear what he intends to do."

"It may be. If he tries it on he'll simply make himself ridiculous. There's only the most superficial resemblance between this and the Gladstone quarrel."

"Those verses in Londoner's Diary were about you, weren't they?"

"Yes. Marlowe's sending them everywhere. They left out the middle verse that mentioned my name."

"I should have thought if they could have been pinned down as definitely referring to you. . . ."

"I still don't understand what happened in the Gladstone case," Marion said.

Roger smiled at her. "It's a trifle complicated." He was still explaining when they turned in at Burlington House, where there was a long queue of taxis and cars waiting to fecundate upon the steps of the Academy.

Inside, some of the artists themselves moved among the crowd, like amiable spiders weaving little knots of friends and acolytes under their pictures. Almost at once Sir Percy met a friend. Roger and Marion strolled on together.

After a minute Roger said. "Tell me, Marion, what do you personally think about my quarrel with the Marlowes?"

She hesitated, not looking at him, turned a page in her catalogue. "Does it matter what I think?"

"I find it matters to me."

She stared at the catalogue, allowed the pages to flip over, closed it. "You're very flattering."

"I never flatter people."

Abruptly she said: "If you ask me—if I can have any opinion at all, and of course I don't understand journalism—I should have liked you never to have written the articles. Now that they have been written I'd be glad to see the thing settled as quickly and as—as honourably as possible, because I think it affects my father's opinion of you."

"It doesn't affect yours?"

She hesitated, rather breathless. It was like running down a slope—each step bigger than the last. "I don't think so."

"I hope that means what I think it means."

"I don't know what you think it means."

"At least, that you have trust in me."

"I think so!"

"Because if there is trouble over this I shall want to feel mat my special friends—and particularly you—are with me."

She said quietly: "I hope there won't be trouble."

"I hope not——"

"Hullo, Dad."

Roger turned and saw Michael at his elbow.

They had not met since the evening of Michael's disastrous

house-warming. Michael looked pale and thinner, his cheekbones more prominent. They stared at each other.

"Well, Michael. ... How did you get in?" Roger's voice for understandable reasons was not friendly.

"Bartlett came this morning and he gave me his catalogue to come in on this afternoon."

"You know Miss Laycock, of course."

"Yes, of course."

The conversation remained formal, Michael particularly uncertain, not knowing how far Roger blamed him for his present troubles. Eventually he smiled at Marion and said: "I always like to look at paintings with my father. Have you noticed? he knows exactly what he thinks about a picture and how to say it. I can never be that intelligent."

She smiled back and glanced at Roger. Michael, looking quickly from Roger to Marion, suddenly and sharply saw the extraordinary and astonishing possibility that existed there, a possibility which he himself had suggested in angry sarcasm—but only in sarcasm—three weeks ago.

"But ... perhaps you know about painting yourself, Miss Laycock," he ended lamely, his mind still boggling.

"No. This is my first Private View."

"It seems to me the people here are viewing each other rather than the paintings. What a collection of hats!"

"It's a two-way exhibition," said Roger.

Just then Sir Percy Laycock caught up with them. He nodded to Michael and said:

"I didn't know your son was coming."

"Nor I," said Roger.

"I've been trying to get near the new portrait of the Queen, but there's such a press."

"I hear it isn't awfully good."

They moved on to one of the rooms which was slightly less crowded. Michael's thoughts had been racing, covering infinities of ground. He found himself at Laycock's elbow and carefully avoided falling over his stick. Laycock looked at him and Michael suddenly smiled his beautiful smile and said:

"You know, sir, I'd like to apologise for that night you came to dinner. I somehow got off on the wrong foot and everything I said went wrong. I must have sounded very boorish and unpleasant to you. Bad manners isn't usually a family failing."

Sir Percy straightened his spectacles. "People sometimes take a meeting or two to understand each other. Maybe the fault wasn't all one way that night. I say let's forget it."

"I'd certainly be glad to," said Michael.

They went round the room as a quartet, talking equably, like a family. Michael's apology had helped a lot. More people were coming in now, and Marion and her father went ahead of the Shorns into the next room.

"That was quite a piece of work," Roger said dryly. "I didn't know you had it in you."

"Well, why not? I thought it might help."

"Help what?"

Michael sheered away from the direct answer. "I pretty nearly queered your pitch with the Laycocks that evening. It seemed my opportunity to patch things up."

"You've queered my pitch much more seriously since then."

Frowning, Michael pushed his hair back. "I *know*. I was coming to that. But at least that wasn't deliberate."

Roger stared about him at the pictures. "What depresses me in an exhibition like this is the habit-forming consequences of insufficient inspiration. Not ten paintings in this whole show *had* to be painted. The rest were dead before they were begotten."

Michael said: "I seem to have been quite a hair shirt for you since I came home. Of course I'd not a notion you were Moonraker. I can't tell you how mad I am that I messed that up for you as well."

Roger glanced at his son. "Women who pry into other people's desks should be whipped in good eighteenth-century style."

Michael flushed but kept his temper. "It wasn't in the desk, it was on top. Or so she said and I believe her."

"You're still seeing her?"

"No. She wrote me afterwards saying what she'd done."

"And recoiling I suppose in holy horror from the pair of us."

"No. ... But it's just not possible to keep up a carefree acquaintance with this feud raging."

"Is that why you look as if you haven't been eating anything?"

"I'm all right. .... Except that I'd like a change of job."

"Tired already?"

"Not of work. But of this work. There's no future in it for me."

Roger said: "Have patience. You're not twenty-two yet. Stick it for twelve months. Then I may have something interesting to offer."

"I don't know what's wrong with time," Michael muttered. "It seems to be against all of us today."

Roger smiled and bowed to the French Ambassador, whom he had met once. "It's a common complaint in youth. We'd better join the Laycocks or we shall lose them in this crush."

They moved into the next room. In the doorway Sir Percy and Marion were looking at a piece of sculpture. As he joined them Roger came face to face with Don.

Henry de Courville was with Don. Henry knew Roger slightly. They would all certainly have moved on without speaking, but there were people pressing in and out of the bottleneck of the doorway.

Don nodded and half smiled at the younger man. "Hullo, Michael. Didn't expect to see you here."

"No. .... How's Joanna? Isn't she with you?"

"No, she had a rehearsal."

"And ... Bennie?"

"I think she's well enough." Don tried to edge away.

Conversationally, Henry said to Roger: "That was a good piece of verse Don wrote, don't you think?"

"I don't know what business it is of yours."

The Laycocks were listening to this, and Marion's eyes moved anxiously to Roger.

Don spoke to Roger for the first time "I also wrote to Heath. If the verses aren't sufficiently libellous, that letter is."

"Mardi, where are you, I've lost you!" said a voice behind them. "Ah, there you are! Did you see that weird pink outfit?"

Roger said: "I'm warning you, Don. If all this comes out in court your father's reputation will be in much worse shape than it is now."

"A copy of the letter and the verses will be sent to every newspaper," Henry said. "You'll be given all reasonable grounds."

Michael glanced angrily at de Courville and then said: "Look, you two. Why don't we get together somewhere and talk it over. Why not get out of this crush and discuss it in private—argue it out in a friendly way. After all you've *been* friends for years. There's no point in washing all our dirty linen in public."

"Your father might have thought of that earlier," said Don.

"Well, maybe, but the damage is done. Why be vindictive?"

Don looked at Michael with an almost gentle curiosity. "Is that how you really see it?"

"Well, I quite understand——"

Roger stopped him with a hand on his arm. The Laycocks had not moved away.

"Listen, Don. In your anger—and apparently with the encouragement of this gentleman—you're getting yourself out on a limb. The plagiarism has already been proved by the article in *The Observer*. I can prove the unprofessional conduct just as easily. But——"

"Then prove it."

"It will be at your expense."

"We'll see."

Roger said: "But if it will help to settle this in a civilised way I'm quite prepared to offer you an apology here and now. I'm extremely sorry that I've hurt you and offended you. I can understand how you feel and very much wish it could have been otherwise. If you like I'll put that apology in writing and you can pin it in the Suggestions Book."

"And are you willing to take back what you said in *The Gazette*?"

"About your father?"

"Of course. What you say about me is neither here nor there."

Roger shook his head. "I obviously can't take back the truth."

Don smiled slightly. "Then I'm sorry. There's no sale."

"Then there's nothing more to be said, is there?"

"Quite a lot."

"Publicly?"

"Oh, yes, publicly. I shall go on blackguarding you for ever."

Roger made a gesture which asked the world—or at any rate the Laycocks—to comprehend and acknowledge that he could do no more.

"It's up to you. But don't say that you haven't been warned."

When he was free Roger rang Robinson at his home number.

Robinson said: "I think you're crazy. Of course he's angling for you to take legal action. Therefore to take it is playing his game. What do a few rude letters matter?"

"They could matter. If they went on indefinitely."

"Nonsense. The first lesson a journalist should learn is sticks and stones may break my bones but words etc. I sang it in my cradle."

"Yes," said Roger. "Maybe you did." He was in no position to explain his peculiar sensitiveness to abuse at the present time.

"And I'm right. Forget it."

"All the same," said Roger, "I'd like to know where I stand if I do decide to fight him."

"In what way?"

"Last time we met you said *The Gazette* stood behind its contributors. What could that mean in this case?"

There was a pause at the other end. Roger could visualise the *ci-devant* distinguished face twisted into loose furrows of distaste.

"It could mean a lot or a little. I don't see the point of your rushing into a legal action just to satisfy your injured pride. Do you want our space, you mean?"

"I think it's gone further than space now. Certainly I'll not sue unless compelled. But if I am compelled?"

"If you're compelled we'll advance five hundred for costs. If you lose, which seems improbable, we'll foot the rest of the bill. It's all publicity."

"Thank you," said Roger. "That was what I wanted to know."

"It's all publicity, as I say, but I'm still *certain* you're a fool even to think of accepting his challenge. One thing. Before you take any definite step see our solicitors. They'll know better than we do what the chances are of your succeeding."

"I'll do that," said Roger.

Four days later he began proceedings for libel.

When he left his father Michael picked up his brief-case at the door and walked along Piccadilly. But he walked in the opposite direction from his flat. His mood got bleaker with every step.

All the evidences of money at the Academy today had particularly hit at him because of his new lack of it. In a way, although he had wanted a place of his own, being away from his father meant being away from the centre of things and in a backwater where there was more likelihood than ever of being overlooked and forgotten. His present job was not only a dead end but the wrong dead end. He was all set for frustration and mediocrity, a grain in the desert, moving as the wind blew, without any chance of being able to show enterprise or initiative. There were a hundred million like him. Cannon fodder, John Sucker, the man in the street: they all applied. To become a personality, one, not one of the many, was the greatest single need.

What was worse, his love for Bennie was at a dead end too. He had not even seen her since the night of the party, and he knew now that a bigger obstacle than ever separated them. While this stupid feud raged he had no chance at all of coming closer to her. He couldn't really blame her if she sided with Don. He felt as if a gigantic confidence trick had been played on him. He was left to angry despair.

He turned up Shaftesbury Avenue and made his way to the Middle Pocket. Rather to his surprise Dick Ballance let him in.

"Well, well, come right in, man. Peter's here. How did you know?"

The big Negro was in a green gaberdine jacket zipped up the

front, with fawn trousers and fawn and white casuals. In the inner room there was no sign of the proprietor, but with Peter Waldo was the big young man with the stunted nose. Only a single light burned by the piano to back up the anaemic daylight.

"How did you know we were talking about you, dear boy? You remember Boy Kenny?"

"Too well."

"Now, now, no hard feelings. Pour him a slug, Dick, to soften up that iron heart."

There was a clink and bobble as Dick Ballance put some whisky in a glass. "Like a reefer, brother?"

Michael shook his head.

"Have one of mine," said Kenny. "They kill you slower, like." Michael shook his head again.

"Awkward, ain't he?"

"Michael's the least awkward of men," said Peter, "but he feels a justifiable anger at the destruction of his elderly radiogram. We have had it on our conscience, Michael. Indeed just before you came in we were discussing a way of providing you with a magnificent new one, value one hundred and eighty guineas, in part exchange."

Ballance played a soft chord on the piano, and the light gleamed on the shining skin of his face. "Not me, brothers," he said. "Leave me out. I like my fun other ways."

"It's a crazy idea anyhow," said Boy fingering his white foulard tie. "Who'd be such a fool? Not me."

"What's the matter?" Peter Waldo inquired pleasantly. "Why be scared?"

"Shut up about scared. Who're you to talk? I've done more than you ever will!"

"It astonishes me, Boy, it really does, how unintelligently you and your little gang behave sometimes. You told me you once did a smash an' grab."

"Well, man," said Dick Ballance, rising from the piano stool; "kindly hand me my parachute. This is where I bale out."

"So we did," said Boy truculently. "And got away with it!"

Peter Waldo was flicking a bottle opener round on his finger. "Nobody but a fool ever attempts smash and grab. It's clumsy, it's violent and it's vulgar. I suppose you learned that sort of thing at Borstal?"

"Anyone can talk," said Boy, drawing at a stub of cigarette. "You certainly can. Anyway, if the radiogram's for him, let him do the job instead of me."

"I don't know what you're driving at," Michael said impatiently. "Are you thinking of stealing the thing?"

Peter coughed. "Put bluntly, that was the idea."

"Oh, don't talk rot."

Dick Ballance had gone into the darker part of the deserted night club but he had not left them. They could hear him moving about behind the bar. Peter Waldo got nip and walked across the dance floor.

"It's not altogether rot, Michael. Sometimes it's necessary for one's self-respect to cock a snook at authority. This in a way would be both a test and a protest. It would be a protest against all the debased cheap shoddy swindles of today that get by in the name of society and good taste and law and order. And it would be a test of one's own intelligence and guts."

It was not often that Peter jarred on Michael, but he did today. Michael was sick of empty attitudes. "So what?"

"Well, in that very handsome store, Charles Richards and Co., on the first floor there is a handsome radiogram, offering you stereophonic sound and costing one hundred and eighty guineas. There are three assistants in the gramophone department, the manager and two girls. At twelve-thirty every day one of the girls goes to lunch. At one-fifteen the manager goes. At one-thirty the first girl comes back and the other girl goes. That means that from one-fifteen onwards only one assistant is available to serve customers. Got that?"

"For what it's worth."

Peter glanced at his friend. "Now at Kimbers, the carriers, just off King's Road, there are always at least three plain vans standing idle between one and two while the drivers have their lunch. They're all Morris vans, all with identical keys. Anyway I have keys to fit. The men have their meal in the back of the building and no one will hear a van drive away. At ten minutes past one next Monday Boy and I will walk up in white coats and take one of the vans."

"So you say," observed Boy.

"We shall drive it to the side entrance of Charles Richards's and walk up to the first floor. There we shall go across to the gramophone, grumbling a good deal, cover it in a white dust sheet, carry it downstairs and into the van and then deliver it to your flat. Afterwards we will leave the van in some convenient parking lot, return to your flat and tune in to Listen With Mother."

Ballance had come slowly back while Peter was speaking. He stood by the piano and pressed down three treble keys with his fingers. Michael said: "What if you were challenged?"

"We shall say we're taking it back to the works for testing—manager's orders."

Michael finished his drink and yawned offensively. "Anybody heard the cricket scores?"

"You don't think I'm in earnest?" Peter said.

"I know you're not." Michael looked from one to the other with contempt. "It's not so much smash and grab as talk and gab that you two specialise in."

"'Ere," said Boy. "Lay off that."

"Care to bet me?" said Peter.

"I won't bet you can't do it. I'll bet you ten pounds you won't even try!"

Peter looked at Dick. "You'll hold the stakes, dear boy?"

The Negro shrugged. "It's not my business, man; it's not my line at all; I don't believe in taking risks unless the risks is worth while."

"I make one condition," Peter said to Michael. He did not seem put out by the other's attitude. "And that's that you should be there to see it happen. Go into Richards's at one o'clock on Monday and ask the price of a TV set. That way you'll be on the spot, and at the same time you'll be able to engage the attention of the one assistant. Whatever happens you don't know us, have never seen us before. Agreed?"

"Oh, forget it," Michael said sulkily. "Got any new calypsoes, Dick?"

"*Dick's* right," muttered Boy, cleaning his nails with the nails of the other hand. "If you're going to take a chance like that, take it for something big or not at all."

Peter leaned over the piano and lifted Ballance's hands off the keys just as he was going to play. "Darling boy, it isn't just the money you get out of a thing like this, it's the intelligence you put in. I'm trying to *prove* something to you, Boy. If I suggested we should knock an old woman down in a dark lane and steal her bag you'd think that a smart idea. To you breaking the law is something done with a jemmy and a knuckleduster. It needn't be just that. And I now also want to prove something to Michael as well."

Michael finished his drink and left soon, after, with Peter's acceptance of his challenge not withdrawn. Of course it would be withdrawn, he told himself irritably as he walked away, but he was not going to be the one to make the first move. Peter's windy nonsense needed an occasional prick of reality to deflate it, to keep it on the ground.

Yet under this assumption Michael was slightly uneasy. They had been talking about the thing before he got there. Dick Ballance had been emphatic in his refusal to be mixed up in it. And despite his nonsense, Peter had flair and intelligence and sometimes determination of a high order. Once you accepted one of his slightly zany propositions the rest followed logically enough. In this case, if you accepted the fact that you were going to steal a radiogram.
. . .

Oh, yes, it might come off. But who would try? Not he. Not even to the extent of being a spectator. Yet was he prepared to back out, to withdraw?

Well, there would be some way out. He was damned if he was going to climb down at this stage. Monday was three days off.

Chapter Fourteen

Letter from Messrs Price & Cobb, solicitors, of Cripplegate, E.C.I. to D. J. A. Marlowe Esq.

Dear Sir,

Our client Mr Roger Shorn has consulted us with regard to a letter you wrote to the Secretary of the Hanover Club, and also with regard to certain verses written in the Suggestions Book of that club and signed by you. These grossly libellous communications refer by name to our client. We are instructed that the handwriting is yours and we do not think you will wish to deny your authorship. On this assumption we must demand your unequivocal assurance that you will write first to our client a full apology for your behaviour in terms to be settled by ourselves, and secondly to the Secretary of the Hanover Club apologising for your letter and for this entry in the Suggestions Book and requesting its immediate deletion and destruction and asking for a copy of each of these letters to be displayed prominently on the Club Notice Board. In default of such assurance our instructions are to commence proceedings against you forthwith without further reference to you and to claim appropriate damages.

We await hearing from you within the next seven days.

Yours faithfully.

Letter from Messrs Tranter, Page & Whitehouse of Chancery Lane, W.C. to Messrs Price & Cobb of Cripplegate, E.G.I.

Dear Sirs,

Our client Mr D. J. A. Marlowe has handed us your letter of the 10th instant.

We are instructed to accept service on his behalf of any process in such action as you may institute.

Yours faithfully.

Letter from Messrs Price & Cobb to Messrs Tranter, Page & Whitehouse.

Dear Sirs,

We duly received your communication of the 15th inst., and now enclose the writ together with a copy for service. Will you please return the writ endorsed with your acceptance of service?

Yours faithfully.

Enclosure:
In the High Court of Justice
Queen's Bench Division.
Writ of Summons
Between Roger Norman Shorn
Plaintiff
And Donald John Anthony Marlowe
Defendant.

Elizabeth the Second by the Grace of God, of the United Kingdom of Great Britain and Northern Ireland and of our Other Realms and Territories Queen, Head of the Commonwealth, Defender of the Faiths.

Donald John Anthony Marlowe of 126 Trevor Square, S.W.7 in the County of London, We Command You that within eight days after service of this writ on you, inclusive of the day of such service, you do cause an appearance to be entered for you in an action at the suit of Roger Norman Shorn of 69 Belgrave Street, S.W.I.

And take notice, that in default of your so doing, the plaintiff may proceed therein, and judgement may be given in your absence.

Witness, Henry Viscount Aldershot Lord High Chancellor of Great Britain.

On Wednesday afternoon, coming off duty early, Bennie did not leave the tube at her usual station but went on to Charing Cross and from there took a bus to Aldwych. Then she walked up to the Opera House and, after a little interrogation, was allowed in.

The auditorium was dark, and stage hands were working on the set for the night's opera performance. But there was music off, and Bennie found the orchestra in the Crush Bar playing *Petroushka*. She stood listening behind a curtain until the music stopped.

"Good," said Don. "I think we've time for this movement just once more."

Players eased their positions, turning back their music, wiping mouthpieces, tuning strings. A murmur of talk.

Don said: "There's just one thing, fiddles, in the third bar after 91, the *pp* start was good but I want a really big crescendo up to the C, a bar before you start the tune. We didn't quite make it last time."

Various members of the orchestra indicated that they understood, though one or two looked too tired to be interested in advice. As they were about to go on Don caught sight of Bennie and raised an eyebrow as well as his baton. The orchestra played the movement through. When it was over he came across to her.

"You do look trim and smart. Is this a formal call?"

"I came right on; I haven't been home. I wanted to talk to you, Don."

"More trouble?"

"No, not specially." The leader came across and spoke to Don and was introduced. When he had moved away, Bennie said: "How is it going?"

"What, this? So—so. They're putting me on to do the four acts of *Swan Lake* tomorrow without a single orchestral rehearsal."

"Heavens! Can you?"

"Oh, yes." Don picked up his coat and put it on. "This is trickier and *Les Ambassadeurs* is trickiest. I'm not sure yet whether some of the score is playable; Bellegarde has been excelling himself. Can you climb hundreds of steps?"

"Yes, why?"

"My room is on a level with the gods. I've got to collect a few things."

They walked through the bar and then round The Grand Tier till they came to a door marked "Private" and they went through. As they began to climb the stairs Bennie said: "Has there been anything more about the libel action?"

"Let's see, when did I phone you? Yes. Things are getting under way."

"It's going on?"

"Oh, it's going on."

"You sound quite cheerful about it."

"Not cheerful. But it's what I wanted."

"I don't understand, Don. I'm a duffer about the law. Explain."

He said: "It's the only way of hitting back at a man who defames the dead. *I* libel *Roger* and go on libeling him, calling him a coward and a liar and a disgrace to his profession, on and on, spreading this wherever he goes, until he is forced in self-defence to bring an action against *me*. That is what he has now done. And I shall plead justification."

"Justification?"

"Yes. Namely that what I've said about him is true, that he is a coward and a liar to malign a dead man—*falsely*. In the action when it comes off, although I am defending, I force him to bring evidence for what he has said about the dead man in order to prove that he is not a coward and a liar. The case then turns on the evidence that he's got. If it sticks, if he proves that he had a reasonable cause against the dead man, then he wins his case against me, because my statements about him are unjustified. If he fails to prove that he had a reasonable case against the dead man, he loses his case against me, because it shows him up to have been a coward and a liar."

Bennie puckered her brow. "Very complicated. Do the lawyers think it will be all right?"

"They're not enthusiastic. Here we are at last." Don threw open the door of his room and followed Bennie in.

"But in that case why have you gone on with it?"

"They haven't got the convictions I have."

"About Daddy? No, maybe not. But they represent the legal outlook, and it will be the legal outlook which will decide. What's their objection?"

"I didn't say they objected, I said they were not full of enthusiasm. They think I've gone a bit far, and they regard the proposition as a tricky one. For that matter, so does Joanna."

"Joanna?"

"Yes, she's dead against the idea of an action. She thinks somehow it must be settled out of court."

"And what happens if you go on and Roger wins?"

"He'll get damages—which might be heavy—with costs—which certainly will be."

Bennie sat down and took off her hat. "Once you get into the clutches of the law anything can happen."

Don said: "Would you rather we took the whole thing lying down?"

"No, of course not. But I don't like the idea of his being the plaintiff. I don't like the idea of your putting yourself in the wrong."

"It's the cock-eyed way the law works. Anyway, it worked in the Gladstone case."

"I've seen it mentioned. That was the same?"

He offered her a cigarette and when she accepted it, lit it for her. "It's the same general principle. Whitehouse would be happier if the details were more similar."

"In that case Gladstone's character was vindicated?"

"Absolutely."

"And the case cost Glandstone's sons nothing?"

"Nothing much."

Bennie drew at her cigarette. Don thought she never looked really at home with a cigarette; it was that deceptive dark-eyed innocence which made one believe it was the first she had ever had. "Don, dear, I've never been fonder of you than I am at this moment."

"Very sisterly."

"No ... Because this thing—even if you win all along the line and it costs you nothing in money—it's bound to be a drain on your time and thought and concentration just when you need them most."

"There are occasions in life when one has to be a spendthrift."

Don put too much music into an attaché case and tried to shut the lid. The catches wouldn't click. Bennie said: "I came to ask you something, Don; but now I'm here I hardly like to."

"Is it about Michael?"

She looked at him quickly. "How did you know?"

"I looked at my horoscope."

She said after a while: "I haven't seen him since all this began, since the night when I found the letter. He's asked me to meet him several times but I didn't very well feel I could. He's asked me again for tomorrow night. Before I say yes or no, I want to know what you think."

Don took out a chunk of the music and put it on the table. He carefully persuaded the case to shut. "What *I* think. Well, just at the moment they're not my favourite breed. But I've nothing specially against Michael. You can't very well visit the sins of the father. . . ."

"That's what he says."

"Is he in love with you?"

She looked at him and her eyes were more limpid than ever. "Probably."

"And you?"

She shook her head.

Don said: "Well, thank God for that anyway. If you had Roger for your father-in-law it would give me colic."

"But I *like* him," she said. "Michael, I mean. I know he knows far too much at second hand, and he's a bit wild; but really he's kind and generous and I feel sorry for him. And if I go on refusing to see him I feel a prig and rather a fool."

Don put on a light raincoat and picked up his attaché case and the extra book of music. "I've got the car round the corner. Is it raining much?"

"No. . . . You see, Michael says why should I make a feud with him when he's living on his own, working on his own and hardly ever sees Roger?"

Don said: "My dear, I don't want to develop a Montague-Capulet thing out of this."

"Well, your quarrel with Roger is my quarrel. You know that——"

"I know that. But it's really up to you, Bennie."

"I'm not asking you to lay down the law. I'm asking you if you mind, *really* mind."

Don grinned slowly. "All women are the same; they manœuvre you round until they've got you in a position where you can only nod. So you nod. And that's called free-will."

He opened the door and waited for Bennie to go ahead of him. She said: "I'm sorry, darling, I didn't mean to. Tell me the truth; what do you really feel about it? Come out of your corner. It's rather important to me."

"Of course Michael's right. This is no coffee and pistols for four. But keep underground if you can. The Press might find it an interesting tit-bit."

At about the time Don said this, Joanna was telephoning Roger and making an appointment to meet him at his flat on the following evening.

Chapter Fifteen

She saw Don off at six-fifteen. A few days ago she had offered to go with him. Sometimes he liked her there, sometimes not. This was a not. He said he'd got prickly heat about the whole thing. It wasn't *Swan Lake* that worried him; if necessary he could conduct it from an invalid chair; but from what he had seen of the *corps de ballet* they seemed only less individual-minded than his twenty-two fiddles; anyway if he was going to make a hash of it he would prefer to do so in front of 2,200 comparative strangers, always supposing so many were so improvident as to pay for admission, not to mention those few critics who might feel it necessary to write a small paragraph for tomorrow's papers, all of whom, being bored to death with such a bread and butter programme, would no doubt commission their maiden aunts to occupy their seats instead.

"Yes, darling," said Joanna. "I've put your spare hankies in your tail pocket. If you don't use them, leave them there for next time. Can you manage your tie?"

"Before the end of the evening it'll look like an arum lily that's been left out of water for a week."

"Eat your sandwiches. There's plenty of time."

"You did get petrol this morning?"

"Six gallons, and they checked the oil. Anyway it's only two miles."

"Well, I wouldn't want to run out of juice in Piccadilly in the rain. What will you do while I'm gone?"

She took out his silk scarf and let it fall out of its folds. "Read or sew or something."

He put on his waistcoat and clipped the elastic round the back. "That sounds a great deal more attractive to me than standing up on a rostrum waving a futile bit of cane at a lot of eccentric-featured men and women with brass tubes and spheroid furnishings made out of trees and the intestines of cats."

She handed him his coat. "Would you swop?"

He said: "Your eyes have a gold glinty look tonight. I haven't an idea in the world what you're thinking."

She opened her eyes a little wider, to help him.

"Of practically nothing, Don, except a prayerful wish that your *Swan Lake* will be better than all previous *Swan Lakes*."

"It could well be the most original. Phone Leningrad and tell them to watch Tschaikovsky's grave. If there's movement, it'll mean he's turning over in it."

He put on his coat and took the scarf from her. "Would I swop? No, but we arrange our lives badly. We hardly ever have our feet in the fender at the same time. What are you doing tomorrow?"

"Tomorrow? Practically nothing."

"Book me a seat on the other side of the fire."

When she had watched him drive away she let the curtains fall and sat for a few minutes at the dressing-table eating the sandwiches he had left. Then she mixed herself a fairly strong Martini and took a bath. After it she brushed her hair quietly and unhurriedly, staring at herself, her face in repose almost as if she were sleeping. When she had combed her hair into shape she put on a black jersey frock with a cowl neck and black suède shoes.

There was plenty of time. It was still not seven-thirty. To Roger she had said eight.

She mixed herself another Martini and picked up her scarlet coat and carried both down to the drawing-room. In the half light she watched the clock on the mantelpiece move to seven-thirty.

The audience at Covent Garden would all be in now, murmuring a little but ready to fall into silence when the lights began to die. The orchestra all there, timing up finished; a few seconds' silence, then Don would come, wending his way among the players; there'd be a freckle of applause which would grow as he reached the rostrum; he'd face the audience, a bow slightly to the left, one to the right, then he'd turn to the orchestra, glance around and down at the watching faces, assure himself that all were ready, raise his baton. . . .

Joanna raised her glass, finishing the cocktail, switched, off the electric fire, put on her coat, picked up her bag. It was still raining. She went to the telephone and rang for a taxi; when it came she was at the front door. She closed it behind her, glanced quickly up and down the street. There was no one apparently about, but reporters had a gift for keeping out of sight if they wanted to; she had no intention of providing them with fresh headlines.

"Piccadilly Circus, please. The tube."

The taxi put her down at the Regent Street entrance. She went down and came out again at Shaftesbury Avenue. There she took a taxi for Belgrave Street.

He was waiting for her and opened the door immediately she rang.

"Darling, this *is* good of you. I'm enchanted."

She smiled at him and followed him into his flat, allowed him to slip her coat off her shoulders. He was in a dinner jacket; she watched his sallow but youthful face, its distinguished lines, the keen wrinkles round the narrowed eyes.

He said: "Drink, smoke?"

"Drink, please. . . . A Martini if you have one."

"I'll mix you that special one. Sit down, darling; don't look lost and hesitant."

The electric fire was on, and she folded herself on the edge of an easy chair beside it. There was silence while he mixed the drink.

She said: "This *is* a lovely room."

"I'm much prouder of it since you came."

He brought die drink to her and she nodded her thanks. All his senses were at a stretch, trying to make out what her feelings were for him in the immensely changed situation since they had last met. So far there was no lead.

He picked up his own drink and took the seat opposite her, sipped his drink.

"Have you had dinner?"

"I had sandwiches with Don. It's all I want."

He said: "You're the only woman I've ever known who has ever made my heart miss a beat in this particular way. I wish I knew what it was; it's not just beauty and charm—though I give them top marks. It's perhaps a feeling for your intellect and a subtlety that goes along with my own."

"Birds of a feather," said Joanna.

There seemed to be no danger signals for him here. "You don't know how delighted I am to hear you say that. And relieved."

"Relieved?"

"Well. . . ." He made a disclaiming gesture.

She sipped her drink. "In a way it's a relief to me too, being in your company again."

"I imagine Don can be rather trying."

"I don't find him trying—only different."

Her eyes were down, he could only see her eyelids. She said: "Tell me, darling, did you sleep with me that time in Sussex just for the joy of going through John Marlowe's private papers?"

Here it came. "You ask *me* that?"

"Should I not?"

"Certainly you should not."

She said: "Well, you have to admit it was a very convenient way of combining business with pleasure."

"Darling, don't be silly. It's true I lied to you about John Marlowe. I was interested in him, and had been interested in him before he died. I always suspect that kind of holy eminence. But I did nothing until my editor indicated that he didn't hold a high opinion of him either. . . ."

He offered her a cigarette but she shook her head. She had her legs crossed above the knee and bent so that she was sitting sideways. His eyes travelled over the line of her thigh and hip.

"We soon found our suspicions about him were well founded. He was a sinful old devil. When I met you at the Colcutts' I drove you round that way because I wanted to see the Old Millhouse again for myself, and because I wanted *you* to myself for as long as possible. I always want you. That's not my fault."

"Keep to the point."

"That is precisely the point. I was interested in you that night. John Marlowe was only an excuse to stop."

"But these letters you refer to—you got them then?"

"Would you hate me for it if I said did?"

"I'm chiefly interested in your motives."

"My motives were what I've told you. But I made *some* use of a sudden opportunity. It just happened that way."

"You happened to be able to steal the wife and the letters as well."

"Oh come, darling," he said. "I didn't exactly steal you."

"No. . . . It was almost a gift, wasn't it?"

"Why analyse? Let's be grateful that it happened; and for the other times that it has happened since."

"Oh, the other times," she said. "In this flat. March the 9th and March 19th. I remember quite well."

"It's been too long."

While he topped up her glass he put his other hand on her arm just above the wrist. It was a warm light pressure.

"This libel action," she said.

"Ah."

"I want it withdrawn, Roger."

He had finished with her glass. His fingers closed round her wrist. He kissed her. She turned her mouth slightly away.

He said against her face: "Do you think I want it to go on?"

"Well, you're the plaintiff."

"Ah . . . I'd settle tomorrow if I could, but it's gone beyond the point of no return."

"Why?"

He took the bottle back to the cupboard. "In the first place, Don won't withdraw his threats to go on abusing me all over the town. Will he? Can you persuade him to?"

"No."

"In the second place, I have my reputation to consider. I can't afford not to accept the challenge."

"Can you afford to accept it?"

"Why do you want the libel action withdrawn?"

"Isn't it to everyone's advantage?"

"Not to mine now."

She uncurled herself and stood up, brushing her hands down the front of her fock. "Don hasn't a bean outside the money he makes—and that's hand-to-mouth existence. If he loses this case it will break him—literally. He'll go bankrupt."

"Isn't that an argument to put to him, not to me?"

She said: "It's even possible, if this libel comes to court and everything is dragged out and pawed over, that our affair may come out."

"Oh, so that's it, is it?"

"Not more than a proper part of it." When he did not speak she said: "I don't want this to happen, Roger. I think it would be a bad thing for all of us if this quarrel was fought out in the open."

He hesitated. They were still fencing with each other, but he began to suspect that they were fencing for different things. "Darling Joanna, I wish I could help."

"You still can."

He shook his head regretfully. "No. It's just not possible. . . . Is it his knowing about us that worries you?—would it make so much difference. Have you decided what you're going to do?"

"I think I have," she said.

There was silence for a few moments.

"Roger, d'you find me very difficult?"

"At times only."

"I grew up in an odd way, I suppose. My family life was never quite ordinary, as you know."

"My dear, I wouldn't want you any other way."

She picked up from the mantelshelf a delicate crinoline figure in pink porcelain. "This is lovely. Isn't it new?"

"Yes. Chelsea, about 1750."

She said thoughtfully: "A child's mind shouldn't have to grow up watchful, should it, probing all the time into what is meant, not what is said? With my father and mother always sniping at each other, I grew up in a permanent 'situation'. Life was perpetually subtle, artificial, alert. Perhaps that's why when I met you we seemed to understand each other so well."

"Thank you."

"Oh, it's a way to live." She put the porcelain figure back. "Being married to Don is another way."

He watched her.

"It's different company," she said. "There isn't really anything hidden, implied, difficult at all."

"How shallow."

"You could call it that. And dull, in a sense. But also, after a time, refreshing. I don't know if it's ever occurred to you, my dear, but, whatever their father was, Don and Bennie are *good* people. I don't at all mean good as being without fault but as being without meanness, without envy, without artifice, sometimes without diplomacy."

She was standing leaning against the mantelshelf, one arm along it. Although not listening to every word she said he was conscious that the meeting between them was going further downhill. "It still sounds tiresome to me."

"In two years I've had to adjust myself. It's not always been easy. It isn't always now."

"Joanna, I don't know why you need to beat all this out of yourself. So long as you find your relaxation and happiness here."

He put one hand gently under her armpit. The other moved to her tautened breast, slid over it and round to draw her into his arms.

She said: "You're not listening."

"Yes, I am. What are you trying to tell me?"

"That it's over between us, Roger. Whatever happens between Don and me."

He smiled into her eyes and kissed her. She made no move this time to accept or to draw away.

He said: "You're saying this not to convince me but to convince yourself. It won't do, darling. You're bored to death with Don and you know it. Put it to the proof, to the comparison!"

"I have done," she said. "That's why I'm not coming back to you."

"You . . . bitch!" he said, gently, amusedly, still not believing.

She didn't move. "All right. I am a bitch. That's in the specifications."

"And what is going to happen between you and Don?"

"If he finds out? I don't know. It would be outside his wavelength that the woman he loved. . . . He'd want a reason that doesn't exist."

"Are you sure it doesn't?"

"Not his sort. What should I say to him? That ever since I broke it off with you I've had a tendency to glance backwards? Or should I simply say that while he was away I got so lonely and disenchanted I could have jumped off a cliff, that I looked for somebody's chest to cry on and that yours was the nearest?"

"You didn't cry on it."

"No, because I wanted to be made love to. Well, there it is. I wanted you to take me. You did. I wanted to drown things."

"We drowned them."

"Oh, yes," she admitted, "we drowned them all right."

There was silence for a few moments.

"And can do so again."

She slipped slowly away from him, picked up her drink. "But I don't want to again. When I got home after that last time—the last time I'd been here—I faced up to those facts too. Perhaps I've proved something to myself after all. Perhaps I've grown out of you—rather late."

With his foot he flicked off half the electric fire; it was an admission of defeat. "You've worked yourself into this state of mind because I'm Moonraker and because of the libel action and because you think I've behaved rather badly. I've offended your vanity and your sense of propriety. I'm desperately sorry for that—for both our sakes."

She shook her head. "I've no vanity where you're concerned.

And one doesn't love or stop loving because of—of whether a man cheats or plays fair. It would be deliriously easy if it worked that way. Anyhow ... it was over for me before I knew you were Moonraker."

"You didn't say so when I phoned you two weeks ago."

"The only thing I hadn't decided then was whether I could go on living with Don, and live with myself at the same time."

"And now you have? I must say that makes my own hypocrisy seem pretty slim."

She was silent for a long moment, considering this, considering his change of tone. "Even if I had left him it wouldn't have meant coming to you."

"Why not?"

"I'm sorry, Roger, I didn't come here to quarrel with you. ... But I couldn't have. With you, in the end, I wouldn't quite exist as a separate person. It isn't merely sex, though it's that as well; it's the intense—intense possessiveness of a human being without pity. ... I think that must be why Michael had to find another home."

That touched him on a raw spot. He stared at her as at a stranger, succeeded temporarily in seeing her as of no importance in his life. They were two a penny, women like her, kicking around every studio. Anyway, there was nothing duller than a reformed wife.

"I'll get your coat."

But when he came back he knew they were not two a penny. There was only one Joanna, however many carbons might exist. He helped her into her coat, desiring her and hating her at the same time. He wondered in a moment of sudden insight whether she felt the same about him.

"You still haven't told me why you came."

"I thought there might have been the possibility of coming to some sort of an understanding. You told me once we talked the same language. Maybe I had illusions as to what that meant."

"You mean you thought I might help you to pick up the odd bits and pieces of your marriage?"

"I thought you might agree not to do any more to chop it down. ... It was a pretty hopeless idea, wasn't it?"

"Well, I promise to do nothing I can reasonably avoid. I promise that because I still want your goodwill." He bent and kissed her neck. "You see, I know one of these days you'll come back to me."

She half-smiled, but for the first time nervously and broke away from him. "I've tried to be honest, Roger. Let's leave it at that."

"All right," he said. "But don't let it be four years this time."

"Are you so very sure of yourself?"

He shrugged. "Shall I get you a taxi?"

"No ... I'll pick one up outside. Good night."

Chapter Sixteen

Michael said: "I'll put some more discs on. There's a mass of these older ones you haven't heard."

"The radiogram's terrific," Bennie said. "Did you say Peter *gave* it you?"

"He let me have it for ten pounds." Uneasiness stirred in Michael like a cat disturbed in sleep. "I won't have the thing in here," he'd said when they brought it up the steps; "you'll have to sell it or get rid of it somehow." "Darling boy, we did it all for you. Remember?" "A joke's a joke, Peter. If you——" "A gramophone's a gramophone, Michael, and we want ten pounds, don't we, Boy? My dear chap, there's no danger now. We've run the risks, you get the benefit."

That had been ten days ago. Grumbling, he'd said he'd keep the thing for a week or so till they decided what to do with it. But in a week its tone and look had captured him. He would part with it now with regret. And the first feeling of alarm had passed. The first week or so was in fact the danger period. After that . . . well, it made his old records sound like new. Not that it wouldn't have to go in the end, of course.

"Does he own a couple of oilfields?" Bennie asked.

"Who?"

"Peter."

"Oh, no, but there's a lot of money in his family."

They had been out to a snack meal and then a film together. After the cinema Michael had asked her back to his flat for coffee. But she was on the night flight to Zurich and she tried not to keep glancing at her watch.

"What time's your plane—one a.m.? You've got ages yet."

"We have to report at L.A.P. an hour and a half before the time of the flight."

He knelt down, going through some of the records scattered on the floor; then he glanced up at her, pushing back his hair, smiling that rather lost, charming smile that seemed so personal and yet so lonely. "What d'you do: play patience with the crew till the passengers turn up?"

"No, I'm busy all the time, believe me!"

"What made you take up a thing like that? It isn't natural to think of you droning off into the night while I turn over and go to sleep."

She smiled. "I like doing things."

They listened to the rest of the record. While it was changing he said: "Thanks for coming back with me tonight."

"I've enjoyed it. I've enjoyed the whole evening."

"I mean coming back here means extra, in view of that first night."

"I've forgotten it."

Silence fell between them again. Then, she looked at her watch and started up. "I can't wait until the end, Michael. I must go; I've got to change yet. So sorry!"

He pressed the stop switch. "That's all right, but just wait a few minutes more. I'll run you home and then out to the airport. That'll save twenty minutes."

"There's no need to do that. You have to——"

"Think no more of it. I want to do it. And I'll show you what my old steam wagon will do with the throttle against the stop. Air-travel will seem slow by comparison."

She doubtfully subsided into her armchair.

"Bennie, I want to talk to you."

She watched him with grave clear eyes as he came round her chair and brought a stool up and sat on it. She showed no signs of supposing that this was a move to ensnare her.

"That's a pretty frock," he said after a minute.

"Was that what you were going to say?"

144

"No. . . . For the first time in my life I'm tongue-tied."

"Let me untie it."

"Ah. You could so easily."

"How?"

He frowned doubtfully at his hand, then looked up suddenly. His eyes were deeply concentrated on her. "Will you marry me, Bennie?"

Neither of them moved for quite a while. Then she put her hand over his.

"I . . . don't think so, Michael."

He blinked, as if coming out of a dream. "Why not?"

"I—don't know that I love you."

"Is there some other man?"

"No. No one."

"I love you, you know."

"Yes, I know."

"I suppose it's pretty obvious. What's wrong with me?"

She smiled gravely, her dark eyes never leaving his face. "There's no right or wrong in this. If I loved you I'd say yes—instantly."

He got up slowly and stood over her. "If I believed you meant it, saying no, it would be like a death sentence."

"Michael, you mustn't say that!"

"But I do."

She half-frowned, half-smiled in perplexity, slid out from under his shadow and took his arm. "We've only known each other a few weeks. Aren't you rather rushing your fences?"

"You mean you might change your mind?"

"How can I say? I don't want you to think——"

"Is it because I haven't any money?"

"Darling, do you *really* think that could make any difference?"

"Earlier tonight you were saying you go to all these airports and never have a real chance of exploring the countries, Greece, Switzerland, Austria—you said you longed some day to have money to go over them at your leisure."

"So I do, but—Michael, don't cheapen what you've said by

putting it in any sort of scale, least of all one in which money figures. It doesn't. It really couldn't."

"What have I to do then, to make things right with you?"

"If I knew I'd tell you. But there isn't any way of knowing." She let go of his arm.

After a few seconds he said: "I'm afraid of somebody else getting you."

"Well, there's no one in sight, I promise you. Anyway, you might fall for some other girl in the meantime——"

"I shan't."

"You might. Never's a long time. If you're still as interested in six months——"

He turned, looked as if he was going to get hold of her, did not. "In six months it'll be different?"

She said: "Michael, drop it I can't say. I'm frantically sorry. Throw me out if you want to."

He took the records off the gramophone, put them in their sleeves. "I'll take you home."

"You don't have to come to L.A.P. I've still just time to make the Underground."

"Nonsense. I want to come."

They went out to the waiting car, and after a struggle got the old Delage to go. Then they roared round to Bennie's flat and Michael tinkered with the engine by the light of a street lamp while Bennie flew upstairs and changed and grabbed her equipment. When she came back his head was still inside the engine but he pulled down the great bonnet and fastened its leather strap.

"All right?" she asked.

"I've had ignition trouble this week. Nothing to worry about."

They lurched out into the Fulham road as if they were riding an obstinate donkey. Michael somehow couldn't balance the clutch and the accelerator to keep the revs up and the speed down. They bucketed along, and every time they were stopped at traffic lights the engine fizzled out and Bennie had to do her stuff with the choke. Once or twice the engine wouldn't re-start until the lights were red again. Cars and buses hooted behind them, and one

146

taxi-driver leaned out as he passed and said: "Where did yer buy it: jumble sale?"

When the old car got going again it would lurch forward in a strangulated fashion, mewing and missing and exploding. By the time the trouble had cleared they had to brake for the next lights.

"It'll be all right—as soon as we get out of me traffic," Michael panted between jerks. "Driving a car like this—in London is like putting a thoroughbred—between shafts." Bennie had dissolved in laughter, and kept apologising breathlessly because she saw Michael didn't like it.

They reached Hammersmith somehow and took the High Road, but at one of the busiest crossings the car gave a terrific burp and stopped altogether. More cars hooted and policemen put in their headland impatient hands pushed. Michael leaped out and began tinkering with the engine. He told Bennie to press the starter and pull the plug at the same time, and the engine fired instantly. Michael slapped the bonnet down and leaped in before the revs had died. They roared out into the traffic like a rocket that had lost its stick.

"I could put it—right in fifteen minutes," he shouted; "maybe—less. But—we haven't that much time."

"If you can—take me as far as—Hounslow West I can—get a bus."

He patted Bennie's knee. "Fasten your—safety belt."

They staggered along with great intermittent gulps of power, overtaking cars and lorries, squeezing by inches between a bus and an island, racing to a traffic light and then exploding past all the waiting cars as it turned green. On the Great West Road Michael jammed his foot down. The traffic had thinned, and now that they were really in motion it seemed as if nothing but a brick wall could stop them. But without any apparent reason as they squealed round a round-about the engine gave another of its terrific burps and expired. They coasted on for about five hundred yards. Michael kept slipping into gear and letting in the clutch but nothing happened except a series of strangulated jerks. He steered in towards the pavement.

"I'll get a new set of points in the morning. Difficulty with an old car. . . . Now let's see. . . ."

Bennie slid out and watched him for a minute or two. "What a blissful engine."

"How long have we got now?"

"About twelve minutes."

"Don't worry. I'll just check that it's not petrol starvation. The auto-vac petrol feed sometimes gives trouble."

One minute stretched into five. Michael slid in and used the starter again. Nothing happened. "I'll have to watch this," he said. "The battery is low."

They got out again and Michael took out one of the plugs. A few cars were still going past.

"Michael," she said.

"Yes?"

"Would you think it foul of me if I thumbed a lift?"

"Just wait another minute while I put this, back."

"I think it'll be too late."

"They'll forgive you for once, won't they?"

"Oh, yes. . . ."

"I'll give up after this." He put the plug back and got in again. The car seemed about to start but the battery was almost dead and just coughed once *whurm—whurm* like a tired old tubercular cow. "I'll give it a jerk with the handle."

"Michael, will you forgive me?" she said, and slipped out and stood in the road. Two or three cars went past and then a red Austin-Healey two-seater slowed up.

"I'm terribly sorry to stop you," Bennie said, "but are you going anywhere near London Airport? Our car's broken down and I'm late for my flight."

The young man inside looked at the old car then he looked at her. "I wasn't going that way but I will."

"Oh, I couldn't bother you if——"

"It's no trouble. Honestly. Jump in."

Bennie turned. "*Sorry* to rat on you, Michael. If you'll forgive me. . . ."

"Sure, sure, go ahead."

Bennie ran around the Austin-Healey and slid into the passenger's seat. "It's terribly good of you," Michael heard, and: "What time's your flight?" . . . "Phew, we'll have to move." Michael saw a lifted hand, heard the high-pitched drone of a modern exhaust, and the red car was gone.

He ground his teeth and took hold of the starting handle and gave it a vicious jerk. The heavy engine turned over but would not fire. He tried again and again. Then he lost his temper and went at it like a madman until the sweat was running down his face and his hands were too wet to take a grip. Finally he stopped, panting and gasping, and aimed a vicious kick at the wheel. He turned his back on the car and began to walk back the way he had come.

"The advantage of an old taxi," said Peter Waldo, "is that it goes, darling boy. Not rewarding aesthetically, but the engine turns over for ever like a sewing machine."

"Thanks for coming out," Michael said bleakly.

"What will you do with that motor coach you've left behind?"

"Let it stay there till it rots on its wheels and someone carts it away for scrap."

Peter glanced at his friend. "Harsh words, my boy. By tomorrow you'll be cooing over it again like a nursing mother."

After a minute Michael said explosively: "You don't *understand*. You've no soul for machines. It's a *beautifully* made car, far better than much of this modern rubbish. If I could only keep it in repair. A hundred pounds would make all the difference. But as it is. . . ."

"With a hundred pounds you'd do better to buy yourself a Vespa."

Michael was silent. Since the affair of the radiogram he had come to take Peter and his ideas more seriously. Against his better judgement he had been impressed by that adventure.

"Maybe you'd like to get me a new car the way you got me a new radio."

"It's a thought."

"And a dangerous one. Forget it."

"Not dangerous to me at all."

"Why not?"

"Because no one but a cretin would steal an article which he had to use in public."

"Quite a lot appear to get stolen in a year."

"Yes. By Teddy Boys, ticket-of-leave soldiers, petty gangsters—and of course by the regular car gangs who drive them away to depots for re-spraying and new number plates. No, darling boy, I don't propose to steal a car for you or to encourage you to steal one for yourself. It's not recommended in Waldo's Try-Anything-Once Course. You must walk, my lad. Learn to live the hard way."

"I *want* money," said Michael, savagely. "I'm prepared to work for it—if I can work on the right job. But I'm not willing to sweat at something useless for ever. The world is pie-eyed. It's far more important for a man to have money in his twenties than at any time in his life. Instead he's expected to work eight hours a day for fourpence a week at a dead-end job so that he can be comfortably off when he's fifty-nine. And when he's fifty-nine he sits on his coronaries and thinks: "God if I were only young!""

"Another and another cup to drown the memory of this impertinence," Peter murmured.

"What? Well, don't you agree?"

"Of course. And more so than ever today, since none of us are ever likely to live to be fifty-nine. But we're up against a system, dear boy, a system sanctified by long usage, a code of law drafted by old men for the protection of old men. All over the country at any given moment, at *every* moment, there are young people feeling exactly as you and I do. But we can't unite, we can't kick, except as individuals, and those that do kick usually end up in approved schools or in prison or as burnt-out firebrands worse off than when they started. You've got to be terribly intelligent to get away with anything and you've got to take risks."

"You've taken risks already."

"In an amateur way, yes. For a bet. That doesn't get us anywhere."

They went on in silence. Peter said as he swerved round a man:

"One of the pleasures of driving an old taxi is being hailed by blind types who don't see the meter has been taken off. Of course if the girl is pretty enough one can always stop."

"Some people stop for girls when they haven't got taxis," muttered Michael. "I'd like to bet he's dated her up for next week-end."

"That's another delusion of youth," said Peter, "that love is free. No girl is ever free. Bought women are much cheaper in the long run. Besides, they're a limited liability."

"It isn't always as simple as that."

"I know. One gets caught in the coils of the serpent. Tell me, d'you want to go to your flat or shall we move on somewhere?"

"Oh, let's stop for a drink. I owe you that."

"From time to time I do meet people who escape from the treadmill," Peter said.

"Such as?"

"But they take risks and they're clever. It's a question of weighing up the odds. "I've often been tempted to follow them."

"Into what?"

Peter peered at his passenger with his disorientated gaze. "Look, Michael, are you serious about this?"

"Why shouldn't I be?"

"Only because at the moment you're flamingly angry because you've been humiliated on the Great West Road. What I have in mind doesn't need anger; it needs guts, courage, intelligence. If——"

"Which you suppose I haven't got?"

"Which I know you've got. But you've two sides to your nature, darling boy. One's gentle, cheerful, easy-going; the other side's a good lot darker, and quite tough. But for the sort of thing you're proposing we should talk about you've got to be on the ball all the time."

"Go on. Say what's in your mind."

They drove on. "I'm thinking along these lines," said Peter. "There's money to be had if you go the right way about it. Cheap and easy money, I think. But it's crime. If you get caught the old men will put you away for a couple of years. Him that takes what isn't his'n. . . ."

"I know. I know."

"You wouldn't be able to go out courting your Bennie then."

"I can't now. But that's the risk. What's the reward?"

"As I see it," said Peter, "people who do this sort of thing are usually too ambitious. They reason—if I could just do that one job I'd be rich for life. No more risks, no more litters; just this one. So they set about a bank and try to grab a hundred thousand. Banks have safety devices, burglar alarms. They're well guarded. The job's tried; the odds are twenty to one against and the one doesn't come up; two or three intelligent but greedy men go behind bars. Or you see a jewellery shop with diamonds worth eighty thousand; you try an armed stick-up, a messenger is bumped on the head, the get-away goes wrong; robbery with violence; you wouldn't come out till your glorious twenties were spent, Michael."

"What's the answer?"

"Small profits and quick returns. With the small job the police are almost helpless. They're not really a very bright body of men, and unless they're helped by a lack of intelligence on the other side, they don't begin to get round to it. There are eight million people in London, darling boy. They can't all be protected. There's money everywhere for the picking, but you've got to use your loaf: never the same sort of job twice, never the same neighbourhood, never the same technique. It's all a question of keeping a step ahead of the law instead of a step behind. Once you get behind you've had it."

Michael lit a cigarette. As he held the lighter he was surprised to see his hand wasn't quite steady. "Sounds interesting."

"It is interesting. But it's no joke. Now supposing you and I went into partnership. We're both tough, young, intelligent, and if necessary athletic. Supposing we did six jobs a year. That's six nights a year—six risks, but small risks. Each time we aim to get three thousand pounds' worth of stuff. On an average, I mean. That's very modest but I aim to be modest. Stuff up to three thousand pounds isn't guarded much. It isn't big stuff. Three good fur coats or a dozen rings or so much Georgian silver or a few antiques. We get rid of them for half the value. That's——"

"How?"

"Boy Kenny. He knows every fence in London."

"I don't like Kenny."

"He's all right. He knows his way around. I found that out over the radiogram. For a time we'd need an 'L' on our backs, and he could help with practical know-how. Afterwards maybe we could discard him."

"What does this all add up to?"

"It could add up to about nine thousand pounds a year divisible between—for a start—the three of us. Free of tax, of course. It's not a king's ransom but single men could live off it."

So could a married man. "You wouldn't want Boy's friends in on this. He seems to have a few hangers-on."

"He fancies himself as their leader. But he'd drop them at a word from us. He pretends not to be impressed being in with me, but he is."

"Where are we?" Michael asked. "I've lost my bearings."

"Just coming off the Old Brompton Road."

Michael on his uncomfortable box seat stared out through the windscreen. It was just beginning to rain. He felt as if he were at some junction in his life, that he had lost his bearings there too. In one direction Bennie was receding rapidly. But the other offered a way of cutting her off. Whatever she said, he didn't believe she was unaffected by money. Nobody could be. It was the lubricating oil without which life couldn't continue to run. She meant, of course, that she was not a gold-digger; but that was quite a different thing.

He said: "Peter, how much would it take for a course in civil engineering?"

"I don't know. Maybe a thousand pounds."

"And how much would it cost to live for three years married?".
. . . He answered his own question. "Maybe another three thousand
. . . living quietly."

"It has been done."

"Four thousand pounds," Michael said, toying with the thought. "So little—and yet so much."

In the old days men went overseas to make their fortune, to carve out some sort of a fate for themselves by pitting their skill against nature or against the skill of others. That was no longer possible. What Peter suggested was possible, but there was no point in deceiving oneself as to what it really amounted to.

Peter sighed. "Ah, well, I thought for a moment you were serious."

His tone nettled Michael. "Come back to my place. I want to talk it over with you now."

Peter looked at him by the light from a passing neon sign that suddenly coloured their faces a startling red. "You remember I said once I thought it necessary for one's self respect to cock a snook at authority from time to time."

"Yes."

"This way we might even succeed in giving it a kick in the crutch."

Chapter Seventeen

Mr Vincent Doutelle said: "Well, Mr Marlowe, we propose to plead four defences. (1) That these verses are in fact not libellous. (2) That the letter you wrote to the secretary of the Hanover Club was an occasion of qualified privilege: i.e. that you wrote in legitimate defence of your own interests. (3) Justification, namely that the facts and imputations in these verses and in the letter are true. (4) Fair Comment, namely that in so far as the words complained of are a statement of fact they are true, and in so far as they consist of an expression of your opinions they are a fair comment upon a matter of public interest."

"I don't understand a word of it," said Don. "I sweated my brains out to compose verses and a letter that would specially hit the plaintiff where it hurt most. Why say now I didn't mean them?"

"Well, we all understand that that was your intention, Mr Marlowe, but I trust it's also your intention to win this case, and I have to advise you that we must have a defence on paper to meet all eventualities. Indeed, until we can find evidence for your convictions, we're in better shape to fight on the alternative pleas than on the main one."

Don said: "This quarrel has blown up at the most difficult time for me. I haven't yet had the chance to do all I intended to do. In a week or two I hope to be freer."

"Well, Mr Borgward here will be drafting the Pleadings. In the meantime, Mr Whitehouse, if we can get further information by means of interrogatories of the grounds Shorn had for writing the articles on Sir John Marlowe. . . ."

"Yes, we can try. It's a complicated issue . . . . We have offered

Mr Donald Marlowe the services of a private inquiry agency, but he feels that to begin with at least he is the most suitable person to make these inquiries into Shorn's accusations."

"I quite agree. For example, you are the only one, Mr Marlowe, who can approach Miss Chislehurst personally. A lot can be done sometimes in this way." Counsel folded his handkerchief corner to corner and put it back m his pocket. "It's vitally important to know just where we stand at the earliest possible moment." He peered at Don, who returned his stare.

"What do you consider the prospects?"

Doutelle smoothed his smooth cheek. "If there were a chance of a not-too-expensive settlement out of court I should strongly advise you to take it. But you wouldn't, would you?"

"No."

"Well, a great deal depends on what turns up in the interrogatories. I think from the preliminary exchanges the other side are going to be rather naughty. But at the moment everything really is in your hands, my dear sir. I'm afraid, for instance, that any jury will be impressed by the apparent similarities in the two books. Bring us proof that your father got his source material for those chapters from somewhere other than Chislehurst—notes made before he met Chislehurst—some admission from the sister—anything of that sort—and we shall be in a much better position to fight it out."

The following week Don pressed the bell of a tiny modern bungalow on the outskirts of Blakiston and when someone narrowly opened the door he said: "Could I speak to Miss Chislehurst, please."

"I am Miss Chislehurst." The nine-inch gap became six.

"I'm John Marlowe's son. I should be grateful if you could see me for a few minutes."

She stared at him with unwinking eyes, a stout old lady with a bulging face like a purse that has never been opened for charity. She wore a faded serge dress the colour of a nurse's uniform with a heavy black knitted cardigan over it and a jet brooch pinned to her lapel like a long-service medal.

"I've nothing to say to you, Mr Marlowe."

"I'm sorry. It's rather important."

She swelled up. "I know. I've had nothing but reporters. Buzz, buzz, they've come, back door and front. I've said nothing to any of them—you'd think I'd committed a crime. . . ." She was shutting the door.

"I'm not a reporter, Miss Chislehurst. I'm only anxious to talk to you."

"Well, I don't care to talk to you——" Just in time he put his foot in the door. She stared at him indignantly. "If you don't go away I'll call the police! I've done it twice already."

"Miss Chislehurst, you gave an interview at the beginning of all this—you must have done. That's why the other reporters came down here——"

"That first man deceived me; he took me in; I wouldn't have said anything to him if I'd known; it's not my concern to——"

"Well, if you saw him it's only fair you should see me——"

"I want to have no truck with the son of John Marlowe. Let me close this door!"

"Miss Chislehurst, d'you realise you are going to be subpoenaed to appear in court in a libel action that will be coming on soon?"

That stopped her. She examined him closely with her opinionated eyes. "Why? I've done nothing."

"You're the only material witness left to what passed between John Marlowe and George Chislehurst. You're certain to be called."

She hesitated. "If this is a trick. . . ."

"It's no trick."

She looked at her watch, holding it well away from her and screwing up her eyes. "I can't see the time without my glasses."

"It's a quarter to three."

"Well, I can talk to you for five minutes. But I'm due at a Working Party. I can't stop longer than that."

He followed her into the small living-room which was full of enormous clerical furniture that stood about in it as if waiting for a sale. There were religious pictures among the books and a calendar of saints. On the sideboard was a Victorian knife-box and a big silver-plated cruet with six cut-glass bottles. The table was covered with a dark-red plush cloth, with a heavy silk fringe. Miss Chislehurst faced him across this. "Well?"

"I wonder if you'd tell me what you told Mr Shorn when he came down?"

"Was that his name? He represented himself as a publisher interested in reissuing my brother's book."

"As I've told you, I'm John Marlowe's son; but this is the first I've ever heard of any complaints your brother had or any quarrel that occurred between——"

"Quarrel indeed! The upset, the anguish ended my brother's life! When Sir John came down to the funeral I said to him——"

"Just a minute, Miss Chislehurst, could you start from the beginning? D'you remember for instance exactly when they first met?"

She stared at him for a long time.

"How should I know when they first met? They didn't know each other before George was inducted into St Anne's, that's all I can tell you."

"When was that?"

"In 1941. Right in the middle of the Plymouth blitz. I remember——"

"But, Miss Chislehurst, you must have some idea of when my father first called at the house."

"I haven't an idea in the world. You don't suppose I lived with my brother, do you?. . . . Oh, I see you did think that. I loved my brother *devotedly* but I never lived with him; we had certain fundamental differences of *opinion*; I lived in Minehead until he was taken ill; then I gave up my house there to come to look after him. Alas, he lived only a few months. Your father's action, that was what did it."

Don took a few breaths for mental adjustment. "I see. . . . Then you don't actually know about this quarrel at first hand?"

"At first hand! My brother was still alive when I answered his call, wasn't he? I learned enough from him about the way your father stole his ideas and perverted them to his own ends!"

Don moved round the table and stumbled over a stool. "I don't understand, if Mr Chislehurst had a fair complaint, why he didn't make some public statement when the book was published. It would have been——"

"He was still corresponding with your father, writing him letters of complaint at his betrayal, when he was struck down. When I reached him he was paralysed all down his right side. He couldn't even *hold* a pen!"

"I wonder if you have any of the correspondence—any of my father's letters? That might be useful——"

"There were some letters but I burnt them. I felt I wanted to have no more to do with it."

"Did you give any to Mr Shorn?"

"I certainly did not."

The black marble clock on the mantelpiece had stopped at half past nine. He said: "The trouble is I can't find any letters at my end. Whether they've been stolen or lost or burnt, I don't know; but Shorn claims he has got hold of some."

"Well, I can't help that, can I?"

"No, but it's likely to make your appearance in court more than ever necessary."

This was the lever. "I can't appear in court! There's nothing I can say."

"I'm afraid it won't be left to you, Miss Chislehurst. The other side will subpoena you to confirm what you told Mr Shorn."

"I'll make a statement, that's all. They can't *force* me. And now it's time to go. I shall be late for my Working Party." She buttoned her black cardigan carefully up to the neck. She looked him over and picked up her gloves and went to another door and took down a fawn mackintosh. "I'm sorry, I can't help you."

"I'm sorry too."

He waited for her to go out of the room first, but suspiciously she waved him on. She took keys off a nail and put them into her bag, then saw him out and slammed the door after her. She tried it twice to make sure it was locked. Her eyes went over the bungalow to see that all the windows were shut.

"My brother," she said, "was inclined to blame it on that woman."

"What woman?"

"He said your father changed a lot after he came under her influence, deteriorated. If it hadn't been for her, George thinks he wouldn't have done such a shameful thing. She was always with him, George said, influencing him for ill, turning him from the right."

"What woman?"

"A Mrs Delaney. Some divorcee he picked up with. After all what else could you expect from a creature like that?"

Mrs Norah Gibbs said: "I'm sorry, Mr Marlowe, I've lost touch with Narissa. The last time I heard from her was about twelve months ago when she sent me a postcard from Cairo. It was her first visit since the trouble over there."

"How long did you know her, Mrs Gibbs?"

"All the time she was in Sunningdale, but that was only a little over a year. After her divorce she took the house opposite and lived there more or less alone. She was quite wealthy, of course, and she used to entertain. We had very good times."

"Anything you can tell me might help. What was this about Egypt?"

"Well, her grandmother was an Egyptian. Her father was in banking there. He left her a lot of money. She travelled a good bit when she was young—then she married Bob Delaney but I gather the weather was never exactly set fair. Anyway, in the end she divorced him. That was how she met Sir John Marlowe."

"How?" said Don carefully.

"Well, he was her counsel, wasn't he? After it was over she moved here, and when the divorce became absolute she told me she was going to marry Sir John."

"Did he come down to see her here?"

"Oh, yes, he was at several of the week-ends. He was always so gay and Narissa so obviously enjoyed his company."

"How did it go wrong?"

"I never knew, though you could see she was broken up about it all. What with one thing on top of the other——"

"What thing?"

"Well, you know it was the time of the Suez crisis. One day everything was fine, then suddenly there was war and Egypt seized all British assets. All her money, all the property her father had left her was there. Then on top of that, John Marlowe broke off the engagement. It was a shattering blow."

"Did he break it off or did she?"

"Oh, he did. She told me that. She was terribly upset. She said to me, I remember—in a half humorous way—'Norah, I have been left at the post. The wedding is off, *finito*. John is not going on with it.' And when I asked her why, she said, nearly breaking down, 'Oh, forget it, it does not bear talking of. I am too knocked over to think straight.'"

"And after that did she move away from here?"

"Yes, she went back to London. I intended seeing her but I was away for a time and when I went up she had moved again."

"Any idea why she is referred to as 'the notorious Mrs Delaney'?"

"She dressed well and lived well and had an expensive car and went to the races. But so do people even higher up the queue. You could say it of *Mr* Delaney maybe."

"Who else did you meet at these parties? Neighbours of yours?"

"I was her only friend round here. She had people down from town for the week-end. I expect I can give you their names if I think a minute or two."

"Did she ever mention where Mr Delaney lived?"

"In St John's Wood—that was where she lived before they were divorced. He's a company director."

"Did you ever meet Stanley Salem?"

"No." Mrs Gibbs was thoughtful. "My husband did once, in his business, though that was nothing to do with Mrs Delaney. Derek always says that Stanley Salem to him is the supreme example of the trickster who got to the top by playing one great name off against another. The Chancellor of the Exchequer only had to be in the same room with him at some official function, Derek says, and the next week Salem would introduce himself to the Governor of the Bank of England on the strength of his friendship with the Chancellor. In the end he built himself up into a person of wealth and importance. Derek says if it hadn't happened he wouldn't have believed it could happen."

"But he crashed in the end."

"Yes," said Mrs Gibbs. "But I don't think I ever heard how."

Don thought, now I know what selling vacuum cleaners is like. As for Narissa Delaney—has she slipped out of people's lives accidentally or deliberately? And will her husband know any more? And is this her husband? Three R. Delaneys in the phone book but only one in St John's Wood.

The door opened. A blonde girl in a low black taffeta blouse and a straight cut skirt.

"Is Mr Delaney in?"

"What name is it?"

"Marlowe."

"Come in, Joe!" a man's voice called from somewhere behind her.

She said over her shoulder: "It isn't Joe, sugar." She turned back and eyed Don. "What would you be wanting?"

"I came to ask. . . ." The hall space behind the girl was no longer empty. A middle-aged man, with a square-jawed boyish face, a tight mouth and a lock of fair hair falling over his brow, looked at Don's tie, at his ear, and then beyond him to see if there was anyone else there.

"Yes?"

"I came to see you about Narissa."

"There was a pause. The girl tightened the screw on her earring, and her bracelets jangled.

"Come in," said the man.

Don followed him into a living-room with chocolate-coloured rugs over a parquet floor, and angular furniture in steel and light wood. There was a good strong smell of Dior and Coronas. Behind him the girl's heels clacked in her black mules as she shut the door and followed them. Delaney pointed to a seat.

"Well what can I do for you?"

Don eased himself slowly into a chair with cantilever arms. "You remember my name, I expect, Mr Delaney? Two or three years ago your wife was friendly with my father, Sir John Marlowe."

"She certainly was."

"Well, I hope that explains a lot."

"Hardly enough. Has Narissa sent you?"

"Did you ever meet my father?"

"In the divorce courts, and I never wanted to see him again."

"Any particular reason?"

"Only that I had the pleasure of being cross-examined by him."

"I think my father was going to marry your—to marry Mrs Delaney. Have you any idea what went wrong?"

"How would I know? Narissa became a poor woman for one thing. Hasn't she told you?"

"She won't talk about it."

Delaney looked him over. "Pour a drink, Dolly. Whisky, Mr Marlowe?"

"Thank you."

Dolly went across, her legs unfree but provocative in their straight skirt; she looked as if she was bruising them against each other as she walked.

"Well what have you come about? I can hardly believe she's sent me a message."

Don said: "She thought it ought to be the other way round."

"How d'you mean? That a proposal ought to come from me?"

Dolly opened the bleached wood cocktail cabinet, which stood in a corner on legs as stiff as a wooden soldier's. "Soda, Mr Marlowe?"

"Water, please." Don's eyes lingered on a large photograph of a tall dark woman in a white evening cape.

Delaney said: "You can talk in front of Dolly; she's one of the family."

Don said: "Do you see anything of Stanley Salem these days?"

"I saw him in February when he came out. I saw him half a dozen times. What's that got to do with it?"

"Where is he now?"

"Buenos Aires, I expect. That's where he said he was going, and I don't blame him after what he's been through. Sometimes I wish I'd gone with him. It's good to have a final canter before you're turned out to grass."

"We're doing all right here, sugar," said the girl. She brought the glass to Don and then took one to Delaney and perched on the narrow arm of his chair in a series of disparate curves.

Delaney said: "Of course she got out of it well when she hadn't the money but she can't pretend that any longer. There's been this settlement. She's lying low now. Her solicitors pretend they don't know anything. Tell me where she is, first, and then we can talk."

"No," said Don, "*you* tell *me* where she is."

While he was sipping his drink no one spoke. Then Delaney murmured: "Say that again."

"Oh, I get it now!" Dolly exclaimed. "You're Don Marlowe the conductor. I heard you do a thing at Westminster Hall last year. Is it the libel action you've come about? I read about it in the *Mirror* a few weeks ago."

Bob Delaney took up his glass and drained it. The glass clattered slightly when he set it down. "I must be getting old. I was a fool to suppose you had come from her. Dolly, when he's finished his whisky, show him out."

"Perhaps we could help each other," said Don.

"How?"

"I want to find Mrs Delaney. You probably know her as well as anyone living. Tell me where to look. I'll do the looking."

"What good will that do me?"

"I might be able to answer that if I know why you wanted her."

"There were trust funds, settled on us when we married. When she divorced me she tried to take the lot. After the Suez crisis she said it wasn't coming through. That was true then but it isn't true now. She's hock deep in money again. I'm entitled to my share."

"Can't you see the trustees?"

164

"They're Egyptians. She's a quarter Gyppo herself. D'you think they'll listen to me?"

"But if you found your wife?"

"My ex-wife. I'd like to find my ex-wife."

"So would I."

"My dear chap, it's hopeless. When a woman like that leaves the field she isn't found till she wants to be. She changes her name and goes and lives in Bermuda or the South of France. Her money doesn't have to come into this country. There's no contact."

"How did Stanley Salem come into all this?"

Mr Delaney looked weary. "Stanley had his faults but at one time he was a friend of mine. I'm honestly not interested in you, Mr Marlowe. Especially I'm not interested in anything that's going to help your father—even if he is dead now."

"Oh, come," said Dolly. "Give the boy a break. Wouldn't it help us all if we found Narissa?"

The Under Treasurer of the Upper Temple said: "Of course Lord Queenswood was absolutely right in his letter to *The Times*. So far as I know Sir John's reputation was never in question."

"These articles," said Don, "are difficult to deny because they state that nothing was put on record, that John Marlowe was given the opportunity to resign to save a public scandal. Could that come about?"

"Let me put it this way," said the Under Treasurer. "If a barrister goes off the rails in his personal life—to such an extent, that is, of its becoming notorious—it could happen that he would be taken aside by the Treasurer and given a word of warning. If he persisted and if his conduct was sufficiently scandalous, it's possible that he might then be invited to retire. In that way it would be entirely unofficial and no record would be left. But actual professional misconduct is another matter."

"What d'you mean by professional misconduct?"

"Well, if he is found to be touting for business, or persistently interviewing a client without the presence of a solicitor—or arranging with a solicitor for payment of a commission—any such thing as that would automatically come through me—then I am compelled to report it to the Treasurer whose duty it is to inquire into the facts; and if there's any grounds at all for the accusation he must put the matter before the Benchers of the Inn. Any inquiry of any sort, even the least, is put on record." The Under Treasurer pointed to the drawers behind him. "The files are here. If there had been anything at all it would be in the records."

"And there is nothing?"

"On, no, there is nothing."

"Who was Treasurer that year?"

"Sir Frank Bles. He's retired now and lives in Devonshire, but I can give you his address if you want to see him."

Don said: "I called on the solicitor who acted for Mrs Delaney in her divorce, but he was pretty close as she was his client. I gather he doesn't have her address now. The only other information I got was that she didn't know my father before the action or specially ask for him to represent her. . . . Then there's this veiled nonsense about his misconduct as Recorder. I was thinking of going to Cheltenham when I can spare the time and making a few inquiries. Whom would you recommend me to see?"

The Under Treasurer rubbed a pencil up and down his cheek. "I don't think you would discover much to help you there, Mr Marlowe. It all works from London. If there were any sort of scandal or dissatisfaction in the Circuit over the Recorder's conduct at the Borough Sessions, it would find its way to the Lord Chancellor, who would be very quick to act. I would say that if you have any influence and could arrange a meeting with the Lord Chancellor, he would know everything there was to know."

The Rt. Hon. Henry Arthur Babington-Allen, Viscount Aldershot, G.C.V.O., said: "I got Queenswood's note and I'm glad to have this opportunity of seeing you, Marlowe, if only to confirm what you must already be sure of in your own mind. I knew your father well, of course, though he was my junior by six years."

"What I want to know, sir, is what reason he gave you for his retirement."

"That he had been overworking, that he was tired, that he wanted to devote more time to his writing."

"Was that why he gave up the Recordership?"

"When he wrote to me I replied to point out that this was not an onerous appointment, entailing as it did only a few days' attendance each quarter, that if he retained it it would keep him in touch with the law.' Lord Aldershot frowned. "I was under the impression that I had persuaded him not to resign this appointment. But he wrote a few days later and said he felt he would be happier to cut right away."

"For the same reason?"

"Mainly, yes."

"But there was some other reason, sir?"

His Lordship clasped his hands behind him and gazed out over his garden to the yellow rhododendrons at the end. "I'm not sure of the exact sequence of events at this distance of time, but I believe it was in September of that year that your father tried a criminal charge brought against a man called Salem. After evidence for the Crown had been heard Salem's counsel submitted that there was no case to answer, and John Marlowe ruled in his favour. Salem was discharged. Afterwards for a number of reasons Marlowe seemed much concerned about the principles on which he had acted. When he wrote me saying that on due consideration he had decided to resign the Recordership after all, I felt that this case was still exercising his mind. It worried him, and I think it just tipped the scale."

"You don't think it should have done?"

"No, I do not."

"I'm glad of that. But can you tell me what it was about the case that worried him?"

"Partly a matter of law. But there was one other point." Don waited.

"He did at the time write me a personal letter of explanation—between friends, as it were. As it was not in any way an official communication, I don't see why you should not read it—provided I can find it after all this time. I'll look when we go indoors."

"Thank you very much."

They strolled again across the lawn, but His Lordship turned back when they came within reach of the wind as it blew through the trees. "Treacherous month. The Borgias should have been born in May. Your father might well have been a judge in another twelve months. . . ."

"A pity."

"Yes, a great pity. A great waste."

There was silence for a few moments. "Do you know anything about grafting azaleas?" asked Lord Aldershot. "I'll show you in the greenhouse an experiment I've been trying." He frowned again, as at a long memory. "It must be twenty years since I first saw J.M., as we used to call him. He was addressing the Court of Appeal, appealing against a judgement in the County Court in which his client, a farmer, had lost an action for trespass against a riding school which it was alleged had done damage to his property. One of the judges; Bartram I think it was, interrupted him to say: 'Nevertheless, Mr Marlowe, it must be admitted that your client behaved towards these ladies on horseback with a singular lack of courtesy and gallantry'. Marlowe at once replied, 'My Lord, with due respect I submit that, as this was the third infringement, my client was entitled to consider that the age of cavalry was past'."

They went into the greenhouse.

"Odd," said the Lord Chancellor, "I can't recall the details of my own case that day. It was litigation over a commercial contract, that's all I recollect."

"I hope you won it, sir."

"I hope you win yours," said his Lordship.

Chapter Eighteen

At about the time Don was interviewing the Lord Chancellor Bennie was seeking less exalted company. As she turned in at the side door of Marlborough House, the Church Army Hostel in Paddington, an old woman in a tattered jumper and skirt, with reins of grey hair straggling out from under a tea-cosy hat, was standing on the doorstep talking to herself.

"If it snows," she said, "but then if it snows. I would hate to be caught out. Ah, Miss Marlowe, d'you think? . . . you know how frail I am, but if I don't go this minute I shall be late for work. If the snow catches me . . . I should really be in bed."

"No, Miss Roberts, there's no risk of snow. You're *standing* in the wind, there. Cheer up, dear. You'll be better for the walk, it'll warm you."

She slipped past Miss Roberts into the grim tiled passage and heard Sister Frey's voice from the foot of the stairs. "I'm very sorry, but we just haven't room at the moment. If you come back in two or three days. . . ."

"Well, I call it more than a disgrace; it's a bloody insult! What are these dumps for if they can't put a girl up?" A door slammed and the girl, an angry, tarted-up woman of fifty, shoved past Bennie and clattered down the stone steps. Another door slammed and there was silence. Bennie opened the door of Sister Frey's room and put in her head.

Sister Frey turned and blew out a breath, and then laughed. She was a slim-featured pale girl in her late twenties, bearing the sole responsibility of a home for a hundred women, many of them aged and many of them difficult, in one of the seediest and shabbiest areas of North London. Although she looked frail, the responsibility didn't seem to bear her down; her face showed only kindness and a rare serenity in one so young.

She said: "I wouldn't have taken that one if we'd *had* room. I know her sort, roaring drunk every Saturday night and a gin fight in the dormitory. No, thanks."

Bennie said: "Sorry about Tuesday. I had an emergency duty and couldn't get out of it."

"I see you've brought some new books."

"Well, chiefly magazines. D'you think anybody does do anything here now in the evenings except watch the telly?"

"Yes, gossip," said Mary Frey. "After air, food and water, that's the fourth primary need. Bennie, when you go upstairs you'll find Mrs Holland in bed with flu. Talk to her for a minute or two, will you? Or listen to her. She needs company."

The home was on three floors, the dormitories big, light but tiled and institution-like in the Victorian fashion. Attempts had been made to soften them with gay curtains and bright prints. Most of the women were permanent residents, and nearly all went out to work: charwomen, washers-up, scrubbers-down, sweepers and scourers, they represented a small pool of semi-casual labour on which the city round them drew as it needed; they were a part of the forgotten and the unnoticed, the wizened woman washing the office stairs, the stout body clattering crockery m the university kitchen; the potato peeler in the cafeteria, the grey-haired brusher-out of yard and basement.

A few of the women were still about. Bennie found Mrs Holland on the top floor and sat consoling her for a time; then she did odd jobs until lunch-time when she had a meal and a chat with Mary Frey before she left.

She decided to walk home. The area round the hostel was one of tiny shops and warehouses and neglected shabby streets, but a little further south it degenerated into something else. In a few paces one walked suddenly out of a conventional semi-slum into a new London of the coloured people. The influx from the West Indies, like some foreign fluid injected into the body of the city, had settled in unassimilated hydatids wherever the resistance was lowest . . . Little Harlems like this sprang up, not full of law-breakers but full of people accepting lower standards than even their immediate neighbours——"

She was surprised to hear her name called and saw Peter Waldo across the street beside his taxi talking to a big man in a black suit with a polka-dot scarf. She waved back and walked on, but after a minute the taxi caught up with her.

Peter said: "Well, this is a surprise! Doing a little fashionable slumming?"

"No, I'm just walking home." The other man had gone.

"Then let me give you a lift. Do you wish to ride sumptuous, or will you sit with me? I'd warn you it's one of those folding seats that always fold at the wrong time."

"I'll risk it."

When she was beside him he looked at her for a moment. A half-dozen Negro children stood and jeered as they drove off.

"I know you're a brave little girl but I really wouldn't think this is the best way for a stroll after dark."

"I usually take a bus then. That was Boy Kenny you were talking to, wasn't it?"

"Yes. But *he's* quite harmless, bless him. He's just a big crazy kid who wouldn't hurt a hair of your head—unless you struggled."

"He's older than you, Peter."

"Oh, in years, yes. But in development. . . . It's interesting to notice the progression. First he was a Borstal Boy, then he was a Teddy Boy, now he's just Boy, saddled for ever with a name that'll become more ludicrous with every year that passes."

"Why do you make a friend of him?"

He glanced at her. "I don't know that I am making a *friend* of him. I studied biology once, and maybe I like to look at people as if they were under a glass."

"Do they wriggle?"

"Sometimes. One has the illusion of omniscience while recognising it always as illusion."

"Not worth much, that, is it?"

"It's worth what anything is worth in this world, my dear. The fleeting pleasure that presses a bell. A drink, a pretty girl, a sense of power, a joke, doing something others can't do—they're all keys on a cash register. You press down the appropriate key and 'ting!'. Nice. Pretty sound. Pleasant feeling. Just that. Then it's gone. Nothing left. Move on to the next."

In no time at all they were in the recognisable London of the Edgware Road. From there it was only a few gear changes to the dignified opulence of Park Lane.

Bennie said: "I've just come from seeing a girl who spends all her time looking after difficult old women. There's nothing wrong with her: she's young, quite pretty, got a sense of humour, but she's made that her job, poorly paid, long hours. I don't feel she's playing on quite the same register."

"But of course she is, darling. There are many different keys; it only depends which ones for her make the best 'ting'. Probably she was crossed in love or is sexually timid or needs treatment by a psychiatrist to bring her into the normal zone. But why bother? She sees herself as St Theresa, rescuing, bending over sickbeds, advising and comforting. Don't tell me she's sacrificing her life. She's doing what she likes doing. She's seeking and finding power."

"In fact in your view," said Bennie, "everything we do is selfish."

"What else? We are nothing but ourselves, and in ourselves we're nothing but a few secretions and sensations. The empire builder, the nurse, the Teddy Boy, the burglar, the so-called saint, they're all fundamentally the same person reacting differently to slightly different stimuli. Just like the blind worm or the sea anemone."

"I'm not quite keeping up with you," she said. "Is this an aquarium universe or a cash register one?"

"Naughty." They drove on in silence until they reached the traffic lights out of the Park. "Tell me, are you going to marry Michael?"

She did not speak until the lights went green. "What does Michael think?"

"He doesn't confide his inmost thoughts in me. Only it is quite clear that he won't be happy till he gets you, one way or another."

"And you think I'm more likely to be got one way than the other?"

"It's the impression I've formed."

"You really needn't go any further than this, Peter. I'm taking you out of your way."

"No, you're not. I'm going on to see Michael now. Coming?"

"I can't. I wish I could."

He said: "I think if you were to go and live with him for a few months and got it out of your systems it would be much better than marriage, for both of you."

"It all depends, doesn't it," she said, "which key makes the loudest 'ting'?"

"How well you learn your homework. Actually, Bennie, Michael's prepared to make a lot of sacrifices for you. You underrate him."

"I'm sorry," she said. "I wouldn't want you to think that."

He looked at her to see if she was serious and saw that she was. She got down slowly and closed the door behind her. "Thank you, Peter, for bringing me home."

"I didn't expect you until this afternoon," Michael said. "I've only just got in."

Peter went to the side table and poured himself a drink. "I've fixed our first assignment."

"What?" Michael looked up too quickly.

"For next Friday. I've been working on it for more than a week."

"I wondered where you'd got to." Michael lit another cigarette from the stub of the old one, feeling a sudden need to chain-smoke. The tips of his fingers were tingling.

"There wasn't the opportunity to tell you before. Ever hear of a village called Tordean?"

"No."

"It's in Berkshire. About fifty miles from London. Ever heard of Any Questions, Ignorant Child?"

"The radio programme? Who hasn't?"

"Who hasn't? The Any Questions programme is being broadcast next Friday from the Village Hall of Tordean. The hall holds two hundred. Admission is by ticket only, and the tickets have already been distributed. There aren't many local bigwigs but what there are have received tickets. There are three good houses in the village. The audience have to occupy their seats by seven-thirty. The programme is over at nine-fifteen. During that time the village will be empty."

"How do you know all this?"

"I have an aunt in Nebury; I stayed with her last week-end."

Michael frowned impatiently through the smoke. "What's the proposition? D'you mean one would. . . ." He hesitated over the word. ". . . break in somewhere?"

"Getting into any ordinary private house is like cutting the crust on a gooseberry pie. I've left that to our natural energy and enterprise."

"Is there anything worth—having? There might be nothing but dust and Victorian furniture."

"One house, I'm told by my innocent aunt, has a good collection of eighteenth- and nineteenth-century sketches. The owner of the second house has two cars and a houseboat on the Thames; I shall be surprised if you don't find a good fur coat or two and some decent silver."

"You say 'you' as if——"

"I'll take the first house, you the second. The third has an invalid and two servants living in, so it ought to be skipped. Boy is driving the car——"

"Do we need him?"

"Very much so. He's disposing of the stuff. My dear Michael you may not love him but he's indispensable in these early stages. Once we get on our feet we can drop him if need be."

"Always providing," said Michael, "that he's willing to be dropped."

"You're not losing heart already?"

Michael hesitated. Since that conversation with Peter he had had lots of second thoughts. Several times he had half decided to pull out. Sometimes he hoped Peter had forgotten about it or had chosen to look on their talk as the improbable vapourings of two young men on a dark and rainy night. Yet the old urge, the old discontent remained.

"I thought, if we did this sort of thing, we'd plan it together. We both risk the same. Yet here the whole exercise is apparently tied up and arrangements made even with Boy before I'm told the first thing about it."

Peter sipped his drink. "I see your point. I thought you'd be pleased to be saved the staff work."

"In a sense I am. But I want to feel I'm going into this with my eyes open."

"Well, aren't you now? Do you want us to drop it?"

Michael hesitated again, aware that Peter was watching him. This was the point of no return. This was where your bluff was called—the last moment to say, stop. Until this moment he was a law-abiding citizen and all society was his friend. After it, if he said go on, he was on the other side of the fence.

Yet society was his friend only at a price—the price of conformity and nonentity and monotony and frustration. And Bennie? On the side of society, no doubt; but unreachable because of it.

He put out his cigarette half-smoked. "No, of course we'll not drop it. Tell me more."

On the following Saturday Joanna went to a cocktail party at the Savoy given by one of the executives of an ITV circuit, and almost the first person she saw there was Roger with a tall brown-haired girl who looked rather out of her element. Roger was solicitous. That spelt only one thing.

It was nearly four weeks since her visit to Roger's flat; and at this first, seeing, of him again Joanna's alert brain dug for a second or two in search of the old feelings. In the past she had been capable of the worst enormities, of not really wanting for herself but not wanting others to have—unpardonable sensations outside her control. Now she dug and they were not there. She hastily took a cocktail and drank to that.

Towards the end of the party she saw the girl slip out, and at once he came across and spoke to her.

"Joanna. Where's Don today?" It was as if the quarrel, even her last visit, had never been.

"Covent Garden. . . . No, he'll be finished by now."

"I was at my solicitor's this morning."

Perhaps it was the clairvoyance of three gins, but for the first time ever she thought he looked less than tidy, less than handsome. His good looks seemed to derive not so much from distinction of feature as from fastidiousness of expression.

She said: "Are you going to call Mrs Delaney?"

"Why do you ask?"

"Because she must know so much about all the things you accuse John Marlowe of."

"Other people do besides."

"Don has been trying to find her. If she told you what you know, you'll have to produce her as a witness, surely."

"She didn't. And I've never met her."

As Joanna was about to speak again, a flash flickered near them. Roger narrowed his brows. "Sometimes I disapprove of my own breed. If it's one of our papers I'll try to stop that."

"Isn't it all part of the same technique?"

"What technique?"

She didn't use the word she was going to. "Interference, where it's not wanted. If you stop that, why not the libel action?"

"We become the prisoners of our own attitudes. Don much more than I."

It was on the tip of her tongue to say, Roger, why do you hate Don so? But she almost knew what his answer would be. He would raise his eyebrows and say, I? I don't hate anyone—implying that it was far too uncivilised an emotion for him to feel. Yet everyone was civilised only to the Plimsoll line. It was a mistake he made in counterpoise—a mistake about himself. People like him had the advantage of detachment most of the time. But just once in a while reason wasn't enough even for them—and then they were capable of the unreasoning shift of weight, the emotional misjudgement, that lesser people would never think of.

The girl was coming back. Roger said: "Anyway, it will be months yet before the action comes on. Perhaps it will give him time to think again. . . . Oh, Marion." There was an ironical gleam in his eye. "I don't think you know Mrs Marlowe, do you? Joanna, may I introduce you to a friend of mine, Miss Laycock."

She had arranged to meet Don at Simpson's afterwards. He greeted her with the slightly masked expression that he kept for her in public.

"I wonder how many years of married life it will take," he said, "before I can see you come into a room without feeling as if I was suddenly going down in a lift."

"It's hunger, darling. I'm hours late. Terribly sorry."

"I've been spending my time breathlessly reading the account of some men who drove into a village in Berkshire last night and ransacked the place while all the population were listening in the Village Hall to Any Questions."

"Did I put the catch down when I left? I can't remember."

"You look happy."

"I am. I am. . . . Yet really I loathe cocktail parties. I always come away *blind* with smoke, lit up like a church, and no appetite."

"We'll fix those in reverse order. What will you eat?"

The waiter came up and Don ordered. When the waiter had gone Don said: "Apart from gin, why so high-spirited?"

"Don't you want me to be?"

"Yes, but it's unusual for you to look quite like this. I want a hand-out. Fair shares for all."

"There's nothing to share—exactly. D'you ever get a sensation of being suddenly—emancipated, set free?"

"Invariably, after four gins."

"Yes, all right. But not just that. . . . How was this afternoon?"

"You may well ask. On Thursday I got a good *Daphnis and Chloe* from the orchestra and a bad one from the stage. Today I got a good one from the stage and a bad one from the orchestra. Absolute hell. The conductor should be the point of fusion, the creator of the occasion. If becomes to grief, so does everyone else."

Food was brought, and conversation stopped until they were

served. She said: "I expect everyone told you how perfectly ghastly you were?"

"No. But what they muttered into their beards God only knows."

"*Daphnis and Chloe* is no joy-ride. And who was it this afternoon? Carton and Trianon? Not exactly Fonteyn and Somes."

"You can't blame them for my shortcomings."

"Don't forget I watched them at rehearsal last week. I expect today their costumes made them half a beat slower even than when I saw them. What do you think that does to your tempo?"

Don said reflectively: "I like you like this. It's another facet of perfection."

"Well, I'm drunk. It does help."

"No, you're not remotely drunk. You're excited."

"Let's argue about it. . . . But did I hear the word perfection? Oh, oh . . . you've been warned."

"In what way are you imperfect?"

"I wish I could tell you."

"Well, do."

"Putting me on a pedestal—terribly dangerous. I've no head for heights."

"Then come down for a change. Think I won't be able to take it?"

"I don't know."

They looked at each other for several seconds. He saw that the extra brilliance in her eyes was caused by tears. It had never happened in their married life before, and the realisation set off a sudden communication of feeling between them that threatened to swallow them both.

He said: "Darling, what is it?"

"Nothing. But. . . ."

"Go on."

She blinked suddenly and put a finger to the corner of her eye. "Nothing. . . . Think nothing of it."

He withdrew his hand from hers as the waiter approached. "Red currant jelly, madam?. . . . And horse-radish sauce for you, sir?"

She said: "Did you—did you go to the estate agents about the cottage?"

Don tried to collect his thoughts. "Yes, they advise against an auction—think we may get more if it's put up privately. If there's anything you want out of it we ought—ought to get it."

"Bennie might want something."

The waiter left them. Don stared at his food. "D'you know I'm not interested in this now?"

"But you must be. Pay no attention to me, darling. It's just a sort of breaking-up day at St Trinians."

There was a long silence while the emotional charge grew less. Rather uncertainly they began to eat. "How are you fixed I next week?" she said.

"In what way?"

"For going to the cottage."

"Hopeless, with *Les Ambassadeurs* on the carpet. And you?"

"I'm free on Wednesday, after I've recommended some divinely new quick-drying paint. 'Darling, did you do all this yourself, and all while I've been away, this one week-end?' 'Pet, it's nothing, pet; you just buy the paint ready-mixed in these sleekly-styled colourful tins and brush it on.' 'But, darling, isn't it very expensive, darling?' 'Not a bit, pet, nine shillings and threepence a *large* tin, ready-mixed and subtly glowing. You'll love to try it in the nursery, *won't* you!'"

"And Thursday and Friday?"

"Beautifully, beautifully free as air."

"Thursday and Friday I shall be stewing all day at Colet Gardens. ... D'you think you could take Bennie down to Sussex?"

"I can if she wants to go."

Don made another effort to keep the conversation on an even keel. "Did I tell you that Whitehouse is—is putting someone on to see if they can trace Narissa Delaney in Cairo?"

"No."

"And I've got this. This is new." He took out his pocket-book and handed her a dipping. "Mrs Delaney at the time of her divorce."

Joanna looked at the dark handsome face. "I've seen her somewhere. I know her face."

"Recently? When?"

"I'm not sure. But I think so. I've certainly seen her before."

Chapter Nineteen

Friday was the only day Bennie could manage in the following week, so Joanna called for her at nine.

They had never been much alone together except for the enforced meetings after John Marlowe's death. There was no particular coolness between them—only an absence of perfect ease, such as can exist when one man is the link between women of quite different temper and outlook. Both were aware of Joanna's greater sophistication, Bennie a little shy of it, Joanna afraid to seem to condescend.

Bennie apologised for getting her sister-in-law up so early but her next flight was at four that afternoon. Then they talked of Don's work: it was the first night of *Les Ambassadeurs*, but Don would be with Joanna in the audience; Sargent was conducting the first three performances, Don taking over next Friday. While they were waiting at a traffic light Bennie said:

"I feel guilty over this lawsuit, Joanna. I'm not pulling my weight."

"You support what Don does, and I imagine that's all anyone can do."

"I still see Michael."

"Did you read the evening paper on Monday?"

"No."

"Oh. Only from that you would have gathered that I still see Roger."

Bennie said: "Oh?"

"There was a cocktail party last Saturday given by a TV circuit. I had to go and Roger was there. He spoke to me and I answered. While I was speaking—and I seemed to be smiling—the Press took a snap. It came out over the caption: 'Friendly Lawsuit. Mr Roger Shorn sees no cause for litigation in Mrs Don Marlowe's party quip.'

Bennie whistled soundlessly. "Was Don annexed?"

"Mildly, yes. Chiefly because I hadn't told him Roger was there."

"For any reason?"

Joanna shrugged her well-tailored shoulders. She was her collected self again today, quite a long way removed from the excited and exciting person of last Saturday. "There didn't seem any point."

Presently Bennie said: "We came past here on Sunday."

"Who did?"

"Michael and I. We went out for the day."

"It was fine too."

"Glorious. . . . We went first to a swimming pool at a hotel about ten miles from here. We swam and had lunch and then went to Cowdray Park to watch the polo. Afterwards Michael said he'd seen so many horses he felt like riding one, so luckily I was able to find him one of my old riding schools near Midhurst and we hired a couple of hacks. Then we had dinner in Brighton and got home about midnight."

Joanna raised an eyebrow. "Quite a day. Did you go in that old car?"

"No. I expected to but he turned up in an M.G. Apparently he'd changed it during the week."

"Roger's very generous."

"Well, I said that, but he said it wasn't Roger's doing at all. He'd had a windfall from his mother. Some insurance or other. He seemed rather vague about it."

"Does Don know you're seeing him? Not that it matters."

"Yes, I told him. He didn't seem to mind. Except he said he wouldn't specially welcome a Shorn as a brother-in-law."

"Any likelihood?"

". . . No."

They reached the cottage about eleven. They only had to go over the place for the last time and earmark one or two things that Bennie thought she would like. It was a melancholy business with peculiar memories for them both, and they were through it by noon. Bennie lingered for a few minutes by herself taking her last look, then she pulled the front door to behind her and followed Joanna to the car.

They had a snack lunch in Midhurst and got into the car again at a quarter past one

Bennie said: "On Sunday Michael was telling me about Roger. It can't have been a particularly rock-solid household he grew up in. I feel sorry for him."

"I always did."

"Oh, of course you've known them longer than we have. . . . But I didn't realise before that he felt himself so much in the wrong groove."

"Who, Michael?"

"Yes. I happened to mention engineering and he at once began to talk about it, and talk well, using names I'd never heard, like "Rankine and Lindenthal and Freyssinet. Apparently . . . does this bore you?"

"No, of course not."

"Apparently he did classics at school but from about sixteen desperately wanted to switch to science or engineering, but Roger persuaded him not to—said there was nothing duller than to become a third-rate scientist and that he could do nothing for him in that world but any amount for him in arts or literature. After a time I think Michael began to feel trapped. He said he made one or two half-hearted attempts to change over while he was at Cambridge, but they all went wrong and in the end he came not to care what happened." Bennie stirred in her seat. "Of course it's easy to say he should have tried harder. I don't know. He says his father is terrifically persuasive."

"He is."

"Anyway, you can't doubt that Michael is sincere. When he talk about engineering his face lights up, fairly glows. It was quite an eye-opener to me."

After a minute Joanna said: "Did you mean what you said before lunch? About there being no likelihood that you and he. . . ."

"I was certain when I told Don about it. Now I'm not quite so sure."

Joanna waited for her to say more but she did not. Joanna started the car.

Bennie was wrestling with the need to talk to someone, and couldn't decide whether her sister-in-law was the most suitable person possible or the most unsuitable. It depended on one's estimate of her association with the family of Shorn. . . .

Her mind went back to Sunday, to them sitting on the grass by the swimming pool, their skins drying in the sun, his wide friendly admiring dark eyes. Then squatting beside the, pitch at Cowdray Park, listening to the thud of hooves and watching the players gallop, turn and race, swing sticks, the ball flying, turn and race again. For a few minutes, for no reason that she knew, a great depression had come over him there: you could see it fairly fall upon his face as if he were remembering something he badly wanted to forget; the muscles of his neck and jaw tensed; he was suddenly, potentially, darkly strong.

Later when they rode together the sun was slanting, and a breeze that came up from the sea had made the young leaves turn and glint like wild silk. It was while they had ambled through the sunshot lanes that they had talked about engineering, and he had talked of the possibility that enough money might come to him for him to be able to throw up his job with Bartlett & Leak and take a course in civil engineering. Somehow that had not seemed clear to her; there was a hint of ambiguity about the way he spoke——

A car turned out of a side road and Joanna had to brake suddenly. She swore gently but explicitly under her breath.

"Joanna," Bennie said. "What do you really think of Michael?"

"I? I don't know him very well. I suppose I ought to know him. Certainly I like him as far as it goes."

"I think—in spite of what I've said—I think I'm in rather deep water just now."

"About him?"

"Yes. . . . Last month he asked me to marry him. I said no. He

184

took it rather badly. We haven't stopped seeing each other, because he didn't want to. It seems to mean a lot to him, and I'm not keen to hurt him more. We—we get on well together—argue sometimes but have fun. There's so much that I like about him. But I don't think I'm really in love with him."

Joanna said quietly: "And what's the particular deep water?"

"Not knowing which way we're heading."

"That all?"

"It could be enough."

"Yes, it could be enough."

"This must all seem frightfully juvenile to you."

"Why should it?"

"Other people have fine strong emotions urging them this way or that. I stand shivering on the edge not knowing what to do."

"Doesn't it answer your question—the fact that you don't know what to do?"

Bennie said: "Most things I know. But not this. Sometimes what I feel seems to be on the verge of love. Maybe it's all I *can* feel. Emotion's a personal thing, isn't it? Nobody can relate it except to what they've felt before. What have I felt before? Calf-love when I was sixteen. ... Michael's intelligent, good looking, kind, and—devoted. What am I waiting for? A signal from the port officer to land?"

There was a long silence."

"I had a man when I was your age," said Joanna quietly, "Don knows, so it's no secret. It didn't last. I didn't marry him. But I felt a lot for him—did for a long time. It works its way into the system. You feel it in the knees, the pit of the stomach, the throat. I didn't go with him because I felt sorry for him, as apparently you're considering——"

"Oh, it's more than that. But your thing didn't work?"

"Not after a time. Darling, are you asking me for advice or what?"

"Maybe."

"What sort of advice do you want—as your sister-in-law or as a girl with a few of the corners rubbed off?"

"Not as a sister-in-law."

Joanna hesitated, her tawny eyes narrowed under straightened brows as she stared at the road. "Personally I hate advice—it always comes either from people who think they've done everything or from people you know have done nothing. If I say, yes of course you must go and live with him, I may be pushing you into a hole you'll never properly get out of—it *takes* getting out of, you know: If I say no, of course you mustn't, I'm trying to deny you the line I took." She stopped. "But perhaps you hadn't thought of anything but marriage. Is that it?"

"No . . . either's a possibility—I think."

"If it's marriage or nothing, then definitely nothing, darling. If you want to try what living with a man's like, it's not so awfully important being sure you're whole-hearted about it. You may think it will give you better know-how later on. You may want to see what it's like. I wouldn't at all blame you for that. You may like the thought of the excitement. You may feel enough for Michael to want him for his own sake—as I did for this other man. But marriage . . . if you're not perfectly sure in your own mind about every slant of it, you'd be crazy even to have it on the agenda. In spite of easy divorce, a broken marriage is a *mess* like no other."

Bennie flipped her gloves. "I like hearing you talk."

"Light me a cigarette, will you? After that I need one."

Bennie laughed. "Sorry."

"The difficulty is. . . . Thank you. That's better. . . . The difficulty with you, Bennie, is you're much more stable than I am, and this very stability is a bit of a decoy duck for you at the moment. Isn't it? I'd guess that, although you *think* you accept either way out, something—the way you were brought up or what you believe or something in your nature is going to make you awfully reluctant to take the easier one. You're not the mistress type, Bennie—and I don't mean that bitchily: any man would get his money's worth in you—but although I could maybe see you as the mistress of a married man if you felt that way for him and he couldn't get a divorce, I can't quite get the picture of you living with someone for six months for fun or for the experiment. . . ."

"Go on."

"When this lorry's out of the way. . . . Well, what I mean is that I should think there is a certain amount of danger of your *marrying* Michael rather as an experiment and coming badly to grief in the process."

"After last Sunday I think perhaps it would be all right."

"What particularly happened last Sunday?"

"Nothing, except that everything went so well. There was a warmth—in me—that hadn't been there before."

"Let me see, do we turn here? Straight on? What's the hurry, Bennie? Have you got to make up your mind by Wednesday or lose your stake money?"

"No. . . . I'd gladly delay. But there's an urgency in him that I can't quite explain—not just sex. He's communicated it to me I feel that I can perhaps help him more now than at any other time—that if he gets me now it will—stabilise him. Put him right with himself and so help him to put himself right with the world."

Joanna raised a delicate eyebrow. "There we *are* getting a little fancy, aren't we? If you're going to bring in the crazy mixed-up kid element, then I gracefully retire. If this is all tied up in your mind with Florence Nightingale and Sigmund Freud, then I——"

"No, it's not. Really it's not——"

"And it shouldn't be, darling. I don't believe a word. Michael's not so frustrated, so short of reserves that he can't last the course if he really wants you. Take your time. Waiting will do him more good than harm. His trouble all his life has been having too much too soon."

"Except perhaps love."

"And take care of that. I don't get the idea that you want to be a mother substitute?"

"No. . . ." Bennie laughed. "I try to see the obvious pitfalls."

Joanna said: "I think I've done what I tried not to do—come the heavy sister-in-law. I'm only thankful to feel that nobody ever takes notice of advice they ask for."

Bennie said: "What d'you think of Roger Shorn? You know him better than any of us."

They went through Guildford and turned off on the road for Woking and Chertsey. They were both exploring the further implications of the question. At length Joanna, having left it too long to make her intended rejoinder, said: "D'you mean as a father?"

"No, just as a person."

"Do you think it would throw light on Michael's problems?"

"All our problems."

"Well . . . he can be the most enchanting company when he sets out to be. I know no man with more charm." Joanna pressed out her cigarette in the ash-tray. "He's madly fond of women, and they're fond of him. I think at the end they turn away from him—some even before he turns from them—because they discover that they only exist to fill in his picture. Deep in him, carefully kept under lock and key, is the most enormous egoism on earth. All experience, all pleasure, all love—so called—all interest, centres on that. There's no give—only the appearance of give, the appearance of consideration, the appearance of generosity, the appearance of sympathy and understanding, because they build up in someone else the mood he wants to build up. So all his acts—no matter what they appear to be—are really votive offerings to himself."

"Oh," said Bennie quietly.

"He can also be the Champion Tearer-Down when it comes to art or—or reputation. And yet he's not dishonest. And I'd take his judgement before almost anyone else's. Because of his sense of fairness and balance."

"Fairness?"

"Yes . . . which itself runs him into contradictions. I don't know if you understand me, but he—he can speak kinder of his enemies than his friends—not because he likes them better but because his judgement, his sense of balance corrects his goodwill or ill-will almost at the source. He often says: 'I'm devoted to young So-and-So, but. . . .' And he really does like him, but his eye for the flaw. . . ."

"It must be fun having a man like that as a father."

"It doesn't leave much room for wonder." Joanna had been listening to herself with a certain amount of interest. Talking about Roger confidentially with someone for almost the first time, her thoughts had made their own shape as she went on. Yet a month ago she wouldn't have talked like this. Did one discover other people through a discovery of oneself?

Bennie said: "Then how did you feel when Roger first made those charges against Daddy?"

"When I knew it was Roger," Joanna said carefully, "I certainly took far more notice of them."

"You think he believes they're true?"

"I feel sure he does. But, Bennie, I don't know him so well that I can see into the depths of his—his motives. It could be envy of Don and of your father, just for being what they are. I'm sure he thinks Don has got on too well too soon. And in a way it could be the jealousy of a sophisticated man for those who know instinctively—and show it—that sophistication alone isn't enough. Or . . . Do we go through Staines?"

"Yes."

"Or it could be a quite genuine expression of his sense of balance and proportion, an honest attempt to shoot down what he would look on as a preposterous sham. . . . Or it could be one masquerading as the other, unknown even to himself. Proof? If he hadn't got proofs he couldn't go on. But they may not be so very watertight. Remember he began this anonymously. He never expected to be dragged out into the light, his own name tacked on to it. *He* didn't want this libel action. But he couldn't afford to admit himself to be a complete liar, and nothing else would satisfy Don."

"Do you wish that something less would?"

"Yes. I think we're running into a fight with no holds barred, and no one's going to come out of it any better than they went in."

"In the meantime if I suddenly married Michael. . . ."

"Well, it would be a scoop for the Press. But that wouldn't stop you if you felt like it—I hope."

"No," said Bennie.

Chapter Twenty

In Peter Waldo's flat Peter was leaning against a table in the centre of the room, his elbows on it, reading a book. At the window Michael stared down on the traffic of Portland Place and smoked a cigarette to hide his tension at this sudden summons. Boy Kenny was sprawled in a chair. He was wearing a black gaberdine suit from one of the "American" shops in Charing Cross Road and a navy blue shirt with a narrow white tie. His black-faced wrist watch was on the inside of his wrist with a wide heavy silver expanding strap. There was a grease mark on the breast-pocket of his jacket, and the top of a comb showed why.

Still reading his book, Peter said: "Ingenious, these alarms. This mercury gadget, for instance. Practically makes a safe safe for democracy."

"Who's thinking of breaking into a safe?" said Boy. "I thought you was above that."

"Not above it. I just don't think it's our line of country. But when I enter a profession I believe in having a working knowledge of all its branches. . . . You've brought the rest of the money, I suppose?"

"I couldn't get what I ought to've done for those etchings. Man who took 'em didn't want them, says they're hot, he'll have to flog them abroad, see, cost more money. It's rake off, rake off all the way, he says. Not like silver you can melt down. Melt those down, he says, an' you get ashes."

"All right, we'll dispense with the emotional content. How much did you get?"

"Three hundred."

Peter Waldo turned a page and straightened up. "The one Goya was worth more than three hundred."

"Maybe. But who's going to give it you for that sort of stuff?"

"Twenty-three etchings and sketches," said Peter. "A life's collection. At a minimum they were worth fourteen hundred."

"I done my best. If you don't like it, shop elsewhere."

Peter Waldo looked at the sprawling inimical figure in the chair. His eyes were slightly adrift, as if he were seeing not Boy Kenny but an abstract and distasteful principle.

"Where's the money?"

Boy indicated with his thumb the cheap fibre attaché-case he bad brought. Peter did not move but in turn gestured to Michael. Michael went across and brought the case to the table and opened it. Inside was a mass of loose pound notes, as twisted and bent as leaves swept up in a dust-pan.

"You go on," Peter said to Michael. "I never could count above thirty-five."

With a feeling in his spine Michael lifted out the notes and began to count Peter said: "People are disgusting the way they treat money."

"Some types aren't well bred, now, are they?" said Boy. Silence fell. Michael said: "I make it a hundred and ninety-nine."

"Scheming bastard," said Boy. "He must of given me one short."

"You said three hundred," said Peter.

"Oh, I've taken my cut."

Peter looked more directly at Boy. Boy struck a match with his thumb nail and lit a cigarette. He flicked the match still alight into the grate where it lay smoking.

"Any objections?"

Peter took out his note-case and offered a ten-shilling note to Michael. "Give me a hundred. We won't quibble with this awkward little man."

In silence the deal was done. Michael split his money into four twenty-fives, putting each lot into a different pocket. As he did so he thought: that's for Bennie, that's for me, that's for civil engineering, that's for living costs. It was the only way his mind could rationalise and accept the event.

"The other stuff?" said Peter.

"It's still in the garage. Pity there wasn't more silver."

"What about the furs?"

"Cool off a bit. I got a man from Stepney interested. But you not got to be too eager—that's the way to send the price down."

Peter's money was still on the table. He made no move to pick it up. "I suppose we can look for three or four hundred each out of our trial run. It's not as much as we should have got, but it's something. The new job in prospect is more ambitious."

Michael's mind came back sharply from the thought of Bennie. "A new job?"

"Earlier than I expected but it happens to have cropped up and it can't wait."

With his thumb and forefinger Boy took the cigarette from one corner of his mouth, and blew the smoke in a narrow stream from the other. "Got something good?"

"Can it be that you are now going to take an interest in your work?"

"I don't know what you're talking about."

"Only that I felt your part in disposing of the goods was putting a strain on your resources."

Boy frowned. "Clip it. What's the job?"

"I was at a dinner last night with my mother and eight other people. Two of the others were a Mr Hamilton White and his third wife. He's a New York lawyer and rich. His wife is quite a looker, but not at all worried at the thought of gilding the lily. Mr While has been supplying Mrs White with some very handsome jewellery, and what she wore last night must have been worth ten or fifteen thousand pounds."

"If they're not paste," said Boy, rubbing his decayed nose.

"Mrs White, as well as being a looker, has the look of someone who would want to be at the jewellers on the day. To give Mr Hamilton White credit, he has the look of someone who has forgotten that imitations exist."

"So?"

"The Whites have accepted an invitation to spend the weekend—this next week-end—with Lord Mules at his house near Henley. I happen to know the house."

Michael found the muscles of his arms cramped, and to relax them he yawned and stretched.

"How?"

"I went there to dinner with my mother in February. I thought then what an easy house it would be to get into."

"See," said Boy, jocular in an elephantine way, "criminal instincts from the start."

Michael said: "You're not suggesting we should break into a house when it's full of guests?"

"Why not? That's the time when no one will be expecting us."

"In the middle of the night when everyone is asleep?"

"No. I mean about ten p.m. Get up, Boy, out of my best armchair and come here."

After a minute they were all round the table. Peter said: "It's not a very big house. Look." He picked out three of the cleaner pound notes and put them on the table in the form of an H. "Centre piece is the hall. Front door here—stairs opposite. Drawing-room on the left, with french windows—study and conservatory behind. Mules employs a man and wife—man serves at table, wife cooks. I don't *think* the front door has a catch—just a normal handle with key and bolt which wouldn't be locked in the evening. Best time to go in would be during a meal, but thanks to daylight saving we couldn't do it at this time of the year, even though they dine late. Next best is ten o'clock or as soon as the light goes out in the dining-room. What's happening then? People are fed. Back they go to the drawing-room; manservant brings coffee and liqueurs. When he's done that he goes to the kitchen and helps his wife clear away and wash up. For half an hour or more there's no traffic in the hall. Servants are busy. Men and women have all been to powder their noses. Too early to go to bed. Impolite to leave until eleven. So in we go and up the stairs."

"What happens if the front door is locked?" Michael asked.

"We go in through the dining-room instead. There'll certainly be windows open."

"And how do we know which bedroom to try?"

"We don't. There can't be more than six. Why worry? There may be pickings in the other rooms too. Mrs White has a black mink. And that doesn't mean a couple of hundred from your miserly fences, Boy."

Boy Kenny shrugged. "You don't realise you've missed the one thing that tapes up the whole plan. This dopey will be wearing her jewels when she's down having dinner. Fine lot of use it'll be searching her room when she's carrying it all in the shop window."

"Darling boy, Mrs White is spending three nights with the Mules. That means a different frock each night. And that means different jewellery. Oh, I know, there's a basic equipment, but on the top of that she'll ring the changes to suit what she's wearing. And Mr White, being a man of taste, won't let her glitter too much. I shall be surprised if we don't get away with twenty thousand pounds' worth from her alone."

They thought it over—each in his own way. Calculations. Ten from the fences. Threes into ten. What I could do with three thousand three hundred.

Peter said: "It's bigger stuff than I'd intended, but I don't think the risk's greater. The trouble with the big jobs is when the risk increases in proportion."

Michael said: "But the risk *is* greater, far more than the first one. Supposing somebody runs upstairs for a handkerchief. Suppose they ring for more coffee. Any of twenty things——"

"If someone surprises us they'll be too surprised themselves to stop us getting away."

"Supposing, unknown to you, they have a dog——"

"They have."

"Then——"

"Not unknown to me. That's what will make them careless. But before we go on let me counsel you that there isn't any way to get rich quick without any risk at all——"

"I don't like dogs," said Boy.

"You wouldn't like this one. He's a big Chow with a bad temper and the loudest bark in Henley. And he's in the garden every day from nine in the morning until eleven at night. Last week they had trouble with him because he bit the postman. Lord Mules was telling us about it at the party."

"Poison's not easy to work," Boy muttered. "And you're not always sure with a crow first hit."

Peter Waldo began to gather up his notes and arrange them into neat piles of ten. Boy watched him as if he couldn't keep his eyes off the money.

Peter said: "I happen to be fond of dogs. You touch that Chow with a crowbar and I'll use it on you."

"I don't get it," said Michael.

"Between now and Sunday, darling boy, I hope to make a round of the pet shops and dogs' homes. I propose to buy a bitch in season."

"Oh," said Michael. "Would it——"

Boy said: "What's the idea?"

"It seems that you're both unaware of the facts of life or didn't have the advantage of holidays on a farm. I can tell you that no dog yet born will resist the temptation. It turns the wildest man-eater into a lap-dog. You just walk up to the gate with the bitch. If the dog should bark *before* he catches the scent, he'll stop as soon as he does. But if you approach from the right direction he'll get the scent first. Then all you have to do is open the gate and he'll trot out and follow you as gently as a lamb."

"Any dog?" said Boy.

"Wouldn't you?"

Boy shook out another cigarette and stuck it in a corner of his mouth, did the match-lighting trick and flicked the smoking stick out of the open window. "I don't like it. It's too clever. It's pretty-pretty."

"It's brilliant," said Michael. "That part of it. It's the other part of it I don't like."

They argued for a few minutes, then Peter said: "It's two to one, Boy. Anyway, I'm the one to take the risk with the dog. If it goes wrong, I carry the can, you don't start. If I go right then you two come in."

"Yes, but you have the easy end."

"It's unavoidable. Too many people know me there. Whatever pretty mask I wore, there'd be the danger of being recognised."

They went on and on, picking over the details. Again Peter said, directing his remark at Michael as if excusing himself: "We weren't going into the big stuff, but this is too big a plum to miss. There's no point in taking a risk for two thousand when you can take an equal risk for twenty."

"Twenty thousand," said Boy, moving his wet cigarette end round in his lips. "I'd do a lot for that."

"You don't need to do a lot. Just do what you're told. And above all no violence if anything goes wrong."

They fixed it for the following Sunday evening, the third night of the Whites' stay. Peter felt it was the night when it was least likely that there would be guests from outside. They went down twice during the week and made a study of the house. On the second visit Boy went near enough to the gate to set the Chow barking. He had a deep angry note and they moved quickly off.

Michael had arranged to see Bennie on the Sunday morning, but on the Friday he phoned her and made an excuse. He didn't feel he would have the mental ease to enjoy being with her, and she was pretty acute.

Saturday was a trying day. The office did not open, and by afternoon he regretted not having pressed Peter to act on Saturday instead of Sunday. The twenty-four hours would seem a week long, and if it could have happened tonight he would have been able to meet Bennie tomorrow morning with the thing off his mind.

He had plenty of work to do for his office, but the very sight of the thin carbon sheets of typescript made him restless. So he pottered through the day, and it wasn't until well on in the afternoon that he lost himself for a while in studying some cross-section drawings of the Tirso dam in Sardinia.

He left his car more or less permanently outside the flat, and presently he went to the window and stared out at it, wondering if a mechanical job would suit him better. The exhaust was "puttering" a bit. He knew a garage where on a Saturday afternoon he might have the use of an inspection pit.

A girl in a grey uniform was coming down the street on the opposite side and turned his thoughts to Bennie. Then something bumped inside him when he saw it was Bennie and that she was crossing the street to call on him.

He ran to kick a pair of slippers under a chair, grab a frying-pan out of the grate. Ash-trays to be emptied, two old bottles thrust away, dust on a table, push back his hair, twist his tie straight, the bell went; damn the rugs, why did they always kick up; he went to the door. "Bennie!"

She smiled up at him from a lower step. "I'm just off duty and. . . ."

"Marvellous! Why didn't we think of this before?" He drew her inside and hugged her and kissed her.

She said against his face: "I can't stop terribly long, Michael; but when I got out of the tube I somehow turned west instead of south."

"That's the nicest thing you've ever done. Let me fix you a drink."

"No, thanks. Oh, what a lovely chair! Is it meant for rest, or only for ornament?"

"Both when you sit in it."

"You certainly buy expensive things," she said. "I suppose this is part of the legacy?"

"Legacy?"

"Insurance or whatever it is."

"Oh, yes. Yes, that's so. Tell me, how long can you stop? Have we the evening free?"

"Michael," I'm sorry but I haven't been up to see Sister Frey today. I usually go Saturday evenings. I don't do much but I try not to let her down."

"Does it matter?"

She looked at him, smiled rather quizzically. "Darling, I can't answer that in two words. I like doing what I can, and she's my friend."

"Are you mine too?"

"Can you doubt it?"

Michael said: "I'm so sorry about tomorrow. Something cropped up and——"

"It doesn't matter at all." They talked easily and companionably for a while, and then Bennie made tea and they squatted together on the rug before the electric fire.

Michael said: "You've got such lovely legs, Bennie. I didn't realise how lovely they'd be until you came swimming with me."

"They don't feel awfully good when I've been standing on them from London to Munich." It wasn't very clever but she had to say something.

"I wish I could take you out of that job."

"Whether I like it or not?"

"I wish you'd like what I offer you."

The cake was rather stale and he apologised for ft. The ideal thing was to have a service flat like Peter Waldo.

"Are you going out with him and Boy Kenny tomorrow?"

He regretted he'd let the name slip. "Would you mind?"

"How could I?—for myself."

"But you do for me?"

"No. . . . You exist in your own right, Michael. It's only that I. . . ."

"Go on."

"I don't understand the particular attraction."

"I don't like Kenny myself. He's Peter's friend."

"And Peter is yours?"

"Yes. I find him quite fun." Three thousand three hundred each from tomorrow night, if all went well. If all went well. But that wasn't fun, that was dangerous nerve-stretching work. Supposing he had it now, all in notes, in the house, said to Bennie, here take it, in a heap at your feet, I want to buy *you*; all this I'll give; could she refuse?

She said: "Have you known him long?"

He blinked the expression out of his eyes so that she shouldn't see it. "Two years, off and on. Under his nonsense he's quite a serious chap. We agree on many things."

"What things?"

Michael frowned. "Well, on much of the stupidity of life, the—the lack of imagination, the deliberate screen of lies that people of older generations put up to hide their incompetence and their blunderings. Above all perhaps a feeling of a lack of *time*. Maybe I feel that even more than Peter. How many years have we got? Or months even? Yet everything goes bumbling along in the same middle-aged, criminally inept way. Society seems to know and care as much about what's going on—*really* going on—as a bunch of fat old ladies playing bridge while there's a fire in the cellar!"

She leaned back on her hands. "I suppose I'm just one of the great deluded. You see, I still carry on, accepting the pattern as it is, taking things on trust."

He said: "It's much easier to go slow if you feel you can afford to wait. That's why I may sometimes seem to want to cut corners. ... Tell me, Bennie, was it true what you said the night the old car broke down? You didn't refuse to marry me just because I hadn't any money?"

"If I had I wouldn't be a very good bargain—even at a cut price."

There was silence. He said: "I wonder if it would help you to—to make up your mind if I promised to stop seeing Peter Waldo and Boy?"

"Michael, it mustn't ever be my business to choose your friends."

"But if I promised to cut them out—say in two weeks' time—cut them right out, it would help?"

She got up and sat in the chair, for once slightly unsure at his closeness. "It's for you to decide alone. You *must* do exactly what you want to do."

"If you don't like them," he said, "I don't like them. Give me a week or two to break things gentry. I'll drop quietly out of me circle."

"Almost I wish you wouldn't."

"Why not?"

"Whether I like it or not I become—obligated."

"In this I shall do whatever you say, so you become obligated either way."

She hesitated, picked up her hat and twisted it in her fingers. Her eyes glimmered and she shrugged, making a humorous official disclaimer.

"Well?" he said.

"Oh, drop them, then," she said. "It's just a feeling I have. . . ."

He went to bed early and slept well but woke at seven. He lay for a time looking out of the window listening to the sparrows chirping and wondered why his stomach had a hard knot in it.

He got up at ten, cooked himself an egg, went out for the papers, bathed and shaved and smoked and studied the cricket and the racing.

Peter Waldo came about one.

"Hullo," said Michael. "What's wrong? I thought we weren't meeting till five." He stopped when he saw Peter's face and followed him in. He had never seen Peter look like that before.

"What's wrong?"

"Do you ever read your Sunday papers?"

"Yes. But not carefully. What's the matter with you?"

Waldo took a newspaper out of his pocket and slapped it on the table. "Read that." He went to the window.

Michael picked up the paper and found a piece ringed on the front page.

"Masked robbery in Henley. Last night, while entertaining distinguished guests at Greenlea, Henley-on-Thames, 59-year-old industrialist Lord Mules found his home invaded by a masked man who entered the house as dusk fell and began to rifle the bedrooms. Surprised by guest Joseph Murphy of Chalfont St Peter, the intruder escaped by way of a back staircase and through the kitchen quarters. Some jewellery is missing but the thief was interrupted before most of the valuables in the bedrooms could be seized. Lord Mules's pedigree watchdog Kong was found clubbed to death in the garden by the river."

Michael put the paper down. For a few seconds his brain wouldn't work.

"What the devil? Somebody else has. . . ."

Peter turned from the window. "Somebody else has."

He was staring so fixedly at Michael that briefly Michael thought he was being suspected. Then he saw.

"You think it was. . . ."

"Yes, I think it was."

"*What* a—dirty piece of underhand——"

"No doubt he thought it would be better if he hadn't to divide the spoils by three."

Michael picked up a packet of cigarettes and offered one to Peter. Peter shook his head. Michael flicked his lighter. He had read the account as if it was a report of a job they had done. It had been like reading in the papers about the Any Questions adventure—only this time it *hadn't* happened—to them. A few seconds later he began to feel "there but for the Grace of God". . . and then relief that now at any rate he could relax because they hadn't any need to do anything tonight.

But then there was no money either. A golden chance. It seemed easier now it hadn't to be done.

"*What* a swine!. . . . But can we be sure it was Boy?"

"It was the precise arrangement—one night before time, and bungled by a clumsy fool. And killing the dog . . . I'll get him for that."

Michael picked up the paper again. "What are you going to do?"

"I've sent a message to him, asking him to be here by one-thirty. If he doesn't come that's double proof."

"Suppose he comes and tries to bluff it out. That's what I'd do if I were in his shoes."

"Would you?" said Peter.

Michael let his cigarette smoulder.

"I wonder how much he got?"

"About two thousand pounds' worm. I phoned Paul Mules to sympathise."

"That was pretty risky, wasn't it?"

"I was entitled to ring an acquaintance I'd dined with last week. Or does that make you tremble?"

"Oh, shut up, Peter. I'm as disappointed as you. But there's nothing to be done now."

"Except wait."

Silence fell. More and more Michael realised what this meant. His offer to Bennie to drop out of the Waldo circle had been on the assumption that before he left he would have money enough.

"Does this mean," he said, "that we shan't get any more share-out from the first job?"

Peter Waldo was biting the skin round his fingers. "If he's ratted on the second deal we-shall see no more of the first."

"Do you know where he lives?"

"I know where he lived."

"And if we found him?"

"Just so. If we found him. . . . And he got away with practically nothing in the end, the crooked, diseased bastard."

"I never liked him or trusted him," said Michael.

"I know. You never liked him or trusted him, did you? I'm the one who led you into this, you poor unfortunate boy. I'm the one who thought up the foolish arrangements and wouldn't listen to reason when all the time you had better suggestions in the pipe-line. Now if——"

"Shut *up*, Peter! What's the good of picking a row with me! It isn't my fault and it isn't yours. We've been let down, that's all. We've just got to begin over again."

"Presently," said Peter. "At the moment we'll wait."

One-thirty came and then two. Neither of them was hungry, but they had a couple of drinks together and Peter began to calm down; the veins in his temples subsided and the innocence crept slowly back into his eyes as if only anger had scared it away.

Michael said: "Did you get the bitch?"

"Yes, she's at home in my flat looking very sorry for herself, and the dog upstairs is howling."

Michael began to laugh. "Sorry, but it does seem rather funny."

"I'd see the funny side more if he hadn't killed the Chow."

About four they cut up some bread and opened a tin of tongue and a bottle of wine

"How much have you left of the first haul?" Peter said.

"About sixty."

"Don't despair, darling boy. I'm not without ideas for the future, and now that we're free of that corroded Cockney——"

"We're also without any means of disposing of the stuff."

"That can be overcome. This evening what do you say if we go down to the Middle Pocket, just to see if there's any sign of Boy?"

"Let's do that," said Michael.

It was a windy night and the hanging signs in Wardour Street were squeaking and wheezing like old men in an asthma clinic. Peter parked the taxi just off Brewer Street.

They went up the stairs to the night club. The proprietor was there to welcome them in, but his smile was a little ill at ease, as if the tom-toms had already been beating. A girl with fish-net stockings and gold suspenders sold them cigarettes, and they walked down the central corridor into the club.

At the piano Dick Ballance played a love song, and the smoke from his cigarette clung about him like clouds around Fujiyama. Six or eight couples rocked in the half light. Michael went to the bar and bought two beers and a whisky. A girl he knew slightly came up, but he waved her away. Peter was drooping against the trellis. He went back to him.

Peter said: "Would you recognise Boy's friends?"

"I'm not sure."

"What about those three?"

Michael looked across the dance floor. "Could be."

The dance ended. Michael carried the whisky across to the piano. Dick flashed a smile that was like a lighthouse, warning them of rocks. "Hullo, boys, what you been doing with yourselves this week? Thanks, man; I sure am thirsty; here's mud in your pipe, man; thanks a million."

Peter drooped over the piano. "Seen Boy tonight?"

Dick rolled his eyes and wiped his mouth with the back of his hand; then he wiped his hand. "Good, that sure is good, by gosh. Boy? No, I don't think I seen him round tonight. Why, you lost him?"

"That's our impression."

Dick played a soft arpeggio. "Too bad. I guess he'll turn up."

"I guess he won't. We've been doubled, Dick. It makes me rather ashamed for him."

"Here, you have one of mine; you too, man, that side's quite safe, not even Turkish. What's he done? He should know better than to play it that way with you. You two are smart boys and no mistake."

"Know where we could find him?"

"Me? Ho, ho! I don't know nothing about the habits of those types. Excuse me, I got to start again. Boss don't dig me lazing around."

They waited beside the piano while Dick played the next two pieces. Two men Michael remembered as seeing with Kenny now came into the first bar and sat at the stools there. They had the stamp of their breed. When the music stopped Michael said: "Who are those two, Dick?"

Dick's hands were sweating. "Those two? Keep away from them. They're fast men." He began to talk quickly, through his own arpeggios. "Look, I like you two boys, see, and I say to you, clear out. There's trouble on tonight. I don't know what. It's not my business to know what, see, I'm the innocent little nigger boy. Maybe it's nothing to do with you, but maybe it has, see. But if they're laying for you, then now's the time to beat it before they all turn up." Dick Ballance wiped his pink palms again. "By gosh, it gives me a surprise that Boy has outed on you. I guess you got to give that thought. But not here, brothers, not here."

"Half a dozen gutless scroungers," muttered Michael. "They haven't got an unpadded shoulder among them."

"You could be right, man. I don't know how tough they come. But anyway do me a favour, man, and move away from here. Come an' see me at my barber-shop if you want advice."

They drifted back to the bar and had another drink. One of the men in the further bar came through the dance hall and joined the other two. Heads bent together.

"And now?" said Michael.

"Out of here," said Peter.

"Whatever for?"

"I think Dick's advice is good. He's shivering on the sidelines, chiefly anxious to keep his own feet dry, but he knows what he's talking about. Either Boy's already been here tonight or he's left word."

"I'll go and ask those three if they've seen him."

"*No.*" Peter took his arm. "They may be rats, but collectively they'll fight."

"Should that matter?"

"It matters if they carry flick knives. It's common sense to move. Don't hurry your drink. We *may* get out without trouble."

They began to take their leave in a leisurely way, waving to Dick, stopping to joke with the cigarette girl. Five men watched them move, from under frowning eyebrow, through cigarette smoke, sidelong with raised glass. They seemed to lack a decisive word among them, an incident to make them go. Peter kept up a running commentary under his breath. "Five against two, the odds are on our side; as punters they favour ten to one. But when we get out, make for civilisation just in case. Leave the cab for the moment, we'll collect that with the milk; Piccadilly is three minutes walk and gorillas hate bright lights; thank you, dear, no, we didn't bring hats, just our own sweet smiles. . . ."

Out in the street a man and two women were arguing at the open door of a car; a taxi was rounding the corner; a boy and a girl cuddled in a doorway; somebody moved in the shadow of a car parked on the opposite side of the road.

"This way," said Peter.

They walked down the length of the street; as they turned to look back two men came out of the night club. A crowd of fellows came towards them arms linked, talking and arguing and shouting. Some of them were of the same kind. Peter stepped into the road and Michael reluctantly followed him. A car hooted sharply behind them. They got out of its way and the driver glared. But somehow they were past the crowd. In three minutes they were in Piccadilly.

"A show of force," said Peter. "He thinks to scare us off."

"And did just that. We ought to have stuck it out."

"I've seen a little more of this world than you have. Let's fight them with different weapons. I've got to make a telephone call. Come on."

They went down into the Piccadilly tube station and found an unoccupied box. Peter put in his money and beckoned Michael to squeeze in with him. Michael stared at the dialling finger unbelievingly.

"It's ringing," said Peter quietly.

"What are you up to——"

"Oh, can I speak to the duty officer please? My name doesn't matter. I have some information for him."

"Peter, what the hell——"

Peter frowned and shook his head. "Duty sergeant? Yes, that will do. Hullo. I'm phoning you to give you information about some stolen property. I think you will be interested to hear about it. It is at present in a garage in Flange Street, Kensal Green. Not far from the cemetery. Yes, the south side. The number of the house is twelve and the garage is between the house and the greengrocer's shop, number ten. I'm not absolutely sure, but I think you will find there some of the stuff that was stolen last night from Lord Mules's house at Henley. If that's not there you will find other things that will make it worth a visit. . . . Never mind about that. Now listen. Don't go and get it. Send a couple of men to watch the garage. Sooner or later—they may have to wait a week—the thieves will come for it. That will be the time to get them. Bye. . . ."

He hung up.

Michael said: "You *fool*! What d'you think you're involving us in?"

Peter's face was full of high-strung amusement. "Boy will be sorry he killed that dog."

Chapter Twenty-One

Unlike his son, Roger found his affairs going well. Because he was in the news a weekly magazine had offered him £2,000 for a series of articles on coming political figures. "Make them as hot as you like," the editor told him. "We'll cool them down if we have to." And unlike his son, who had so much more time, he was in no hurry over his new love affair. He could have plotted it all out in advance on a drawing-board or explained it at brigade headquarters in the ops room to junior officers under his command.

What he could not have passed on was his own personal zest which he brought sincerely enough to this odd courtship. His cynical and adult brain continued to rate the odds while it got full value out of the enjoyment of the chase. Even though she was a girl he wouldn't normally have raised an eye to, there was more piquancy in this than in his affair last year with Fran. (He remembered once making a flattering if not quite original remark to Fran and she had replied: "Sweetie, break up the act, this isn't the 200th Performance, try to think you learned your lines last night.")

One day he overheard Marion say she hadn't been lucky with tickets for Wimbledon this year and that she was dying to go. So he arranged it all without her knowing that he had even heard her. Lunch first at the Caprice, a chauffeur-driven hired car—no fuss over parking—seats in the Press Box, dinner afterwards at Claridge's. Everywhere he went head waiters knew him, men touched their caps, others said, "Good afternoon, Mr Shorn." "Good evening, Mr Shorn." It all built up, it was subtle flattery for the girl without a word being spoken.

Under his attentions Marion had come out. Looking at her, Roger decided that when he could get his hands on her he would be able to make her striking enough not to disgrace the recollection of the other women he had had. If someone who really knew his job tackled her hair—not from one of the fashionable chi-chi *salons* but a man with classical principles in mind—a virtue could be made of its shortcomings, the curls could be got rid of and its heaviness given the strength and beauty of sculpture. You couldn't do a lot with her face, but he was inclined to think that the frame would make all the difference.

It was difficult to think of marriage again after all these years. Marriage meant the complete invasion of privacy, whereas in the conditional liaisons of the past thirteen years he had been able to keep part of his life separate and to himself. It seemed to him now that the first moves towards his present position in the world had dated from the end of the excesses of his third marriage. He and Rachel had driven each other into wild tempers he could hardly now believe in. Looking back, he felt that that had been the lowest ebb of his life; from the moment he let her go he had begun to climb away from his own fallibility of disposition towards this new eminence of composure and culture and autonomy.

But Marion was a different kettle of fish; and if Sir Percy played fair with him, he was prepared to play fair with her. Although she couldn't be expected to see it as such yet, she was part of a triangular bargain and he would keep his side.

After dinner they went back to his flat for coffee and a cigarette before he took her home. She had been slow to do this at first, but she had gradually got into the way of it and now it was taken as a matter of course.

Tonight when she sipped her coffee she sighed and said: "Ooh, it's been lovely. Thanks a million, Roger. You *are* kind to me. Why is it? Didn't you ever have a favourite niece?"

Roger winced inwardly and stirred his cup and smiled. "My dear Marion, I'm far too selfish a person to interest myself in nieces, favourite or otherwise. You should know that."

"I do hear stories about you sometimes."

"Such as?"

She laughed. "I never believe half I hear."

"They're probably true. I'm not a very admirable man."

"There," she said more slowly, "opinions might differ."

"We're all to some extent chameleons, changing according to our foliage or company. I can only tell you that, at whatever low level I started, I've been a much improved human being since I met you."

"Ah." She laughed again. "I don't believe that for a second. I'm no reformer."

"Intentionally, no. We none of us know what we are inadvertently. Do you remember that thing that Michaelangelo wrote? 'The might of one fair face sublimes my love, For it hath weaned my heart from low desires.' How does it go on after that?"

He looked at her. She had flushed to the roots of her hair. She said in a low voice: "Roger, don't, please. How can I . . . how can that be?. . . ."

He got up and put his coffee cup on the table, walked to the mantelpiece. Was this the moment? Why not? It was the moment at any rate to probe the enemy's defences. "Dear Marion, ignorant mortals that we are, it isn't any good asking how or why of an accomplished fact. Only what we are to do about it, once it is recognised."

She said faintly: "It is recognised?"

"Isn't it?"

When she didn't answer he came back and sat on the settee beside her. "Isn't it?"

She still did not speak. He took her hand interestedly, turned it palm up, felt a sudden tremor in it. There was no need now for reconnaissance units.

"Darling, you must have realised. I *hope* you've realised. I don't believe for a moment that my rather shaky restraint can have taken in anyone as intelligent as you are."

"Restraint. . . ." she said.

"Often I've felt like apologising for it, but I was so afraid of losing you if I spoke too soon."

"It's strange," she said, "that someone should be afraid of losing me."

"I was," he said.

She looked at him. "Past tense now?"

"It's still for you to say."

She looked down at his hand on hers, then covered it with her other. "I haven't words, Roger. Not like you. I can only say if you want me . . . then you will not lose me. . . ."

For the first time ever he kissed her. It was a clean, chaste kiss, but before they separated he moved his lips against hers to assure her there was nothing lukewarm in his feelings. He straightened up thinking; all over her body nerve ends are sending their impulses.

She said: "I think I'd better go."

"You had."

Behind him he heard her get up, reach for her coat. He turned and said: "No, not yet. Let's—let's talk sensibly for a minute." He gently took the coat from her, took her in his arms. His fingers moved gently down her back. A longer kiss this time. Oh, yes, she'd be all right. Thank God there seemed no risk of her being frigid.

"This isn't sensible," she said, terribly out of breath.

He released her and smiled delightedly. At all such times he had a sense of power; now more than usual because of all that her love and dependence on him meant.

"What's the matter?" she asked.

He said: "I'm so—so relieved, Marion. So relieved."

She smiled back, half laughing, half puzzled. "Darling, dearest, weren't you sure of me?"

He said: "I'll never be sure of you until we're married and I can keep you under lock and key."

"Dearest, dearest," she said. "Dearest Roger, I never *dreamed*. You know two months ago I never dreamed of this! I wouldn't have thought you'd look the side I was on. That first time we came to see you, you seemed so charming but so utterly unapproachable in your—your culture and your taste and your reading. One knew your judgements of things were right the minute you spoke them, but one could never anticipate them. It was impossible that you should take the slightest interest in me. And then that day we met by chance in the Art Gallery. I thought you were just being polite out of friendship for my father. I was so terribly flattered and nervous."

He said: "I was afraid you'd make some excuse and go. It was such a lovely coincidence. Ever since that first meeting I'd been trying to think of some way of seeing you again."

She looked at him eagerly. "Was it so? Was it really like that?"

He nodded, his face lit up with his smile. He kissed her again and she clung to him.

"Oh, Heavens!" she said. "I must go. This is frightful! I'm so happy I could cry!"

"Calm, calm, calm." He held her at arm's length, smiling. "What *about* your father? How will he take this?"

She smiled. "I don't think he'd better know—yet."

He stroked her arms. "Why not?"

"He needs preparing. He hasn't a notion in his head that anything like this may happen."

"But surely he must have an inkling. You've been out with me six or seven rimes in the last month."

"Yes, dearest, but I haven't told him."

He stared at her. "You haven't *told* him?"

"No. I didn't want to."

"But I thought. . . ."

"Have I deceived you too? I'm sorry, dearest. I thought if he knew he'd only start asking awkward questions when I didn't know the answers myself! Now I do, perhaps I can begin a system of education! But he's terribly strict and because I love him I try to humour him. Don't worry," she said, noticing the change in Roger's manner; "he's really quite easy to lead but very hard to drive. It's a question of time and patience."

Roger made the best of it. "I'd hate to offend him. He's been so very kind to me."

"We won't, I think, if we take it easily, but we'll *have* to go easily. I'll get him to invite you to the house again." Still seeking for the qualification in Roger's expression, she said: "Do you mind? Do you mind keeping it secret for a few more weeks?"

"No. . . . No, it isn't that at all."

"Dearest, if it's going to make any difference to your feeling about me, I'll go straight away and tell him tonight. His consent wouldn't make any *difference* in the long run. I'll marry you tomorrow if you say so."

Roger narrowed his eyes at her, his face still warm and affectionate. "Of course we'll wait. Take your time. Prepare the ground. Undermine his defences. So long as we can go on seeing each other in the meantime."

She laughed. "Of course. You see, I so much wanted to come out with you when you asked me, and I knew if I mentioned it to him that even if he didn't actually say no he might so hedge it about with disapproval that part of the fun would be gone."

"Does he frown on me in particular or on all men who——"

"Oh, I don't think . . . in fact I'm sure he likes you. But he might be surprised at the thought of your being his future son-in-law. Don't misunderstand me, dearest. It's only that he might think of the difference in age—and I suppose in experience."

"Yes, I must look very sere and yellow to you."

"You don't look anything of the sort, and you know you don't. But I'm an only child, and parents part more reluctantly and want more satisfying than when they have three or four to get rid or I'm afraid Daddy will make rather an inquest of the whole thing." She was thoughtful. "I'm wondering. . . ."

"Yes?"

"I think we ought to go carefully for a while—even about seeing each other—till I prepare the ground. When it didn't matter I didn't care. But now it becomes much more important that he shouldn't feel we've been pulling a fast one on him."

"I didn't know we had been."

"I'm *sorry*. But you do see how much I wanted to come. Anyway there's one thing Daddy won't be able to say, thank Heaven, and that's that you're marrying me for my money. . . . D'you know, I think it will be better if we don't go again to such public places as Wimbledon. Perhaps we could meet here sometimes, or in a cinema or——"

"Here is best."

They kissed again. His sense of triumph was temporarily less.

As she was about to leave she said: "There's one other thing—the little action. Do you know when it's going to be heard?"

"Not certainly. I was hoping it might come on before the end of the present sittings, but I don't think there's much hope of that now."

She looked intently at him. "Is it going to be all right?"

"My solicitors say so. They don't think I can possibly lose."

"And when will it be, if not soon?"

"Probably early October."

"Oh, dear, what an age!"

"Does it make any difference to us?"

"No ... I only think that, once that's out of the way, it will make it much easier for me to approach Daddy about this."

Roger had tickets for the following Wednesday also, but he was very willing to agree that they shouldn't be seen in public again. The last thing he wanted was to be accused of stealing Marion away by underhand means. It was possible, even probable, that a marriage to her, even in the teeth of Sir Percy's opposition, might turn out well for him in the end. But in the big-game hunt that occupied him at the moment Sir Percy's *present* and *immediate* goodwill was of surpreme importance. The trustee-directors of *The Globe* were being cagey about Laycock's advances, but there was no question whatsoever that they would jump at his help and his money if conditions agreeable to both sides could be drawn up. The way might yet be long and the bargaining hard, but Roger knew agreement could be reached. If it was reached Sir Percy would either stipulate for him a seat on the board or, what he really coveted, would offer him the editorship. That meant a salary of the size he liked and power of the sort he wanted. It meant an end for ever to being at the call of people like Alexander and Robinson.

In future, if this came off, he would be on the other side of the desk. To gain that Roger was prepared to do a great deal.

He remembered he had seen Michael only twice in the last month. This year there would be no breaking up, no cheerful talkative dinners together in his flat during the early weeks of August, no holiday at Antibes. He phoned Michael and asked if he could get off on Wednesday afternoon.

They met in the box at ten past five. Michael slipped into the seat beside him and smiled a greeting before settling to watch. Roger thought he had lost weight and looked pale and pasty. Too many late nights, too many snack meals, too many girls. It was a familiar pattern. What could one do on twelve pounds ten a week? Roger felt a twinge of conscience at letting him loose in the city.

The game was a cut and thrust men's singles. One player scowled at the umpire, queried line decisions, muttered under his breath and sulked. "Let's go out for a bit," Roger said at the end of the second set. "I can't stand these hairy-legged prima donnas."

"I didn't know you were interested in tennis."

"I'm not; but I had the tickets. I brought a girl on Monday but decided today to invite you instead."

"Rather an anti-climax."

"Not an unagreeable one. Wimbledon acts as a giant catharsis for women. They lose their individuality in some sort of psychological purgation."

"Anyway I was glad to come."

They went out into the main thoroughfare between the scoreboards. After pushing through the crowd and queuing for a drink they sat on the grass and talked.

Roger found it pleasant to be with his son again. Women were wonderful but exacting. His own standards in their company were exacting. Michael was easy to be with. And Michael, after the wear and tear of the last few weeks, found it easy too.

It was eight days since he had done with Peter—not quarrelling but absolutely and decisively finishing with him on the spot in the Piccadilly tube after the telephone call. That was wild man's work, Michael said, to inform on Kenny when Kenny might do the same back, and he was having no more of it. Maybe, as Peter argued, Boy, if caught, wouldn't dare to say anything about them for fear of getting in deeper himself. (And in any case there was no proof.) But Michael didn't like the idea of a few hints being dropped in the wrong places. Although Peter had found the tyres of his taxi slashed and the number plates torn off, Michael cared little or nothing for the spite of a few barrow boys. He *was* worried about the police. And he felt he had been shoved head first into a war of nerves that could do no one any good. He was angry enough about being let down and about the killing of the dog, but one had to keep some sense of proportion.

So his, promise to Bennie had been fulfilled ahead of time. And he was back on his own resources except for a few pounds he still kept under his bed.

Roger said: "D'you like living on your own?"

"Yes, fine."

"What d'you do with your time? You don't come and see me."

"I thought my last visit was disastrous enough."

"Yes, well.... The next time need not be. D'you still see Bennie?"

"Yes."

"You look a trifle etiolated in the sunlight. D'you get out of town much?"

"I went down to the coast a few Sundays ago. And you. Dad?"

Roger laughed. "I don't want to pry into your affairs. I was always on my own and I came out all right. But remember if you want any help or advice I'm always on tap. I've done my best to give you a pretty wide-awake outlook; but I'm an experienced and seasoned warrior and there's nothing like having been in the fight for twenty years to put you wise to things."

"Thanks," Michael said. It was very much on his tongue then to tell his father everything from the beginning. It was all waiting to spill out in a complicated tale of doubt and annoyance and half failure.

But however near it all was to being told, it would never have come. The closeness of the relationship made the gap wider; even their liking for each other did not help; Michael could more easily have told it all to a passing tramp. In that moment he felt the Catholics were off the track to call a confessor "father".

After a pause that seemed long to him he eventually muttered "Thanks" again and scrambled to his feet. Roger, seeing the darkness and uncertainty in his face, nearly said something further but decided not to. The offer was there. He could do no more.

They spent three hours there and then took bus and tube back to London. They had a snack meal at a public house and then separated, Michael having promised to have lunch with his father at the club on the Friday. Michael got a bus home the rest of the way and turned down his street whistling under his breath, the only whistling he ever did, when he was content.

Today had shown up to him the stretch at which he had been living since the time of the Any Questions robbery. For weeks he had been taut as a wire, chain-smoking when he could and drinking quite a lot in the evenings. The sun and the rest today had done as much good as his father's company. Almost he would have been willing to wipe out the last weeks and return to the era of youth and dependence and day dreams.

He let himself in, first by the door common to all the flats, then by his own personal door. Letters scraped as he pushed it open. He went into the big living-room and switched on the light though it was not yet quite dark, drew the curtains and went to collect his post.

Two bills and a plain envelope with a printed address. He recognised this as Peter Waldo's script and quickly tore it open.

Dear M,
They got him this morning about noon, together with another man called Adam. Revenge on an enemy is a second life. Kong will sleep quieter now.
Peter.
P.S. Do get yourself a telephone.

There wasn't much to drink in the flat. Michael found his throat very dry, and tried to open the one bottle of Worthington. He went round the flat, aimlessly opening and shutting drawers and cupboards, looking for a flipper. After a few minutes he stooped in the middle of the living-room and began to prise off the top with a key. His hands were greasy and kept slipping. The top came off. The warm weather had made the beer lively and it frothed all over his fingers before he could find a glass. When he got it in the glass he could hardly drink it for the head.

He stood there sipping and wiping the froth off his lips.

All his new peace of mind had fizzled away in a second. He was down in the ring again. Now what? How did Peter come to know so soon what had happened? In spite of their break it would be better to see him at once.

Michael swallowed his drink, picked out a cigarette and lit it. Then he switched off the light and went to the door. When he opened it two men were standing there.

The nerves in his body seemed to jump about two feet while in fact he showed no outward surprise.

"Mr Michael Shorn?"

"Yes?"

"I wonder if we could have a word with you? We're police officers and we wanted to ask you a few questions."

They were back in the room. Michael, his hands in his pockets and his black hair in a shock over his forehead, stood with his back to the empty fireplace; one plain-clothes policeman stood by the window admiring the view, the other turned the pages of his notebook as if looking casually for something he had mislaid.

"What can I do for you?"

The policeman by the window said: "Do you know a man called Boy Kenny?"

So this was it. "I've spoken to him once or twice."

"Where did you meet him?"

"In a night club in Pawle Street off Wardour Street. The Middle Pocket it's called."

"Oh, yes. I know the place. It's changed its name several times in the last few years."

"Has it? I didn't know."

"Did you also meet a man called Adam there?"

"I don't remember him."

"A big man with a dash of the tar brush. Thick woolly hair."

"No."

"Have you ever had business dealings with Kenny, Mr Shorn?"

"Why? Is he in trouble?"

"Just a little. We're checking up on some of his friends."

"I don't think you could rate me in on that. What has he done?"

"Can you remember when you last saw him?"

Michael's frown deepened. "It was at the night club two or three weeks ago."

"Was he in company? Did you know anyone he was with?"

"I can't say that I remember."

"Has he ever been here?"

"I don't think—oh, yes, he did come to a party once."

The policeman by the window continued to admire the view. The other made a note in his book. Silence fell. They're waiting for me to talk, Michael thought. Well, let them wait.

To his suprise he found himself saying: "What's this all about? Why have you come here? Kenny is nothing to me."

The man by the window said: "We're only checking up, Mr Shorn. Kenny was arrested this morning in possession of stolen property. We found your name and address in his pocket book."

"My address? Well, that's pretty surprising. Weren't there others?"

"Oh, yes, there were others. We're working through them."

So Boy hadn't talked. Relief drummed in his ears. But it was still a dangerous link.

"Can you suggest why he should have bothered to have your name and address?"

"Didn't you ask him?"

The man by the window smiled grimly. "Well, that isn't the point, is it? We're asking you."

Michael said: "I don't know what goes on in the mind of a man like that. He may have thought he could touch me for a loan or use my name somehow."

And then he noticed the policeman with the notebook looking at the radiogram.

As a child Michael had had one persistent nightmare of being chased by an immeasurable terror down endless dark passages. It had begun soon after Roger had married a second time, and it had recurred at intervals all his life. He felt an echo of it now. He was at the end of the passage; sunshine and green grass and the voices of friends were not far away, but across the mouth of the passage the steel talons were closing. . . .

"Well, thank you, Mr Shorn," said the man by the window. "I'm sorry you can't help us."

"I'm sorry."

"Do you often go to the Middle Pocket?"

"I've dropped it off."

"A good thing, I'd say. It's getting an unsavoury reputation."

"Time it was closed," said Michael.

"You think so? Well, I'll pass that on to the appropriate quarters."

Michael laughed politely as the man by the window began to move out.

"That's a lovely radiogram you have, Mr Shorn," said the man with the notebook. "It's a new one, isn't it? I've seen them advertised."

"Not quite new. I bought it second hand from a friend who didn't like the tone."

"Not from Boy Kenny, I suppose?"

"He wouldn't have a thing like this."

"You can never tell with someone like Kenny what he'll have. Has he ever offered to sell you anything cheap? An etching or Georgian silver or a Swiss clock or a wrist watch?"

Michael shook his head. "I'm sorry. I haven't got any stolen property for you. For that I think you'll have to try some of his real friends."

The man with the notebook smiled. "Well, you see, until we go round and make this check-up, we don't know who *were* his real friends, do we?"

No, thought Michael, as he showed them out, he was never a real friend of mine. Peter is responsible for this mess entirely.

He felt he had got through the interview pretty well. He had given nothing away. Yet he bitterly resented his own fright—his hands trembling, his knees turned to jelly. The mere authority of the law was enough, like the judge's wig, the red robes, the trumpets; they were impositions upon the spirit, part of a centuries old sham.

The first and most obvious thing was to get rid of the radiogram.

Chapter Twenty-Two

Boy Kenny and his friend Adam got three months. Peter Waldo was furious.

"They nearly ducked it altogether. There was nothing in the garage from the Henley robbery and only three things from Tordean; he must have sold more than he told us. There was only that ring that Boy thought was real and turned out not to be, a wrist watch and the fur you took—none of them valuable. They couldn't pin anything else on them. Three of their beautiful friends, all respectability and white silk mufflers and greased hair, went into the witness-box and swore that Boy had been at Epsom with them on the evening of the Any Questions affair. The police tried an identification parade for the man who saw him at Henley, but it didn't work. So the magistrate rules that there is no case to be sent for trial on that charge. Then they agree to be dealt with summarily on a charge of receiving, and he gives them three months each, the fool. Any innocent type who happens to drive a car when he's disqualified can get twice as much as that. It shows you how topsy-turvy the laws of this benighted country have become."

"D'you think they know we gave them away?"

"I wouldn't put it past their powers of deduction, and. . . ."

"And?"

"Well, there's room in the world for us all, but perhaps Boy and Adam may not think so when they come out."

"Oh, to hell with them," Michael said contemptuously.

"You may be right. Anyway, it leaves time for some nice quiet job to be pulled off before then."

"You can do it on your own," Michael said.

On a hot afternoon in late July Don called in to see Paul Whitehouse.

Whitehouse said: "I'm sorry we've been so unsuccessful in tracing Mrs Delaney. It doesn't of course mean we're giving up; but we're anxious so far as possible not to run up the costs on your behalf."

Don said: "The costs will have to take care of themselves. You've no news from Egypt?"

"I'm afraid a good deal of feeling exists there still, so that our inquiries are not always met with the best will to help. However, there's time yet."

"Any approximate date?"

"The Michaelmas Sittings begin on October 1 and we're not too far down the list. I should have thought late October."

"That will suit me. I shall be out of work then."

Paul Whitehouse smiled uneasily. He was never quite sure about his client's humour. "I may say we had a good deal of trouble with the interrogatories. Junior counsel, Mr Borgward, and our clerk were before the Master several times trying to get more precise details of the accusations levelled at your father."

"And the proofs?"

"Not the proofs. Proofs are for the judge and jury. I wish we could feel that Miss Chislehurst was not going to be so hostile. She can do a great deal of damage."

"And means to," Don said.

"Yes, well, it's the other side that's bringing her into court, isn't it? She may not feel too kindly disposed towards them if she is put in the box against her will."

"I'm certain she's not on very strong ground and knows it. Doutelle ought to shake something out of her."

"With such a witness the danger is one may well shake out something one doesn't want."

Don got up and took a few paces about the office, like a lion at feeding time. "Doutelle asked for evidence disproving the Moonraker articles as cast-iron as we could make it. Well, some sides of the case he ought to feel happier about; now that we've got that barrister who was at Cheltenham on the Salem case to give evidence—what's his name?. . . ."

"Taylor Hutton."

"Taylor Hutton, now that he's giving evidence we should be able to plug that hole satisfactorily. But the Chislehurst angle is a disaster."

"I think if Mr Doutelle gives the impression that we have a hard fight on our hands it's mainly for that reason. And of course that fact that you abused Shorn in those rather—er—unduly extravagant terms. I wish you had come to me for advice first."

"I did."

"Yes, but not on that point."

"Well, you would have advised against it."

"Maybe . . . yes, I suppose I should. But the libel could have been couched more moderately. It's easier, for instance, to justify calling a man a liar and a coward than to justify the use of words like louse and skunk and jackal."

"Doesn't it amount to very much the same thing?"

"Not quite in law. Anyway, I think we have to face the situation and do the best we can with it. By the way, Doutelle has advised a smallish payment into court. It's not unusual, and he suggests twenty-five pounds. It's a long shot but it might save you costs."

"How?"

"Well, it is in effect an offer of settlement. They won't take it of course, but it puts the onus on them of continuing; and it's a valuable insurance for you if the outcome isn't clear cut. . . . Oh, yes, and there's another development. We know that two *Gazette* reporters have been assigned to this case during the last month or so. They've been making a lot of new inquiries into your father's private life and reputation. From that it looks as if our opposite numbers are pressing for extra proofs too."

That night Don was due to give the first of the two concerts which had been allotted him at the Albert Hall that season, but between leaving the lawyers and taking up his baton he had a flaming row with Joanna, which seemed to shoot suddenly out of nothing at all.

Joanna had had a hard day: a telerecording at Television House which went as wrong as it could go: an ungrateful part, a delayed beginning because of a technical breakdown, a "scene" between the chief actor and the producer, both pansies, and a long argument at the end about cutting three minutes of the first scene. Coming away she met Roger who had been upstairs recording a talk; and although for her the fatal charm was no longer working and even the word "darling" on his lips had a staleness that cloyed, he yet contrived to get under her skin with a remark or two which hurt and at the same time disturbed.

They separated at the door but not before Don, coming up Kingsway, had seen whom she was with. There it had all begun. He suggested angrily that she might be more choosey of her company, and suddenly they were knee deep in the worst quarrel of their married life. From small beginnings the sky was suddenly the limit on both sides, and by the time they reached the parked car even their future together seemed in question. They drove in the car along the Strand until she demanded to be put down so that she didn't have to bear him any longer. Then, stopping in a "No Waiting" area, they managed to cool off a bit before the first policeman came.

Even so she left him there, refusing a suggestion that they should have a drink together. At the last moment, as a sort of gesture, she apologised to the policeman and took all the blame for the delay on herself, thus probably saving Don a ticket and indicating that she still had thought for his welfare.

She had been going to the concert, and for a while after she left Don she couldn't make up her mind what to do. But at the last minute she caught a taxi and got in just as the orchestra was tuning up.

She normally liked listening to Don, but tonight with the desolate exhausted ashes of the row inside her, she found it hard to uncouple the personal issues from the musical ones. It took an overture and half of Max Bruch to put things right.

Looking at her husband she suspected, not for the first time, that the rather simple man of everyday life was not so simple as he seemed. Certainly he didn't give that impression when angry; nor when playing the piano in the quietness of his own home; nor now, not even the back view which was all she could see. It was as if the stability of his everyday life was hardly more than a compass by which he navigated on a good deal of uncharted sea.

The first part of the concert went well. The solo violinist was a woman and a favourite. Don retired to his room, felt his collar and decided it would last; and wondered what in hell had got into him that he should quarrel with Joanna so. She was as high strung as a pony, and he ought to know it. He had had no particular excuse for being tetchy himself. He had been rehearsing all morning, but this orchestra and this programme presented no problems. Also the first pressures of the ballet season were over. *Les Ambassadeurs* had had a mixed Press, but it was drawing full houses whenever it was put on, and de Courville and Bellegarde seemed satisfied. From now on it was a period of consolidation until November, by which time his contract would have expired.

Well, was it the libel action that was getting under his skin? What had she said today? "I don't feel anything at this moment except *utter* exasperation and despair. I wish to Heaven we'd never heard of the action! I asked you and begged you to drop the thing before we got too involved; now it's seeped right through into our bones. We can't do anything, we can't think anything, we can't *breathe* without worrying how that's going to be affected. If only for ten minutes you were possibly able to forget it." "The minute you see Roger you seem to have no difficulty in forgetting it completely." "What has Roger to do with this? Surely this is between ourselves. If we don't come to terms with each other, temperamentally, then we shall have lost more than the libel action before it begins!"

Was that true? Yes, certainly it must be true. Yet how could he drop it at this late stage? Only by going to Roger or writing to Roger and eating his words. And even then, if he did all that, would it really leave them free to live their own lives?

When the second half was due to begin he walked slowly out along the passage and on to the platform where the orchestra were waiting for him; he bowed to the audience, smiled at the leader, glanced briefly at the microphone, raised his stick.

Dvorak's *New World*; a sure-fire hit with any popular audience. The violas and the 'cellos gave out the first sombre phrase; then came the warning note of the horn, followed by the woodwind picking up the introductory theme. The music died for a second before the full orchestra made its emphatic entry. In that silence a flashlight clicked from one of the boxes at the side, flickering through the darkened amphitheatre like lightning. Then came another one and a third.

Don put his baton down. The first notes of the full orchestra never came; instead a few strangled mews from fiddle and flute died to nothing as the players lowered their instruments and looked at their conductor in surprise. There was complete silence in the auditorium and then a whispering, growing murmur. Don turned back the page to the opening of the symphony. He leaned down to the leader, Paul Lane.

He said: "These bastards have no right in the hall. We'll start again."

Lane nodded mutely, smiled, and passed the word to the violinist next to him. But all the orchestra had quickly guessed his intentions.

"Press photographers," said the woman next to Joanna. "They shouldn't be allowed."

"They're not," said her companion. "Must have smuggled their cameras in."

"I expect it's with Marlowe being in the news."

The murmur was growing in the hall; Don raised both arms to quiet it; it began to die. But he didn't hurry to begin again. For a moment anger had almost blinded him. He was determined now to give the orchestra time to settle down and he was determined to have absolute silence. He got it. As he was at last about to restart he remembered this was all being broadcast.

The Symphony went through to its end. At the finish the audience gave him an ovation. He wondered if it was in appreciation of the music or out of sympathy. His collar was fairly dripping now as if it had been softened in warm water.

He said to the leader: "So sorry we had to do our homework over again."

"It's a disgraceful piece of interference. You did quite the right thing."

"Were they thrown out? I couldn't see."

"They left anyway."

"Well, it's you chaps who had the worst of it. I only got the flash on my starboard beam."

The last piece was the *Midsummer Night's Dream Suite*. It went through without a hitch. After the usual applause the audience began to stream out. Many of them discussed it. Joanna heard one woman say: "Poor fellow; it put him right off." "Well, I don't know about that; didn't he stop on purpose?" "Of course, he did," said Joanna in annoyance, and they stared at her, slightly knowing her face and wondering who she was. "It's the best Scherzo I've heard for three years," said a tall woman in corduroy trousers. "Much quicker to walk to the tube. I always do." "This libel action," said someone. "You know his father was a frightful sham." "I say the Press ought to be muzzled. They're getting that no one has any privacy." "That slow movement, 'Going Home', it makes you want to cry." "But I said to him: 'Bella's right', I said. 'You can't get away with that.'"

Joanna hung back, letting the threads of people unravel at the exits. In a few minutes she would go behind and see Don; now instead of being a matter of doubt it was a necessity. Her eye was caught by a mink wrap worn by a tall dark woman in the terrace immediately below the boxes. Mutation. Lovely shade and shape. Then she looked at the woman. Mrs Delaney.

Instead of waiting patiently in the emptying hall Joanna snatched up her gloves and ran sideways along her row, got out into the aisle and reached the door with the last of the crowd, tried to squeeze through with frequent apologies, was stuck, free, stuck again, she pushed ruthlessly into the circular corridor. The exits for the terraces in this confusing building. ... She ran along, side-stepping and dodging. Another knot. A woman turned and frowned at her. "Do forgive me," said Joanna, "it's rather important," and "please excuse me I'm anxious to. . . ." "We're all trying to get out, miss," said a man.

She found the entrances to the terraces, pushed in past a few stragglers, but the seats were now all empty and she had come in by an entrance two doors too far back. She ran back down the crowded corridors. Another knot of people; she glanced quickly from face to face; nothing here.

Out in the cloudy summer evening the audience streamed towards the buses, blocked the pavements; taxis and cars drew up; other people were making for the car park.

She turned towards the car park, overtaking groups, glancing about. A lot of people looked at her with her striking figure and hair. She made for the entrance to the park, still peering as doors slammed, engines revved.

She stayed about ten minutes watching cars as they went past. Then at last she gave up, angry with herself for not having been able to do the impossible thing.

She didn't want to miss Don, and knew that he lost no time in leaving. She went back into the Albert Hall, which was now deserted. She recognised some of the orchestra on their way out, and one or two smiled and raised their hats as they passed.

At the turn of the corridor she stopped. She knew suddenly where she had seen Mrs Delaney before. It had, of course, been that face which had looked in at the window of the Old Millhouse on the night when she had visited it with Roger. She was no longer certain that she immediately wanted to catch Don, no longer certain what she was going to say to him.

Chapter Twenty-Three

The summer was still at its height when Marion Laycock told Roger that her father was being difficult.

"I've gone about it ever so slowly, as we agreed. I just brought you more into the conversation. At first I thought it was working; he seemed very well disposed—you know, praised your ability and judgement. But then last night he said suddenly: 'I hope you're not getting a schoolgirl crush on Roger Shorn'. I said: 'Daddy, I'm not a schoolgirl and haven't been for four years'. He said: 'That doesn't really answer my question, does it?' and I said: 'I don't suppose Roger Shorn knows I exist', and he said: 'Oh, yes, he does, that was obvious the last time he came to dinner', so I said: 'Well I'm very flattered to know it', and he said, looking at me over his glasses: 'Marion, you still haven't answered my question'."

"Then?"

"I still thought it better to be careful so I just replied: 'I like him awfully. And I think what you suppose were his attentions to me was just his natural courtesy to all women. But I must say that if it wasn't for his age I should think him one of the nicest boy friends it was possible to have.'"

Roger suppressed a shudder. "Go on."

"That must sound rather nauseating to you," she said, showing him that he must suppress his shudders more expertly. "But you have to realise that Daddy isn't yet awake to the fact that I'm a grown woman. There's a time-lag in his brain where I am concerned, and I have to treat with him on that level. Anyway, then he said: 'You must know I've nothing against Roger Shorn as a person. But you have to realise that he's very much a man of the world, living in a sophisticated society that you have never known and, I rather hope, never will know. Although, if these negotiations go through, I shall welcome him as a business colleague, I don't think he's the sort of person I want my daughter to imagine herself in love with.'"

"Oh, dear. And do you imagine that?"

She gave his hand a squeeze. "I said to him: '*You're* doing the imagining. Daddy, not I. So tell me now once and for all what you imagine you've got against him.' He looked a bit testy and said: 'I've nothing whatever against him in the broad sense of the word. I've told you. But where you're concerned I like to be very fussy indeed. And there's this libel action pending. I shall want to know what comes of that.'" Marion looked at Roger doubtfully. "I'm sorry, dearest, don't be offended with me. You asked me to repeat exactly what he said."

"I'm glad you have," said Roger. "It enables me to see what I'm up against."

"Of course it can't make any difference in the long run." When he didn't answer she said: "Can it?"

"No," he said, with slight, deliberate hesitation. "If I'm sure of your love I'm sure of everything."

"Be sure of everything," she said.

Roger had been undecided for a long time whether as a matter of policy he should seduce Marion. At first he had had no such thought; he would have been willing to follow the normal seasonal progression: engagement, father's consent, social wedding; it all seemed set fair for the conventional lead-up to the conventional exercise.

But a tide was running against him. In this he stood to gain more and to lose more than he had ever expected. Negotiations over *The Globe* were coming to the crucial stages. His relationship in a business way with Percy Laycock had gone ahead very quickly, and he had no real need of Marion, as he had once supposed he might have. Indeed on the short view he was rather sorry he had tangled with her, for it spelt danger where there need have been no danger. His first idea had been the better one, to tie Michael up with the daughter while leaving his own movements free.

But that was past. To jilt Marion now would bring him the worst of both worlds, however tactfully he might try it. But didn't secret meetings really run him into the same risk? If they were discovered he would lose Sir Percy's goodwill in *The Globe* transactions, and his present hold over Marion might just not be strong enough in the face of her father's veto.

What followed? If he saw Marion aright she would not surrender herself lightly, but once he was established as her lover she would be bound to him by ties that couldn't exist in any other way. Whichever side up the coin fell he was then in a winning position.

Big stakes. The only other consideration was that he liked it. One afternoon in early September they met at a little tea shop in Wigmore Street. It was enough off their normal routes to make recognition unlikely, and it was quiet and secluded. They had not seen each other for eight days, but they hadn't a great deal to say.

After tea he said: "Darling, how early must you really be back?"

"I should be home by seven."

"Your father's in to dinner?"

"Well, no. . . . But I told the cook I'd be back."

"When will your father be in?"

"He's in Manchester. He might be home late tonight, or he might stay overnight."

"Come to my flat for an hour or two. It's easier, to talk there. Then we can have dinner at a place I know in Chelsea and afterwards I can see you home. There's really no reason to be in just to please the servants."

". . . . I suppose I could phone."

"Of course you could. Well, come to my flat first anyway. I promise I'll be good."

She glanced at him in slight surprise, for she had not expected him to be anything else. He was content for the moment that he had put the thought in her head.

In his flat he slipped into the living-room while Marion was taking off her coat, and switched on the fire and part lowered the blind. When she came in she glanced towards the window but made no comment and sank into the settee holding her knee in her hands.

"It's so very restful in this room, Roger. I long to live here. I wouldn't spoil it for you?"

"You'd provide the only things it at present lacks. I'm longing for the time when you'll be here every day and all day——"

"I love to hear you say so."

"—and all that that means," he added.

After a minute she looked away. He went on considering her.

She said abruptly: "I saw Michael on Tuesday."

Roger accepted the switch of subject. Move two had been registered.

"Did you?"

"Yes. We walked down Davies Street together. I found him terribly nice. Quite, quite different from what I first thought."

"I'm glad. Even though it makes me rather jealous."

"Oh," she laughed. "As if there were any reason! I'm the one who should be jealous."

"*Why?* How can you say that?"

He sounded hurt and she said hastily: "I didn't mean of any woman now. I meant only of—of all the women in the past."

He frowned at the fire. "You know, you don't really need to be."

"Dearest," Marion said, coming to him. "I'd no wish to offend you. You see, I must be aware that there have been many others—whereas with me there have been no others. At times it—it frightens me."

He took her head slowly in his hands, regarded seriously, reverently the equine bones of her face, narrow but resourceful, the heavy waved hair, the dark loyal eyes. This was the worst of her, her face. But it would wear, it wasn't pretty-pretty; and she had a good body.

"You mustn't be frightened."

"I am. Sometimes I'm frightened of you and of the comparisons you must make."

"That's terrible! It mustn't ever be."

"But it is, Roger."

"I could change that."

"How?"

"Darling," he said. "Do I have to tell you how?"

He felt a tremor pass through her body. He thought, if she'd had three drinks now instead of one. . . .

He released her very suddenly.

She said: "What's the matter, dearest?"

"You're thinking of the other women."

"No, I'm not."

"How can I convince you that they never meant what you mean?"

He stopped. It was a long time since he had used this approach. Now, only now, because of Fran, and partly because of Joanna, he had become self-conscious of his own ways, although Joanna never had the cynicism of Fran.

"What were you going to say?" Marion asked.

"I was going to say that you're completely wrong if you suppose any comparisons I make in my mind weigh against you. How can I convince you that it's the other way round? I began life on the wrong foot, as it were, particularly in my relations with women, and I've been out of step ever since. You offer me a way back, a new way, that there has never been before for me. I want you to try to forget everything but us. If I am your first man, I want you to think of yourself as my first woman. That's how I look on it."

"If I could think that I should be very proud."

"You must think that because it is true."

An hour later it happened. It all seemed so unexpected, so unpremeditated, that she couldn't have believed even if she had been told that the fire had been switched on in his bedroom and the curtains drawn ever since they came in at five. One thing after another this afternoon had undermined her resistance—which had never really been a resistance to him but to her conscience and her upbringing. She was herself unaware of her scruples failing until the last moment and she found herself in his bedroom with his cool gentle fingers sliding the zip of her frock.

Then when it was over she burst into tears and clung to him while he stroked her fallen brown hair. Again came the incongruous spectre of his memories of Fran to plague him; but now unexpectedly they helped him to a new tenderness towards Marion. The girl in her untutored awkward grace caught a moment at his unguarded self.

"Darling, I'm sorry; did I hurt you?"

"*I'm* sorry. I expect I was terrible."

"You were wonderful. Why are you crying?"

"I think you must hate me."

"If I've made you think that, then how utterly I've failed."

"Perhaps," she said, "I mean that I hate myself."

"Why should you hate yourself? Why should you be anything but happy? I am. If you're not happy in five minutes I shall know that you don't love me."

"Oh, *that* isn't true. I love you so much but I. . . . Roger, I don't want you to say just the easy comforting things. If you despise me at this minute, tell me. Promise that, whatever else, between ourselves you will never pretend."

He stared at her. She was holding the sheet before her, hiding her breasts. Her arms were strong and creamy, the shoulder blades prominent. Few women, even the most beautiful, Roger had long ago decided, look attractive when they are crying, it was a delusion. This one was no worse than most, and better than some because in her distress she had put on a kind of dignity.

He said: "Nothing that has happened this afternoon could possibly make me hate or despise you. I only love you more and more and more. And want you more. If you're unhappy now, I must be the one to be despised."

She managed to find a handkerchief and wiped her face. "I'm not—unhappy if that's how you truly feel. I only—desperately wanted you to tell me the truth. I was so awful so afraid, so—embarrassed, that now I am . . . abased. Is that the word? If it were not for that I should be happy. If it were not for that I should be proud."

234

He saw that the corner had been turned, that all was, as usual, going to be well.

"Be proud," he said. "I'm proud. I'm very proud."

Chapter Twenty-Four

Bennie got engaged to Michael on the nineteenth of September, but she said tell no one until after the action. She didn't know whether as a result of it Don would take any more kindly to the idea of Michael as a brother-in-law, but at least the quarrel would be past and not still fomenting.

Michael's acquiescence came hard; he was so heady with delight that he was bursting to tell everyone. But at least there was the consolation of buying the ring. Still heady, he took Bennie with him to Burlington Arcade. In the shop the well-tailored assistant said: "Engagement rings? But of *course*, sir. Something like *this*, sir?" A tray was slid out, diamonds winked on black velvet; prices were staggering. "Have you something less expensive?" Bennie asked. The well-bred face by showing no change of expression seemed to Michael to register contempt. "But of *course*, madam. What sort of price?" "About thirty-five pounds," Michael said. "Less," said Bennie. "Twenty-five is plenty."

The assistant bowed and went away. Michael noticed that despite the utter courtesy of their welcome they were constantly under observation while their own assistant was gone. It turned his mind to the life he had nearly taken up.

"These, madam, are inexpensive and *very* good value. This at forty-five. . . . *Must* it be diamonds? This little secondhand ruby ring is exceptional value at thirty-five. The setting of course is Victorian, but . . . Or then *again*——"

"Thanks," said Michael, "we don't want any of those. Come on, Bennie, we'll look elsewhere."

"But, Michael, I think——"

"Come on."

Outside the shop he looked at her with flushed face and said angrily: "I'm sorry, Bennie. It's just I can't stand it."

"Stand what?"

"These dead-pan shop-walkers! They represent all I hate most in life ... the sham gentility, the smooth lies; they're like—like social eunuchs. It's all part of this ridiculous conspiracy to choke one in cotton-wool. ..." She was surprised to see that his hands were trembling.

"Darling, any shop you go into offers you the expensive things first. But what does it matter, or how you are served? There were some quite pretty little rings——"

"Pretty *little* rings!"

"Well, if they're little, does that matter either? I don't mind. Why should you? A curtain ring will do."

"All right, then," he said furiously, "we'll try Woolworths!"

"Don't worry," she said, taking his arm. "When you have money I'll help you to spend it. I love being extravagant. But it isn't the—the one essential, and you know it just as well as I do."

Presently they went into another shop and bought a ring for twenty pounds. He fumed all the way back to their car. "What future is there for us?" he said. "I remain an office boy and you an air skivvy and we get married and live in two barren rooms and meet accidentally about four times a week! That isn't married life as it should be!"

Getting impatient she said: "Well, what do you suggest?"

He at once retracted. "Oh, I'm talking through my hat, Bennie. It's only that I want everything of the best for you."

"Don't worry. It'll come. We're not the only ones who have to make do. Look at the people about you, darling."

"Yes, I know. ..."

One of the people about them, who saw them turn out of Clifford Street and roar up Bond Street, was Joanna. She saw Michael look at Bennie and Bennie's smiling answer. She didn't catch the gleam on Beanie's finger as her hand lay on the side of the car, but the exchange of glances was enough. She went on with her window shopping in a thoughtful mood but did not mention anything to Don when she got home.

Nor had she ever mentioned her sight of Mrs Delaney in the Albert Hall.

Don had just come from Whitehouse who told him the Old Millhouse was at last sold. The price wasn't good, but it had been worth waiting for. As the new people only wanted curtains and carpets the rest of the furniture would be auctioned. When all was settled he might expect to clear four thousand, and the same for Bennie, but he had asked White-house to keep his share to put against the costs of the action.

"If we lose it."

"Yes." Their talk round and about this one preoccupying subject was always rather guarded now; they discussed it as little as possible.

He had also heard that morning that George Bratt was coming back as arranged, so that his contract with the Royal Ballet would not be renewed.

"Did Henry tell you just like that?"

"No, but that's what it amounts to."

She stood beside him at the piano. In her Capucci shoes she was nearly as tall as he was. "Well, I suppose that's all we expected in the first place. You'll be the first on the list if he ever does decide to retire."

"I wouldn't even be sure of that."

"Oh, come."

"Well, I could have done better." He hesitated, decided not to revert to the sore subject. He sat down at the piano and began to play again, punsing now and then to dab at the score with a pencil.

When he finished she said: "You have some recording on, haven't you?"

Two overtures. Then there's a thing in Manchester in November, and of course the concert in Edinburgh on October 22. That's the one important job pending because it's to do with the Burns Centenary celebrations, and I shall be in the same programme with two foreign conductors."

They discussed ways and means. This house was too expensive

for them, they should get a small flat somewhere. It was a recurring theme, but they always put off a decision because the house suited them perfectly and they kept hoping next month would be better. Of course this money from his father might just put them on—if it ever came ... Joanna was playing in a revival of *The Lady's Not for Burning* on October 21; it was important to her because it was the sort of part she wanted. But it might mean she could not get up to Edinburgh for his concert. ...

While this was going on she had moved to the white-painted bookshelves which were stacked with books on music and the theatre. Occasionally she took one down, not looking at it, ran a pointed finger along the top.

Suddenly she said: "Don, this thing still means as much to you, doesn't it ... I don't mean just the money, I mean putting things right about your father?"

He closed the music. "I think it's got to. I'm *sorry*. I don't think there's any turning back now."

"I wasn't going to ask you to. But I just wanted to be sure."

"Why?"

"I just wanted to be absolutely sure. What date is the auction of the furniture? October the sixth? I think I'll go down."

"For any particular reason?"

"It's a feeling I have."

He fished among the music beside the stool but did not take any of it out. "Go by all means if you want to, though I don't see. ..." He paused and looked at her, aware that penetrate. "Please don't worry about it, Joanna. It'll soon be over now."

"Yes," she said. "It'll soon be over now."

Michael had seen Peter only twice since July, and it was by chance that they met now. Michael had taken Bennie out to the airport for her afternoon flight, and when he came back he turned in at the Three Crowns and Peter was there.

It had been a mixed day for Michael. On Thursday when she promised to marry him everything had been infused with a golden glow; for the first time in his life he had felt drunk without touching liquor. Today should have been the same, but instead he had been brought up against the financial facts of life. He had been made bitterly aware of the different value placed on a few bits of diamond chips in a thin gold circle by a London shop and by Boy's fences.

And that was only the symbol for everything else. Marriage for him and Bennie would almost literally have to start in two bare rooms. And his romantic hope of becoming an engineer was finally going to be blown away. Of course he would marry her on any terms—that was not in question—but he had none of her disregard for the luxuries.

After the one outburst in the Burlington Arcade he had hidden his feelings from Bennie; they'd been terribly happy together over lunch, laughing more than they had ever done before so that one crazy joke led to another. What made it funnier was their perfect awareness that no one else would see anything mildly amusing in what they were laughing at. It was lovers' laughter. Yet at the heart of it Michael felt a stone.

When she had left him the coldness and the desolation came back; she was his only shield against it; perhaps when they were married she would become a permanent shield; but now she was gone.

Peter offered him a beer as if they had never had any disagreement, and soon they were talking. It was easy for Michael to go on with his story.

Peter said: "The trouble with you, darling boy, is that your pride is bigger than your purpose. You're crazy about this girl and you want to lavish everything on her. You can't bear to think that you're not able to load her with mink and jewels. Very praiseworthy. But you haven't a bean to do it with. You're in a dead-end job but can't get out of it. You take up a life of crime and then get cold feet before you're properly launched——"

"I get cold feet the way you run things."

"Peter nodded. "Yes, I certainly made a hash of that last affair. However, the hash has led to nothing, has it? We're no worse off for the experience."

"We're worse off—or feel it—for not being better off. If Kenny hadn't let us down I might well have had enough capital to get married in the way I wanted, to do all the things I planned."

"You probably would have. However, don't let me hold that out as a further enticement. You come to me for diagnosis and I tell you what's wrong, not how to cure it."

They had two more rounds and stayed an hour. Peter never drank much, and Michael's three pints was not excessive. But just as they were leaving Michael asked the question he had wanted to ask all evening. "Are you working with someone else now?"

"No. I looked on it as a slice of life. But I felt that if both my partners had—backed out, it was time for me to stop too."

"Well look. ..."

They had left the pub and walked towards Michael's car.

"Look at what?"

"If you get any thoughts about one more job, let me know."

"Oh, I often get thoughts. I had thoughts about one last week but I went no further with them."

'What was it?"

Peter opened the door of the M.G. "If you're interested I'll make a few more inquiries. But it would definitely be something for two to do."

Michael got in. The desolation was round him again. "All right," he said. "If it's anything good I'll try it, this once."

"Car still going all right?"

"Yes, fine."

Peter shut the door.

Chapter Twenty-Five

In the following week Sir Percy Laycock gave a dinner-party in a private room at Claridge's to the Mander Brothers, their lawyer, a third director of *The Globe* called Burnett, Roger and himself. This was another sort of engagement party from Michael's.

Roger did not welcome Burnett's presence tonight, and was surprised that he was here. Burnett had little money involved, but he had had long practical experience as a working journalist and was more closely concerned than any other director with the day-to-day running of *The Globe*. Inevitably Roger's suggestions for a new editorial policy involved criticisms of the old, and usually he had been successful in keeping Burnett out of the top-level discussions.

Newspaper policies were hardly mentioned until the coffee and brandy were served. Then a general rather unprecise discussion broke out, which went on until Burnett said to Roger: "You know, Mr Shorn, I like these new ideas of yours, but I must say they're going to be a gamble."

"Which particularly?" said Roger carefully, aware that silence had immediately fallen.

"Well, I see your arguments, of course. You say our paper only runs twelve pages a day while papers like the *Daily Express* are up to sixteen—how can we expect to compete? Maybe that's true. But this idea of pushing up to sixteen right away without being sure of more advertising is a blazing risk. An extra four pages a day could cost you, *will* cost you, ten thousand a week. That will be all loss to begin."

"That's what we've budgeted for," Roger agreed. "For some

weeks, perhaps three months. From then on we shall begin to pick up."

"Well, of course you'll attract some extra advertising. But you'll have to show your circulation figures to get it."

"You know my answer to that. More features—constantly more features. With extra pages you can spread yourself. Look what's happened to *The Sunday Times*."

"Yes, but that's weekly. And there were immense resources behind it. Daily's another kettle of fish. And don't forget another thing. Suppose, just suppose, you increase our circulation by half a million. Until you get your advertising, you *increase your loss* by, say, fifty per cent. So your loss per week rockets to fifteen thousand; and the new advertising beats the loss down to the original ten thousand. Where do you go from there?"

Roger noticed that Sir Percy was watching him closely. He suddenly realised that Burnett was here at Laycock's express invitation. What Roger still did not understand was why.

He said evenly. "My dear Burnett, all this has been thrashed out before. I should have failed utterly as Sir Percy Laycock's adviser if I had not warned him of the most obvious pitfalls." He turned. "Haven't I done so?"

"Yes," said Laycock, but a shade non-committally.

"From the beginning I pointed out the risks and the opportunities. I told him that in my view a quarter of a million pounds was the *initial* stake. Another quarter of a million may have to be engaged. It is a big investment for a big prize: a flourishing left-centre newspaper, vital without being vulgar, informed without being stodgy, not the first with the news—that's out-dated—but information *about* the news that the others don't get. . . ."

He went on talking; and once or twice Burnett interrupted him. But on the whole he knew he was carrying his listeners along. Again he wondered why it should be necessary at this late stage.

Once Burnett said: "You talk about editors. You know, editors hardly matter these days. It's the business manager of a newspaper who counts most—how he organises his forces. Production's everything."

"Certainly production's everything. But that's the *business* of the editor. Editorials, of course, mean practically nothing. It's *how* the editor deals with his news. That's how policy is influenced today. . . ."

Eventually the dinner-party broke up. The others left but Roger stayed, interested to know if he would hear what was behind this cross-examination. Laycock ordered more brandy and they talked superficially for a while. Then he said:

"You know, Shorn, I've often thought of asking you, but never have, what you hope *personally* to gain in this. You must make a very handsome living the way you are now. Editorship of *The Globe* is a big responsibility."

"Which I should welcome, if it was offered me. And freelance work, however well paid, is chancy and uncertain. Besides, a columnist is constantly in fetters to his masters. I want to be free to do something big while there's still time."

"But in *The Globe* you'd still be subject to me and the other directors."

Roger smiled. "I think I should get a reasonably free hand. I should expect it."

Sir Percy sipped his brandy. "Would that apply also to my daughter?"

Roger blinked. So that was it.

"I don't know what you mean."

"Well. . . . I hear from Marion you've been seeing more of each other these last few months than I knew about."

Roger said: "I've seen her—once in ten days perhaps. Not more. I assumed she told you about it and you didn't object."

"No, she didn't tell me about it. Not till yesterday when something slipped out, accidentally I think."

A waiter came in and brought two clean ash-trays. When he had gone Roger said: "I took Marion to Wimbledon once, because I knew she wanted to go and I had tickets. We have been to the opera once and have met occasionally for lunch. I don't think it's anything that the strictest parent could object to."

244

"Well, maybe yes and maybe no. Marion seems to have grown rather fond of you."

"I confess I have grown rather fond of Marion." When Sir Percy looked at him sharply Roger went on: "It's not so surprising, is it? She's a highly intelligent girl, with a great deal of charm and a well-balanced mind and judgement of her own. I greatly admire her."

Sir Percy shifted his stiff leg. "That's very well, Shorn. I'm glad you think she's a nice girl. But one has to look at it all round. You have a son as old as she is. You've been married three times, apart from—anything else. You've knocked about a lot and are very much a man of the world. It adds up. And there's this libel action. I don't say I'm blaming you for any of this. I'm only stating it as I see it, as anyone would see it. I've a great admiration for your intellectual capacity—look at the way you've been talking tonight. But that's as a business associate. I think there is danger in being friendly with an impressionable young girl who may take you more seriously than you intend."

Roger said: "Has it struck you that there's equal danger for me—that I may feel this thing even more deeply than she does?"

There was silence. Laycock said: "Then by God, it's time something was done about it!"

Roger nipped the end of his Romalo No. 2. "I'm more than sorry, Sir Percy, to worry you in any way. Obviously it's not to my benefit that I should offend you now. But I promise you the entanglement's not of my seeking. I took her out first simply as a friendly gesture towards you both, nothing more. I thought you knew all about it and approved. I looked on her as I would a daughter. It was only when I got to know her better that I found her so advanced—and so fascinating. Perhaps you don't realise. Even then I should never have thought—would hardly have dared to think of anything more if she hadn't given me to understand that she'd welcome it. Then for a time I tried to put a stop to it; we didn't see each other; but it wasn't any use." He paused to light his cigar. When it was going he went on: "Why should I look for any attachment? As I say, the last thing I want now is to quarrel with you. But even the most experienced of us fall into these traps. The problem is how to get out. I tell you I'm in love with your daughter and would like to marry her. Nothing would give me greater delight. But if you forbid it, then I'm willing to co-operate in any way you think fit."

"Hm," said Sir Percy, and drained his brandy. "Hm!"

"I honestly don't think," Roger said, "that it will help if you forbid Marion to see me. She has a lively sense of indepeadence and a strong generous will. The surest way of cementing this thing would be to send her off to Switzerland or the South of France—and if it didn't cement it she would in all probability throw herself away on the first man she met, who might be even more unsuitable than I am."

Sir Percy fidgeted suspiciously. "You know how to put things to your advantage, Shorn. I'm not saying you're the most unsuitable man in the world. What I'm saying is that she is my only child and I want to do the best for her; and this development leaves me very worried indeed."

"I've had sleepless nights myself," said Roger.

There was silence for a time. Sir Percy fumbled with his stick. "I think we'd best be going. Not much good will come of sitting here."

Roger said: "I hope concern over this won't affect your judgement in the matter of *The Globe*. So far as that goes, if it's the sort of opportunity you want, then I'd advise you to take it; because I can't see the same set of circumstances occurring again. Whether I become editor is another matter altogether. There are plenty of good editors in the world."

Sir Percy got up, and Roger politely followed suit. "That's as may be. But so far as Marion is concerned I can only tell you I am very disturbed."

Roger said: "If it will help I'll undertake to see as little as possible of her over the next months. Much the best way is to leave it alone, then it may cool off of its own accord."

"I'd be grateful," Sir Percy said slowly, "if at any rate you'd not see her at all until this action is over. There's bound to be a lot of unpleasant Press publicity, which I wouldn't want Marion involved in."

"I'll do my best."

They went out to the lift. As they walked together through the discreetly-lit chandeliered foyer Roger said: "There's an irony in all this, you know."

"I don't follow you."

"Only that I brought this libel action partly to satisfy you."

"I don't know what you mean, Shorn."

"Well, the natural thing was to ignore this silly challenge that Don Marlowe flung at me. My editor told me to. My friends told me to. But I had just met you and had a great respect for your opinion—and you seemed to think it unsatisfactory to leave it there. It would have been easier and less expensive for everyone if I had."

"Possibly in the——"

"But I didn't. I went ahead. So I am shortly going to run into the expense and the 'unpleasant publicity' you speak of, chiefly to clear myself in the eyes of someone to whom it clearly couldn't have mattered less."

They got near the door and stopped. Sir Percy waved away a liveried attendant. "That's not strictly true, Shorn; really it's not. It does matter, it must matter, not only to me but to everyone. Personally, I don't think you could honourably have refused to bring this action; and if you went ahead partly because I said what I did, then I'm glad. My favourable view of your talents hasn't changed in the least since then. You ought to know that. But where Marion comes in you touch a very sensitive spot, a very sensitive spot indeed. She's all I have, and I want her to be happy. It's the most important thing of all, and I'm not at all sure yet that she would be happy with you. That's not a criticism of you as a person but of circumstances as they exist. I hope you don't mind my frankness."

"I admire you for it."

"Well, there it is, there it is." They passed through the revolving doors and stood on the step. It was a fine night. "I'm sorry about

247

this. I'm sorry it has had to happen. Ah, I see my car is just down the street. No, don't bother, doorman, I'll walk to it."

"Good night," Roger said.

They shook hands. "I hope your action will go well. I believe it is still very important—for all of us." Laycock tapped Roger's arm. "Good night."

Chapter Twenty-Six

Joanna turned down an engagement for the sixth of October. She made her plans and could only leave the outcome to decide itself. A feeling of fatalism had sedimented in her mind.

The auction began at 10 a.m. The big low living-room was quite full, the people the usual mixed bag. Some recognised her and wished her good morning, others stared enviously and then lost interest.

She had a catalogue and took a careful note of what each piece fetched and who bought it. When she didn't know or couldn't catch the names she put Mrs A. or Mr B. against the item. Occasionally she bid but she bought nothing.

By lunch much of the important stuff had gone, and over a hasty lunch in a café she summed up her findings. Local people had bought quite a lot, especially a Mrs Carter who had a shop in Midhurst. A selective buyer was a Mr Barnard whom she didn't know. After lunch she went back and followed the sale until the end. The last item went about 5.30.

The next morning she drove down again and was in Chichester by eleven. She went into the offices of the auctioneer and asked to see him. She said: "I wonder if you could be so very kind as to help me? I was at the sale yesterday but missed buying one or two personal things that my husband wanted. Most of those things seemed to have been bought by a Mr Barnard. We thought we might inquire if he would re-sell them. Could you give me his address?"

"Well, yes, certainly, Mrs Marlowe. But I have to tell you that

Mr Barnard was representing Thorpe, Mills and Thorpe, a firm of solicitors. I don't think he was buying for himself."

"Then perhaps you could give me the address where these things were to be sent?"

"Fred, where were those things for Barnard to go? Got the address?"

"Sure, wait a minute." The auctioneer's clerk came out with a book, which he thumbed through. "Here it is, ma'am Mrs Beaconsfield, Chatterton House, Hurtmore Road, Godalming."

It was about an hour's drive, and then she had to find the house. It was on the outskirts of the town, set back in its own grounds among beeches and pines; but when you got to it it was quite small, brick-built, with leaded panes and a tiled veranda.

She had left the car in the road and walked up the gravel path. The house looked deserted and she half hoped it might be; but she pulled the bell and almost at once someone opened it, and at once she knew that her search was ended.

Narissa Delaney was a tall woman, and looked taller for being two steps higher than her visitor. She was dark, with a broad white forehead and wide finely shadowed cheek-bones, a sensuous but composed mouth, rich black hair winged back.

"Mrs Beaconsfield?"

"Yes?"

"I am Joanna Marlowe."

Her expression did not change. "Yes?"

"You are Mrs Delaney, aren't you?"

"Yes."

Joanna followed the other woman into a sitting-room looking out over the back lawn.

"How did you trace me?"

"I went to the sale yesterday and took note of the man buying most of Sir John's personal things."

"He had instructions not to say."

"He didn't say. I got your address from the auctioneer."

Mrs Delaney took down a silver cigarette-box, offered it to Joanna, who took one. "What can I do for you?"

"Thank you. ... No, I have a light." Joanna felt herself over-coloured in this sombre room. The trees were growing too near the windows. "I came to see you about the libel action."

Mrs Delaney put her cigarette in a long holder and took her time over lighting it.

"I have been away. Since March until nearly September I have been in the Bahamas."

"I thought that might be the explanation."

"Of what?"

"You'll know about the articles in *The Gazette*—about my I husband's father."

"I have heard of them, yes."

"And of the action that's pending?"

"Something." The tone was not helpful.

"Mrs Delaney, I think perhaps you could do more than anyone to contradict some of the things said about him in those articles."

"I don't know everything that was said in the articles."

"You know we've been trying to trace you?"

Mrs Delaney looked at her visitor. "Haven't we met before?"

"I don't think so."

"Oh, well. ... Perhaps it is the photographs I have seen." The liquid brilliance of the eyes was filmed. "Yes, I knew you were trying to trace me."

"This libel action starts next week—Monday or Tuesday. I'd like you to see my husband before then."

"What good would it do?"

"You must want to disprove these lies about John Marlowe, if you know them to be lies."

"My memory of John Marlowe is complete. I know and understand what he was. Why should I care what people say of him?"

"Doesn't his reputation mean anything?"

"Reputation? Words in the mouths of a few trivial people. Why should I sully my memories by dragging them out in a court of law for the papers to paw over? I have had enough of newspapers.

Your husband should have taken no notice. By forcing this action he is playing them at their own game."

"And hoping to win."

Mrs Delaney shrugged. "I suppose now you know where I am you can force me to appear even if I don't want to."

"Well. . . . we'd rather have you as a friendly witness."

"I am neither friendly nor unfriendly. Only a little disgusted with so much that life has brought."

Joanna said: "Are you willing to help us?"

"How do you know that anything I said in the law court would be favourable to you?"

"A woman doesn't collect the personal things of a man she dislikes. Nor——"

"Nor?"

"It doesn't matter."

"But I remember now. I saw you at the cottage last February, didn't I, with a man; you called in one Sunday and nearly caught me. I have a key of the house and had gone there for a few minutes, as I did once or twice about that time, just to be there alone."

"Yes," said Joanna.

"I slipped out of the back and then came round and saw you as I passed the window."

"It was rather a shock."

Mrs Delaney moved quietly across the room, sat on the arm of a chair by the window. The filtered light fell on her face and showed the fine lines like arrow heads at the corners of her eyes. "There is another reason why I have not come forward. After John's death I was so upset that I only wanted to get away. When I came back I changed my name to avoid being persecuted."

"By the Press do you mean?"

"No. By my ex-husband. Robert Delaney."

"I'm sorry."

"When I married him my father settled a trust fund on us jointly. When I began to divorce him, Robert at first said he would not defend. Then when he found that if he was the guilty party he would lose his interest in the trust, he chose to fight. That was when I met your father-in-law. Afterwards ... after I had won, Robert pestered me for what he considered his rights, though he no longer had any legal claim. In those days I had a lot of money, so I agreed to make him an allowance equal to the amount he would have had through the trust. Then I lost my money. ..." She shrugged. "Now that I have some of it back I know that as soon as Robert can find me he will begin all over again."

"I see."

"If I once go into court. ... And almost certainly my appearance would be useless. ..."

"I wish you'd let Don judge that."

"He is sure to clutch at any straw."

"I don't think so."

"Don't you? ... I wonder about that. ... It's strange that I never met him. His sister was enchanting, though so young. I used to think that they were neglectful of their father until I found it was part of a deliberate policy on his part to give them absolute freedom, indeed, slightly to keep them at arm's length. He was going to invite them down—and you—one day to tell you he intended to marry me. You had just become engaged to his son, hadn't you—three years ago this month?"

"Yes. We were engaged on the first of October and married on the thirtieth of November. ... Why did you never marry him, then?"

"He never told you?"

"No."

"Nor his children?. ... I knew he did not at the beginning, but I thought sometime he would have let it out."

"No."

Mrs Delaney said: "He was a strange man, full of contradictions. Witty—serious minded. Easy-going—stiff backed. Principled—earthly. Perhaps after all it will be a good thing if I meet his son."

"Thank you. I think you should."

"But no promises. I will keep all that to decide when we meet."

"Could it be today sometime? If you are going to give evidence it's urgent he should know what it is."

Mrs Delaney tapped her fingers.

"Tomorrow evening?" said Joanna.

"... Very well. Tomorrow. Tell him he can come after dinner—about nine. Will you come with him?"

"I think you should have this talk alone."

They went to the door together. Mrs Delaney said: "Who was the man you were with that day in February? That wasn't John's son."

".... Don was away until April." Joanna pulled on her gloves, sliding the black kid fingers. "That was Roger Shorn, the man who wrote the articles in *The Sunday Gazette.*"

There was a short pause. An assessment was going on between two adult, highly intelligent women. It was as subtle and as silent as the onset of frost.

Joanna said: "He was driving me home from a friend's house and we called in at the cottage. He claimed then to be an admirer of Don's father. But while we were there, though I didn't know it at the time, he took some letters; he has used these as a basis for some of the statements he has made. I don't know what they were but I imagine they were from George Chislehurst."

"George Chislehurst," said Mrs Delaney. But she was not thinking of what she said.

Joanna looked up. Her eyes were cool and steady. "My husband doesn't know of my visit with Roger Shorn. I think he wouldn't understand."

Mrs Delaney's gesture was a polite disclaimer of responsibility. "But I take it, in view of your coming here, that your loyalty is still to your husband?"

"Yes. . . ."

"Don't you think you should tell him?"

"No."

"Well, there is no reason why I should, Mrs Marlowe."

"Thank you," Joanna said in the same level tone. "That's what I wanted to know."

Chapter Twenty-Seven

"Wipe that dirt off your eyebrow," said Peter. "We don't want to overdo it. How does this hat look?"

"All right," Michael said. "How long have we got?"

"Ten minutes."

They sat side by side in an old lorry in a private garage in Brook Green. Michael broke a cigarette and put one half behind his ear. The other half he lighted.

This was the job. During the last two weeks they had made their plans, cautiously, with intelligence and attention to detail. The idea seemed to Michael well thought out, impudent maybe but not inherently risky. He was more sure of its success than he had been of either of the others.

A Mr and Mrs Bernard Gilbert lived at 241 Sloane Street. Gilbert was in oil, and they had a big house in Kent where they spent every week-end. During the last four years Mrs Gilbert had been prominent in the sale rooms buying anything that took her fancy. Much of this no doubt was now in Kent; but, since they gave dinner-parties in London, a good deal was bound to be in the house in Sloane Street.

All this by itself meant nothing. What gave it significance was a demolition and rebuilding scheme for numbers 225-231 Sloane Street. Woodrit & Carlow was the firm employed, and a great gap already existed in the street where some of the buildings had come down. A high corrugated-iron barrier had been put up to keep the dust and rubble off the street, and behind it cranes worked and men dug and hammered and picked.

The houses due to come down were part of the same row as

241 but at the opposite end. The first two were already down, but the demolition of 229 had not yet begun, although it was now empty.

The employees of Messrs Woodrit & Carlow dropped tools the moment noon struck on a Saturday morning and by twelve-fifteen the site was usually empty.

"Right," said Peter, and Michael started the engine and drove out of the garage. They had bought the old lorry cheap two weeks ago and had spent a good deal of time getting it up to look right. As they rattled up the King's Road half past twelve was striking.

There was no way in to the demolition from Sloane Street, but Michael turned up Pavilion Road and then by way of the mews. At the entrance to the demolitions where the back gardens of the houses had been he went slowly so that if anyone was still about he could appear to be driving in to turn round.

But everyone had gone.

He drove bumping across the uneven ground, over a concrete path, past a pile of old mattresses, circled a mound of rubble and old window frames, avoided a flower-bed and stopped beside the gaping rain of a basement window. Propped against the window was a broken board: "*J. Goldstein. Society Photographer, Studio Hours 10–5.*"

They got out, lifted ladders from the back of the lorry, then pick-axe and shovel. Observed by the unobserving eyes of twenty houses round, they carried the ladders through the blitz-like debris of No. 227 and came to No. 229.

"It's no good down here," said Peter. "These basement walls are practically foundations. Up there, I should think."

"Further back," said Michael. "We'll be less on view from the road and the ladder's on a better foundation."

They carried the longer ladder back and propped it against the wall of the house where the floor joists of the ground floor of No. 227 had been. A piece of the floor at the back about three yards square still existed.

"I'll start," said Michael.

"No. Bring the other ladder. We'll work together."

As they climbed the ladders, so they raised themselves above the protective iron hoarding. By the time they were at the level where they wished to work they could not only be seen from all the houses but were in full view of people walking on the opposite side of Sloane Street.

Michael put his pick-axe down and took the half cigarette from behind his ear and carefully lit it. "You, mate, or me? Who starts?"

"You pick, boy. I'll shovel."

Michael lifted his pick and brought it down with a thud into the wall.

Although the brick was for the most part weathered and hardened by time, it had corroded here and there so that, while his pick often didn't make much headway, every now and then it would sink in to give him leverage. After ten minutes there was a small hole but he was sweating a lot.

"Take it easy," said Peter. "Don't forget you're being paid by the hour."

Michael straightened up and gave a hitch at his trousers. Some of the Saturday rush hour was thinning, and when it had all gone they would be much more isolated. As he looked about him two youths on the front of a 19 bus grinned at him and said something to each other. They were almost exactly on a level with him at twenty yards distance. He pulled his cap down an inch and began again.

Another ten minutes and the hole was larger.

"Anything?" said Peter, who was shovelling away the stuff Michael got out.

"Yes. Lath and plaster now."

"Let me try."

They changed places. Michael leaned on the shovel and wiped his brow with his forearm. Two policemen were walking on the other side of the road. One of them seemed to glance across, but he evidently didn't notice anything strange.

"We'd better get a bit more of this down first," Peter said. "We don't want to look as if we're simply knocking a hole."

By two they had made a jagged opening four feet square. Then

Michael went back to the lorry for a saw. They sawed through the laths, and in a shower of dust and plaster he pushed his way into the empty kitchen of No. 229.

"O.K." he said. "Are you coming?"

"No. I'll stay here. Don't be long. The sooner we're away now the better."

Michael made a quick survey of the condemned house, up to the top story, examined the dormer window of the attic, came down again. Peter was shovelling rubble off the edge of the flooring and tipping it into the basement below.

"Right," said Michael again. "Let's go."

"Take your time," said Peter, leaning on his shovel. "Remember all the people who may be watching us. You go down. I'll follow in a minute or two."

Michael carried one ladder away and stacked it against a wall. Beside the wall was an old dentist's chair, broken and oozing horse-hair padding as from an open wound. He walked back to the lorry and got in. In a while Peter joined him. Michael kicked the starter and drove off.

In all human affairs there is an element of chance. If Michael had driven round Cadogan Gardens and down Sloane Street they would have seen the taxi drawing up outside No. 241 and a tall stout man carry his suitcase to the door of the house and let himself in. Instead Michael turned left out of the mews and then right at Symons Street.

Even the most careful staff work would have been unlikely to have discovered the arrangement between Mr Bernard Gilbert and his brother Captain Oliver Gilbert whereby Captain Gilbert used his brother's town house at week-ends whenever he chose. Bernard Gilbert was notified by postcard and left a bed prepared; but Captain Gilbert was in the Diplomatic Service and was sometimes not seen in London for years. Just now he had been in Kenya, and after briefing in London he was to fly to New York on the 15th for a lecture tour.

Today Captain Gilbert, having travelled through the night, went briefly upstairs for a bath and shave, changed his clothes and then went out to his club.

Peter and Michael spent what was left of the day in Michael's flat. Michael lay on his decrepit settee, moving only every half hour or so to change his records. Peter chain-smoked on a chair by the window, but not nervously. His hands and his manner were passive. He seemed at rest.

Michael made coffee about six. Over it Peter said: "I miss the Middle Pocket. That had a legitimate flavour, give it its due. The others are either too respectable or too sleazy."

"Have you ever seen Dick Ballance since that night?"

"Twice. He says there'd be no trouble going there again now, but maybe it's better to be sure."

"I hope you can flog this stuff when we get it."

"I know I can. There's a tremendous demand in France and of course in America. I've been promised fair prices."

"I'm glad."

"Well, naturally."

"But specially, as this is my last job."

Peter didn't say anything.

"Will you go on?" Michael asked after a while.

Peter shrugged. "Not for a time anyway. Dear Ma-ma has gone to Estoril for the winter, and I shall probably join her. It's always interesting to see her face when I turn up somewhere unexpectedly."

"Why particularly?"

"I'm her problem child, dear boy. Privately I believe she thinks I'll do her in some day."

"But why?"

"Ma-ma's a great one for the psychiatrists. She's always having a go with one, and, as soon as I lifted an unorthodox finger, off I went too. They've been a familiar figure in my life ever since I can remember. Then when I was in my late teens I beat up a butcher boy because I saw him kick a pony. He went to hospital and I went in triumph to a new skull thumper. Unfortunately this new man fairly loaded Ma-ma with guilt by telling her she'd let me down. Then I believe he dropped the word Orestes into the conversation, and she's never completely recovered her nerve since. I only have to brood a while and she thinks her moment has come."

"It's an interesting idea."

"In fact you're a much better brooder than I am. If she had you to deal with she'd be scared right out of her pants. . . . Personally I'd never so much as touch a hair of the silly old woman's head."

Michael poured himself more coffee. "What is this thing you have about animals, Peter?"

Peter raised his eyebrows. "Have I?"

"I think so."

". . . . I don't know. . . . To me animals are the blind alleys in evolution's struggle to evolve the perfect creature—man. . . . But somewhere along the way, out of perfection has come infinite evil. So I can't bear to see these—these less perfect creatures humiliated or hurt by a form of life that has forfeited any right it may ever have had to be considered superior."

When darkness fell they went out and had a meal. Michael was for going ahead very soon but Peter said patience.

They went back to Michael's flat and spent the evening reading and listening to the radio. About midnight they put on old clothes and took out two battered brown valises Michael had bought early in the week. They parked the M.G. near Olympia, picked up the old lorry and made a devious way to Pavilion Road.

It was a dark night, and as they turned in at the demolitions only a few of the square eyes of the houses round were lit; not nearly so many as on a mid-week night. The street lights from Sloane Street were not bright, and Michael stopped the old lorry in the shadow of a partly demolished wall, killed the engine and switched off the lights.

They changed into gym shoes, put on thin gloves, carried the ladder back to the place where they had been a few hours ago, went up with the bags and through the wall into the empty house to the top floor. Here there was a dormer window which opened without trouble.

Climbing over the roofs was moderately tricky. They were invisible from below, but they had five intervening roofs to negotiate before they came to No. 241 and they had no means of knowing how many of the houses were occupied over the week-end.

So the prime need was quietness. Even then the difficulty was not great. There was always a comfortably wide parapet, sloping slates could be edged round, there were broad areas of flat roof, occasionally a chimney stack to be skirted. The only real danger lay in the bags which were big and unwieldy to carry.

The dormer window of No. 241 was latched on the inside. Peter had been practising for two weeks. He took a roll of broad tape from his bag, cut a strip and brushed it with a quick-drying gum. Then he pressed it over the glass until it stuck. While he was holding it there Michael cut another piece of the tape. So they went on until the whole pane was covered. After waiting until the gum was dry Peter took a blanket out of the bag, held it to the window and gently pressed. There was a light cracking sound, then another. He took the blanket away. The window had broken through but the glass was sticking to the tape. He slowly wriggled his gloved hand between two pieces of the tape until he was through the hole and could reach the catch. The hinges creaked. While Michael held his bag Peter let himself down into the room.

The two bags were passed in; Michael followed. They were in a room exactly like the one they had left seven doors away except that this one was furnished. A bed, a dressing-table, frocks behind the door. Michael latched the window half open and pulled the curtains.

Peter switched on his pencil-beam torch. "Three-point landing. It's all a matter of technique."

"Yes."

"Ground floor first and work up."

"That's a good miniature to have in an attic bedroom," Michael muttered.

"Slip it in your pocket when we leave—if there's room for it."

When they opened the door on to the landing another bedroom door faced them, and stairs led down. All the way down this flight and the next were miniatures and small oil paintings. On the ground floor there were three rooms because a kitchen had been built out at the back to serve the dining-room.

They drew the curtains both front and back; but the curtains at the front, being on big bone rings, made a rattle as they were slowly pulled, and it was this that disturbed Captain Gilbert from his first deep sleep.

Both rooms they found were full of good pieces. Among other things in the dining-room were a pair of silver salvers of early eighteenth-century design, an Elizabethan silver-gilt goblet, a Queen Anne chocolate pot, a Meissen tea service. Michael hesitated over the china for he could neither bear to leave it nor bear to damage it. Presently there was a sound at the door, and he turned to see Peter with his bag half full, watching him.

"I've got a Degas drawing and a superb little Epstein head of a sleeping child. God knows what they're worth."

"I'd like to keep some of these things myself," said Michael. "Look at this gold and enamel box."

"Leave space. We've three bedrooms yet, and if I know people like this they'll have bought so much stuff that there will be pickings everywhere."

"Peter, I've been thinking. There's so much here, and we've five hours of darkness. Why not a second journey?"

"Maybe. See how it works out this time. Anyway there's no hurry. I'll go on up."

"Have you pulled the curtains back in the front room?"

"No, they made such a clatter. Watch your step coming up the stairs; there's a window looking out at the back that hasn't any curtains."

Peter went out, and Michael picked up a pair of *famille rose* octagonal plates enamelled in colours. But he decided to leave all the china, for his bag was three-quarters full already, and heavy. He zipped it up and carried it across to the drawing-room to give that room a quick glance over in case Peter had missed something obvious.

The other pictures were undisturbed. He made a round of them and stopped at a small flower palming. It didn't appear to be signed, but the art sense he had picked up from his father suggested it was a Fantin Latour. If so it might be the biggest prize of the lot. He lifted it down. As he did so there was a loud bump on the floor above.

Damn Peter for a clumsy fool! These houses were narrow and thin, and some nervous old lady next door might ring up the police. The picture under his arm and the bag in his other hand, he went up the stairs.

Half-way he stopped. There was a light on. This was beyond reason. And then he heard a voice.

For an insane second it came to him to hope that Peter had accidentally switched on a radio. Then sickly, he heard Peter's voice:

". . . yes, it does rather, doesn't it?"

"So you've nothing to say for yourself, eh?"

"What can I say? You can't suppose that I've called about the rent."

Peter had dropped something on the floor to warn him.

Still rather insanely carrying both the picture and his bag he came to the top of the stairs. Peter was standing in a bedroom, his hands half-raised. He looked pale and he kept blinking his eyes as if in smoke. A stout dark man stood in the doorway in his pyjamas; he was holding a small automatic pistol.

"Lucky I'm a light sleeper, isn't it?"

"Oh, I'd have come into your bedroom and wakened you."

"Well, now we'll just waken the police."

As the man turned to the phone Michael stepped in and swung his heavy bag at the man's head.

He went down. The pistol exploded and a window shattered. The man had fallen in a heap, the receiver swinging, the automatic somewhere under him; Michael switched off the light.

He slid out through the door, and in ten seconds Peter was beside him.

"Up!"

They ran up the stairs; as they came to the top flight the man downstairs came out, started firing: *thrump, thrump,* into the woodwork. They were in the bedroom; there was a key m the door; Michael turned it.

Peter was already at the window. "Come on."

They got out. "Pity you lost your bag," said Peter. Michael saw he was carrying his.

Not a pleasant journey back. "Take your time," Michael said. "He'll be ten minutes breaking that door. And if he goes down and out into the street he won't know where we're coming out. Oh-ho, clumsy."

"Didn't see that guttering."

They made two houses, began the third; all was quiet now; yet one couldn't imagine glass clattering into a London main street even in the middle of the night without attracting some attention. And the revolver shots.

The third done. "Who the hell *was* he?" Peter muttered. "Man should be arrested, shooting like a drunken cow-hand."

The fourth. One more. Michael paused to put his nose over the parapet. "He's out and looking up. He can't find a policeman. There's another man talking to him."

Fifth. Nearly there. "This bag's heavy," said Peter. "Hope there'll be enough for two. Can you take it while I get in."

Michael took it. Sound of a car down below. If the people below crossed the street and looked the right way he could still be seen.

"Right," said Peter.

Michael swung in the bag and followed. To be away from the spaces of the London roof tops.

Peter was running lightly down the stairs ahead of him; Michael followed more slowly. The kitchen and the hole; Peter was peering out.

"All quiet, I think. I'll go and try."

He left the bag until he was on the ladder. Then Michael handed it to him. He went down; Michael followed; ground again, solid ground. Peter was a shadow ahead, dodging towards the lorry. He was there, lifted the bag into the back, climbed into the cab; Michael caught him up.

"This engine'll make a row."

"Got to chance it. We've got to get away before the whole area is cordoned off."

Michael started the engine, let in the clutch too fiercely; the engine stalled.

"Gently does it."

The second time was better; but they had not backed the lorry before leaving it; Michael shunted it round, catching one wing on a wall, the engine roaring.

"Turn right when you get out."

They went lurching and jolting over the rough ground, came to the mews; not blocked. Screeching of tyres as they came into Pavilion Road.

"Lights," said Peter. "And slower a bit. Left here."

They eased their way round a corner. Car coming towards them. It kept on its own side. Taxi.

"Right here."

No one followed.

"Slower, boy."

They came out into Pont Street.

"Well," said Peter and let out an uncertain breath. "That was a near miss. Thanks for the back-hand volley."

"We should have stopped and tied him up and gone on with the job," said Michael. "As soon as anything blows off we lose our heads."

"I don't like thick-ear stuff."

"Sometimes it's necessary."

"Cigarette?"

Michael shook his head.

They drove on through the deserted streets.

"It might be wise to make a detour," said Peter.

"I don't feel like any more detours."

It was just after three when they came to their garage. They drove in and Michael cut the engine. He said: "This is another tricky part."

"How come?"

"That man shot me in the leg and I'm bleeding like a pig. How do I get home without leaving bloodstains?"

Michael sat in the garage while Peter went for the car. Wrapped in the car rug and the blanket, he made the journey without staining the leather. Once in the house Peter had a look. The wound was in the upper part of the thigh, well towards the back.

"God, this will have left a trail! And all over the seat of the lorry."

"Would you rather we'd stopped for repairs in Sloane Street?"

Peter was dabbing at the wound. It had almost stopped bleeding, but the delayed effects were showing in Michael; he was pale and sweaty from shock.

"The bullet's still in, isn't it? That means a doctor of some sort."

"Dangerous."

"Dangerous either way."

Peter said: "I'll tape you up now and see if I can get someone tomorrow." He began to tear a sheet into strips.

Michael screwed round to look at the wound. "What sort of a gun was it?"

"A .25 automatic, I think. It's a perfectly clean puncture. It would heal on its own."

"Not with the bullet in."

"Oh, I expect it could. My tutor at Cambridge still had bits of shrapnel in him that he'd carried for thirty years."

"I'd prefer not to carry this."

Peter began to bandage the place. Now that the emergency was over, his own hands were not steady.

Michael said: "How do I go about things until this does heal? I was seeing Bennie tomorrow—I'll have to cancel that."

"Say you fell and ricked your back. I'll phone Bennie for you, if you like."

"No, take a note round tonight before she gets back. She didn't know I was seeing you. Take it as you go home."

Peter's face twitched. "I wasn't going home. But on second thoughts I will. I don't like that bag over there. It'll be safer in Portland Place."

Michael wrote:

Darling,

To my fury old Bartlett wants me to go to Liverpool for a Book Week they're having there. It's maddening but I can't refuse. I tried to catch you before you left but it was too late. I hope to be back about Thursday, in time perhaps to see something of the libel action, if it isn't all over by then. I shall rejoice if it is.

Darling, I love you so much.

Michael.

He didn't sleep. The throbbing kept up most of the night, and when he tried to get out of bed about nine next morning it was as if all the muscles had seized up, and every movement was an agony. He was weak too and still shaky.

Eventually, like someone with acute arthritis, he forced himself inch by inch to raise himself, to edge out of bed, to lower his feet. Then he stood up and nearly fainted.

Kneeling on the floor he crawled to the kitchen, drank whisky, switched on the kettle. When he had made tea he buttered a chunk of bread and crawled back to bed. The wound had now quite stopped bleeding.

Peter came about eleven. He had his own key so was able to let himself in. He stood in the doorway of the bedroom looking at Michael with his innocent dazed blue eyes.

"Bad?"

"Have you brought the papers?"

"There are some in the car if you want them. But it's too early to mention us. Tomorrow's rags will flutter, no doubt."

"Did you manage the stuff?"

"It's stowed away. But we'll have to watch our step. It has occurred to me that you are really luckier than I am. At least you weren't seen. I wonder how accurately that fat thug will be able to describe me."

"Have you done anything about a doctor yet?"

"No. I came to see how you were first. I wasn't up at crack."

"Did you deliver the letter?"

"Yes. Now I'll get you some breakfast."

Michael said he wasn't hungry, but in the end he ate something and felt better for it. Peter went off and did not show again until five in the afternoon.

"It's all laid on. A man called Gros is coming to see you, but he won't come until after dark. Now I'll get your lunch. Meals are a bit off time today."

"D'you know anything about him?"

"Not much except that he's a fifth-year student at St James's who periodically runs into debt and works it off this way."

"He probably doesn't know a damned thing."

"Oh, yes, he's done his surgery. In any case I'm told he's been working on little jobs like this on the side for years."

They spent the time playing cards, though Michael was in too much pain to concentrate. Peter was restless and kept looking at his watch. At times his eyes seemed to have a film over them like a cat's.

"Look," Michael said at last, "don't wait if you don't want to. I can get along."

"No, no. No, no. I'll stay till Doctor has been."

This visitor didn't come until nearly eleven. Then the bell rang, and Peter led in a plump short young man with wispy fair hair that was thinning to a bald patch on the crown. He looked quite thirty, and high living had already sewn little pockets under his eyes. He was wearing a Harris tweed hacking jacket over a T-shirt, with corduroy trousers and brown suede shoes.

"Evening, old man. 'Fraid I'm a little late. Busy these days. Swotting most of the time." His glance flickered once swiftly round the room, making sure they were alone. "Nice place you have here," he added perfunctorily. "Bit of trouble, eh? I expect you're pretty uncomfortable. When did this happen?"

"At a party last night," said Michael. "Things got a bit wild at the end. You know the sort of thing."

"Don't I just." Gros came into the room on crêpe soles. Michael could see a big stain on his trousers.

"My friend doesn't want anyone to know what happened," said Peter. "Might lose his job, you understand."

"Don't I understand," said Gros unbelieving. "Parties. They're hell. Let's see, did we say twenty pounds?"

"It's here." Peter pointed to an envelope on the table. "Care to count it?"

"No, no, that's not necessary between friends." The envelope was taken up in the plump capable fingers, felt once for thickness between thumb and tobacco-stained forefinger, slipped into his pocket. "Parties, they're hell. So are the girls. Now, old man, let's see the bomb damage. We'll try not to be rough."

He bent over Michael breathing whisky and the peppermint he was still chewing. The pupils of his pale grey eyes were haloed with a paler band. He uncovered the bullet hole, pulling away the bandages where they were stuck together with dried blood.

"Well, well. Clean as a whistle, eh? Don't think it's taken anything in with it either." He opened his attaché-case and rattled about. "Pretty deep, old man, that's the only trouble. We'll have to take it carefully."

"Ever done this sort of thing before?" Michael asked.

"My dear chap, I'm always on the go. All the people who want things done on the quiet. You'd be surprised. I believe it's the Health Service. People don't trust the ordinary G.P. nowadays. And I don't blame 'em."

"All right. Get on with it."

"Any more light? Shadowy, y'know. . . . Ah, thanks, that's better. And I shall need some boiled water. Towels? Ah, yes, goody." Peter went out. Gros probed the wound. Michael grunted.

Time passed. Gros said: "Bloody thing's gone off course. I'll give you a local, old man. It may help a bit. Never can tell with a bullet, once the bloody thing's inside you."

He gave an injection and stood up. Peter had been looking bleakly at a Sunday newspaper.

"Ever go to the Panhandle?" Gros said. "Jolly little spot. They

269

certainly have a line in girls. But you've got to pay, my God. The price goes up with the vital statistics." He laughed. Nobody laughed with him.

Michael wiped the sweat off his forehead with a corner of the sheet.

"Any easier yet? Give it another minute." Gros belched behind his hand. "Pardon. D'you happen to have a cigarette?"

"There's a packet on the mantelpiece."

Presently he got to work again. Michael could stand it better this time. After a few minutes Gros stood up.

"Got it?" Michael asked.

Gros flattened his thin hair and reached for his cigarette which had been smouldering in the ash-tray.

"No. 'Fraid not, old man."

Michael rolled over. "What's the trouble?"

"Know anything about anatomy? No, well, it doesn't matter. The bullet seems to have missed the bone and lodged against the femoral artery. Never can tell what they'll do, once they're inside you."

"Well, can't you get it?"

"I can *touch* it. I can touch it with my probe, but I can feel it pulsating. Afraid you'll have to go to hospital."

Michael tried to sit up, and winced. "I tell you I can't do that. Why can't you take it out?"

The ash from the cigarette drifted down the front of the Harris jacket. "It must be lying right alongside the artery. If I start yanking at it I'm likely to damage the artery. Get me? If you start bleeding there, brother, you go on bleeding. Too high up for a tourniquet, y'see."

Peter said: "People in the old days had their legs off anywhere an accident happened."

"That's butcher's work, old man."

In the silence they all listened to a door opening and footsteps going to the flat upstairs.

Michael said: "Look, you know I don't want to go to hospital.

Do you know the name of a qualified man who would do this job here?"

"Think I don't know what I'm talking about? No qualified man would take the risk. Want to bet on it?" Gros blinked through the smoke. "I'll take a hundred to eight."

"Yes, but——"

"It's got to be done at a hospital. If it goes wrong there they can operate at once. No trouble then."

A further silence fell while Gros lit another cigarette.

Michael said: "And if I don't have the bullet taken out?"

Gros shrugged. "The wound will heal—seven to ten days. It's not likely to go septic, bullets are usually sterile. I should say that's your best bet, chum."

"Permanently?"

"Not permanently, good God, no. If you leave the bloody thing there too long it may erode the vessel and give you trouble that way."

"Well, how long can I leave it?"

"It'll probably be all right for two or three months. Take it easy, of course."

Michael let out a slow breath. "That seems to be the answer."

"It'd be my answer if I badly wanted to keep it quiet. . . . In the meantime I'll give you a shot of penicillin, be on the safe side. You're a bit sweaty now, but I expect it's me mucking about in the hole. If you run a temperature, send for me and I can drop round again tomorrow evening."

"At twenty pounds a time?"

"Well, health's everything, don't you think? Not but that I mightn't make it fifteen next time. We've got to help each other in this world. That's what I said to my girl friend last night."

"Did she agree?" Peter asked.

Gros smiled slyly. "No." He pinched off the tip of the cigarette in the ash-tray, and slipped the end into his cigarette case where there were half a dozen ends already.

"Let's hope you won't need me again, old man. No reason why

you should. With luck you'll be on your feet again in a couple of days."

Chapter Twenty-Eight

On Monday Whitehouse said: "Not until Wednesday or Thursday, I think. The Lord Chief going ill has put things a day behind, and this enticement case has lasted longer than anyone expected. But definitely this week."

On Monday Michael tried to get up, but again had to go through all the painful business of loosening muscles which during the night had clamped themselves round the wound in a knot. As the day wore on he was able to get about with a stick. Peter didn't come until the afternoon, when they spent an hour reading the papers together. "Captain Gilbert, brother of the owner, who had returned from Kenya only that day. . . ." "One thief, wounded, left bloodstains as far as the empty lot where they had parked their car. The other, a young man of good appearance. . . ." "Some eight thousand pounds' worth of valuables and *objets d'art*. . . ." "Police are anxious to trace . . ."

"We left tyre marks," said Peter, "and your old bag."

On Tuesday Bennie waited for the 11 a.m. post and nearly missed her plane. She had thought there would be a letter from Michael giving his address in Liverpool. On Wednesday Roger called to see his son.

By now the worst of the pain had gone and Michael could get about on a stick for short periods. There had been no return of the fever and therefore no return of Gros.

When the bell rang Michael limped cautiously to the door and was startled to see his father.

"Hullo. Can I come in? I'm glad to see you're up."

Michael opened the door wider. "How did you know?"

"I met Bartlett at the club. He told me you'd been away this week with a sprained back. I thought I'd call."

"Oh, thanks. I'm fine now, thanks."

"Well, you don't look fine. You look terrible. Have you shaved today?"

"Not yet. I've been getting some breakfast."

"What does the doctor say? Is it a slipped disc?"

"Oh, no. Just a sprain."

"How did it happen?"

"I'm afraid I made rather a fool of myself. Went to a party on Saturday night, slipped on the stairs. Peter Waldo brought me home in a taxi, and I've been here ever since."

"Peter Waldo? Oh, yes, I remember." Roger, in his usual quietly distinguished clothes, looked out of place as he stood in the chaos of the living-room. "Have you got anyone to do for you? How long will you be before you're all right again?"

"Another couple of days. Not more." Michael let himself slowly down into a chair. "Dad, I think I ought to tell you something, although it's supposed to be a secret until after the action. I'm engaged to be married to Bennie."

Roger's eyes flickered. "I can't say the news pleases me. Does Don know?"

"Not yet. When does the action come on?"

"Friday probably."

"I see. Well, I hope it will turn out all right for you."

"As a matter of fact I was just on my way to my solicitors. Another witness has come to light—the woman Delaney that John Marlowe nearly married. Apparently she's going to give evidence for the other side, and I'm just going along to hear a summary of it. I don't know what it is yet, but I gather it will mean an alteration in the way we put our case."

"Well, it'll be a good thing when it's all over."

Roger eyed his son. "Look, Michael, I know you've your own life to live; you're going to be independent and marry Bennie Marlowe et cetera. But why don't you come home and occupy your old bedroom for a few days and get properly looked after?

This flat and your much prized independence will still be here next week when you're well again."

Michael spent a few seconds untying and retying the cord of his dressing-gown. As at Wimbledon, he found the old childhood and adolescent ties clinging when he had thought them quite cut away. He was like a sailor who has a nostalgic feeling for the safe anchorage he has left behind for ever.

"No," he said sharply. "I can't do that."

Roger put the handle of his rolled umbrella thoughtfully against his teeth. "Just as you say, Michael."

Michael eased his leg, careful not to show the spasm of pain. "Sorry," he said. "I get frightfully irritable being pinned down like this. Sorry."

"My dear boy, I was only trying to help. Are you getting on all right with Bartlett? Or are you still hankering after engineering?"

"It's a pretty forlorn hope."

Roger put his umbrella down. "I want to tell you something, Michael. If you'll keep in step with me for another few months I'll not leave you with Bartlett a day longer than I can help. I have big plans."

"What sort of plans?"

"Well, I may be able to offer you more the sort of job you might like. Not engineering in its narrowest sense but possibly an approach to industry and engineering through journalism. Something that will give you an opportunity to show your keenness and insight. Certainly a job with plenty of scope and a substantial salary."

Michael stared at him, not sure if there was some catch. "I'd like that."

"Well, it could be yours in a matter of months."

"You mean it?"

"Of course I mean it."

"Well, of course I'd like that very much. I—Bennie wants to go on working after we're married but I'm determined she shan't."

"I'm not doing this for one of the Marlowes, I'm doing it for you."

They talked a few minutes longer. As they went to the door Michael said: "I still don't know quite the sort of job you mean."

"Well, I'm thinking aloud now, but something in the nature of industrial correspondent—or motoring correspondent—for a big newspaper. Something that would entail travel abroad and opportunities to study engineering projects of all sorts at first hand."

Michael didn't speak until his father was on the top step.

"I'd really love that."

"Good."

Michael still stared at his father. "God, I wish I'd known about it a couple of weeks earlier!"

"Why?"

"Oh . . . it doesn't matter."

"Tell me."

"I'm afraid I can't. Never mind, it's good to know it now, and . . . thanks. You're . . ." he hesitated, ". . . such a good sort."

Roger smiled. "Everyone wouldn't agree, I'm afraid."

All the week Peter had been pretty good, but on Wednesday evening he came with a more than ever unfocused look in his eyes.

"Money," he said, putting his attaché-ease on the side. "A cut-throat price, but we couldn't hang on this time."

"How much?"

"Eight hundred each."

"For the whole lot?"

"Yes."

"God, that was throwing it away!"

"Maybe." Peter began to light a cigarette. "How's the leg?"

"Better; I can get about the room. But——"

"Good. You see, darling boy, it may soon be every man for himself."

"What d'you mean?"

"Well, I hear that the gun-happy psycho from Kenya has supplied the police with a pretty good description of me. That by itself is unhelpful. But it isn't by itself. Run your eye over this."

He passed a cutting from *The Times*.

"£1000 Reward. Stolen on the night of the 10th/11th October from 241 Sloane Street, S.W.I, fine lacquer and emerald brooch, solitaire diamond ring, Elizabethan loving cup, Epstein, bust of sleeping child, Dégas drawing of a violinist, Louis XIII French crested silver spoons etc. One of the two thieves was wounded with .25 automatic pistol. The above reward will be paid by Moriarty & Co., Lloyds Avenue, Fenchurch Street, E.C.3, to the first person giving such information to them as will lead to the apprehension of the thieves, and to the recovery of the property intact or *pro rata*."

Michael passed the cutting back. "Does it add to our troubles?"

"Think beyond the tips of your toes. A seedy fifth-year medical student with an expensive taste in blondes tried to take a bullet out of you on Sunday. This mentions that one of the thieves is wounded. What are the chances, d'you think, if he sees this, of his wanting to make an easy £1000?"

Michael shifted. "But could he?"

"He hasn't to go to the police—only to the underwriters. Then somebody will check up on the other man who was with you when he called, and that will fix it."

"What are you going to do?"

"Get out while the going's good. The perspective will be better in Estoril."

"I can't very well come with you."

"Well. . . ." Peter hesitated. "I don't want to seem to be ratting on you, but you'd be as welcome with me as a culture of conform bacteria. From now on it will be fatal for us to be seen together."

"They can't really prove . . . oh, yes they can." Michael got up and hobbled to the dressing-table to pour himself a glass of beer.

"We're both in this, I with my face, you with your leg. Let Gilbert once see me and I'm sunk. And you're carrying this bullet around like a visiting card."

"Let me see the money," said Michael.

They tipped out the attaché-case on the bed and divided the notes into bundles of fifty.

"Odd," said Michael. "We do all this for a few bits of paper. Stick 'em in the fire and they'd be gone in smoke. . . ."

Yet against his saner judgement the money warmed him, gave him confidence. If they could only bluff this out, just this once. Someone would take the bullet away privately for hard cash. Abortionists had operating theatres of some sort. His father's promise of a new job opened up vistas that he hadn't been aware of before; it meant that he could begin life with Bennie quite afresh, his main problems no longer problems at all. It was quite staggering. It was better even than he had pictured for himself. In any event he was going straight after this: he had finally learnt his lesson. But if his father's plans went through, even the temptation to break out would be gone.

"If I were you," Peter was saying, "I'd get away abroad for a few weeks somewhere. It would be safer."

"Safer for you but not for me. If I go off everyone will start asking questions. I shall bluff it out."

"You can't bluff away a .25 pistol bullet."

"No, but who's going to see it? In a week I shall be walking normally."

"And in the meantime if Gros sells you up the river?"

Michael swallowed his drink; "I think it's a risk I have to take. The chances are he'll never see the notice."

Peter got up. "And if I go to Estoril? What will you feel about that?"

"Nothing."

"You won't think I've let you down—you being crippled?"

"Why should I? I can walk now. Your staying only doubles the risk."

In a few minutes Peter began to look better. They had a last drink together.

Peter said: "Anyway we'll part company for a few months. I shan't go to Portugal until Sunday. So ring me before then if there's any new development. And let's keep in touch."

"When it blows over, maybe. But not for this kind of thing again. That's settled."

"We've been unlucky," said Peter meditatively. "Anyway, let's be thankful if we don't share a common cell."

Michael wondered afterwards what it was that made him limp off into the unlighted living-room and pull back the curtains to watch Peter drive his battered taxi away for the last time.

By the time he got there Peter was already in the front seat and the self-starter was turning. It whirred reluctantly as if the battery was down; presently the engine fired. Peter backed the taxi until the bumper was touching the kerb, then swung round and made for the Old Brompton Road.

As he did so, about a hundred yards along, a black Wolseley pulled sharply out in front of the taxi-and blocked its way. The taxi stopped. A man got out of the Wolseley and then another man. They went across to the taxi and spoke to Peter. There was an argument. Then one of the men pulled a card out of his pocket and showed it to Peter. They wanted Peter to get down. Peter wouldn't. One of the men put a hand on Peter's arm and half pulled him off his seat. Peter got down. Another man got out of the car. He was wearing the flat cap of a police driver. Peter, still protesting, got into the back of the Wolseley with the man who had taken hold of him. The policeman in the flat cap got in the taxi and drove it into a space among the cars parked by the kerb. He got out again and rejoined the Wolseley. The Wolseley drove off.

There was perhaps half an hour. It couldn't be more. Michael dragged off his pyjamas, struggled into a dark suit, grabbed a tie, threw a few things into a small suitcase. The sweat was pouring off him, partly from pain but mostly from the urgency to get away.

Money in the pockets—wads of it; dark overcoat, trilby, one extra suit, a few shirts.

When he looked out of the living-room window again the street was absolutely quiet. Lamps burned stilly, with the moon above them like an obsolete competitor. In the distance the traffic was murmuring and remote.

The lavatory to the flat looked out at the back over the mews towards Cranley Gardens, this small window being the only one facing east. He dropped the bag through and his stick, and then somehow got out himself. For a few minutes he lay flat on a strip of damp sooty grass, recovering from the effort. Then he hobbled to the wall.

He managed to climb up by way of a dustbin and topple over. Instead of taking the easy way he crossed the mews and made a devious back-alley detour to the road beyond.

There he paused to rest and to watch. A group of girls were giggling in a doorway. Otherwise nothing stirred. Gritting his teeth, he picked up his bag and began to limp towards the Fulham Road.

He spent the night at the Cumberland thinking that that would be the sort of place where he would not be noticed; but he felt people were staring at his limp and at his face, as if between the two they read something strange. He slept very little; when he woke his leg was nagging.

He ate a light breakfast in bed and stayed there till nearly twelve. The struggle to dress when it came was not as bad as he had expected, as if in spite of everything the healing processes were going on. But there was no healing process in his mind.

He went down and paid his bill and sat for a few minutes in the foyer watching the people.

Did this mean the end of his own identity? Did it mean the end of everything, including Bennie? This couldn't be. It just couldn't be. Yet even if disappearance was possible, would she ever be the wife of a man on the run living under a false name? The idiocy of this last robbery, now that it had gone wrong, seemed monumental. And all the time Roger had been working on his behalf, planning a job for him which would provide him both with the sort of occupation he would delight in and enough money to marry Bennie.

He could have banged his head on the floor. Was there no way of getting round it? No way of going to the police and saying it was all done for a wager, we never meant to sell the stuff we stole?

What would Peter's defence be? Would it be better to give oneself up and take the stand with him, get a good barrister in? They might get off as first offenders. Roger might pull strings.

That was baby talk. Whatever you pulled strings for in England, you didn't do it to the law. Nor could a clever lawyer do much. "This young man, led astray by evil influences; I ask you not to blight his career at its outset by giving him a prison sentence. A first offender, only just twenty-one. . . ." A lot the judge would care. Anyway his new job would be gone.

At present, on him in cash, he had eight hundred and twenty-three pounds. What would that buy him? Nothing remotely worth what he had lost. A trip out of the country? A quiet room somewhere in London where he could watch for a week or two to see how things turned? A lot would hinge on what happened to Peter. A quiet room where no one asked questions.

But it would never bring him nearer to Bennie. Not now. Perhaps not ever. It was the end, the end, the end.

The barber's shop was in a side street not far from Hammersmith Broadway. Michael paid off his taxi at the mouth of a ravine of Victorian brick and limped down through the rain. A few stallholders were crouched under their awnings. Orange papers and cigarette packets lay sodden in the gutters. Two women nattered endlessly in a doorway.

Good trade. Both chairs full, three men waiting; chromium gleamed a synthetic welcome; the snip-snip of scissors, the smell of violet hair-oil. Everyone was coloured. Little black wires like multiple watch-springs lay in curls over the floor. A big man growing out of has dove-grey suit moved a grudging inch or two to let Michael sit down.

When one man was finished and the assistant came across to brush his coat Michael said: "Is Dick in?"

"Sah?"

"Dick. Dick Ballance."

Bloodshot eyes looked him over. "What name, sah?"

"Michael Shorn."

"I'll just go see. I'll go see if Mister Ballance is in."

He moved through the bead curtains at the end which tinkled like a French bistro. After a minute he came back. "This way."

Michael followed him into a shabby kitchen, where a stout coloured woman in a tight vermilion silk dress was frying chip potatoes, and then up a flight of stairs. In a tiny sitting-room, in half light because of the heavy lace curtains, Dick Ballance was bulging over a desk. He didn't seem to be doing anything, but perhaps that was because he had stopped doing it as Michael came up the stairs.

"Hullo, boy. Nice to see you. By gosh, it's quite a surprise after all this time. How's that Peter Waldo; going great guns, I guess?"

"I'm in a jam, Dick. I want help."

Ballance wiped his hands cautiously on a yellow silk handkerchief. "Yeh? What sort of a jam?"

"I've got in a mess, and I want to lie low for a couple of weeks—perhaps more. Think you can help?"

Ballance took a fountain-pen out of his breast-pocket and tapped it against his teeth. There were five other pens in his pocket. "Well, man, I could and I couldn't. It might cost you a lot of loot."

"I can pay."

"Mind, it wouldn't be for me; but these landlords. . . . You just have to pay the earth for a hide-out these days."

"How much?"

"There's Negro folk where I would send you. Mind Negro folk?"

"No. Not if there are no questions asked."

"Brother, no questions are never asked."

"That'll suit."

Dick's eyes grew speculative as he fastened the two top buttons of his trousers. "Yah. Yah." He pulled forward an old envelope and scribbled an address on the back. "It'll be maybe about ten pounds a week for one room, man. And it'll be, say, fifty pounds for going in."

"Payable to you?"

"Yah." Dick's eyes shifted the responsibility on to someone on the other side of the street. "I pay half of it out when I see my friend."

"When do I move in?"

"Got any luggage?"

"What I have is near at hand."

"Go right ahead, then. The room'll be ready for you when you get there. I'll give my friend a tinkle right away. But don't expect luxury. It'll be bare."

Chapter Twenty-Nine

On Friday the 16th of October, in the Queen's Bench Division of the High Court of Justice the hearing was begun before Mr Justice Alston of the libel action between Roger Norman Shorn of Belgrave Street and Donald John Anthony Marlowe of Trevor Square. Mr Aubrey Lytton Q.C. and Mr B. J. Partridge appeared for the Plaintiff, Mr Vincent Doutelle Q.C. and Mr H. Borgward for the defendant. Mr K. A. Smith held a watching brief for the Hanover Club, and Mr R. Rogers for *The Sunday Gazette*.

"Great pity the Lord Chief Justice is ill," said Whitehouse. "We might have come before him, and I'd be happier if we had. Alston's very unpredictable."

Mr Lytton opened the case for the plaintiff. ("*The* fashionable man at the moment," said Whitehouse, "but past his best and no great lawyer. I suppose that's why he never quite made the bench.")

"The defendant, Mr Donald Marlowe," Mr Lytton was saying in a throaty, elderly, not too audible voice, "is a young conductor of some eminence. He is the eldest child and only son of the late Sir John Marlowe, Queen's Counsel and Recorder of Cheltenham, who died in January of this year. Sir John Marlowe was a barrister of distinction. At the age of fifty he retired from the Bar, and a year later he published his book *Crossroads*, a work which has become well-known in the world; so that when he died, prematurely and before he was fifty-three, he was mourned by many outside the range of his personal acquaintances.

"This renown was prized by his son: he believed his father's repute to be unassailable. But Mr Roger Shorn, the plaintiff in this case, has assailed it. That, members of the jury, is in essence what this action is about; and when you have heard all the evidence I venture to predict that you will not call into question the *sincerity* or *good faith* with which my client undertook his no doubt distasteful task.

"I say distasteful because there has been friendship between the two families over a number of years, and it cannot have been anything but distasteful for Mr Shorn to put his public duty before his private feelings. But he did so, and staked his reputation upon the truth of the facts he published. You will hear in evidence that in an attempt to heal the breach he repeatedly offered to make a public apology to Mr Marlowe for any unhappiness he had caused. But he would not, he could not, retract what he believed so sincerely to be true."

Mr Lytton at seventy had a weather-beaten and fleshy face with cheeks that quivered in battle. When he addressed the jury he blinked at them repeatedly as if they were too bright a light.

"It may be, it may be, members of the jury, that some play will be made in this action on the natural distaste that Englishmen feel for maligning the dead. It is not a practice any of us wishes to see adopted as a part of our democratic way of life. But great reputations bear a heavy burden. The higher they ride the more unassailable must they be to the inquiries of the biographer, the historian, the seeker after truth. The responsible journalist fails in his responsibility if he allows repute to stand when he sincerely believes it to be undeserved, whether that repute belongs to a dead man or to a living. That was Mr Shorn's dilemma.

"Mr Shorn is forty-two years of age. He has had a distinguished career in letters, has broadcast many times and appeared on television. For a while he was on the 'Critics' programme. He has his own column in *The Sentinel* and another, under the journalistic *nom de plume* of Moonraker in *The Gazette*. It was through his column in *The Gazette* that he chose to make known what he had discovered. . . ."

Joanna glanced about the court, trying to see as much as she could without turning her head. The judge was a florid man, yet his face had an ascetic narrowness and his mouth was astringent between its furrows. There were three women and nine men on the jury and they sat in three rows of four in a jury box hung with green curtains on brass curtain rings. The foreman was a middle-aged Jew with a shock of greying hair sticking up like a fan.

Bennie was beside her. They had met in the Gothic main hall, where the day's cases were posted up in frames, but had not been able to understand what it all meant in terms of finding a way through the dark stone passages. In time Paul Whitehouse had turned up and had taken them to the court which was already full. They had had to push their way through a crowd of thirty or forty people who couldn't get in.

Don was already there, and they took seats next to him. There were a lot of barristers in front. Roger was in court but not Michael. Marion Laycock was sitting with her father. It was the first time Joanna had seen Vincent Doutelle, their own Q.C. He looked like a tall highly polished bird; his was the neatest wig, the newest gown, the best manicured nails. His face gleamed with smooth alert good health. No worm escaped him.

There had been a ripple of amusement through the court but she had missed it.

Mr Lytton said: "It is no laughing matter, members of the jury. These are bitter words, wounding words, written with the most deliberate malice, and exhibited in that place where they were calculated to do the greatest harm to Mr Shorn's professional reputation, namely in his club, which was the meeting-place for his business and social friends. The law of libel is designed to protect the ordinary citizen against being held up to hatred, ridicule or contempt. How more obviously, how more maliciously, could one man hold another up to hatred, ridicule and contempt than by comparing him to the louse, the jackal, the wolf, and calling him a liar and a coward? Following this—if this were not enough—in attempting to justify the writing of these doggerel verses Marlowe wrote to the secretary of the Hanover Club the letter which I will now read to you. . . ."

It was a big wide court in solid unvarnished oak. Above was a public gallery; over to the right was another tiny gallery as if for distinguished strangers, but this was empty. Green curtains behind the judge's chair.

".... The crux of the matter is this. What the defendant in effect is saying is: 'All these things I have said about Roger Shorn are true'. And, since the defendant is now relying only on these broad grounds of justification, that is the *only* issue, members of the jury, which you have to decide. Do you agree that every man is a liar and a coward and a disgrace to his profession as a journalist who chooses to assail responsibly the reputation of the dead? Or do you not? I will put it to you another way. Do we incur the abuse of the present Lord Nelson by mentioning Lady Hamilton in the same breath as his distinguished ancestor? Of course not, members of the jury! Essays are published every day qualifying or setting to rights this or that reputation of the past. Who knows, another essay may be written tomorrow restoring the fallen idol. The moment a man dies he becomes a part of history. This attack upon Mr Roger Shorn is, I suggest, an attempt to put the clock back, an attempt to muzzle the freedom of the Press and to curtail the right of free discussion. No filial piety can for a *moment* excuse it."

Aubrey Lytton looked down at his brief, half turned his head and said in a low voice: "Mr Shorn."

Roger got up and went towards the box. He looked and felt composed and unhurried. Mr Lytton began to take him through his evidence in chief. The judge was looking at the point of his pen as if it didn't satisfy him. Every now and then he would lift himself in his chair and take up a different position. When he did so he usually accompanied it with a suspicious glance at somebody from under his lids.

After Roger had given evidence about the quarrel and the verses in the "Suggestions Book", Mr Lytton said: "What made you first feel, Mr Shorn, that John Marlowe's reputation was open to question?"

"I had heard ugly rumours for some time, but I had been inclined to ignore them. Then one day last January I happened to meet Lord Kinley, the economist, and the conversation turned on Sir John Marlowe's death. Lord Kinley then told me that Sir John had

287

been forced to retire because of some scandal, though he did not know the precise details. I asked him how he knew this much, and he said Sir John had confessed to him in confidence that he was a hypocrite and that his retirement was very far from being voluntary. Lord Kinley said he had never told anyone this while Sir John was alive but that there didn't now seem quite the same necessity to keep silent about it."

"What did you do then?"

"Lord Kinley's comment was so much in line with these other rumours I had heard that I consulted my editor. He agreed that it was a matter of some public interest and suggested I should make further inquiries."

"Which you did?"

"Which I did. And as a result of them I interviewed a Mr Malcolm Sunway, a barrister of the Upper Temple. Mr Sunway occupied chambers near to those of Sir John's, and he confirmed the unsavoury rumours that had been current at the time of Sir John's retirement. He was not able to give me precise details, because he asserted that the whole scandal had been carefully hushed up, but he said it was common knowledge that Sir John had been forced to resign. He thought that most of the trouble derived from Sir John's imprudent friendship with a Mrs Delaney and a Mr Stanley Salem."

"Then?"

"I tried to trace Mrs Delaney but failed. However I learned that she was a woman of doubtful repute whose husband had been warned off the turf. Sir John acted for Mrs Delaney when she divorced her husband. I later interviewed a Miss Dolly Riley, who is a close friend of Mr Robert Delaney, and she informed me that Mrs Delaney became Sir John's mistress during or at about the time of her divorce. In confirmation of this a letter came into my hands, written to Sir John Marlowe by Mrs Delaney in March, three years ago."

"Is this the letter?" Copies of a slip of paper that Mr Lytton held were passed to the judge and the foreman of the jury. Lytton read out:

"Darling John, I'm so *desperately* looking forward to seeing you again after last week. I never remember a happier or more wonderful rime. For me it was like the beginning of a new life. Phone me, please.

Narissa."

Lytton looked up. "Narissa, my Lord, is Mrs Delaney's first name."

The judge said: "That was written on the twelfth of March? When was Mrs Delaney's divorce made absolute?"

"On the twenty-ninth of March, my Lord. .... What was your next move, Mr Shorn?"

"I then tried to trace Mr Stanley Salem. I discovered that he was in prison. He had been a notorious shady financier and confidence trickster and he was serving a sentence for fraud. I interviewed him when he came out. He had been one of Mr Delaney's greatest friends and also of course he was well known to Mrs Delaney."

"So?"

"In the course of other inquiries, I went down to Cheltenham where Sir John held the office of Recorder. I found that in one case, in October 1956, Salem had come up before Sir John on a charge of false pretences. After strong evidence for the prosecution had been heard, Sir John abruptly ruled on a very unconvincing technical point that there was no case to answer and ordered the prisoner to be discharged."

"I don't quite follow you," said Mr Justice Alston. "I thought you said this Salem had just come out of prison."

"Yes, my Lord. Six months later he was arrested on another charge and sent for trial at the Old Bailey and sentenced to a term of imprisonment. He was released in March of this year. I saw him then before he left for the Argentine."

"What did you ask him?" said Lytton.

"I asked him about the earlier prosecution when he had been discharged at Cheltenham. He was naturally reluctant to talk about it, but when he saw he had nothing to lose he frankly admitted that Sir John Marlowe had been an old friend of his and had taken the opportunity of doing him a good turn."

Mr Lytton pulled out a handkerchief and dabbed his lips. "Now tell us about Sir John's book."

"Well . . . it was while I was making inquiries about Sir John's professional reputation that other information came into my hands, and I decided to interview Miss Chislehurst whose brother wrote the original book, *Man and the Future*. She said she was utterly disgusted with John Marlowe's behaviour and at the shameless way in which he had stolen her brother's work. She told me of the worry which was induced by this plagiarism and which preyed on the Reverend George Chislehurst's mind and resulted in his last illness."

"Were you able to obtain any outside confirmation of what she said?"

"Yes. At about this time, quite by accident, a letter from George Chislehurst to John Marlowe came into my possession."

"Yes."

"Is this it?"

More papers were passed round. "As you will see, my Lord, it is dated September of two years ago—the month before Mr Chislehurst died. It begins:

"Dear John Marlowe, I have given your letter the fullest possible consideration, but I cannot change by *one degree* my attitude as to the *entirely unauthorised* use you have made of my ideas in your book. What you have done, in view of our one-time friendship, is utterly unethical. Above all it is un-Christian. I cannot protest too strongly against it. I can no longer believe that you are a man of honour.

Yours etc.
George Chislehurst."

Lytton went on: "Did you obtain a copy of George Chislehurst's book?"

"Yes. I compared it page by page with John Marlowe's. The plagiarism is most flagrant and obvious."

Mr Lytton fumbled the handkerchief away under his shabby bombazine gown. "Were these the facts that induced you to write your two articles about Sir John Marlowe?"

"Yes. I was convinced that it was my duty to the public as a journalist to publish what I had discovered."

"May I ask what your feelings were as you proceeded with your investigations?"

Roger glanced briefly across to where Don and Joanna and Bennie were sitting. It was the first time he had looked their way.

"Reluctance—particularly when so much more was unearthed than I had ever expected I very much regretted that I had to make these charges. I never felt any ill-will towards any of the Marlowes living or dead."

"Why did you choose the columns of *The Gazette* for your exposure?"

"Because it was *The Gazette* that instructed me to make the inquiries in the first place."

"Did you, when the Marlowes found out your identity, make any attempt to heal the breach?"

"Yes. I met Mr Don Marlowe several times—also his wife once or twice. On all occasions I did what I could. Even when these verses had been written I tried to prevent the quarrel being dragged into court."

"Was that because you were afraid of the outcome?"

"Not for a moment. I only wanted to save them the needless pain of hearing my evidence and of having all this unpleasant publicity over again."

"Thank you, Mr Shorn." Aubrey Lytton lowered himself back on to his seat.

There was no question about the impression Roger had made on the court. Mr Justice Alston pulled at his bottom lip and looked across at Mr Doutelle. Mr Doutelle got up, stretching his body like a jackdaw on a branch, flapped his black gown once or twice and then was still.

"Tell me, Mr Shorn, do you regard yourself as a responsible journalist?"

"Certainly I do."

"You write what you believe to be the truth."

"Yes."

"The whole truth and nothing but the truth?"

"I try to."

"You try to. Even when it gives great pain and offence to people whose friendship you purport to value?"

"There are things I have been taught to value more."

"Such as what?"

"My duty to the public as a journalist."

"Do you think, supposing these charges you made are true, that the public is any happier for knowing of them?"

"I think it is better informed."

"Oh, yes, the sacred cause of information. Now tell me, just now you said you would gladly have avoided this action if you could, in order to spare your one-time friends the Marlowes the needless pain it would cause them."

"Yes."

"Did it not occur to you that the needless pain would never have arisen if you had not written these pieces of cheap journalism?"

"That may be your view of them. It's not mine."

"Would you not agree that the editorial policy of *The Gazette* has been strongly antagonistic for several years, not only to Sir John Marlowe personally but to his philosophy?"

"Wouldn't it be better to ask the editor that?"

"I am asking you."

Roger hesitated. "In our view Sir John Marlowe was in danger of becoming a legendary figure. On insufficient grounds. It was necessary to see him in perspective."

"To debunk him."

"To put him in perspective by publishing the facts that had come into our possession."

Mr Doutelle rubbed his long nose. "Mr Shorn, if by any chance these articles were *not* true, if they were all based on a few bits of erroneous information carelessly compiled and insufficiently checked, would you agree with me that they were scurrilous and disgraceful?"

"They were not so written."

"But *if* they had been so written, would you not agree that the writer was a disgrace to his profession?"

"I would say that he wasn't doing his job."

"No more than that? Come, Mr Shorn, you are on your own estimate a journalist of repute. Would you not say that a man who maligned another man after his death, on the strength of a few bits of unconfirmed tittle-tattle, should be 'classed with the skunk and the liar and the funk and expected to live with the same'? Doesn't that really sum up the situation very well?"

"I would call him careless and cruel. But that is not the——"

"Careless and cruel. Thank you."

"But that is very far from being the case here."

Mr Doutelle brooded a moment, as over an inedible crust. "Now you say you chose *The Gazette* in which to publish these relevations, because it was *The Gazette* which instructed you to make these inquiries in the first place?"

"Yes."

"Your column in *The Gazette* also no doubt had the advantage over your column in *The Sentinel* in that it enabled you to remain anonymous."

"That did not enter into it."

"But if your identity had not been discovered, would you not have maintained your friendship with Mr Don Marlowe, even while in the process of making these terrible accusations against his father?"

"I did have the hope that my relationship with the living Marlowes would continue unimpaired because I bore them no ill-will and indeed valued their friendship."

"Is it not your avowed duty in your column to expose hypocrisy,

Mr Shorn? Standing here in this court of law, are you not embarrassed to tell us of your own?"

"My Lord," said Mr Lytton, rising, "I must protest most strongly against the manner in which my learned friend is conducting this cross-examination."

His Lordship raised his lids an inch. "What have you to say to that, Mr Doutelle?"

"If your Lordship pleases, I will ask the witness a different question. . . . Mr Shorn, at the time you wrote these articles Sir John Marlowe had been dead only four months. If you felt the way you do, why didn't you attack him while he was still alive?"

"Exactly what I said," muttered Sir Percy Laycock.

"Shh," whispered Marion.

"I thought nothing at all of it until the time of his death when I had that conversation with Lord Kinley."

"But it's very convenient for you, isn't it, that he cannot now defend himself?"

"It would have made no difference."

"Not even to *The Gazette*?"

"Whatever its shortcomings, *The Gazette* isn't afraid of trouble, Mr Doutelle."

"According to your conversation with Lord Kinley Sir John Marlowe confessed to being a fraud because his retirement was not voluntary. Did that surprise you?"

"At the time very much."

"Did you express your surprise to Lord Kinley?"

"Yes, I think I said something to him."

"You don't remember?"

"Not exactly."

"Do you remember if Lord Kinley made any attempt to explain his extraordinary statement?"

"Isn't Lord Kinley going to be called?"

"Yes, but we are concerned at the moment with your processes of thought. I am anxious to know how it is that you can apparently quote this bald statement out of context and nothing more. Where were you at the time? What was happening?"

"It was at a dinner of the Clothworker's Guild. After dinner we were talking and smoking, and Sir John's death came up. Lord Kinley made that remark, but I believe before much more could be said the conversation was turned."

"There were others present who heard this remark?"

"Oh, yes, four or five others."

"Mr Shorn, you have just told the court that whether Sir John was alive or dead made no difference to you or to *The Sunday Gazette*."

"That's true."

"Are you suggesting that if Sir John had been alive you would have written or *The Sunday Gazette* would have dared to publish such articles on so little evidence?"

"You were asking me what *led* to our inquiries. Obviously if Sir John had been alive we would have sent a man round to get a statement from him right away."

"Did it ever occur to you that, Sir John being dead, the nearest person from whom you could have inquired would have been his son?"

"It occurred to me, but I felt that he would probably not be in a position to know the facts. Indeed that has proved to be correct. I also felt that even if he was aware that something was wrong he would naturally try to cover up for his father."

"But you know Mr Marlowe. You were a friend of his. No reporter was necessary. You only had to ask him the next time you met him at the club. Could you not have gone on to other sources if that one failed?"

"For the reasons I have told you I did not do so. Sometimes it is essential for a journalist to write on behalf of his paper, however individually responsible he may wish to be."

By one-thirty there was a long queue outside the court, and when the principals returned it was crammed with people standing four deep at the back. "There's Warner Robinson," said Don. "The big chap with the loose jowls and the thin hair."

"Is he going to give evidence?"

"I don't know. That's Laurence Heath, secretary of the Hanover; he's evidently got away from his operating table. And Knowles; and I think that's the Editor of *The Sentinel*. Behind him is Lord Queenswood, the man with the pince-nez; I don't see Michael here, Bennie."

"No, he's in Liverpool."

The court-associate was motioning Roger to re-enter the witness-box. He had just got there when the judge entered and they all rose. When he had bowed to the court and sat down they seated themselves again, all except Roger—and Mr Doutelle, who was bent over his brief.

After a minute he straightened up and gave his wings a flap.

"Now, Mr Shorn, let us get on with these other accusations which you have brought. You said you were told by a Miss Dolly Riley that Mrs. Delaney became Sir John Marlowe's mistress. When were you told that?"

"I had heard it from other sources. She confirmed it when I interviewed her in August of this year."

"Did you know that Miss Riley was born near Aintree and that until twelve months ago had never been to London except on a visit?"

Roger smiled slightly. "I know that Miss Riley is at present living with Mr Robert Delaney, Mrs Delaney's ex-husband."

"Do you think that establishes her as an authority on something that happened in London two years before she left the North of England?"

"I should have thought even you would agree that she would be likely to have first-hand information on it from Mr Delaney."

"And you think her testimony is sufficient evidence on which to base your charge that Sir John Marlowe and Mrs Delaney were intimate at a time when Sir John was appearing professionally on Mrs Delaney's behalf?"

"I never said that."

His Lordship turned over his papers. "'During or at about the time of the divorce', were his words, Mr Doutelle."

"Yes," Roger said. "That was in my examination today—not in

the articles. I think there is sufficient *totality* of evidence that that was true. At or about the time."

"What other evidence is there?"

"The evidence of the letter which has been read you, from Mrs Delaney to Sir John, written before her divorce was made absolute. The fact that Mrs Delaney and Sir John became engaged to be married soon afterwards. The help he gave Stanley Salem. All these add up to the one general conclusion."

"It seems to me, Mr Shorn, that you do not appreciate the difference between evidence and assumption. Do you, for instance, when you look down the announcements of forthcoming marriages in *The Times* every morning—do you necessarily assume that all those couples have been sleeping together for six months already?"

"No. Only a certain proportion of them."

There was a murmur of amusement.

Mr Jusnce Alston moved his head. "Are you asking us accept that answer, Mr Shorn, as evidence of your attitude mind when you sit down to write your articles?"

"No, my Lord," said Roger quickly. "I'm afraid I allow myself to be provoked into making that remark."

Mr Doutelle tipped his wig forward. "In fact, Mr Shorn isn't it true that your whole approach to your column in *The Gazette* is precisely summed up by what you have just said namely that you are ready on all occasions to believe the worst of your fellow men?"

"Not without evidence. We should not keep our jobs a day if we did."

"But is not such a ready belief a necessary part of the gossip columnist's equipment, so that the equivalent of an anonymous letter may be circulated every Sunday by the blessings of modern science to three million readers?"

"Certainly not."

"I don't think I want to sit this out," whispered Marion.

"They finish at four," said her father. "I'd prefer not to go yet."

But Mr Doutelle had by no means finished. What other evidence, as distinct from rumour, was there that Sir John had been unofficially compelled to retire? Mr Malcolm Sunway.

"Ah, Mr Sunway. He should be an expert on disciplinary action. Did you know that three years ago he was disbarred, for accepting a bribe in a commercial case?"

"Yes, I did."

"Did you know that Sir John Marlowe was a member of the Professional Conduct Committee that investigated his case?"

"I'm not sure if I did at the time. Does it matter?"

"I should have thought that from your experience of the odiousness of human nature you would have supposed it did."

"I sincerely believe Mr Sunway to be speaking the truth—from inside knowledge and without malice."

His Lordship lifted himself up and his position. "To hear the truth about a man, Mr Shorn, do you always go to his enemies?"

"No, my Lord. But the law. ..." Roger stopped.

"Go on," said the judge.

Roger said, picking his words now: "All professional bodies, especially the law with its great reputation for probity, are anxious to avoid publicity over minor scandals in their own ranks. It seemed to me that in a case such as this we were likely to hear more of the truth from outside the profession, or from one who had lately become an outsider."

Mr Justice Alston frowned thoughtfully at his pen. "The law, Mr Shorn, does not welcome the inquiring journalist, but that is because the inquiring journalist usually gets his facts wrong. You would be mistaken in supposing that the law attempts to cover up in its own interests any scandal which may affect itself. Adequate publicity is always given to disciplinary action taken by the Bar."

"Yes, my Lord." Roger knew he was on delicate ground here.

Mr Justice Alston looked at the clock. "Go on, Mr Doutelle."

Mr Doutelle said: "Now this information that Sir John Marlowe stopped a case and discharged the prisoner because the prisoner, a notorious swindler, was his friend—what evidence have you of this statement?"

"Evidence that the case was stopped. Look up the records. If you examine them you will see that there was an absolutely fool-proof case against Salem. Why else was it stopped? The one local journalist who was covering the case was astonished that it should be. Evidence of Stanley Salem's own statement to me that it was stopped by Sir John because Sir John was a friend of his and because he, Salem, had influence over Sir John's girl friend, meaning Mrs Delaney."

"Do you know that Stanley Salem has claimed at one time or another to be on terms of close friendship with the Duke of Kent, with Onassis, with Queen Juliana, among other? None of them in fact had ever met him."

"Salem was Robert Delaney's closest friend, that's indisputable. Obviously Salem must have met John Marlowe many times. It was an irregularity of the most flagrant kind and contrary to his oaths of office that Marlowe should have presided over the case at all."

The barrister had a word with his solicitor. "There's another matter I hope you'll be able to help me over. Mr Shorn. Today you have put in as evidence these letters, private letters, property belonging to Sir John Marlowe. Could you tell the court how these letters came into your possession?"

"Does that matter?"

His Lordship said: "You know, Mr Doutelle, I'm inclined to agree with the witness there."

"If your Lordship pleases, I submit that the manner by which the witness obtained these letters may be very relevant to justification as it is pleaded here."

The judge looked down at his notes for a moment. "Well, Mr Shorn?"

"I prefer not to say, my Lord."

Doutelle said: "Did you buy them?"

The judge looked at Mr Lytton, who a moment ago had half risen from his seat in protest. "I think, Mr Doutelle, if you want to persist with that question I shall first have to rule on its admissibility."

"Well, will he tell us *why* he prefers not to say?"

Roger straightened up. "Because it could involve someone else."

"Do you mean the letters were given you?"

"Not exactly, my Lord."

"Well," said the judge, "there you are. You must make the best of it, Mr Doutelle."

"I am quite content to leave it there, my Lord. I think that the jury will know what to assume."

"I'm sure I should not."

"I mean, my Lord, that they will safely assume that the letters came into Mr Shorn's possession in a way which reflects discredit upon him."

"Not even necessarily that. It might only reflect discredit on the person Mr Shorn prefers not to tell us about."

"As your Lordship pleases."

Mr Justice Alston again looked at the clock. "Are you nearly finished, Mr Doutelle?"

"No, I shall be some time yet, my Lord."

"Then I think this would be an appropriate moment to rise. Members of the jury, you will please remember not to discuss the case or any of the evidence with anyone during the adjournment, or let anyone speak to you about it."

They all got up, Marion rather unsteadily, as the judge walked out. Roger flexed his hands where they had been gripping the edge of the box. Then he came down too.

The first day was over.

Chapter Thirty

Before they left, Don had a word with Whitehouse. "Not bad," said the solicitor; "but Shorn is first-rate in the box. That impression of sincerity and integrity. I think, in spite of all we now know, that a lot will turn on the sort of showing Mrs Delaney makes."

"What do you think the judge feels about it so far?"

"Well, one would expect him to be a little on our side; but I'm a trifle uncertain of Alston. It's still possible that when he sums up he'll bend over backwards just to show he has no prejudice against Shorn."

"Do you want me any more?"

"No, I think not. I'll ring you in case of need."

When they had separated Don said to Bennie; "Come back and have tea with us."

"Thank you, but I've my week-end shopping to do. Can I come on Sunday?"

"Can she come on Sunday?" Don said to Joanna.

"All day if she likes," said Joanna. "We shall all be on edge, and it helps if we can be edgy together."

"I'm on duty part of Sunday, but I'd love to come to tea."

Bennie watched them get into their car and drive off. She stood a moment uncertain on the pavement. She had not heard a word from Michael since last Sunday, not even a postcard, and she was feeling worried. Her refusal to go home tea with Don had been more on this account than any other.

She turned back into the Law Courts and found an unoccupied telephone booth. She rang Barlett and Leak. "Could you tell me if Mr Michael Shorn is there?"

"I'm sorry, Mr Shorn is away ill at the moment. Can I help you?"

"Ill? Er—no, thank you, it's just a personal matter. When did he come back from Liverpool?"

"Liverpool? I didn't know he'd been."

"Yes, but surely you sent him there to attend a Book Week?"

"Not us, madam. He fell and sprained his back last weekend. We understand he'll be in the office again early next week."

"Oh—er, thank you. I . . . must have misunderstood what he said."

She came out and stood by the box. People were streaming down from the Law Courts, among them a few barristers still in their wigs and gowns. Two men went past in black suits and black trilby hats. One said: "But it's perfectly plain under the Forfeiture Act of 1870, section four. A sum not exceeding £100 by way of satisfaction."

She went out of the courts and walked to the Temple Underground. She caught a tube for South Kensington. She got out and walked to Roland Gardens. She went up the steps and pressed his bell.

No reply.

After trying three or four times and then turning the handle to see if the door was locked she stood on the stone balustrade of the steps to peer into the living-room. Nothing stirred. She climbed down and tried to see into his bedroom. No one.

She walked back down the street. As she did so a tall man in a mackintosh came from behind a car at the end of the street and walked towards her on the other side. He didn't look at her and they both went straight on, but she had the impression that he had been watching her.

She found another telephone box and rang Roger.

He answered almost at once. Briefly and irritably: "Yes?"

She imagined him just coming in from that day in the witness-box, still with his coat on, the telephone ringing. "Is Mr Michael Shorn there, please?"

"No, he's not. Who wants him?"

"Oh, it doesn't matter. I——"

"You'll find him at 191 Roland Gardens."

"Thank you very much." She rang off.

She walked back to her own flat. Pat was in and ironing a frock. She wanted to know all about the day in court and rather absently Bennie told her. Pat said: "Oh, there is a letter for you. I put it on your bed."

Bennie went in and, seeing Michael's writing, fumblingly tore the envelope.

Darling Bennie,

I don't know how to start this letter or what to say to you. I can only begin by putting it baldly—that I have done something pretty silly and am now in a spot of trouble with the police. I can't bear to think what you will feel when I tell you this. I can only try to explain by saying that my idea was to have money for when we got married. As you know, I have always kicked bitterly against the idea that I should not be able to give you some of the smaller luxuries of life. I thought that by taking one risk, if I had luck, I might be able to do many of the things I dreamed of doing for you. Well, the luck ran out on me.

Darling, darling Bennie. I suppose, feeling the way you do about right and wrong, this may be more or less the write-off for me. I try to tell myself that it isn't, that you will find it in your heart to excuse and forgive. Then—perhaps—in a few weeks or months we shall be together again, and—somehow—this will all be forgotten like a particularly nasty dream. Don't *worry* about me I'm very safe at the moment where I am, and I'll let you know about once a week how it goes. Later, when things have cooled off, I'll send you my address—or even come and see you. I'm not so very far away.

Don't tell Dad you've had this letter. I expect the police will have been round to see him by now, and the less he knows the less he'll have to hide. If they come to see you, as they well may, please tell them nothing.

I can't tell you how mad I am with myself that I have got

in this mess—and should even be dragging you into it in this way. Really Bennie, I can't tell you how sorry I am to upset you. I can't begin to tell you. I could jump under any one of the trains I see from my window. I would if it were not for loving you. That's the one thing I cling to. I hope you find it in your forgiving heart to love me too.

Devotedly, dejectedly,

Your Michael

"What is it?" said Pat. "Bad news?"

"No, not really, I. . . ."

"Sit down, you look like a sheet. I'll get you something to drink."

"No, it's all right."

She held on to the end of the table and lowered herself into a chair while Pat went hurriedly to the cupboard.

"We've no brandy, only gin. Was it something in the letter to upset you?"

"I think it's the stuffy court. No air all day—packed like sardines."

"Were there so many? Here, try this."

She drank the gin, choked, coughed. What had she done with the letter? Was it still on the bed? Ah, in her pocket.

"Was the letter from Michael?" said Pat.

She'd seen the writing on the envelope. "Yes."

"Don't tell me he has let you down. After all his persistence when you did not want him."

"No, it's nothing like that." She could see Pat was only half convinced but she let it go.

After a few minutes the blood began to come back to her face. Pat, seeing she wanted to be left alone, went on with her ironing. Bennie went back into her bedroom. She took down some nylon stockings she had washed that morning, put them into a drawer. The sick feeling kept coming over her. She dusted a freckle of powder off the dressing-table, unfastened a small parcel of laundry, put the things away. A shirt blouse had lost a button and she sewed one on. When she put that away she saw in the bottom of the drawer the bathing costume she had last worn at the pool in Surrey.

After a while she came out and went through into the tiny kitchenette, began rummaging about. "What is it you want, dear?" Pat said.

"I was looking for last Monday's *Evening News*."

"Monday's? That is a long time. Oh, is this it?"

"Thank you." Bennie took it back into her bedroom.

She fumbled about with the pages, dropped a sheet and had to pick it up. "Sloane Street Robbery." There it was. "Thieves in their twenties. One, a very tall young man, with a public school accent, was surprised. . . . The other was wounded in the leg by Captain Gilbert's automatic . . . trail of blood . . . made off in car or van parked in vacant lot nearby.". . . . "Darling, old Bartlett wants me to go to Liverpool for a Book Week. I hope to be home about Thursday." "Not us, madam. He fell and sprained his back."

She took out her letter and read it again. The postmark was London, W.10.

The next morning, after a sleepless night, she went as usual to the hostel.

Sister Frey was concerned as soon as she saw her. "Bennie, what's the matter with you? You look ill."

"Do I? Does it show that much? No, I'm not ill."

"Then what is it?"

"I just happen to be desperately worried." Bennie began to sort out into three piles the magazines she had brought. She blinked away tears that had got into her eyes. "I really am. It's just one of those things."

"Can't you tell me about it?"

Bennie shook her head. "Sooner you than anyone, but. . . ."

"Don't stop on if you'd rather not."

"I'd rather. It helps to occupy me."

"What time are you off today?"

"Three twenty-five. For Stockholm."

"It's a strange life."

Bennie half smiled. "So's yours."

Sister Frey said: "There's a lot about the libel action in the papers this morning. There seems to be a good leaven of malice in it all."

"Mary, have you a map of the London postal districts? I want to know where W.10 is."

"Yes, I expect so. We seem to have most things. I know we're W.2." Mary Frey went to a drawer and took out a small map. They looked at it together. "W.10. Oh, that's not far away. North Kensington."

"What's this?" Bennie asked, suddenly pointing.

"It's a railway line. It'll be the main line from Paddington to the west."

"Mary, have you got a bigger scale map?"

"On the wall behind you, dear. It's useful, we find, when people here don't know their way about. . . ."

Bennie had turned round and was staring at it. With the help of the postal map she was able to isolate a small area where the line ran through the corner of the W.10 district. "Do you know anything about this part?"

Sister Frey looked at Bennie's finger. "How do you mean, know anything about it?"

"Well, is it a good district, for instance?"

"One of the shadiest, I should think. Notting Dale and the top of Ladbroke Grove. The County Council have been trying to clean it up for years but it's still pretty grim."

"The sort of place anyone might hide if they were wanted by the police?"

"I should trunk just that. Bennie, what is it? Do you know someone who's in trouble?"

"Yes."

"Do you want to find them? Are they somewhere in that district?"

"I think so."

Mary Frey picked up a pile of sheets. "We've four or five women working round there. Why don't you ask them?"

Bennie stared. "What, d'you mean they might know—about people corning and going?"

"Yes. It's just a chance. It might come off."

"Oh, but surely not. I don't know what scale this map is but. . . . There must be thousands of people."

"Well, I gather you think he's somewhere near the railway line. That makes it a pretty small area. And there's a sort of bush telegraph. Of course it was only a suggestion."

"What do these women do? Which are they?"

"Oh, the usual odd jobs. There's—let me see—there's Mrs Carpenter, and Mrs Dean, and Sarah Porteous, and. . . . Anyway, if you think any more of it call round tomorrow evening when you get back and ask them. They'll all be here then."

"All right," said Bennie after a moment. "It'll do no harm. I will."

They had a tail wind on the homeward flight and touched down half an hour ahead of schedule. The TV Personality had been very difficult. He had complained about the gin, and had had to be shown the bottle to prove it was the brand he asked for, he had refused to eat the lunch and had said it was a disgrace no alternatives were provided; he had bought too many cigarettes and disagreed about the rate they gave him for his kroner. When the flight was over he apologised most charmingly for being such a nuisance. Bennie smiled and said nothing, although her head was cracking. People, she found, often went on like that when they were terrified.

Before leaving the airport she asked for special leave for the Wednesday and Thursday in addition to her usual Tuesday, giving the libel action as her reason. She was at the hostel by four.

"Well, I'm in fish and chips," said Mrs Carpenter. "You know, right at the end of Portobello Road. Frying I do for the missus when she's busy and potatoes, my life, I'm sick of the sight of potatoes. Well, dear, it's a queer district; there's some funny 'uns about, that's true. Lots of niggers, some of them in their big chromium cars, it don't seem right. And Teddy Boys. Well, I'll look out. Dark young man, black hair falling over his forehead, possibly a limp. But it's not likely, dear, is it? If he's one of that sort, he'll lie low, won't he? And a tall young man with a long neck? I'll do my best."

"You can never tell," said Mrs Dean. "That's what I say. You can never tell. But it's them streets leading off where the wide boys live. I've a sister in dry cleaning. They come in there. Press this suit; dye this coat; mend this tear … and like as not the tear's been made by a razor. Yes, I'll ask my sister. She knows everything that happens in her street. You wouldn't believe."

"Well, dear, I don't know as *I'm* likely to see 'im," said Miss Porteous. "I'm in the Ladies Convenience just by the bridge. Mind I *'ear* a lot. Is 'e fond of girls? Girls come in there for a *chat*, or if they've someone they want to shake off. But in the daytime it's *quiet*. Too quiet for me. And lonely, like. Sometimes not sixpence in a morning. But I'm leaving end of this month. I got a smashing job at the Knightsbridge one. There you're busy all day. It don't leave you time to get depressed."

Mrs Richter said: "I help in the little shop where newspapers are sold and cigarettes and curling pins—oh, and chewing-gum and pencils and all those things. Yes, it is near the railway. All day long we are hearing the trains whistle. Many people come in and out. I will watch and I will listen."

"I'm at the Crown," said Mrs Knight; "just round the corner from Telford Road. Scrubbing, most of it is—that and washing glasses. My dear life, we get some types! It don' *do* to ask questions! But I'll *listen*. Oh, yes. I'll listen. There ain't much go on in that area we don't hear about sooner or later. I'll tell the barmaid to keep her ears open too."

When she left, Bennie walked home and telephoned Don to say she would be round later. Then she looked through the telephone book and found that both Peter Waldo and Lady Waldo were in the book. She phoned Peter Waldo's number but there was no reply. She rang Lady Waldo. Lady Waldo, said an impersonal voice, was in Portugal. Could she speak to Peter Waldo? No, the impersonal voice was sorry, Peter Waldo was not there, and rang off.

On Sunday evening Roger met Marion for a drink at a little bar where they had been twice before. It was usually quiet and they could talk. He hadn't seen her to speak to privately for some days.

After he had ordered drinks he said: "Darling, it's so lovely to be with you again. I hope in a week or two when all this is out of the way we shall be able to see more of each other, and openly, not as if there were something to be concealed."

She was wearing a hat with a brim which in the shadowy light of the bar hid the expression in her eyes. "Roger, I felt so awful on Friday. I could hardly stay in the court."

He shrugged, nettled by her tone. All week-end he had been on edge. "Law courts are always like that. Who was it said, 'Private litigation is the civilised equivalent of war and should be expected to be conducted with heat. . . .' What did your father think of it all?"

"He didn't seem very happy about it." (Sir Percy had said: "The more I see of this case the less I care for it.")

They had started off on the wrong foot tonight. Every-thing she said irritated him. She and her father . . . oh, God, how they bored him. . . .

She said: "You were wonderful in the box. But things get twisted round so. Have you to face Doutelle again tomorrow?"

"Yes, but that's nothing to worry about."

"You mean there is something else?" She was learning to read inflexions in his voice in a way few other women ever had.

"Well, yes, I'm afraid so. Mrs Delaney, the woman that Sir John Marlowe was to have married, has decided to come forward at the last moment and give evidence. It's going to put a very different complexion on the case from what I imagined a week ago."

"Why? Why, Roger? What is she going to say?"

"Well, she will obviously give her own version of events. How far the jury will believe her is another matter. But it will count enormously against us."

Marion was looking at him in alarm; but he determined at that moment not to tell her any more. He had dropped the warning; that would have to do. He would certainly not tell her of the morning when he had left Michael and gone to his solicitor and there found Mr Cobb so confounded with Mrs Delaney's evidence that he seemed on the point of suggesting that the case be withdrawn. But they had gone across to see Mr Lytton and fortunately Mr

Lytton had been altogether more comforting. He had said: "I'll not pretend this isn't a tremendous broadside. It'll be touch and go now instead of an easy victory; but I still by no means rule out the possibility of our carrying the day. In fact I think we will. What sort of a woman is this Mrs Delaney? You've not seen her? No. Well, although all she is going to say, and these letters, and the evidence of this man, Lippmann—although all that will in itself be quite shattering at first, there may be a lot of holes to be picked when I cross-examine her. Why, for instance, has she been so reluctant to come forward? Do you mean to say she has nothing to hide? What will the jury really think of this dubious woman in Marlowe's life? I consider now it will be touch and go."

Marion said anxiously: "What are you thinking, dearest?"

"Is your father corning tomorrow?"

"Yes."

He bought more drinks. "Come home with me, Marion. We haven't been together for so long."

She looked at him. "Dearest, I'd adore to, but I mustn't. I only slipped out as it was."

He put his hand over hers. "This isn't going to make any difference to us?"

"Of course it won't. How could it?"

"Even if the case didn't turn out so well?"

"I don't mind what happens so long as you don't personally come out of it badly."

They talked on for about half an hour. She tried once or twice to steer the conversation back to the action, but he headed her off. Eventually when it was nearly time to go she said:

"I know you don't want to talk about it. You even say we shouldn't. But there is one thing I feel I must know. Who did give you those letters, the Marlowe letters?"

He smiled a little. In a queer way he had warmed towards her again, just because of her anxiety for him. "Won't you trust me?"

"Of course." But now she looked put out.

"It involves someone else, as the judge guessed. I don't like letting another person down. Even a journalist has his own particular honour in matters like this."

"That's what I'm afraid of, Roger. If you don't say anything more the jury will assume you stole the letters or got them by some fraud. My father will too."

Her father would too.

Marion said: "It isn't good enough, that someone should shelter behind you and let you take the blame. Is it a woman?"

". . . . No."

"Another journalist?"

"Yes."

"Then bring him into court and make him explain."

"I couldn't do that."

She made a little impatient movement. "Everything that's been said so far, all that Doutelle has said is aimed at your reputation. If they can make you out a thief and a cheat you automatically lose the action."

He got up and passed money across the counter. "It's so clever of you, Marion, to see the issues so clearly. You should have been a lawyer." He got this far smoothly, not meaning anything, then hesitated. Why not? Could one not. . . . "In fact I don't mind telling you about it, but you'll see it really shouldn't go any further."

She waited, watching him with an attentive but loving gaze.

He said: "A colleague of mine—I don't propose to give his name even to you—is writing a book on famous murder trials and wanted some details of one trial in which Marlowe appeared for the defence, so he went to see John Marlowe last December by appointment and interviewed him on it."

Roger took his change, looked at it unseeingly, slipped it into his pocket.

"Go on," said Marion.

"Well, after the interview John Marlowe offered him his notes and papers on the case to take away. This journalist naturally accepted them, and it wasn't until two weeks later that, looking through them, he found that as well as the notes were some letters. He thought of returning them right away but decided he'd send them back when he returned the notes. Before he could do that John Marlowe died. In March, hearing I was doing something on John Marlowe, he handed the letters to me."

"But dearest," Marion said, "why didn't you *say* that in court? There's nothing whatever discreditable to you in it, and not really anything very terrible about the other journalist!"

"To tell you the truth," Roger said candidly, "I thought it would seem too lame altogether. And I'm not willing to get the other fellow in trouble."

"But there's no trouble you can get him into! Dearest, you *must* tell them that in court tomorrow!"

"I'm not sure. I may."

"I'll tell Daddy. I must. It's only fair. You don't mind that?"

"You can if you want to."

"I certainly do!"

Chapter Thirty-One

On the Monday Bennie was on the Paris run. When she got home she rang the hostel, but none of the women had anything to report. Then she rang Don.

He said: "Bennie? We missed you. You have a comforting warm presence sitting next to me on that hard bench."

"What happened, darling?"

"We finished with Roger eventually at half past eleven, but the plaintiff's case didn't close until twenty past four. After Roger left, witnesses were called to give evidence of the way some of the words were understood by them when they read the verses. Then Lord Kinley was called. Apparently Dad shared a taxi with him one night about the time of his retirement, and Kinley said to him how self-sacrificing he thought it was of Dad to give up his career in mid-stream to devote his life to philosophy. Apparently Dad replied irritably that he had never intended that his behaviour should appear self-sacrificing, and that he had not retired at all willingly, and felt himself a fraud. Kinley took it seriously, so in that respect Roger was right. Kinley repeated it after the city dinner. Then came Miss Chislehurst, who was vindictive about the whole thing. Whitehouse said the judge was pretty lenient about what he admitted, so we hope he'll be of the same mind when it's our turn."

"Did Miss Chislehurst say anything fresh?"

"No. Doutelle in cross-examination got out of her the fact that she knew nothing of her brother's friendship with Dad until her brother was taken ill and that when she came to look after him old Chislehurst was already paralysed and hardly able to talk. Then they called Dr Lehmann who wrote the article for *The Observer*, comparing the two books. Borgward cross-examined him for the one or two facts necessary to our case."

"Will Mrs Delaney be giving evidence tomorrow?"

"I think so. It rather depends how long they take over me."

"Poor you. Thank Heaven I haven't to go into the box. How long will it all last, do you think?"

"Whitehouse thinks Wednesday. It'll be an impossible situation if it doesn't end then because I've that important concert in Edinburgh on Thursday. Joanna missed part of this morning for a rehearsal of *The Lady's Not For Burning*, and it's being televised on Wednesday so she may miss that as well. I haven't seen Michael in court at all, by the way."

"No," said Bennie. "He's away on business."

Don said: "Oh, there was one other thing. Doutelle returned to the attack about the two letters this morning. The lawyers had a good squabble about the issues raised in the pleadings or something. However the judge eventually allowed Doutelle's questions, and Roger suddenly brought out a story about how he got the two letters, or how he *says* he got them. Some journalist, he says, whom he refuses to name, interviewed Dad on the Cobham case and Dad gave him his notes and papers on the case, and by accident included in the file some of his private letters. Dad died before the journalist could return the letters, so the journalist passed them on to Roger."

"Daddy was untidy about filing things, but I shouldn't have thought he would be as casual as that."

"Doutelle's view is that Roger has had the week-end to invent an excuse and this is it. Oh, here's Joanna. Do you want to talk to her?"

"Yes, please."

Towards 10 p.m. Bennie said she was going out for a walk, but refused Pat's offer to go with her. She sat in an espresso bar for a time making up her mind, and then she took a taxi to the Middle Pocket.

The same trek up the office stairs, distant music incongruous and unspecified, the door, marked "Council for European

Affiliation"; inside, the brassy blonde was standing before the chromium-framed mirror examining a pin-head mole on her neck.

Bennie said: "I've been here before with Michael Shorn; you remember? I'm not stopping tonight but I have a message for Dick Ballance. Could you let me in?"

Blue eyes peered through slits in the mascara. Bennie put ten shillings on the table.

"All right, dear. How long'll you be?"

"Five minutes. . . ."

Down the beaver-boarded passage into the bar. As she got there the gramophone finished and Dick began to play a slow sleep-walking rhythm. The dim lights had been made even dimmer, and a spot-light changing colour focused on the four couples moving over the floor. She waved away the Cypriot waiter and edged round to the piano.

Dick didn't look up until her shadow fell on the keys. Then she saw that he instantly knew her. He missed a beat.

"Holy snakes, I thought you was my conscience, pussy-footing up behind me like that." He turned back to the piano and caught up the slow sweet rhythm. The dancers were clinging tightly to each other like all-in wrestlers in the last stages of exhaustion.

"I came to see if you could help me."

He went on playing in the bass while he reached with his right hand for the cigarette smouldering at the end of the keys. "Who brought you, sister?"

"I came by myself."

"Holy snakes." He finished the piece and the lights went up. Mild clapping, but he split his face in a grin and waved his purple palms to show there was no more. The dancers drifted back to their seats. Bennie, suddenly realising she might look like a singer who had come to do a turn, dragged a chair forward and sat on it.

"Dick, do you know where Michael is?"

He said, almost before she had finished speaking: "Haven't a *notion*! If I had I'd say, you bet. I'd tell you this very instant! Believe *me*."

"He's in trouble, and he once said you were the sort of person who could always fix things—and I thought perhaps you'd fixed something for him."

"His little joke! Me fix things! Well, I tell you I haven't seen Michael for weeks and weeks and weeks."

"Or Peter Waldo?"

Dick put his cigarette down. "I hear he's going to be out of town for quite some time. They tell me so."

"Who told you so?"

Dick laughed outright. "Little birds. But I haven't seen Peter now for weeks and weeks and weeks. They don't come here no more."

He began to play again. Half-way through, a boy with close-set eyes and a turtle-neck sweater came from the bar and asked Bennie to dance. She smiled and said no. She sat through the dance. When it was over she said:

"Supposing you see anything of him, Dick, will you let me know? I'll give you my address."

"Sure, sure, anything you say. Why don't you go dance with that boy? He's all right. He'll have you a good time."

She passed him an old envelope. "If you do find him I'll give you ten pounds."

"Thanks, thanks. Now I guess I got to play again."

It was no use. For some reason Dick was treating her like a piece of hot coal. Well, she had done all she could. She got up to go, and then saw the faces of the three men sitting at the nearby table. Until now they had been screened by the raised lid of the piano. One of them was Boy Kenny, another was the tall man in the raincoat she had seen outside Michael's flat.

She moved a couple of steps, hesitated. In the moment of her seeing him Boy had just taken a wet stub from his mouth and was lighting a fresh cigarette from it. He was looking at her. Something hadn't improved his appearance or his expression since they last met.

Her mind flew over the situation and decided there was some reason why she should not ask Boy. She went on.

She went on, glad to be gone. At the door the boy in the turtle-neck sweater overtook her again, wanted to take her home. She said no again, more firmly, and slid out.

Mr Doutelle made a very short speech on the following morning, saying that he had a number of witnesses to call and that he would reserve most of his remarks for his closing address. He spoke only for fifteen minutes and then called Mr Donald Marlowe.

Don went to the witness-box, wishing he might have held a baton just for comfort. The court looked different from up here. He was on a level with the judge, very close, staring at him man to man. The judge had reddish hair going grey; perhaps that explained his freckled, farmer-like skin. His wig wasn't on straight, and he had cut himself in shaving.

Don looked down at Doutelle and listened to the first question. After stumbling over the answer and trying to clear his throat and hearing his voice at first too loud and then too soft, he let go a little and found it all came fairly easily, since he knew the general trend the questions would take. The same story over again. His "indignation and anger" at reading the articles, his "discovery" of Moonraker's identity, his wish to "clear his father's name". Listening to himself, it all sounded depressingly stale, as if the months of waiting had taken the sap out of it.

Wasn't there some less pompous way to describe what he had tried to do than "clear his father's name"? Was he very self-righteous standing up here in a white sheet and a halo, admitting to such laudable and dutiful behaviour? No doubt Mr Lytton, who had a nasty look in his elderly eye, would be able to attend to all that.

"In short, Mr Marlowe, when you wrote these verses, were you actuated by any desire other than to force Mr Shorn into court?"

"None."

"Had you any wish to injure Mr Shorn, either professionally or otherwise?"

"No."

"Were you actuated by personal malice of any sort towards the plaintiff?"

"None at all."

So it went on. Half the barristers in the front didn't seem to be listening. There was an Indian law-student here today in a blue turban. From the witness-box Don was able to see up into the public gallery, the peering faces, the resting elbows, the attentive ears. Not an inch of space upstairs or down. House Full notices. *Booking for the new season begins on November 2. The Queueing System will be in operation.* ... The only gap in the well of the court was between Joanna and Bennie where he had been. Mrs Delaney was two rows behind, almost next to Warner Robinson. And Robert Delaney was here, in the front row of the gallery. He didn't look as if he'd recently backed many winners.

Eleven forty-five before the examination in chief was over. By then, although the worst was still to come, the weakness had left his knees. There was a pause before Mr Lytton got up. Nobody seemed in a hurry. The judge lifted himself an inch or two to change his position, and stared into the middle distance from under suspicious lids. A couple of barristers whispered together. The judge's clerk was sharpening a pencil.

Mr Lytton rose, and stood for a moment winding a piece of pink brief tape on and off his fingers.

"Mr Marlowe, can you tell the court exactly when you left home?"

Don stared at him. "Do you mean as to date?"

"I mean in relation to your own life."

"Well ... from Oxford I went straight into the army, not by choice of course. When I came out I started at the Royal Academy and for about a year I lived at home. Then I went to study in Vienna, and when I came back I didn't go home but went into digs."

"Any reason why you didn't go home?"

"Only that I was studying hard, going to concerts, playing the piano, was in and out at all hours."

"What did your father feel about it?"

"He thought it was a good thing."

"So it would be a considerable number of years, six—eight—ten? since you lived with your father?"

"About eight, I suppose."

"Did you see a lot of him during that time?"

"I'm afraid not a great deal. If one wants to be a musician one unfortunately has to develop a one-track mind. . . . Then, at about the time he retired, I got married."

"Not too much of a one-track mind for that?"

"As you remark."

Mr Lytton kept screwing up his eyes as if dazzled by the witness. But he never really looked at Don; he only spoke in Don's general direction, his grey, pachydermatous face wearing a weary, dusty expression as if too many years of exposing human frailty had left him without illusions and without hope.

"Now in these eight years since you left home, how frequently would you say you saw your father?"

"Well, I was abroad part of the time. I——"

"Omitting the period when you were abroad did you see him, say, twice a week?"

"Oh, no."

"Once a week?"

"Before I was married I went home every Sunday evening. Afterwards, and because he was then living in Midhurst, it wasn't so often as that."

"Once a year?" suggested Mr Lytton.

"About once a month, I suppose, or a little oftener."

"So that you consider you have had every opportunity of observing his behaviour during the last eight years?"

"I don't follow you," said Don, following very well.

"I am wondering how you could consider yourself so certain that none of these statements about your father was true?"

"One doesn't need to live with a man every minute of the day to know his character."

"Every minute of the day is a little different from a few minutes once a month. It is true isn't it that, although you were naturally indignant at reading these articles, you knew nothing really to contradict them from first-hand knowledge?"

"I think that my first-hand knowledge of my father over a great many years was enough."

"You mean you had an opinion which, like anybody else's, could have been right or wrong?"

"That may be how you see it."

"It's really a question of how the jury will see it, Mr Marlowe. . . . Tell me, do you feel you were a dutiful son?"

"How can one answer that?" Don said impatiently. "I would have liked to see more of him. But that wouldn't have been a duty because he was always good company."

"His death came as a shock to you?"

"Naturally. One doesn't expect it at fifty-two."

"Perhaps you had promised yourself that in a few years' time when you were better established you would be able to see more of him again?"

"Yes, I had."

"Where are these questions leading, Mr Lytton?" asked his Lordship.

"I was about to ask the defendant, my Lord, if he felt something of a conscience about having seen so little of his father, now that he was dead."

Mr Justice Alston raised his eyelids to Don. "Well?"

Don said: "No, I don't. It's not, I suppose, unnatural to wish one had done more."

"Well?" said the judge, this time to Mr Lytton.

"You wish you had done more . . . Mr Marlowe, I am asking you to consider this very carefully. I am asking you if you are sure as to the motive behind your attack on Mr Shorn. Is not your desire to clear your father's name rather a window dressing, so to speak, sincerely felt of course but largely a surface indignation?"

"Why do you suppose I am incurring all this unpleasantness, then?"

"Would you answer the question directly, please?"

"What is the question?"

"I am asking you if it is not true that the real motivating force for this quarrel derives on your side from a wish to rid yourself of a sense of guilt because you did not do your duty to your father while he was alive."

Don looked at his fingers but made no reply.

"Well, Mr Marlowe," said the judge at length, "what have you to say to that?"

Don said: "I think it's just damned nonsense, my Lord."

There was a titter in the court. Mr Doutelle gave a convulsive movement of disapproval.

His Lordship looked across the court. "It will not assist your case, Mr Marlowe, if you answer the questions in an improper manner."

"I'm sorry, my Lord. It seemed to me that that one had been put in an improper manner."

"You may think so but it is a matter for me to decide, not you."

"I beg your pardon."

"Would you how try to answer the question?"

Don said to Lytton, "In the first place you use the word 'attack'. My 'attack' on Roger Shorn. If I chase a burglar who has stolen my money, am I attacking him? What's the difference, except that Shorn stole my good name? As for trying to tie it all up in a lot of psychological nonsense, I still think the suggestion, begging your Lordship's pardon, what I called it in the first place. If I could have got some sort of a public withdrawal of what had been said I should have jumped at it, but that was never offered."

Mr Justice Alston looked at Aubrey Lytton. "You seem not only to have been answered, Mr Lytton, but to have provoked a speech for the defence."

Mr Lytton said: "*Please* answer the questions, Mr Marlowe, and confine yourself to them. . . . Now tell me, you say you were not actuated by malice in writing these abusive verses?"

"Not malice, no."

"What would you have done if Mr Shorn had ignored this attack?"

"I should have written something else."

"In other words you would have gone on and on and on?"

"I should have gone on and on and on."

"You intended your writings to be defamatory, yet in your original defence you put forward, among other things, a plea of no libel."

"I'm afraid that's a legal point I don't understand. I want the case to be decided on its broadest aspect."

"In other words, justification?"

"Yes."

"You hope to convince the jury that Mr Shorn is a jackal, a wolf, a coward, a skunk, a liar and a louse?"

"Not literally," said Don.

There was a murmur of laughter.

"You left out the fungus, Mr Lytton," said his Lordship. There was more laughter. During it Roger sat with legs crossed and an expression as if nothing in the present court concerned him.

Mr Lytton impatiently cleared his throat. "Now Mr Marlowe, you say you were on the best of terms with your father during his last years?"

"Yes."

"Would you describe him as a secretive man?"

Don hesitated. "I had always thought of him as very frank."

"Did you meet his friends?"

"Some of them."

"Did you ever meet Mrs Delaney?"

"No."

"Did he tell you about her?"

"Not as far as I can remember."

"Don't you think that rather strange for a frank person?"

"I think he wanted to keep his friendship with her a secret from everyone for the time being."

"Why?"

"I have no idea."

"Don't you think his whole attitude showed that he knew he was getting into dubious company?"

"I have only just met Mrs Delaney; but 'dubious company' is the last way I'd think of describing her."

"Did you ask your father for his reasons when he told you he was going to retire?"

322

"He told me he wanted to devote his whole time to writing."

"How did this explanation strike you?"

"I was surprised. Naturally I accepted it."

"If you were surprised, it's not unnatural, therefore, is it that other people should have been surprised, and perhaps not have accepted it quite so easily?"

At the time the litigants were snatching a hasty lunch in order to be back in court for two o'clock, Michael was eating his midday snack and reading the report in *The Times* of yesterday's hearing.

Not that he had any need for hurry. His greatest enemy was time.

Number 10 Wornington Place was at the end of a row of late Victorian houses in a cul-de-sac backing on to the railway. Michael had a room on the top floor. In the basement were two West Indian families, each family paying £2 10s 0d. a week for their room and a share of the coal-house. The front windows of the basement were boarded up but they had windows at the back and electric light and water. (Sometimes too much water because there was a crack in the drainage in the house and it seeped down an inner wall.) On the ground floor was a white labourer who had a wife and three children for his two rooms but no furniture except some old sofas. They slept on the floor and ate off soap boxes. His wages were ten pounds a week and he paid fifteen shillings a week for the rooms, to the infinite chagrin of the owner, who couldn't get them out. A room on the first floor was rented by a Welsh harmonica player who earned something in the pubs on a Saturday night and by running errands for the two Central European girls who shared a room on his floor and occasionally, it seemed, customers. It was he who had given Michael all his information.

The other room on the first floor was in the possession of the owner, a Jamaican and his wife and two children. Four years ago he had bought the house for £3,000 on a ten year lease. By sub-letting he had already paid for the house and could now live off it without working and run a smart second hand Chevrolet. On this floor also was the one bathroom-lavatory, which the Central European girls used as a kitchen.

On the top floor in the two rooms at the front were four coloured men. Three of them went out to work and made good money and were the most respectable people in the house. The fourth wouldn't work and sat at the window all day looking out. He got £2 a week National Assistance and paid 35s. a week rent. The other 5s. he spent on rice, on which he lived.

Michael's room looked out at the back over the great railway tracks to the west. A last-minute liberality had inspired the builder of the houses to give longer windows and window-boxes to these upper rooms, so it was possible to get a good deal of air. The window of the next house was only a few feet away and he often heard the woman first thing in the morning and could have reached the clothes she hung out to dry.

Fresh air was a thing he needed, because the whole house stank of a dank musty odour he had never smelt before. At first he thought it was the drains; but when night fell and he lay down on the iron bed to sleep he found out. He killed half a dozen bugs before falling asleep, and woke badly bitten to spend the hours until dawn starting up every time a little hard plop told him one had fallen from the ceiling on to the bed.

In the morning they were all gone, except those he had killed staining the sheet and the wall, but he began a search of the room and presently prised away a piece of the skirting board, where they clustered in a mass like a brown varnished plank.

That was how he came so quickly to know the Welshman. Rhys good-humouredly lent a hand, telling Michael that anyway he was wasting his time; but Michael gave him a couple of pounds and sent him out for D.D.T. and a hammer and a chisel and some nails. Then he took off all the skirting boards and sprayed and dusted behind them. The landlord, a big shiny man in a check suit, came up to complain, but Michael said he was improving the property.

Between times Michael sat by the window and watched the trains. They were his only escape from himself. Accelerating off on their long journeys, they hammered out every time they went past that if, when his leg was quite better, he could jump one a bit further down the line he would be two or three hundred miles from London by daybreak. It was the thing to do, after he had seen Bennie.

But he couldn't go without seeing her first. He had to know how she felt, whether she was still able to care something for him. If she did, then anything was possible, even to giving himself up.

Over and over in his mind went the bitter regrets. It was of his own choice that he had gone on. He had run into all this by little more than a week. If only Roger had seen him before the robbery and told him what he had to tell him. . . .

He bought three papers every day, and every day he searched them for news of Peter Waldo; but he had missed the day after the arrest was made, and probably his case hadn't yet come up.

The wound was healed and he no longer wore a bandage, but he still found it painful to put full weight on the leg, so that he still limped, and sometimes the muscles would have a spasm of cramp. Always in the morning it was hard to get them moving.

When he had finished reading through the account of the libel action for the second time Michael let the paper drop and rolled up his empty fish and chip papers into a ball. He finished his bottle of beer and stood up. Four hours of daylight yet, with nothing to do but read through the papers and magazines strewn about the bed or on the table. Then darkness and an hour or two out. After that a climb up the stairs to this barren room and two hours to kill before bed.

As he recovered his health the old restlessness came back, but with a stronger sense of drive and direction. He must get out of here and he must begin again—really from the start. He wanted that. Would the police, knowing of the connection, be watching Bennie's flat? He couldn't bear not to know what she thought. He couldn't bear to wait to know. Sometimes he banged his head on the pillow in the night to stop his thoughts going on.

Chapter Thirty-Two

Don was conscious that his own appearance in the box had not been the finished performance that Roger's had been. Nerves had made him stumble and hesitate too often. But the battle was now about to be joined in earnest. The witness who followed him was a tall thin young man of about thirty.

"You are Mr Taylor Hutton, barrister-at-law, of 44 King's Bench Walk?"

The witness said he was.

"Were you at the Borough Sessions at Cheltenham on the 1st October, 1956?. ... Did you appear for the defence, in a case brought by the Crown against a Mr Salem Levitski, before Sir John Marlowe, sitting as Recorder of Cheltenham?. ... Will you tell the court what happened?"

"I appeared for Levitski who was charged with obtaining money by false pretences. He was accused of having defrauded a bank. You—er—wish me to go into details?"

"Briefly, if you can."

"Levitski had a number of businesses standing in the name of various nominees; and by juggling with cheques drawn on his nominees' banking accounts he was able to finance a series of speculative deals, without having much capital behind him. With this sort of system, if one is ingenious enough, large sums of credit can be built up and manipulated on a modest outlay. Then, if a particular gamble in commodities comes off, the gambler has made money and no one has lost any?"

"I hope you are not recommending it, Mr Hutton," said the judge.

"No, my Lord. But in this particular case, on July 12, when the whole edifice was about to collapse, Levitski presented further cheques, themselves worthless, drawn on one of these accounts, and managed to obtain cash for them. Then he quickly paid all the proceeds—together with considerable monies of his own—into another nominee's account, so that earlier cheques which were in course of collection by the bank and which otherwise would have been valueless were met in full. He was charged—mistakenly I still think—*only* in respect of his transactions of July 12, and when the prosecution closed its case I submitted that no case had been made out, because the bank was actually much better off after this final transaction—indeed that there could be no intent to defraud on *this* occasion as the intention was to benefit the bank. It was never disputed that the bank was not injured by the defendant's actions of July 12. I had not had an opportunity of looking closely at the authorities beforehand, but the point seemed a good one to me; and I argued it on general principles."

"Yes, Mr Hutton. And then?"

"Well, my Lord, the prosecution were taken rather by surprise, I think, but we had some legal argument, and then the learned Recorder upheld my submission and directed the jury to find the prisoner not guilty."

"It looks a very arguable point," said the judge, getting really interested at last. "I remember being in court myself when R. v. Pickup was decided many years ago. But there's a later case. . . ."

"Yes, my Lord, I——"

Mr Doutelle cleared his throat. "And what happened then, Mr Hutton? Did you ever see Sir John afterwards?"

"I met him two weeks later here in the Law Courts. He stopped and told me how distressed he was at the ruling he had made which he said was inconsistent with R. v. Kritz 1949, which——"

"Yes, that was the one I was trying to remember," said Mr Justice Alston.

"I tried to reassure Sir John," said the young barrister. "It was presumptuous of me to do so, but I had talked it over with several of my colleagues and some of them had felt that the prosecution was at fault in preferring the wrong charge. Besides Sir John had had to decide without having the cases in front of him. But he appeared unconvinced and seemed to blame himself. It was shortly after that that I heard of his retirement."

"Did you connect his retirement in any way with this case?"

"No, it never entered my head to do so. Judges—with every respect, my Lord—often . . . that is, sometimes. . . ." He hesitated.

"Err?" suggested his Lordship.

"I was going to say, my Lord, have their judgements reversed in the Court of Appeal."

"Except that there is no appeal against an acquittal."

"No, my Lord."

"Go on, Mr Doutelle."

"One final question," said Mr Doutelle. "Will you think very carefully, Mr Hutton, and tell the court whether at any time during this case, Salem Levitski was ever referred to under his assumed name of Stanley Salem?"

"No, he definitely was not."

"Why are you so sure?"

"Because on the following day when I read my paper I was surprised to see a short column referring to his acquittal and calling him Salem levitski, alias Stanley Salem."

"Thank you, Mr Hutton."

Lytton asked only three questions.

"Stanley Salem was a well-known name In 1956, wasn't it, Mr Hutton?"

"Yes, I suppose it was—in certain circles."

"Do you think the police were making a very good job of it if they didn't discover their prisoner's alias?"

"I think they slipped up."

"Do you seriously ask us to believe that *everyone* slipped up—that the name of Stanley Salem—if not actually mentioned—was not 'known' at the trial, even by his own solicitor, even by the learned Recorder?"

"I have no idea what his solicitor knew. I only know that the following day it came as a complete surprise to me."

The next witness was a brisk elderly man who had not been in court more than half an hour when he was called.

"You are Arthur Horace Lippmann and you are a Doctor of Medicine and a Fellow of the Royal College of Physicians? You practise at 210 Harley Street?"

"Yes."

"Can you tell us about one of your patients who visited you on the 28th September, 1956?"

"Yes. An appointment was made a week previously by Sir John Marlowe's secretary, and Sir John came to see me at 10 a.m. on the Monday. He complained of some discomfort and pain in the chest but he said he had not been to see his local physician. I examined him and found that he had an aortic lesion, probably resulting from the rheumatic fever he had suffered as a child."

"What did you tell him?"

"He was so clearly a man of intellect and courage that I could only tell him the truth. Namely that he was unlikely to live longer than two or three years, and only that if he lived a quiet and retired life."

"What was his reaction?"

"He was naturally upset. But after a while philosophical. He told me that he had had great plans for the future, now he would have to revise them. He thanked me, as if I had done him a favour, and prepared to leave. As he was going he asked me not to tell anyone of his visit. Of course it was an unnecessary request, but I remember he said, 'Pity, I hope, is something I shall never have to ask for'."

"Did you ever see him again?"

"Yes. Twelve months later he called again. There was very little change. I think perhaps he had hoped for some miracle."

"Thank you, Dr Lippmann."

The judge looked at Mr Lytton who half rose and with a resigned expression shook his head.

"Mrs Narissa Delaney."

She looked tall and continental in her black suit with the flowered toque, the elegant gloves. She walked to the witness-box and took the oath in a composed undertone. The judge looking at her with interest. Here, so clearly, was the lady in the woodpile. Was this Sir John's bit of stuff? If so, his taste was not to be derided.

"You are Mrs Narissa Delaney, and you live at Chatterton House, Hurtmore Road, Godalming?"

"Yes."

"Will you kindly tell the court when you first met Sir John Marlowe?"

"It was in January, three years ago. I was petitioning for divorce. When my husband decided to contest the case, my solicitor, Mr Mills, advised that we should retain a Q.C. to lead the junior who had first been engaged. I met Sir John two or three times in February during the hearing of the case, and after it was over I called on him to thank him. A little later he wrote inviting me to a small dinner-party at his house."

"Did you at any tune during the hearing of the case see him without your solicitor being present?"

"I never saw him privately at all until I called to thank him two weeks alter the case was over. A friendship then sprang up."

"What do you mean by a friendship?" asked his Lordship.

"He came several times to week-end parties at my house, my Lord. We saw each other sometimes in London. We fell in love." Mrs Delaney made the statement casually, as it were dropped the comment into court. "But because my divorce was not absolute, he insisted that we should be circumspect. He warned me that I might be spied upon by someone called the Queen's. Provost——"

"Proctor. Yes, go on."

"That letter," she said with contempt. "That letter that was read out in court. It is of no concern to me how it is interpreted here, but in fact it was meant innocently enough. It was after a week-end we had spent together as guests at the home of some friends of mine whose name I will give if you need it. For me knowing John *was* the beginning of a new life. I saw no reason why I should not tell him so."

"Quite," said Mr Doutelle. "And after the divorce was made absolute?"

"In view of his position and the way we had first met, John thought it a little early to marry right away. So we planned to announce our engagement in October and be married the following January. We had a private engagement party in May."

"And then?"

"In September, John was unwell. He went to the doctor you have just heard, who told him that he could not live." She made a gesture. "That was the end of my new life."

"You did not marry?"

She put one glove over the edge of the box. "That was something in his nature—I cannot explain—a pathological dislike of being ill, a dislike of being pitied. Of course I wished to marry him. If we had only two years, then we should spend 'binding me to a dying man.' We argued long but I could not move him. At the same time he must have decided he would keep his illness a secret even from his own children."

"Why?"

"For one thing, his son had just himself become engaged and was to be married in the November. John did not wish to cast a cloud on him at that time. But of course it was much more than that. He carried his pride and independence to extreme limits. He loathed the thought that it might get into the paper. Also, I think he had a superstitious hope—strange in him—that if no one knew it might not become quite so true. If everyone was aware of his condition, everyone would be waiting for him to die. If no one knew, he could half delude himself that he had retired voluntarily to write his book, that he was perfectly well, within limits, and could forget his disease."

"What happened when he retired, Mrs Delaney? Did you visit him?"

"As often as he would allow. Once or twice a week. Sometimes I stayed over a week-end. I—did what I could, right up to the end."

There was a pause. The court was stiller than it had been.

"One other thing worried him," she said, "and that was that the newspapers took hold of his retirement and made it seem an act of self-sacrifice. The rich barrister giving up fame and fortune to devote his time to other things. That was something, when he decided to keep his ill-health secret, that he had never anticipated at all. It worried him, for he said he felt a hypocrite because of this unwanted prestige he had gained. That was why he was abrupt with people who spoke to him in that strain, that was why in the end he began to tell people his retirement was not voluntary. It was not to start a slander campaign against himself or to imply that he had been asked to retire: it was simply that he was trying to correct a wrong impression."

"Did you see much of Sir John during the period he was writing *Crossroads*?"

"Of course. All through. I read the page proofs for him and helped him often with corrections."

"Did you know of the quarrel with the Reverend George Chislehurst?"

"Oh, yes. Of course. John talked to me about all that."

"Will you tell us what happened, so far as you know it?"

"Sir John and Mr Chislehurst had been close friends for several years. They were first attracted by their common interest in philosophy, and John thought very much of Chislehurst's book. They would discuss the subject long into the night, often after he had been in court all day. They saw many of the problems of life from different sides, and sometimes disagreed about the solution. But always it was friendly until John published his book." She took off her other glove and folded it beside the first. A square-cut diamond winked in the dull light. "John told his friend of his intention to write that book. They talked of it much together. They agreed together that Sir John should make use of certain material in two chapters of Mr Chislehurst's book and that he should make acknowledgement of his debt in a foreword. Unknown to Mr Chislehurst, Sir John also dedicated the book to him. The book was finished and set up in page proofs, and in this form John sent a copy to his friend. He was—staggered by the reply. Mr Chislehurst was a clergyman and saw the universe through Christian eyes ... John—Sir John Marlowe—did not."

"Could you explain that, Mrs Delaney?"

"I do not mean that he was without—any religion. You might call him perhaps a reverent agnostic. . . . Now this Mr Chislehurst knew, this he had known all along; but for some reason he expected John's book to reach the same—same conclusions as his own. It did not. He flared up, and no apology, no explanation would do. I have saved the letters—and copies of two of John's letters which I typed myself. Perhaps. . . ." She hesitated.

Mr Doutelle produced a bundle of letters and copies were again passed up.

"These have been disclosed?" said His Lordship.

"Yes, my Lord, and the appropriate notices have been given."

"The first," said Mrs Delaney, "is the one that Mr Chislehurst wrote after receiving the page proofs."

Doutelle read: "'Dear John Marlowe, I have read the proofs of your book and have to say at once that I am astonished and *deeply distressed* at what I found there, at the use you have made of the material we agreed you should take from my book *Man and the Future*. Certainly the premises are much the same, but your reasoning from them is *entirely humanist* in origin and not Christian, as mine was. If you do not believe, fundamentally, in a Christian God then you are turning the most precious possession in man's heritage to unworthy ends.'" Doutelle looked up. "There follows two pages of argument, my Lord, and then the last page reads: 'In conclusion I can only ask you to do two things. First, take out the passages which in any way derive from my work. Second, expunge my name from among your acknowledgements and remove the dedication. I would have no part in any false credit which may come to you as a result of this unworthy publication.'"

Counsel put the letter down. "Next is a copy of the reply that Mrs Delaney typed for Sir John." He read:

"My dear George, I am very upset that you should so much dislike this book. I did not know that I had ever pretended to be anything other than I am—though I suppose from your letter we must to some extent have misunderstood each other. I don't *disbelieve* in God. I just don't know. One leaves open the possibility of the

Christian revelation being true. But as far as I see now, there are various manifestation of the truth, and it is our job to make the imaginative effort to comprehend them all. Haven't we argued about that often enough? Anyway, it's from that general standpoint, and with a good deal of thought for man's moral and ethical welfare, that I have tackled this book.

"Believe me, I'm very distressed at this misunderstanding. I'll do what I can to meet you, but it's really too late to make the alterations you want. Anyway, even if the two chapters were re-drafted the result would not be notably different. Of course I can take out the dedication and the acknowledgement. But I wish you would change your mind, old friend, and let them stay. Our many arguments were always a tremendous stimulus to me. I had hoped they would continue. Why not think it over for a day or two? I'll do anything reasonable to please you. But time is short. It is particularly short for me. I can't delay publication now. Your sincere friend, John Marlowe."

In a pause after counsel had finished reading, Mrs Delaney said: "The letter that was read out in court on Friday was Mr Chislehurst's reply to this letter."

Mr Doutelle went on to read four further letters, but they did not greatly advance the point that had already been made.

When he had finished he said: "Mrs Delaney, did you ever meet the Reverend George Chislehurst?"

"Oh, yes. Quite often for a few months."

"What was your impression of him?"

"That he was a man with very strong but rather narrow views—like his sister who gave evidence here yesterday. He was a clever man but dogmatic."

"So far as you know, did Mr Chislehurst expect to gain financially from the publication of Sir John's book?"

"Oh, no. Long before its publication John told him that all proceeds from the book would go to charity and Mr Chislehurst was entirely in agreement."

"Was Sir John a wealthy man?"

"Before he retired he had a very big income. He repeatedly offered to help Mr Chislehurst, but Mr Chislehurst, apart from the hundred pounds he accepted at the beginning, would take nothing. After Sir John retired of course he was quite short of money and could barely make ends meet."

"Now, Mrs Delaney, will you tell us if you knew Salem Levitski?"

"Yes, I did. My husband and I always knew him as Stanley Salem—though we knew his real name was Levitski."

"If you spoke of him, how did you refer to him?"

"Always as Stanley Salem."

"Did Sir John Marlowe meet him at your house?"

"Certainly not. Salem was my husband's friend, not mine. After my divorce I was very glad to see the last of him. I never invited him to my house and Sir John never met him."

"Might he have met him outside?"

"It seems unlikely. I saw John one evening during that first week in October and he was looking ill. I asked him what was the matter, and he said he was annoyed with himself and irritated at a mistake he had made during the Borough Sessions. And he added that what made it worse was that it had been to the benefit of a former friend of mine, whom he hadn't recognised under his real name of Levitski."

"And then?"

"I told him that I thought he was making too much of it. But he said it was no business of a judge's to preside unless he had an unpreoccupied mind. Of course I had no idea then that only three days before he tried this case he had been told he was going to die."

"Did he not tell you immediately of his visit to the doctor?" asked the judge.

"No, my Lord, he didn't tell me for some weeks after that."

"Mrs Delaney," said Mr Doutelle; "do you know of any reason for Sir John Marlowe wishing to favour Stanley Salem on your behalf?"

"None. None whatever."

By now it was well after four. Doutelle glanced hastily at the clock and said: "Returning to the question of these letters you have produced. How did they come into your possession?"

"Some I had before Sir John died. My own letters to him I took possession of afterwards."

"Where did you get them?"

"From his house. I had a key. His son was away, and his daughter and daughter-in-law had left everything undisturbed. After his death I used to go down sometimes for an hour or so. It gave me some comfort to be in the house again. I took some letters and some manuscripts and personal papers then."

"You have heard the plaintiff say how he got possession of these two letters he read to the court. Do you have anything to say about that?"

"What he said is not true."

The judge lowered his pen. "You think it is not true of or you know it is not true?"

"I know it is not true. Although he may have been untidy. John would never have allowed a letter of mine to be among his professional papers."

The judge said: "That may be a reasonable supposition, but surely it is only a supposition."

"Have you any other reason for thinking this?" asked Mr Doutelle.

Mr Lytton rose with an injured air and said: "My Lord, in view of your earlier rulings, I can only formally object to this line of questioning."

The judge nodded and, fingers on bottom lip, looked at Mrs Delaney who was hesitating for the first time since she entered the box.

"A considerable number of letters disappeared at one time," she said.

"What letters?" Doutelle prompted.

"Oh, some dozen letters in a box. These two that Mr Shorn produced were among them."

"Have you any explanation of how they came to disappear?"

"Mr Shorn made his way into the house on a pretext and took them."

"How do you know this?"

"I saw him there."

"Was that before or after Sir John's death?"

"After. Two months after."

"Thank you, Mrs Delaney."

As the court rose Don whispered: "Can you take Bennie back to tea. I'll join you later."

"Where are you going to do?"

He smiled and patted her wrist. "I've got to see someone."

The figure of the last witness walked ahead of them along the stone passages to the main staircase and the hall. As people fanned our Don followed Mrs Delaney but made no attempt to catch up with her. She came out of the Law Courts, crossed the street and walked west. At Waterloo Bridge she was held up by the traffic lights, and he kept his distance until the lights changed. As she turned in at the Savoy Hotel two reporters attempted to speak to her but she would have nothing to do with them.

She went into the lobby of the hotel, and he thought she was going to her room, but after some hesitation she walked right through and came out on the Embankment side. The commissionaire asked her if she wanted a taxi but she shook her head. She crossed to the Embankment and took out a cigarette. Don came up with her then and flicked open his lighter.

She started very slightly, then nodded and bent her head to the flame. "Thank you."

He said: "I suppose technically you're not supposed to discuss the case."

"So the judge said."

"When I heard you in the witness-box this afternoon I was sorry I had forced the issue."

"Why."

"It seemed a bad business to have intruded on you."

"On the other hand," she said, "when I came to give evidence I was glad your wife had found me.'

337

"As I said to you the other evening, all this has made me feel as if I hardly knew Dad the way I ought to have done."

"Does any son ever know is father, or father his son? In rare cases perhaps and then it is very fine. But often, so often, not."

"We never quarreled."

"Oh, no, I am not saying that. He always spoke of you—and your sister—with great affection."

They stood looking over the Thames. Don said: "He was so wrong not to marry you! I still don't understand that. If you only have two years, why lose two years?"

She smiled slightly. "When you were giving evidence this morning I thought how much like him you were, the same flashes of humour, the same impatience—only you at present are less tolerant—the same ability to gain people's liking without seeking to. That is really why I am glad now I came forward. But I am not sure, if it came to the point, you would not act exactly as he did. Would you marry someone, desiring them and yet knowing that if you took them you might die in the act of love? Would you marry someone offering them only the prospect of caring for your invalidism, when you expected to offer them a full and happy life?"

Don said after a minute: "I don't know."

"Of course I agree with you. I did everything to persuade him. But that was how he was. Perhaps all of us are in some degree the poorer for pride."

"When this is over," he said. "I hope you'll—continue the friendship with us all."

She inclined her head again. "I shall be glad to."

A tug hooted as it slid through the water. Don said: "I was interested to know that Roger Shorn had come by those letters in some different way from what he claimed."

"Yes," she said, but did not go on.

"How did you come to see him at the cottage?"

"Mr Marlowe, do you know, whether it is proper or improper to do so, I would rather not say. I would have greatly preferred to say nothing of it in court, but foolishly I allowed mention of it to slip out and your solicitor was most insistent then that I should give evidence on it."

"Why."

"He said it could be of vital importance. So I said that I would go as far as I wanted and no further,"

"I don't know if you'll be pressed for more detail tomorrow."

"Mr Whitehouse said he thought if Roger Shorn had a conscience about it he would tell his counsel not to pursue the matter. If he does I shall say what I wish to say and no more."

As Joanna and Bennie got back to the house Bennie said: "Ever since last week when Don had his interview with Mrs Delaney I've felt pretty sick about it. Why didn't Dad *tell* us? I could very well have given up my job and gone home to look after him—and would have done willingly. He knew I would. I left home in the first place partly because I felt he didn't need me. I was doing nothing there. He was always so busy and so smiling and so self-reliant, working all day and half the night, taking a case in Bristol and then one in Birmingham and then rushing back for a Court of Appeal in London, and so on. I hardly *saw* him."

"Perhaps that's why, when things went wrong, he felt he couldn't claim you back."

"But he only had to *say*. I can't bear to think of him sitting in that cottage for two years waiting for death."

"He didn't. Give him credit for that."

When don came in Bennie was telephoning, and Joanna stood a moment in the shadows watching him. But she could tell from his expression that he still didn't know.

They talked over the case for a few minutes, and then Joanna said: "I don't think I can go through with that play tomorrow, Don. It means I shall be away from the court most of the day."

"Well, there's not much to come, except the two counsels' speeches and the judge's summing up."

"And a trifling matter of the verdict."

"Ah, yes. The young man feels his pockets and wonders what's to pay."

'I don't think he'll have to pay."

"It depends." In spite of all the evidence today, he suspected that the impression Roger had made still lingered with the jury. How far was personality going to count with then in a case of this sort?

"I'd rather drop out of the play. They can get someone else. They'd have to if I were ill."

"But you're not. There's such a thing as breach of contract Anyway, thank Heaven the thing isn't running into Thursday. The concert in Edinburgh would have been a nightmare if it had."

"You'd have gone?"

"What else could I have done? That's why I feel you must carry on tomorrow."

"Yes," she said, "we must all carry on tomorrow."

"What is it, darling? What are you afraid of?"

"Nothing," she said, smiling now but smiling past him as if he were no longer part of her life.

It was the second time Bennie had phoned Marlborough House today. It was Sister Frey's day off but she got in touch with one of the probationers who at lunch time was able to tell her that there was no message for her from any of the inmates. The same answer now.

After she had hung up she stayed about an hour with Don and Joanna but would not stop to supper. She couldn't settle in company, theirs or anyone's. Even Pat's would be irksome and Pat was at home tonight. She felt lost, desolated, spent as if nothing in life she had ever done had been worth a damn, as if all the things she had not done were all that had ever been worth while. She should have been closer to her father instead of going off on her own, so that he would automatically have told her of his illness as he had automatically told Narissa Delaney—a woman who had come from nowhere and gained his confidence and love in a few months And she should have married Michael when he asked her in May, instead of hanging back like something out of Jane Austen. If they had been married none of this would have happened, none of this second and even worse failure. None of it.

She began to wait east, turned, into the Park and made across it in the direction of Marble Arch. It was a fine evening, but the sunset had been watery.

Half-way across the Park she thought she was being followed. There were a lot of people about as the rush hour wasn't yet over, but most of them were crossing in the opposite direction, taking short cuts from their offices. The rumble of the traffic down Park Lane was like trains going over distant bridges. All around the sky was pink with reflected light; only here and there was there darkness in the shadow of great trees.

She stopped under one of them and waited. A man sauntered nearer, but there was a fork in the path and he chose the opposite fork. She watched him go until his figure disappeared among other figures.

She walked down Oxford Street, again seeming to push against a tide of people coming the opposite way. Once she stopped at a window when there was a good reflection, but there was no sign of anyone with an interest in her. She walked as far as Oxford Circus and turned up towards Langham Place. In Portland Place she began to look at numbers.

Peter's flat was in a big block with an attendant in an office in the vestibule, but she saw Waldo among the names on the second floor and walked up. She found the door and pressed the bell.

No answer. Difficult to tell if there was any light. She knocked. No answer. She pressed the bell again.

A door opened suddenly behind her.

A bony middle-aged man with bright black eyes and a pipe. "Can I help you?"

"I was looking for Mr Waldo."

"I'm afraid you won't find him. Down, Pollie. Stop it, old girl." He pushed a dog back with his foot and half closed the door. His eyes looked her over. "He's had an accident. He's in Middlesex Hospital."

"Oh. . . . I didn't know. I'm sorry."

"Well, a sort of accident. The police came and told the concierge. Apparently he was beaten up."

"Beaten up? Peter Waldo—"

"Nobody seems to know quite what happened. Some children found him lying on Clapham Common." The man took his pipe out of his mouth. "You a relative of his?"

"No. Just a friend."

"Well, he's in Middlesex Hospital with a broken rib and multiple injuries to his face and head. They say he'll probably be all right but he's not to see visitors yet."

"I . . . thank you. When did it happen?"

"Must have been last Wednesday or Thursday. That's his bitch I'm keeping in. Heard her whining and scratching when I got in from the B.B.C. on Thursday evening. Poor little beggar was starving. So she's been with me ever since. Shall you be going to see him?"

"I—may be."

"I shall go as soon as he's on the visiting list. I only thought if you saw him first to let him know his dog's all right."

"Thank you very much," said Bennie. "I'll do that."

She went back down the stairs.

Chapter Thirty-Three

Wednesday was wet. A south wind brought fine misty rain hanging indecisively over the city, which stirred like as animal waking in its own steam. Buses splashed through the glittering pools. As the baritone bell of Big Ben struck nine, congeries of umbrellas like a mass of insects newly hatched were crawling across the bridges and down the main streets. A smudge of smoke from a barge on the river drifted undispersed; seagulls rose above it flapping their; wings and crying.

Roger found a letter in his post He turned to the end and saw it was signed "P. Laycock.".

Dear Mr Shorn,

I have listened to the evidence at your libel action for three days, but have another engagement for tomorrow. I think tomorrow will be the end, and I am writing to you before then, so that it shall not seem I am being influenced this way or the other by any verdict the jury may bring in.

It is a bad thing, I think, for one man to sit in judgement on another's actions, and I'm the last person to want to do anything like that. But, all the same, all appointments are to some extent a matter of judgement—evaluation as you might say—and after looking at the matter very carefully over the last three days I have come to the reluctant conclusion that you are not a man I would be happy to see in the editorial chair of *The Globe, The Globe* being the sort of newspaper that it is. I will say no more about the action than that, for it is not my business to do so.

As however all my plans for putting money in *The Globe* were based on a reorganisation of the newspaper of your devising and in the expectation that you would be there as managing editor to carry it through, I have notified the Manders that I am not going ahead with the scheme; though I should be willing to think over a greatly modified scheme set out by Mr Burnett.

If you would like to tell me what value you put on your services as adviser to me during the last few months I shall be glad to pay you.

I am sorry about this.

Yours sincerely,

P. Laycock.

Roger finished his breakfast and had a word or two with Mrs Smith before he left. Out in the street there was the usual wet-day scarcity of taxis. He raised his hand to three before he saw they were engaged.

As he stood there he was taken by a sudden rather frightening feeling that because of the letter his position had been completely changed, that there had been a sudden divesting of regalia, as if he was appearing in plain clothes for the first time after a long term of authority and office. Unknown to himself, too much in his mind had come to conglutinate around the Laycock agreement. Now he was cut off—as if no longer the well-established, often-quoted, prosperous Roger Shorn but the man of earlier years, unknown and unregarded. The feeling didn't make sense, because the letter took from him nothing he at present had; but he couldn't escape it. Fifteen years of prosperity was a skin which had suddenly rubbed raw.

When he got to the Central Hall of the Law Courts he found Mr Cobb, his solicitor, in conversation with Aubrey Lytton, who was winding his bit of brief tape and talking earnestly.

"Oh, good morning, Mr Shorn," said Cobb. "We were discussing the evidence given by Mrs Delaney yesterday afternoon."

"Yes?" said Roger, not encouragingly. He thought Cobb a weakling.

Lytton said: "It will be a bad thing for its effect on the jury if we allow her evidence about the letters to remain unshaken."

"Perhaps you can shake it, then."

"I was hoping to have your guidance. Unless I know where I stand there's always the danger of probing too far and getting the answer one doesn't want."

Roger shook out his umbrella and propped it against the wall. The felling of failure was still strong in him. Yet the winning or losing of this action was no less important because of what he had already lost. In fact, from some personal compulsion of his own it now seemed that he could no longer afford a second failure.

"Of course what she says is untrue."

"You mean that she didn't see you at the cottage?"

"I was there on one occasion after Marlowe's death, but that was nothing more than a casual call and had nothing to do with the letters."

"Can you tell us about it?"

Two brightly-dressed women went past. One said: "But Charles swore he never even *saw* the marks on her neck while they were living together!"

Roger said quietly: "It was in February. I had been spending the week-end with some people in Brighton. Mrs Marlowe was there—young Marlowe's wife—and I drove her back to London on the Sunday afternoon. On the way she suggested we should call at Sir John's cottage because she wanted to pick up a few things there to take back to London. We called there. She found the things and went on. That's all."

"Did you go in yourself."

"Oh, yes, we stayed a couple of hours. I can only suppose this Delaney woman was in the garden. Mrs Marlowe thought at the time that she saw someone."

Mr Lytton looked at his fingernails and blew on them gently. He didn't look at Roger. "I wish, of course, that we'd known of this before, but still ... now that we do ... I don't *think* it will be necessary to recall you. We—er—want to cast doubts on this witness's evidence on as many points as we can, but we shall have to tread delicately. She's a very different person from what I had hoped."

Roger saw Marion come in at the big doors and pause looking about her.

He said: "I didn't mention it before because I didn't want to involve myself in any scandal with Mrs Marlowe, or her with me."

Now that he had said it in so many words Lytton looked at him. "That is another reason why we must tread delicately. But, provided you—er—provided we have all facts, there is no need to leave that inference. You were then on friendly terms with the family. It was not unnatural to call at the Cottage."

Marion had still not seen them. She was short-sighted, and Roger realised that in a few years she would have to wear spectacles.

He said: "One never knows what a jury will think natural or unnatural."

"Quite."

Mr Cobb looked at his watch. "We'd better be moving."

Roger said: "I've no particular wish to have my name linked with Mrs Marlowe's in any way, but the winning of this case is more important to me now than it was even a week ago. I think I'll have to give you freedom to use your discretion."

"Quite," said Lytton, screwing up his eyes. "Very well, we'll do what we can."

"I'll meet you in court," said Roger, and advanced towards Marion with a warm and disarming smile.

Mrs Delaney today was in a black and white silk suit, with a black Baku straw hat. As she went into the witness-box, her eyes briefly met Don's; she gave him the faintest of smiles and looked for Joanna. But Joanna was at Wood Green.

Mr Lytton got up looking tired and elderly, as if the night had been too short for him.

"Mrs Delaney, were you Sir John Marlowe's mistress?"

She looked at her questioner with dignified contempt. "Yes."

346

Although this was the answer he wanted, it seemed to put him off his stroke, as if he had expected to have to trap her into the admission. He was several seconds looking at his brief.

"Are you telling the court that your divorce should never have been made absolute because of your misconduct with the man who represented you then?"

"I am saying nothing of the sort. I did not become Sir John's mistress until May, 1956. Then it continued four months until he was ill."

"Mrs Delaney, I see that you obtained your divorce on the 14th February. And you say you called to see Sir John to thank him for his efforts on your behalf two weeks later. That would be the 28th February?"

"About that. I am not sure as to the day."

"You are not sure as to the day. But it would be about the 28th?"

"Yes."

"Not more than, say, two or three days either side?"

"Not more than that."

"Yet in the letter from you to Sir John produced in this court on Friday, beginning 'Darling John' and telling him that knowing him was like a new life—this letter was dated the 12th March. Correct?"

"If it is on the letter it is right."

"Well, if you will count from the 28th February to the 12th March you will find it is thirteen days, even allowing for Leap Year. Right?"

"Yes. . . ."

"Mrs Delaney, isn't it asking a lot of the court to expect them to believe that in less than a fortnight your relationship with a distinguished barrister ripened from the formal call of practically a stranger, into an intimacy in which you wrote a letter to him beginning 'Darling John'?"

"It may be asking a lot. It happens to be true. I do not know if you appreciate it, Mr Lytton, but it really does not take a very long time to fall in love."

Lytton blinked in her direction. "You were both passionately in love, in fact?"

"I said, we fell in love."

"I don't wish to press you too far, Mrs Delaney, but I put it to you that you were intimate with Sir John Marlowe in January of that year, before your divorce case ever came on."

"That is not true."

Mr Lytton looked at his brief.

"Did you influence Sir John at all in his attitude towards Mr Chislehurst?"

"Certainly not."

"But you must have discussed it together?"

"Of course we discussed it. And Sir John did everything he could to meet Mr Chislehurst's complaints."

"Do you think he really did? In the great honour and publicity that must have come to him in the last eighteen months of his life, did he ever mention Mr Chislehurst's name to the Press?"

"No. Because Mr Chislehurst had forbidden him to do so."

"Did you never suggest to him that sometimes one must break one's undertaking in order to give honour where honour is due?"

"No. When it was clear that the book was going to be such a tremendous success, John wrote again to Mr Chislehurst and asked his permission to include a new preface for the third edition making his position clear. Mr Chislehurst replied that in his view he had had no part in the book."

"Don't you think that after he met you Sir John had very little care or attention to spare for this old clergyman's objections?"

"I do not."

"You would agree that after he met you Sir John moved in a somewhat different society from what he had been used to?"

"I don't understand you."

"I mean a gambling, race-going society unsuitable to a distinguished barrister and potential judge?"

"John mixed in no such society. My husband did. When I left him I left it."

"What about these house-parties you gave? Whom did you invite to them?"

"People I liked."

"People whom you had known when you were still married to Robert Delaney?"

"All my husband's friends were not of one sort. And since we had been living our own lives for some years, I had a number of friends who were not his."

"Was not Stanley Salem a constant visitor at your house in the old days?"

"I can only tell you he was never admitted to my house after my divorce."

"But at the time of the divorce?"

"At the time of the divorce I was living apart from my husband and never saw Salem."

"Did he come to the Divorce Court?"

"I can't remember."

"Why do you suppose, if Salem never knew Sir John, that he should deliberately lie when he came out of prison, saying that he had been discharged by Sir John because of their friendship?"

"It depends how the question was put to him," said Mrs Delaney, glancing at Roger. "But in any case, as you have heard, it was his custom to claim friendship with the great. No doubt he is doing well in South America now on his intimate friendship with the Spanish Royal Family."

"I am only trying to arrive at the truth, Mrs Delaney. I can understand a trickster claiming friendship with the great when he has something to gain. *What had Stanley Salem to gain by telling a lie about a dead man?*"

"I can only repeat what I have said: it depends a great deal on how the question was put to him. There are leading questions in life as well as in court. I do not know what malice may have moved in him."

"Is it true that you lost a great deal of money at the time of the Suez crisis?"

"Yes. Most of my money is in Egypt."

"So that, apart from the bar of his illness, marriage to you would be a much less attractive proposition for Sir John than it had been?"

"That is an offensive suggestion that I don't need to reply to."

"I think, Mr Lytton," said his Lordship, "that the witness has some justification for that answer."

"I beg your Lordship's pardon."

"It is not I whom you have offended."

Counsel did not take the hint. "Mrs Delaney, about the many letters and documents which were in the cottage at the time of Sir John's death, you say that you went through these and took away whatever you chose?"

"I took some letters away which seemed to me personal and private, or letters with which I had been personally concerned."

"Why?"

"They were—a link. They were all I should have left."

"On whose authority did you take the letters?"

"On whose authority? Nobody's but my own."

"Do you know that the property of a deceased person belongs in effect to the legatees?"

Mrs Delaney said: "I have always regarded myself as his next of kin—in everything but name."

"Have you ever offered the relatives or beneficiaries access to these documents which you—appropriated?"

"No."

"Yesterday, Mrs Delaney, you disputed Mr Shorn's account of how two letters came into his possession. Is that so?"

"Yes."

"You dispute it, and furthermore say that at some time after Sir John's death you saw him personally take the letters?"

"I didn't say I saw him taking them. I saw him in the cottage."

"Ah, that's rather different, isn't it When did you see him there?"

Chapter Thirty-Four

Joanna said: *"If I perform what they say I can perform I should have got safely away from here as fast as you bat your eyelid."*

"Ok, indeed; could you indeed?"

"They say I have only to crack a twig, and over the springtime weathercocks, hail and gale———"

"Cloudburst," said the prompt.

Joanna clicked her ringers. *"Cloudburst, hail and gale, whatever you will, come leaping fury foremost."*

"The report may be exaggerated, of course, but where there's smoke. . . ."

Joanna said: *"They also say that I bring back the past; for instance, Helen comes, brushing the maggots from her eyes, and, clearing her throat of several thousand years, she says, 'I loved . . .' but cannot any longer remember names. Sad Helen."* She dried up. "I'm *sorry*. I knew these lines backwards last night."

"We'll break for a few minutes," said Ronnie Graveney, who was producing. "No good over-working the old cells. What was it like, Bert?"

"O.K.," said Bert. "But I don't want Miss Sullivan to turn away as she makes that speech. We're keeping it as a close-up."

Joanna nodded. "All right. I'll remember."

One of the stage hands brought Joanna tea, and she wandered off, script in hand, into the darkness of the auditorium. She went up the stairs to the circle of the one-time theatre and sat under a light trying to read her lines.

Can you be serious? I am Jennet Jourdemayne and I believe in the human mind. Dress rehearsal at three-thirty. Down below there was an argument about a piece of scenery. Lights burned on an empty stage. It looked as gloomy and shoddy and unreal as that, other place. Each was equally a shadow show.

Would there among the millions who stared at her face tonight be anyone able to see behind it into the non-pattern of emotions and impulses and certainties and self-doubts which she knew as herself?

Footsteps behind her. "All right now, dear?" Ronnie Graveney sank into the next seat.

"I'll be all right tonight."

"I'm sure you will. Bad luck they should both be on the same day. I expect your mind's at the Old Bailey."

"The Law Courts."

"Yes. Actually it's quite a break for us—sure to put our audience figures up, and that'll please the sponsors." He added broodingly: "I'll never forget when we did a short thing with old Martha Green. She'd only ten lines to say but her memory box had rusted up about the date of the Crimean War. We had to print the lines on a blackboard and hold them up behind the mike. I thought she was going to ask for her glasses to read 'em!"

"Ronnie," she said. "I'm expecting a phone call at half past one. I expect I can take it in the manager's office?"

"Of course, dear. I'll fix that. Look, would you like time off to phone now? I'm an agreeable little beast."

"I couldn't get through at present, and Don has promised to ring me."

"O.K. . . . What's that?" he shouted at the stage, "Wait a jiffy, I'll be down."

When he had gone she put her cup down and lit a cigarette. Her script opened at another page. *Do you think I can go in gaiety tonight under the threat of tomorrow? If I could sleep——*

Don lunched with Bennie, and with Henry de Courville who turned up suddenly beside them and said he had been in court most of yesterday and today. They discussed the action, or rather Henry talked about it, and someone vaguely owing allegiance to Don's mind and voice observed the courtesies on his behalf. Mr Doutelle had made the closing speech for the defendant and Mr Lytton for the plaintiff. It remained for the judge to sum up. Henry was of the opinion that Don would win handsomely, but Don said Whitehouse was still dubious The Wright-Gladstone action had been almost a walk-over, and yet even after the judge had summed up very one-sidedly in favour of the Gladstones the jury had taken two and a half hours to make up its mind.

About half-way through lunch Don excused himself, saying he had promised to ring Joanna. When he had gone there was an embarrassed silence. Henry said: "It's years since I saw your last, Bennie. D'you remember I came to stay with your father and you were home for the holidays, looking perfectly ravishing even though you were then only in your middle teens?"

Bennie smiled. "Mr Chislehurst was there."

De Courville hesitated. "Don looks pretty upset at the moment. I hope he won't allow all this to get him down."

"I hope not.

"I take it he didn't know Roger had been at the cottage with Joanna in February?"

"I really have no idea."

"My dear, Henry said gently, "I'm not inquiring out of vulgar curiosity. I have Don's well-being very much at heart—both professionally and because he s my friend."

"I'm sorry," Bennie said miserably. "I know that. It's just that I haven't the heart to talk about it."

"I'm sorry too."

Don was coming back.

"I had to ring Joanna," he said to Henry. "I promised to ring her about one-thirty. She's doing a television play. But of course I've told you.

"Don," Henry said, "I was having a chat with the Administrator this morning and he was saying how pleased everyone was with your six-months' season at the Opera House."

"Oh," said Don. "Good."

"As it happened Maria was there at the time, and she said she thought we couldn't afford to lose touch with you now."

Bennie said quickly: "Does that mean——" and stopped.

Henry looked full into her dark eyes and smiled. "It mean simply what it says, that we shan't lose touch with him. There's no appointment going as yet, but we shall certainly use him as a guest conductor as the opportunity arises."

"Don. . . ."

"Yes?"

"Have you been listening?"

"Yes. . . . I'm glad to hear it."

Henry said: "It naturally won't be what you've been doing since May, but it will be something. I thought you'd be pleased to know that your efforts hadn't gone unappreciated."

"Yes. Yes, of course. Thanks for telling me."

Silence fell. Don finished his beer and turned the glass slowly round on the table.

Bennie said: "Is dame Maria's the deciding voice in these things?"

"No. But it's pretty influential."

Another silence. Don pulled back his cuff to look at his watch. "Quarter to. We'll have to be moving."

As they got up Bennie took Don's arm. He smiled at her, looking at her properly for the first time. "When this libel action is over, in a couple of days or so—if it ever is over—we'll celebrate. You, and Henry, and. . . . We'll have a party and celebrate whatever's left to celebrate. Now I think perhaps we'd better get back to see if the judge has made up his mind. . . ."

The court was full of creaks. It seemed that all the benches might have been specially designed to protest at the presence of strangers. So the people at the back had to strain their ears to catch what the judge said. Before he came in his clerk had turned his chair diagonally so that he was facing the jury, and he talked to them in a conversational manner, as if across a fireside.

"All actions for libel," his Lordship was saying, "are actions concerned with reputation; but this case goes further by involving

354

within itself the reputation of a second person, a man no longer living and able to speak on his own behalf. This in fact is a libel action within a libel action, and both parties have—in effect—sought defence in justification.

"The first thing, however, it is necessary for me to tell you is that this action does not succeed or fail by the degrees to which the imputations against Sir John Marlowe succeed or fail. This is an action brought by one man, Roger Shorn against another, Donald Marlowe, who has called him a liar, a coward and a jackal, and a disgrace to his profession. The defence is justification. That means that the defendant says: I am justified in writing this because what I wrote was in substance true. That does not mean that every single word must be true, but it does mean that the gist and substance of the charges made in the verse and the letter, as understood by ordinary people, is true. If you are reasonably satisfied that Roger Shorn has behaved in a way which merits his being called a liar, a coward and a jackal, and a disgrace to his profession, then he can have suffered no damage by being called it, and his action falls to the ground. The law will not permit a man to recover damages for injury to a character which he does not or ought not to possess.

"I very much hope, members of the jury, that you will find it necessary to pronounce upon the reputation of Sir John Marlowe as it has come under examination in this action. You are of course entitled to say anything or nothing according to your estimate of the evidence which has been put before you and you are entitled to disregard anything I may say on the subject. But I will tell you that during the four days of this hearing I have asked myself more than once whether there is another man among us who could have suffered similar calumny after his death and emerged from it all with such unblemished repute?"

Mr Justice Alston did his raising and shifting ritual. "However, I must repeat that this case is *not* decided by whether Sir John Marlowe was utterly guiltless of stealing literary work or whether he was utterly guiltless of unprofessional conduct in his legal career. If this were an action brought by Sir John Marlowe while still alive against Roger shorn, and if Mr Shorn pleaded justification and his statements were shown to be untrue, Mr Shorn would be liable to pay very heavy damages no matter how responsible his motives for writing the articles might be. But that is not the case. It is Sir John Marlowe's son who has called Mr Shorn a liar, a coward, a jackal and a disgrace to his profession. You are asked to decide whether *that* is true. In effect, you are asked to decide whether Mr Shorn, with the data then in his possession, had *reasonable and sufficient grounds for supposing what he did* about Sir John Marlowe. If you consider he had such reasonable and sufficient grounds, and if you consider that he acted in a responsible and conscientious way, then it is to some extent beside the point that he should have been mistaken."

Bennie glanced at Whitehouse and saw him pull his mouth down slightly. The court was very stuffy, and the crowd at one of the doors eddied suddenly as a woman felt faint and had to push her way out. Bennie realised that she had not rung Sister Frey today. She had been too occupied with thinking of Don.

". . . . The act of writing defamatory articles about a man recently dead and unable to defend himself is one which is distasteful to our habit of thought. As a poet has said: 'Vile is the vengeance on the ashes cold And envy base to bark at sleeping fame'. In all this journalist with his great power bears a heavy responsibility to society in maintaining a level of conduct which does not debase or dishonor the already suspect standards of our day. But such a responsibility may at times come into conflict with what he may consider his duty to his paper and his personal ambition to bring off a scoop. When such a conduct takes place, where does his ultimate obligation lie?

"You here come to the crux of the present case. The plaintiff, a journalist of some distinction, discovers what he considers to be facts of a highly defamatory nature about a man recently dead. Is he to conceal them because to publish them is something 'not usually done' in our society? Is it not his duty, as he has stated, to unmask hypocrisy wherever found?"

Mr Justice Alston paused to look suspiciously round the court, to rub his fingers along his bottom lip. "But what are his *other* obligations? They do not end there. What would his attitude have been if the man he was writing about had been alive? Would it not have been to check and counter check his facts with scrupulous care? If he had not done so his paper would have done so, for the law of libel, as I have said, would have protected a living man against reckless and ill-founded charges. Not so with a dead man. Is the obligation therefore any less? Would you not say the facts should be checked with even greater care when the person attacked cannot hit back?

"In this event his son hit back, in the only way open to him. He branded the plaintiff as a liar, a coward, a jackal and a disgrace to his profession. It is for you, members of the jury, to say if you agree with him. I cannot direct you on that. I can only direct you on the issues involved.

"In his book, as you have heard, Sir John has some hard things to say about the Press. 'Tomorrow's Poison' he calls it 'An Oligarchy of third-rate brains'. You may wonder whether certain sections of the Press may have resented this.

"Consider now the phraseology of the articles in which this attack occurs. You may wonder if the style employed is not singularly unsuited to its subject. The plaintiff says that such is the manner expected of him in *The Sunday Gazette*. Yet even if everything he wrote had been proved up to the hilt, does not such a style, you may ask yourselves, seem a grossness, the invective of an anonymous pamphleteer rather than the reasoned statement of a responsible journalist? As for the plaintiff's desire not to lose the friendship of John Marlowe's son, you may ask yourselves what state of mind such an attitude indicates. Is this delicacy—a man fulfilling an unpleasant duty and seeking to limit its effects, or is it hypocrisy, as Mr Doutelle has urged?"

Don stared out through one of the high windows and saw that it was raining. The afternoon was already closing in. He saw one of the jurors trying to swallow a yawn. He didn't wonder. He felt so sick; please let it be over and done. Now at the last the result seemed to mean nothing. He thought, it's an interesting slant on life. Win or lose, I've lost.

". . . . The defence has made a good deal of the manner in which Mr Shorn came by the two letters belonging to Sir John Marlowe. Here there is a conflict of evidence. Mr Shorn states positively that he received them from a colleague who received them in mistake from Sir John Marlowe himself. Mrs Delaney states just as positively that he could not have done so for she saw them in the cottage six weeks after Sir John Marlowe's death. The plaintiff has not called this fellow journalist to corroborate his story; but neither has the defence called Mrs Marlowe, the wife of the defendant, who might have shed some light on an alleged visit with Mr Shorn to Sir John's cottage some weeks after his death. In default of such corroboration you may think that there is little to choose between the two stories. Since the onus is upon the defendant to prove whatever he alleges to establish his defence, I would ask you to consider whether this allegation has been so proved. If not it should be set aside as an irrelevance."

An irrelevance, Don thought. That's it. Who else but a judge could find the exact term? "I was on my way back from the Colcutts'," she had said, "so I thought I'd call round and see if everything was all right. I didn't intend staying long, but I began to dislike the thought of driving any further so I stayed until the morning." The collar of the barrister's gown in front of him was speckled with dandruff. "Don, don't ever expect consistency," she had said, "love's a part of personality, it goes on, it's organic; I'm different." No wonder she was different; the bitch, the *bitch*; and this man at the end of the row, this man; all the time I was in Canada. "Help yourself to the letters, darling, as you've helped yourself to me. You've left me rather dishevelled, but while I put my clothes on you can search the desk." Why did this judge keep on talking? What did it amount to?—legal dust and ashes. Dust and ashes. Well, you've cleared your father's name anyway, old boy, even if it turns out that your wife's a common tart. You did one at the expense of the other. Another fruity paradox. Many people in this court would appreciate it. Many. . . .

". . . . So, members of the jury, let me restate briefly what you have to decide. First, were the allegations made against John

Marlowe true? If you consider they are true then you must of course find for Mr Shorn—for if a man tells the truth he cannot justly be called a liar. If you consider they were *untrue* then, second, did Mr Shorn act like a responsible journalist in making them? For again, if you are certain that he acted with absolute sincerity and good faith he can hardly be a disgrace to his profession. So ... were his allegations unfounded? Were they *unjustifiably* unfounded? Were the checked with ample and sufficient care or were they made with rash irresponsibility? And does the manner of their expression show unjustifiable venom and spite?

"Thirdly, you have to consider the full effect of the language used by Mr Marlowe about the plaintiff. Read *his* words carefully too, members of the jury. On the one hand you may think that such is the sting of calling a man a liar and a disgrace to his profession that—if that accusation be true—the mere addition of other words such as 'jackal' and 'wolf in sheep's clothing' adds little or nothing to the charge. On the other hand you may think that even though Mr Marlowe may have had very good grounds for complaint some of the words and imputations which he used went be yond a true expression of such a complaint.

"Well, there you are. It is for you alone to decide. I have reviewed the evidence solely to assist you, but if you disagree with anything I have said, your disagreement is paramount. Only in matters of law can I instruct you. If you are of the opinion that Mr Marlowe has fully made out his plea of justification, you will find for him. If, on the other hand you come to the conclusion that Mr Marlowe's charges, or any of them, have not in effect been justified and that the plaintiff's reputation had been materially injured, you must find for the plaintiff. *And*, if you find for the plaintiff, you must consider what damage his reputation has suffered, and assess that damage in monetary terms.

"That is all I have to say to you, members of the jury, but if you require any further information on matters of law, or any clarification of the evidence, I shall be available to give it you."

Chapter Thirty-Five

"They'll be a long time," muttered Whitehouse. "I could see that by their faces."

"I'll lay odds of five to two on a verdict in our favour," said Henry de Courville.

"Let them hurry up," Don said. "This place is getting me down."

Bennie had expected most people to leave the court when the jury retired, but it was not so. Doutelle went out and one or two of the other barristers, but the general public stayed solidly where it was. The last act of the drama might be long in coming and take only five minutes when it came, but they were content to wait. The public were great waiters. They would wait hours for this as they would for a glimpse of royalty or for a test match.

Somebody switched on the lights in the four ugly chandeliers. Bennie glanced at Don who, for want of something better to do, had taken an orchestral programme out of his pocket and was thumbing through it. She did not know whether to speak to him or not. Henry, who was sitting on her other side, began to talk to her about his holiday in Ischia.

After half an hour a few people drifted away, and Bennie excused herself and went out into the corridor. She found that scarcely anyone had left, that the corridor was full of people who had come out here for air and to stretch their legs. She walked off quickly and made her way down to the great hall. She found a telephone and rang Sister Frey.

"Bennie? I thought it was you. Yes, we have some news for you—or news of a sort. Mrs Richter rang me about noon. She said she thinks she may have located your friend living in lodgings a few minutes' walk from her shop."

The receiver crackled and Bennie shook it violently. "Did she—give any details?"

"No, And I shouldn't bank too much because she's a Czech and can easily be mistaken. But she seemed quite excited. She said if you go round she'll direct you there."

"You mean round to the shop? What time does she leave?

"It must be six-thirty. She's always back here about seven."

"Are they on the phone at the shop?"

"I don't think so. Anyway she left no number."

Bennie took down the address. "Thank you, Mary. If she rings again, tell her I'll come."

After leaving the box Bennie was in an agony of hesitation. She wanted to go at once, just to make sure if it was a mistake. But she could not leave Don as he was at present. It was only just 4 p.m. There would surely be time enough to get the verdict and then go.

As she was walking back she almost came into Roger pacing the corridor with Marion Laycock. Bennie turned away just in time behind three gowned men. She heard Marion say: "But it's perfectly plain, dearest, what happened. You were covering up for her in some way. It was plain to everyone in the court."

In the court nothing had changed. The judge's clerk was talking quietly to an usher. Most of the barristers were out. It was like an empty stage-set over which a curtain should have come down. But the public sat there waiting. And Don sat there waiting. He turned when Bennie slid in beside him and smiled at her but did not speak.

"No sign of life yet," said Henry.

At half past four de Courville slipped out, said he wanted a smoke and suggested Don should go with him. Don said no, he was all right here; he'd stick it out. Bennie said, would Joanna be free yet? Don frowned as if trying to remember an unfamiliar name, then said no, she wouldn't be home till about eight or later. At five Henry came back. Bennie glanced a couple of times at her watch, comparing it with the clock in the court. It was the rush hour now, and it would take quite a time to get from the Strand to North

Kensington. Best way would be a Circle Line from Temple to Paddington and then a taxi. Half an hour at a minimum.

The third time she looked at her watch Henry asked her if she was on a flight tonight. She said no, but had an appointment for six-fifteen which she was anxious not to break. Henry said, well, if she wanted to go he would stay with Don. She said no, she must stay.

At twenty-five to six the court associate was seen making his way to the door through which the jury had disappeared, and there was a flurry of interest in the court. Mr Lytton came back, blinking his eyes and nervously winding his piece of brief tape. The associate came out of the jury room and went towards the judge's room.

"Probably just a routine inquiry," said Whitehouse, who had also come back. "After a couple of hours the judge sometimes sends in to ask how they are going on and if he can help them."

Silence fell again. Mr Doutelle came back and leaned across to Lytton telling him something. Whitehouse went out. A woman behind Bennie was saying: "The moment they told him he had a coronary he crumpled up. You wouldn't believe. I kept saying to him, I've heard of men who've lived for years."

Whitehouse came back. "They've asked for a short time more. That means they've probably agreed on the essentials."

"Calculating the damages," said Don.

Henry said to Bennie: "Missed your appointment?"

"Not yet."

"If you want to hurry off after the verdict, go right ahead. I shall go home with Don in any case."

The clock moved on. At seven minutes to six there was a sudden stirring as if a wind had blown through the court. People pressed in, barristers hurried back, Roger and Marion returned. The jury filed back. Looking self-conscious they took their seats, and then almost immediately stood up again as the judge came in.

When they were all settled the judge said: "You have arrived at a verdict?"

The foreman said: "Yes, my Lord. We find for the plaintiff, Mr Shorn."

There was silence in the court for a moment; then someone in the public gallery made a loud comment of disapproval.

His Lordship said: "If there is any noise or demonstration I will commit the offenders for contempt of court."

Silence felt again. "In that event," said the judge to the foreman of the jury, "what damages do you find for the plaintiff?"

"Er—ten pounds, my Lord."

The barristers looked quickly at each other.

"Against us, but it's a victory really," Whitehouse muttered in Don's ear. "It's a typical English jury verdict—balancing law and common sense on a tightrope. It's a saving grace indeed that we took the precaution of——"

The foreman was still standing, one hand holding the side of the jury box. "Also, my Lord, we would like to add a rider. . . ."

"Yes?"

"In view of our verdict— in spite of our verdict—we would like to add that we are of the unanimous opinion that the evidence we have heard has completely cleared the late Sir John Marlowe of the accusations made against him."

"Good," said Mr Justice Alston.

Vincent Doutelle was on his feet. "My Lord, may I on behalf of my client express his gratitude to the jury—for that rider?"

"Yes," said his Lordship, "you may certainly do that."

"Before your Lordship enters judgement," continued Doutelle quickly; "there has been a payment into court of twenty-five pounds."

A legal argument bubbled up which Don made no effort to follow. Whitehouse in the meantime was continuing to mutter in his ear. Their payment into court of twenty-five pounds in July, which had been an offer of settlement, meant nothing if they lost the case and substantial damages were given against them. But since the damages awarded were less than this payment, the court regarded the costs incurred *after* the payment as being the responsibility of the plaintiff. This meant that Roger, in spite of his having technically won the action, would have to pay almost all the costs.

Don nodded at this and looked down at his shoes.

"One can only speculate on the way a jury will work things out," Whitehouse went on. "How did they reason? Most of their sympathy clearly was for you—but they may have thought you went a little far in what you wrote ... and maybe, who knows, it may have been their way of saying that while Shorn was mistaken, there was some doubt as to his ill-intentions and he must be given the benefit of it. ...."

Whitehouse was suddenly sucked into the legal argument in front of him. Dora folded his orchestral programme but found it fell to pieces in his fingers.

"A thousand," said Henry de Courville.

"What?"

"As a guess I'd say your costs won't be more than a thousand pounds. I'd reckon that if I were you. And Shorn's will be upwards of ten thousand. On the whole one can hardly quarrel with the outcome. You've achieved your object at a relatively small expense. ...."

The legal bickering had suddenly ended. Don heard the judge saying: "... and finally, members of the jury, thank you for your patience and attention during the whole four days of this complicated case." And at last he realised it was all over.

When the judge had gone people stood and stretched themselves. There was a feeling of anti-climax, perhaps for lack of the clear-cut decision. Friends began to gather round Don, half-congratulatory, half-sympathetic, not quite sure which way to take it. Roger went out of court with his solicitor, and after a moment Marion followed. Outside Warner Robinson caught up with them. His big face carried no special message.

"A Pyrrhic victory, Shorn."

"With no encouragement to advance on Rome."

"Oh, it's done you no harm, no harm at all. People will be reading your column with all the more interest next week."

"I haven't a doubt of that."

"Good. Ring me sometime." Waving aside the reporters of two rival newspapers, Robinson passed on.

Roger turned again to his solicitor. As he spoke he saw that

Marion was waiting for him. He wondered if the events of today, the ambiguities and the unsaid things just below the surface, and now this verdict without triumph, had disillusioned her as the earlier days had disillusioned her father. She did not look so. She looked perplexed and still a bit worried did but above all *loyal*. He realised with an extra feeling of malaise that she was a much stronger character than he had ever realised and that he had inspired in her a passionate devotion that he now had little use for but which it would be against his general disposition altogether to turn down.

Chapter Thirty-Six

Bennie got a taxi just as it discharged its fare outside the Law Courts. She asked the driver to hurry, and he nodded laconically and struck north up Kingsway. They reached Paddington by six twenty-five.

It was raining and the night was dark. Once in the Royal Borough of Kensington, the taxi driver went more slowly, keeping an eye on street names. He obviously didn't come here very often. Tall old houses, once the homes of a prosperous middle class, plaster and paint peeling, men standing at the doors, shabby cars, milk bottles on window-sills, papers blowing. The L.C.C. had been at work; great surgical operations to remove a canker and replace it with brown aseptic blocks of modem flats; but the dacay was going on. Respectability persisted among it, healthy wood among the dry rot.

The driver stopped at a little corner shop outside which a few rain-sodden news posters flapped. It was twenty-five to seven and the shop was shut. Bennie got out and tried the door. It was locked. There was a light in the back of the shop so she knocked. No one came. A blowsy woman pushing a pram came past. "They close at six, dear," she said.

As Bennie turned away there was shuffling feet, and Mrs Richter came out of the alley at the side of the shop.

"Miss Marlowe, I was brushing-up and I heard you knock. I waited thinking you might come."

"I was afraid I was too late! Come in the taxi out of the rain."

"No, it is down the next street. Pay it off and we well walk. A taxi draws attention, do you not think?"

Bennie paid the taxi. "What makes you think you have found—my friend?"

Mrs Richter shrugged her narrow shoulders. "I do not think. But it is this way. There is a Welshman called Rhys. He is a carrier of messages, of news. He is always in and out of the shop. Three days ago he ordered a *Times*. We do not stock it—it is not much in demand here. Each day he collects it—also other dailies. 'Wealthy friend', he says to me with a wink. I say, 'tell me about him'. He winks again and will not tell. But tins morning when he comes in for cigarettes I say to him 'they are for your friend, the young man with the black hair and the limp?' and he stares at me as if I have called up a ghost."

They began to walk down the street. Under the lamps the wit pavements glimmered like cellulose. Bennie said: "Do you know where he is likely to be?"

Mrs Richter buttoned the collar of her dirty raincoat. "I know where Rhys lives. I think if it is the right man he will not be far away."

They turned into a narrow cul-de-sac. The rain had driven most people indoors, but two children argued in thin voices from a doorstep, and a man tinkered, ill-temperedly with an old car, the water dripping into the engine off the brim of his crinkled velour.

"It is that one at the end where Rhys lives," said Mrs Richter.

As they came to the doorstep a train screamed past in the darkness beyond the house, a vivid rush of smoke and furnace and flickering carriages. When it had gone a cat dropped from the wall and slid up to the door of the house waiting for it to be opened. Someone was playing a harmonica.

"It is no good ringing a bell here," said Mrs Richter.

She opened the door and the cat was through in a second, streaking up the lighted stairs. No one about. Mrs Richter knocked on the door on her right. At the second knock it was opened by a big bald man in a stained boiler suit with a pink newspaper in his hand.

"Please," said Mrs Richter, "we want the young man who is new here. The young man with the black hair."

The big man stared at them both suspiciously, then out through the open door to see if anyone was with them.

"Top floor first right," he said and slammed the door in Mrs Richter's face.

Mrs Richter did not blink. "Shall I come up with you, Miss Marlowe?"

"Thank you, no. But ... would you wait? I'll call down—or come down again."

"Of course."

The first flight was uncarpeted, the landing above in darkness. Odd smell. The harmonica player had stopped. Bennie stumbled on a piece of old matting; her heel got caught in a hole in it. Someone was frying chips. She tried to find the switch for the next flight but couldn't, so went up it in the dark.

This was the top. Three doors. Light under two of them. Bennie tapped on the first of them, which was to the right of the stairs. No answer. She pushed back a damp streak of hair and tried the handle. The door opened on a room that was empty of furniture except for a single iron bedstead. The floor was gravelly with dirt. On the bed sitting cross-legged was a Negro. He had short khaki trousers, two sacks over his naked shoulders. He was watching her very intently. Bennie muttered a half-swallowed apology and backed out.

The other door faced her. She knocked loudly, anxious now to have done with it. "Who's that?" said a voice. It was Michael's.

"Bennie," she said.

There was a short pause, a scuffling sound and then the door was open. He gathered her into his arms.

"*Bennie*," he said, in delight, in alarm. "I still don't know how you got here. Did Dick Ballance. ..."

She explained, short of breath after running down and telling Mrs Richter that her guess had been right. But short of breath not just for that. Michael looked pale, otherwise not ill, except for——

"You limp," she said. "So you *were* hurt? Tell me about it."

He had shut the door and locked it again.

She said a second time: "Tell me about it."

"Oh, Bennie, it's so good to see you." He came to her, took her coat, then put his face against her face, smelling her skin, resting there.

She said quietly: "What happened, Michael?"

"God, I've been such a fool!. . . ."

They were silent for a time. Then after a bit she sat on the bed and he took a chair opposite her, less than a foot away. He had gone much thinner.

"I was going to come to see you in a few days. I had to know how you felt about it all. I had to know if you could still give me some part of your love."

She said: "Michael, it isn't a thing you give and take back."

"But knowing how you feel about these things. . . ."

"How do you know how I feel about these things?"

"Well, you have such a strong sense of values, and. . . ."

"I have a sense of values, maybe, but it isn't . . . Michael, I don't love a person because they're *good*. I love them because I love them. Once that is so, there's no good or bad in it."

He went on looking at her. "You don't know how much that means to me."

"I've been sick with worry. Was it your leg?"

He nodded. "It's all right now."

They didn't speak for a long time; they were content to look at each other. Then she said: "Can you tell me?"

He nodded again and began from the beginning, right from the beginning of the first challenge and bet over the radiogram, through the Any Questions affair and the quarrel with Boy, to the last misadventure.

As he talked she noticed the change in him. She hadn't been aware before of a lack of frankness, but now she saw the difference. He was talking no longer to someone whose love he was anxious to gain but to someone who knew him and had no fears.

She suddenly felt she understood him better. She realised the tremendous dynamo of energy and drive there was in him and the necessity of its finding an outlet. Whatever mistakes he had made had been mistakes deriving from this excess, differently directed it was as liable to produce an abundance of good. It could be so directed, not by her but by himself—with normal luck, if it once got moving in the right way. . . . This misadventure might yet help to set it on that way.

As she looked at him she thought that in the space of only a few weeks his face had become much more sensitive; it was a face with power in it that mustn't be wasted.

She was not depressed by the story of petty crime, nor by the fix they were in now: she saw beyond it because by her new understanding of him she could look over the head of the present mess and see how it could be in the future.

"This is like it must always be," she said, speaking her thoughts aloud.

He knew at once what she meant. "I can't tell you how happy I am—and how miserable I am. It doesn't seem possible to be both at the same time."

"What are we going to do?"

The windows rattled as an express went past. Hardly had the sound died away than another train came, a goods train, stammering uncertainly along a siding.

"Thank you at least for the 'we'."

"It's always got to be 'we' from now on, Michael."

"Bennie, you're wonderful"

"No, I'm not wonderful at all. It's only these last few weeks that I've begun to get things straight—really straight—in my own mind."

He touched her damp hair. Then he began to kiss her. He kissed her like a thirsty man after a drought. He said: "I didn't believe you'd ever be so good about it. I thought you'd want me to give myself up."

She didn't answer. He pulled away and looked at her very closely. "Do you?"

She shook her head. "Michael, I don't know. I don't know what's going to be the best thing to do—I mean best for you. It's something we've obviously got to talk over at—at leisure, once we're out of this place."

"I don't see how I can get out of this place until that's decided."

"Well, my darling, it's something I just can't decide for you."

He got up then and walked over to tie window. "I think you have to, Bennie."

She could see all his energies, in prison, turning in on himself and devouring the man she was just beginning to know. "Then it must be no, at least—for the present."

He said: "I've given you some pretty nasty moments since we met. Perhaps that's the nastiest. Anyway, let's leave it open for the moment ... I've been watching the papers, to see if there's any mention of Peter being charged. I must have missed it."

"No, you haven't. Peter's in hospital. He's not been charged by the police."

"But I saw him arrested."

"Where? How?"

He told her. "That's how I knew they were coming for me. I knew I only had a few minutes to get away."

"Peter's in hospital." She told him of her visit to his flat.

"Beaten up?" Michael said incredulously. "It's just not possible. That car was the police. ..."

"Were there policemen in it?"

"Yes. ... Well, I took them for that. It was a Wolseley and one of them had a blue coat and a flat-topped cap. Do you mean. ..." He looked at her. "It could have been Kenny and the others! Peter was always nervous about them!"

She said: "*Think*, Michael. How else do you know you're wanted by the police?"

"*I don't.* ..." He came across and took her hands. His eyes were full of anxiety. "*Listen*, let me think this over carefully. ..."

They went over it together, step by step. It was life and death they should be sure.

"What else connects you with the robbery? *Michael*, what else?"

"Nothing, as far as I know. Bennie ... I think I've been a complete fool—running away from my own—my own shadow!" He put his hands up to his face and limped round the room. "Let me *think*, let me *think*. ... The police haven't been to you?"

"No."

"Nor to Dad as far as you know?"

"No. He was in court today. I think if he'd known anything he would have asked me. . . ."

"Oh, God," he said, and sat down. "I think I'm going to pass out. Give me something to drink . . . I—I. . . ." But before she could move he was up again. "Don't you see, darling, darling; I thought I was wanted by the police, and all I'm involved in is some—some footling little gang feud. Perhaps not even that. Perhaps they've taken it out on Peter, and that. . . ." He let out a gasp. "Thank God! Darling, darling, darling!" He took her in his arms again and smothered her with kisses. "You've brought me not only your—your love and forgiveness, you've brought me my life!"

They hugged each other and tried to laugh; but there was too much relief in the laughter and it caught at them and came close to tears.

They went over it once more, just to be utterly certain. "It means we can *go*," she said. "We can leave here together tonight. Or we could except for one thing. There's still one danger. Boy Kenny."

"Oh! . . . what does he matter?"

"He might. He very well could. I don't want you—left behind a bush on Clapham Common." She told him of her visit to the Middle Pocket.

Michael listened but not very soberly. Perhaps because he was physically much stronger, he had always taken a less serious view than Peter of the Kenny threat. Now his relief was so great that he could hardly count it at all. Only when Bennie told him of her feeling of being followed one evening did he give it some attention.

"You don't think you were followed here?"

"I don't think so. But when we leave I'll go for a taxi first, bring it here. If anybody's watching they'll think you're staying behind. When I bring the taxi you can come out quickly and get straight into it."

He took her hands again. "Bennie, will you marry me *very* soon? Please, very soon. The action's over. There's nothing in our way. There's no more need to wait."

"Yes," she said.

"Tomorrow? Or Friday? One day this week?"

"All right," she said, but with a slight hesitation that he instantly saw.

"With conditions?"

She smiled. "No conditions. But you do see, don't you, it must be on money that's properly ours?"

"Of course." He nodded, but bit at his thumb. "What am I going to do with this other money?"

"You have some here?"

"Yes. All there is. About eight hundred pounds."

She whistled. "Can it go back?"

"No. It's money from the sale of goods. They'll be insured. I could only send this money to the underwriters."

She said: "Couldn't you send it to the police? With an anonymous note saying what it's from and asking them to dispose of it? In a rather twisted way our conscience would be clearer. And—if you were ever traced—it would do you no harm."

Michael thought. "Yes. Of course you're right."

"Darling, it isn't a matter of eight hundred pounds, it's a question of our starting off together on the right foot."

"I know. I know. I wasn't seriously hesitating; of course it's got to go." He stared round the room. "Just think, I can walk out of here tonight, never come back. And we can go on living in London, Bennie! Eight hundred pounds! It's worth eight thousand! It's been—pretty terrible this last week. Tonight I'm a millionaire!"

They sat and talked for a quarter of an hour. Then she helped him to pack his suitcase. He went to a piece of the skirting board and prised it out with a chisel. He had hollowed away the plaster behind, and here, wrapped in four bundles, were the notes. He didn't seem to know what to do with them. Abruptly he gave them to Bennie.

"You keep them. They're yours absolutely to do with what you want."

She took them gingerly. "They won't all go in my bag. Put them in the suitcase."

"No, we'll split them. I can carry half in my pocket."

They glanced round the room. Nothing left.

"Stay here," she said. "I'll get a taxi."

"It may be a job in this district. I know. Go next door. Rhys, the Welshman, says they've got a call box in the hall. Nobody will stop you, and you can ring the taxi rank on Westbourne Green. I've got the number here."

"Right," she said.

"A better idea: I'll come downstairs with you and get Rhys to ring for us. Wasn't there a harmonica playing when you came up?"

They went to the door and he unlocked it and opened it. Coming towards him across the landing were Boy Kenny and Adam.

Chapter Thirty-Seven

Kenny took a jump at the door as Michael slammed it. The door creaked and cracked but the catch held. As the handle was wrenched from the outside Michael turned the key. For the moment there was nothing but the sound of breathing on both sides of the door. Then the footsteps went away and there was the sound of another door opening and voices.

"Oh, *God*," said Bennie, "I've led them to you."

Michael didn't speak, but got hold of the bed and dragged it screaming on its rollers end-on against the door. They lifted the old wooden washstand and leaned it against the top part of the door.

"They'll get in easily if they want to," Michael said. He looked round and picked up the chisel. He was quite calm.

"Oh, *darling*," Bennie breathed. "How can we get help?"

"We can't—not yet. Wait."

As he stopped, some sort of metal was forced against the flimsy catch of the door. The whole door creaked and strained, but the metal snapped first. There was more fumbling and scratching.

"Who's below us?" Bennie said. "Couldn't we——"

"Girls. Anyway in these places nobody interferes unless they have to. Here!"

The window screeched as he flung up the sash. "See this window box: it's iron. That one belongs to the house next door. Think you could reach across?"

"I could try. But you?"

"Yes, easily. There's the drainpipe to hold to. Can you go first?"

"*No*, you," said Bennie. "Then you can help me."

The door was creaking again. Michael wriggled out. As he got out, holding with fingertips to the frame of the window, a mail train went past, making the house shiver. Michael moved one hand to the drainpipe, stretched with his foot for the window-box. The other window was closed and he kicked it in with the toe of his shoe.

Behind them the catch burst. The bed was squealing. Bennie slid one leg out of the window as Michael got across, but before she could follow a hand clutched her by the collar of her frock and hauled her choking into the room. Someone hit her on the side of the face.

Both men in the room. Boy said: "Blast 'im; he's through! Nest door. You go this way: I'll cut him off."

Panting, wicked pink spots on sallow cheeks, he blundered out of the room, swinging a bicycle chain. The other man peered out of the window, hesitated, and hesitated again, looking down. Bennie on her knees, grabbed her bag, waited till Adam's head was out of the window again, then fled from the room, cannoned into the Negro who was crouched on the landing, fell down two stairs, saved herself and went on.

The noise had brought no one out yet. Harmonica still playing. Past it. Down to the ground floor. Front door open. No sign of Boy. Out in the street. Next door open. Light in passage. She went in. Boy's feet disappearing up the stairs. She waited till they'd gone, then slid across to the telephone and dialled 999.

The bedroom door in the other house had delayed Michael. It had been locked and of course no key. His chisel had done the job but by the time he was out he knew there was danger in going down. He waited on the top landing and listened. Footsteps.

The light came on on the first landing.

"Adam!" came Boy's voice, cautiously. "You up there?"

Michael worked round the landing to the next door, but was locked. The furthest door, by the stairs had light under it.

Boy came up four steps of the second flight and then stopped, came up two more.

"Adam!" he called.

Michael fancied he heard some sort of scrapings from the room he had just come through. He dodged across the landing to the lighted door and opened it.

A thin elderly man with a mottled face got up sharply from a chair, and a glass tinkled. "My dear sir, bursting into the—the . . . have you no—no reverence for the house of. . . . Don't hide, Mary, there's nothing, nothing to be ashamed of. . . ." He groped across the room towards a bottle and a glass among the cluttered photographs on the mantelshelf. "I'll lodge a protest with the——"

"Adam!" shouted Boy from the top of the stairs. "He's 'ere! I got 'im!"

Michael grabbed up a bentwood chair by the door and threw it as he turned: Boy swung with his chain as the chair came down on him. He went sprawling across the stair head. As Michael tried to get past he kicked; he got to his knees and caught Michael round the knees; Michael hit him twice in the face. That for Peter. Pleasure in that. Boy half fell back, a flailing foot caught Michael in the shoulder as he too fell; Michael grabbed up his dropped chisel and swung it at Boy's head: changed his aim; it caught Boy on the shoulder bone; he howled with pain, doubled up.

Michael clawed himself to his feet: sounds from the further bedroom: Adam had at last risked the climb.

"My dear sir," said the old man, "this is out—outrageous, brawling . . . have you no reverence——"

Michael pushed past him, got down the first flight; two women: "Oo're you? 'ere, what's all this? what's the row?" Past them, half shoving them out of the way. Down the next flight. Boy was on his feet again; could tell that from the shouts, Adam with him, no time to lose. Bennie.

"Darling!" she said. "Oh, thank God, I thought——"

"Not out of the wood yet."

They turned together and got to the front door.

"No!" said Bennie. There was no one about. "If they catch you in the street. Back here!" She pulled him towards his own house.

"But what——"

"Double back. They won't expect—— Is there anyone you can go to?"

"Rhys!" He led the way into his own house again. They had been moving all the time and only seconds had passed. With luck Kenny would come out and not know where they had gone.

The first floor. *Phil the Pinter's Ball.* A small mischievous tattered man with twisted eyebrows took a harmonica from his lips, stared at the two people who had burst in.

"Shorn, boy, what are you doing here—"

"Go on playing," said Michael. He shut the door and limped quickly to the window; this one looked out at the front; he put his eye to a slit in the bund. "They're out there now."

"Well, won't you sit down, my dear?"

"Please go on playing, Mr Rhys."

"How shall we get out if they wait. . . ." said Michael.

"I've sent for the police."

Michael turned and stared at her in alarm. "For the police?"

"We've nothing to hide now."

"My God, if they. . . ."

"The police?" said the Welshman. "Did you say the police? Here, I don't want none of that. I don't want them here, boy. . . ."

"Don't worry. It won't involve——"

"Oh, will it not! If they come up here——"

"*Shut up*! Or go on playing. We shall be gone in five minutes."

"Take care they don't see you," Bennie urged Michael.

Rhys moved his eyebrows about. Then doubtfully he shook out his harmonica and played a tentative scale or two, eyeing Bennie all the time.

She looked round the room. There was one cupboard and what looked like a chest covered with a blanket. If it came to that Michael might get in the cupboard, if she——

"Boy's gone back in the other house," Michael said. "Adam's keeping watch. I suppose they're sure we couldn't have got to the end of the street."

"They must have followed me when I came," Bennie muttered. "One must have followed me and then phoned for the other."

Rhys began to play *Land of My Fathers*.

"Are you all right, Michael? He didn't——"

"No. I nearly killed him. In some ways I wish I had."

Time passed. Then a noisy argument broke out at the door of the next house. Michael couldn't see what was going on. Adam went quickly forward and out of sight. A car came round the corner, moved slowly down the cul-de-sac, evidently looking for a number.

"They're here," Michael said. "It's really the police this time."

Bennie was at the window. She saw Boy Kenny break away from some other man and bolt quickly for the railway line. He jumped over the wall as the police car stopped.

"Come on," Bennie said.

"But it might be dangerous now."

"It's the one safe time!" She took Michael's hand and pulled him only half-convinced to the door. As they went out the harmonica stopped and Rhys called something after them.

Bennie said: "Just be—as if it's nothing to do with us."

They went down the stairs. Two policemen were at the door of the next house—where of course the phone call had come from—listening to a confused story of what had happened from the people gathered round the steps. There was no sign of Adam. A third policeman had run towards the railway lines.

Michael and Bennie turned out, as one of the policemen and then the other went into the next house. The driver of the police car looked at them suspiciously and seemed about to speak to them, but they kept their eyes on the half-dozen people in the doorway of the house. No sign of Adam. They got past.

"You were right, Bennie," Michael breathed.

"Don't look round, darling. Just walk. We're nearly clear, darling. Just walk."

They got to the end of the cul-de-sac. The police hadn't yet come out. They turned left because there were more lights that way and because it took them away from the railway.

"Are you all right?" she asked again. "Did he——"

"No. I'm all right."

379

"Did you hurt your leg?"

"We could do with a taxi."

"It's hopeless on a wet night, and in this district. Shall we find a box and telephone for one?"

"No. Go on. I shan't be happy till we're out of here."

They went on, waiting every second for running feet. The street they were in was perversely, unnaturally empty; two old cars squatted in the rain; an upturned pram at the top of area steps; one old woman hobbled in the distance.

"Which way is it?"

"I'm not certain. Right, I think."

"I led them to you," she said. "I'll never forget that."

"It's all right now. You've got your bag?"

"Yes."

They came to the end of the street. Michael looked sombrely over his shoulder. The encounter with Boy seemed to have I taken the relief out of him. They turned right. He walked along with a white empty face, his arm loosely in hers.

After another hundred yards they came suddenly into Ladbroke Grove. "This way." He pushed his sodden hair out of his eyes. "Darling, you'll be soaked to the skin."

"D'you think I care? Michael, think. This looks like the end of a—very dark passage. You're free! Thank God for that! Don't bother about Boy and his friend. They can't touch you now!"

A bus came splashing to a standstill and they got on. He wouldn't go upstairs and they collapsed on the nearest seat. She said: "Shall we go to my flat: it's a bit nearer?"

"No, I'd rather get home."

To Bennie, just to be on the bus again was to come out of the nightmare of those decaying streets. And as she had said, it looked like the end of the whole nightmare. Getting on this bus with Michael was putting a seal on a miraculous deliverance. The clock had been put back two weeks. The unbelievable had happened; the past was there for re-living. She squeezed Michael's hand and told him he'd have to pay for her as she daren't open her bag. He smiled, and then twitched with pain as he felt in his pocket for some coins.

"Michael, what is it?"

"Nothing much. My leg has been giving me hell since we left."

"D'you mean the wound?"

"Yes. I don't know if it was the scrap with Boy or whether it was when I was climbing across the windows, but it's been—well. . . ."

"D'you think the wound has opened again? Is it bleeding?"

"I don't think so. But the bullet's still in and I expect that's giving trouble."

She sat up. "You didn't tell me! Have you seen a doctor?"

"Sort of. He said he couldn't interfere, that it would have to be taken out in hospital."

"When? But when?"

"Whenever I could fix it. I couldn't go to a public hospital with a .25 bullet in my leg. That would soon settle things. If I hadn't been stuck away in fear of being arrested I should have had it done in some shady nursing-home before now."

She was silent for a few seconds. "Where exactly is it?"

"Here." He pointed.

"Will you let me see it when you get in? I've had first-aid training."

Michael nodded bleakly. "If you like. Maybe we can get the same doctor to look at it. I have his number."

The bus lurched and splashed down Kensington Church Street. Bennie watched him. There was sweat under his hair, a different dampness from the dampness of rain.

"Darling," she said. "I don't think this is good enough. We'd better go straight to a doctor. You see there might be internal——"

"*No.* Not on any account. When we're just free from the whole business?"

"Yes, but there are worse things than——"

"*Listen.* I'm not going to get in another jam. I'll be all right when I get to bed. We'll have the doctor I had before. . . . There's a taxi-rank round the corner. Get off here."

They slid off the bus at the traffic lights and he led the way through the rain. The rank was empty. They waited on the corner. A taxi with its flag lit turned out of the next street but away from them. They shouted in vain. Mere buses went past. Two engaged taxis and some private cars. Then a taxi at last. They got in somehow, and Michael bit his lip to keep back the grunt of agony as he sat down.

It seemed no way once they were in. Michael climbed out and began to pull himself up the steps. Bennie turned her back on the taxi driver to open her bag and groped for her own money. By the time she had paid, Michael was inside.

She found him sitting in the living-room, his face deadly white as if he was going to faint.

"*Darling*, lie down at once. Let me see where it is."

"A drop of brandy first. Then phone that doctor."

She flew into kitchen and went through the bottles there, found brandy, slopped it in a glass. While she was gone he had found the number.

"Just sip it," she said, "until I've had a chance of looking at the thing. . . ."

"Look afterwards. Phone Gros."

He took the glass and drank some of the brandy while she was dialling.

"Can I speak to Dr Gros, please?"

A guarded voice said: "Who is it?"

"I'm speaking for Mr Michael Shorn. He attended him about ten days ago."

"I'm sorry, Dr Gros is out."

"When will he be back?"

"We're expecting him."

"Could you tell him to come round at once to Roland Gardens? Mr Shorn is very unwell. It's very urgent."

"I'll tell him."

Bennie slammed down the receiver. When she turned she saw something trickling down the side of Michael's shoe. At first in the shadow she thought it was oil.

"Michael!" She went to him in horror.

"The thing's pretty swollen. You'll have a job—to get my clothes off."

She flew into the kitchen where she had seen scissors, fled back, knelt at his feet, began to cut the trousers by the seam. As she did so blood got on her hands. She cut the trousers right up and the thin pants.

"Oh, dear God!" she said.

The leg was very swollen. The way he was sitting she could hardly see the bullet wound, but she could see it was a bad haemorrhage. The blood was forcing its way out along the track of the old wound. Every beat of his heart was pumping the blood into the tissues of his leg and out of his body.

She somehow pulled him down on to the floor, so that he was quite flat, began to put pressure above the artery. It didn't work. Her fingers when she took them away left nasty pits in the swelling of the groin but she had done no good.

"Darling," he said. "It's—bit easier. ..." He was half fainting already.

She snatched up a table napkin, tied it tightly round the thigh below the wound. She couldn't get it anywhere else. Her hands and knees sticky with blood, she managed to drag the telephone directory on to the floor beside her, turned over the pages, which stuck together with the blood.

"Darling," he said. "Did Gros—say he was coming?"

She got the bandage as tight as she could and then lifted the leg and propped it up on the chair. She jumped up to the phone, dialled. The thing rang five times.

"St George's Hospital."

"Will you put me through *at once* to the casualty officer?"

"Casualty officer. Just one moment."

She was trembling so much she could hardly hold the phone. Michael opened his eyes and smiled at her.

"Casualty officer."

She said: "I'm speaking from 191 Roland Gardens. A man is bleeding from a gunshot wound. If you don't get him into hospital *at once* he'll bleed to death. Can you send an ambulance *very* quickly?"

"At 191 Roland Gardens? Yes. What is the name?"

"Marlowe."

"Mrs Marlowe? I'll do that right away. . . ." There was a moment's pause. She could hear him giving instructions. "Now, Mrs Marlowe," said the voice calmly and reassuringly. "I'm sure you can help while the ambulance is on its way. Where is the wound?"

"High up on the inside of the thigh below or just in the buttock. Too high for a tourniquet. I think it has broken into an artery—the femoral artery."

"You're a nurse?"

"An air stewardess."

"Oh, very well, then, you'll know that you can quickly check the bleeding by pressure. You know of course about the Poupart ligament?"

"I *know* about it, but I can't *find* it! There's too much swelling. All the groin is swollen and pulpy. What pressure I can bring makes practically no difference!"

There was a pause. The voice was a little less confident. "How long is it since this happened?"

"I don't know exactly. Probably, fifteen minutes."

Another pause. "It's a man, is it? A young man. I suppose you won't know his blood group?"

"No."

"Well, the ambulance is well on its way now, Mrs Marlowe. I'll see that everything is got ready for the moment he arrives. Don't worry."

"How long will it be getting here?"

"Not more than ten minutes. It will depend a little on the traffic."

When Bennie hung up Michael was lying in a pool of blood.

"Oh, dear God!" she said, tears starting on to her lashes. He was practically unconscious now. She felt around the swollen limb and above it, pressing into the groin again. Any pressure might help a little to keep back the pumping blood. "Oh, dear God, what can I do? What can I do? What can I do?"

She felt for Michael's pulse. It was shallow and quick. She put her face against his; his skin was cold and sweaty. His eyelids flickered but he didn't come round. Her tears fell on his face.

She stood up, went out into the hall, switched on the hall light, opened the front door. It was still raining. Why did she ever let him dismiss the first taxi; why hadn't she insisted on going straight to the nearest hospital; why hadn't she *now* got a taxi; if there was a taxi even now, it would get them to the hospital in less than twenty minutes; why hadn't she done that to begin with. Oh, God, save him, even if it means his leg; oh, God, send the ambulance; I can't go back into that room and watch him bleeding to death. She had a picture vivid in her mind of the great arteries branching and stemming from each other, with the heart endlessly pumping through them a relatively small quantity of blood. One breach in that main system. Seven or eight pints, that's all; if he loses a pint every four minutes; oh, *God*, where's the ambulance? "*Taxi!*" she screamed as one turned in at the end of the road; she ran down the steps; even now it would save time; even now, if they could carry him m; the taxi had been turning round; it went off, turning into Brompton Road. She stopped and ran back, stumbling up the steps, went in to the door of the flat, stood on the threshold, swaying. The pool of blood had spread; it had soaked the rug and was creeping off the edge in a thick red finger along the floorboard, moving like snake towards the wall. It was like his life creeping away into a corner.

She went across and knelt beside him; his face was deathly; she tried pressure again; hold on; just for ten minutes more; hold on.

A bell. At the end of the street. She flew to the door, screamed at them; they were on the other side and past; the driver crashed his gears getting in reverse and roared back towards her.

Ambulance doors open; two men: "This way," she said. They followed her with a stretcher. They went up to him. One man made a face at the sight of Michael's pallor. They picked him up. On the stretcher. As they went out someone from upstairs was peering down. "Has there been an accident?"

In. They helped Bennie up. The car was off before the doors

were closed. One man was in with Bennie. "Have you any blood here?" "No," he said. "Don't worry, we won't be long now."

The ambulance squealed out on to the Fulham Road, roared past buses, clanging bell, charged a traffic light and squeezed between a string of cars. Turning again. Bennie had no sense of direction; the ambulance man was trying to do what she had tried, to stop the flow with pressure. It was dripping on the floor already. But it was slower. Another lurch. The man said apologetically: "We take this route; it saves the nasty turn at the top of Sloane Street."

Bennie didn't reply. Her nerves had gone now. She sat quite still, holding Michael's head in her lap. The blood on her hands had got into his hair.

"Belgrave Square," said the man. "Two minutes now."

Bennie thought: I did this once before—on a different trip—from Roland Gardens to Belgrave Street; the night when Michael gave his house-warming party and I found that his father was Moonraker; we rushed along much this same route in Michael's old Delage—such a long time ago, it seems; half an age; very carefree then; Michael and Peter and Boy and Pat and me and the girl called Kathie; it was just the same as this, squealing up to traffic lights, swerving round corners, lurching in and out of the traffic. What has gone wrong since then? Everything has gone wrong. Would it have all been different if she'd married Michael then? Would she have been a steadying influence? Had he done all these things, got into this impossible mess because he wasn't sure she would marry him? how could one have seen this end? What clairvoyance did life ask? Or was the pattern laid down? the puppets dancing with a show of freedom but with the futility of dummies on wires. . . .

The ambulance jerked to a stop, then crawled a few yards further. The ambulance man flung open the doors. The other man was already out, and he jumped in the back. Bennie was relieved of the weight in her arms. She said: "I don't think there's any hurry now."

They stared at her, then looked at Michael in the shadowy light. Not commenting, they lowered the stretcher and carried it into the hospital.

The casualty officer was waiting for them. He looked at Michael, then glanced swiftly at Bennie. He felt for Michael's pulse. They lifted the stretcher on to a trolley and wheeled it along a passage into a surgical ward. No one stopped Bennie and she followed.

Another trolley already prepared for giving a blood transfusion was wheeled alongside. The doctor muttered something to a nurse, who came up with a hypodermic. He injected it Coramine, Bennie thought. While he was doing this a second nurse was taking a sample of the blood too readily available, and she hurried away with it.

The doctor slit away Michael's sleeve and stared at the arm, then took a knife from the transfusion trolley and cut through the skin to the flattened vein. He picked up the vein in a pair of fine forceps and inserted his needle; the nurse ran a little of the Universal Donor blood from the bottle to replace the air in the tubing, then made the connection to the needle. The doctor muttered again, and there were a few seconds of complete silence while the blood began to run into the vein. So perhaps it wasn't too late.

About two ounces went from the bottle, then the flow seemed to check.

"Put some pressure on. . . ."

The nurse fixed an indiarubber inflating bulb to one of the tubes of the bottle and began gently to pump. The blood moved again; Michael gave a sort of inward sigh. Hope. But the bluish pallor didn't change.

The blood moved less quickly. The doctor injected again and waited. One of the ambulance men had noisy breathing, but that was the only sound. It was too much the only sound. Bennie didn't take her eyes from Michael's face. It was Michael's face no more.

The doctor bit his lip and glanced at the ambulance man with a slight shake of the head.

Running footsteps, and the first nurse came back carrying a bottle of the correct blood group. She looked at Michael, then she looked at the doctor, and came more slowly in and set the bottle down.

After a while the doctor straightened up. "It's no good. I'm afraid he's gone."

Chapter Thirty-Eight

Joanna had thought she couldn't go on with the play, because something in Don's voice when he telephoned her had said enough. She thought of pretending to be ill and getting away from the studios, going back to the house and taking her things and being gone before Don came home. But as the memory of his voice slightly faded she began to tell herself that she had imagined half of it.

When it came to the point the play went through without a hitch; somehow better than usual from her point of view, and when it was over she felt tired out but a bit easier in mind. She came out into the rain of North London still relaxed; but the comfortable fiction that had helped her to go on was no longer with her. She knew Don knew. She was composed because there wasn't anything more.

The taxi ride was a long one, and all through it her mind was quiet, not thinking much. Only on her own doorstep did her nerves come awake. She fumbled in her bag, found the key, went in.

There was a light in the living-room. Did one go in as if nothing . . . pretend to the last . . .?

"Hullo!" she called.

"Hullo."

He was standing by the fireplace, in which a small fire flickered. He was lighting a cigarette. She could have run upstairs, taken off her coat. . . .

"So it's more or less all right about the libel action," she said.

"What?"

"The libel action."

"More or less." He flicked his lighter shut. "How did you know?"

"The evening papers. 'Ten Pounds Damages for Shorn. But Sir John Marlowe's Reputation Cleared.'"

"Oh. I haven't seen them." He looked at the end of his cigarette. "Are you wet?"

"Not bad. I got a taxi. Will the action cost us much?"

"Apparently not. We made some sort of a legal move in July in case there was this sort of verdict, so most of the costs fall on them."

"Good. It's *so* good about your father."

She came into the room and fumbled a cigarette out of the box. He didn't offer his lighter, and she found a match.

He said: "I've been watching your play."

She looked up through the smoke. "Oh?"

"Henry came back with me after the verdict—stayed and had a drink. When he left I switched on and saw the last two acts."

"Like it?"

"Yes."

A brief silence fell, and to cover it she knelt to the fire and began to poke it. "This coal is poor stuff."

He said: "I thought you were better than I've ever seen you before. You were terrific."

"Oh ... that's nice to know."

He said: "I sat here in the dark looking at you, particularly in the close-ups. It was queer."

"Was it?"

"Yes. You looked all that I imagine Fry would want his character to look—seductive, feminine, essentially pure in heart. I sat speculating."

"On what?"

"On all that beauty, all that apparent purity, and wondering how it could hide so much rottenness, so much ugliness, so much sham."

In spite of being expected, it was a vile moment.

"What makes you say that?"

"You should know."

She stood up. "Yes . . . I suppose I do."

Neither spoke for a moment.

"Is that all there is to say?"

Her intellect, her adultness, blocked each sentence as it came into her mind. "There isn't anything I can say that won't sound like a cheap excuse."

"Suppose you make the cheap excuses—they may be better than nothing. I want to know in what way I've failed you. I want to—just to begin to understand. . . ."

She drew at her cigarette as if trying to draw nervous stability from it. "What am I accused of?"

"Christ!" he said suddenly, savagely. "You're accused of nothing. I'm your husband, not the Public Prosecutor. We've left the court; remember? We're not yet in the next one. I only want to know *why*. Why, while my back was turned, did you give yourself to—to Roger? Roger of all people. Am I a failure to you sexually?"

"*No.*"

"Or morally, or some other way?"

"No."

"Is Roger more fun?"

"No."

"Or are neither of us sufficient on our own? Which of us is the second string?"

"Stop," she said breathlessly.

He waited. "Well?"

She made a big effort to be calm. She put her hand on the mantelpiece.

"Don, I told you: I'm not making excuses. I don't think now it's any good saying anything at all. The damage is done. But I can say—I can try to say about three things. The first is that Roger was the man before we were married. I thought I'd got him out of my system. I hadn't. I have now. That's really about all. I'm *sorry.*"

"*Sorry.* . . ."

Her mouth was filled with a coppery taste. She groped for reasons she had once found to give Roger, reasons she had given calmly enough then: there weren't any now. It made a difference talking to the person you'd let down. "It must sound—pretty shoddy to you."

"It sounds unconvincing."

"But I think you must know one other thing. It began while you were away. It ended before you came back. And I knew nothing about this attack on your father. If he got those letters while he was with me he got them unknown to me."

For the first time he looked at her,

"And these happy meetings you've been having with him since?"

"What meetings?"

"At the party at the Savoy? At Television House? Were you laughing together at your lovely memories?"

She dropped the cigarette into the hearth and put her hand up to her face. "Yes, damn you, yes, if you want to think that! What else can I expect you to think! It's all in the picture, isn't it? Maybe it's the right picture! What was it you said: rottenness, ugliness, sham? You saw me tonight didn't you, looking—looking the way you said, and thought that's how she's been looking ever since I came home, lying in my arms, in my bed, and all the time acting like a mongrel bitch, slinking round to Roger when my back's turned, letting me down, letting me down worse than any common tart! That's what you thought, wasn't it!"

She stared at him, her eyes blazing with tears. His heart twisted inside him.

"Yes," he said. "I thought exactly that."

"Then what do you want me to do? When shall I go?"

"Whenever you like. The sooner the better."

"I'll go tonight. I'll be glad to get out of this sanctimonious atmosphere of——"

"Sanctimonious!" he said. "Dear Christ, is it sanctimonious to expect ordinary honesty, ordinary fair dealing, ordinary decency? If you'd wanted to go to him why didn't you say so? I wouldn't have stood in your way. You could have——"

"I *didn't* want to go to him! I *don't* want to go to him!——"

He said: "You like it both ways. I don't. I'm sorry."

That finished it.

"Don't worry," she said. "You'll not be troubled again."

As she got to the door he said: "*I'll* go. I'll sleep somewhere else tonight. You can leave in the morning."

She turned. The wildness of narrow temples and fine jaw line were like stone from which emotion had eroded the flesh. "Give me an hour to pack a few things."

He pushed past her into the hall, not intentionally clumsy, but uncertain with anger and pain. He looked at her dragging at words that lost their meaning before they were spoken and so were not spoken and so were not spoken.

"Good-bye." He went out.

The rain had nearly stopped, but after twelve hours everything was sodden; water trickled in the gutters, feet squelched, tyres hissed as if they were punctured, darkness and the sparse lamps turned streets into shallow canals.

He walked for a time without knowing anything, trying to walk away from the havoc he carried inside him. When she came home he hadn't intended it to be like that; he hadn't really; he'd thought that it should at least be civilised and reasonable; yet he couldn't blame either himself or her for the way it had turned out; there was too much inevitability in what had to be done and said; this was the sure end, the only end. Yet every now and then grief pulled at him like some child neglected for its stronger brothers.

In the streets there were a lot of people still about; somewhere a clock was striking, but he had neither energy nor interest to see the time; he stumbled on past lighted shop windows where people stopped and gazed. Christmas woollies for the fuller figure. See our Teenage Department. French Empire chairs, Venetian chandeliers. You want the best seats, we have them. Wembley Stadium, Wednesday night.

He turned off the main road into another side-street. His mind went back now and then to the four-day court action, the remarks of his friends at the end. Did any of them know the real joke of it all?

At the verdict Roger had smiled his self-contained smile. He had lost morally. He had even lost financially; but that wouldn't worry him, as *The Gazette* would foot the bill. In all that he cared about he was complete victor of the field. "Debunking is a disease of civilisation," he had said at the club. "Modern man likes to think, I'm no good but neither is my neighbour." What did it matter to him that a few insinuations about a dead man did not stand up? His theory about human nature had been proved completely and triumphantly right.

What a mess there had been behind the scenes! How Roger must have smiled. Joanna had given herself to gone back to him—gone back to him, if her story was right—while he was away, as coolly, as casually. ... Or perhaps not coolly. Roger had only to look at a woman. It was all like an illustrated guide to his belief in the cheapness and vulgarity of life. It made Don's defence of his father look like the posturings of an indignant cuckold in a Vanbrugh play.

Well, maybe one had to be everything once. It was certainly something he'd never expected to be. Maybe it was a useful corrective. He was still too ingenuous. You had to get civilised. "I'm no good, but neither is my neighbour." Lesson one: how to vomit up the over-sweet pap of idealism.

He turned down a narrow street badly lit at either end. A couple were clasped in each other's arms in the shadow of a doorway. The conventional posture. Further along a cat prowled round an ashy dust-bin, and another arched its back on a wall. The same preliminaries to copulation. Why in God's name was one taught to suppose that of two essentially similar acts, the human had the greater significance? Joanna's view, since she had been carefully tutored by Roger even before her marriage, would no doubt be that her husband was a sap to care. Lesson two was to despise your neighbour and despise yourself; from that all knowledge flowed, and all gratification. Snap out of it, Don, dear, why make a fuss? There'll be plenty ready to console you; when the candle is taken away every woman is alike.

He came to the end of the narrow street. He leaned against a wall, out of breath. Cars were passing along a broad street. The red flower of London bloomed in the night sky behind the tall houses; the window squares were like yellow seeds set in irregular patterns. The glow seemed to be the product of some obscene orchid house in which all the vices were crossed and interbred.

"All right, mate?" said a voice. A little man in a long coat was looking up at him.

"I'm—O.K. Thanks."

A cigarette-end showed up a round moustached face, bright eyes. "Had a drop too much?"

"No. It's not that."

"Like me to get you a taxi?"

"No, thanks. Thanks all the same." He went on, surprised he had looked so strange that even a passer-by noticed.

Movement got him no freer of pain. There was no level on which he could see the future. There was no retreat for his mind. The balance of life had been tipped too far.

He stopped again, staring about him. He was in Belgrave Street.

It was raining. He hadn't noticed it until a thin trickle of water slid from his hair inside his collar. This was where Roger lived. It was about eight months since he had been here for a cocktail-party. This no doubt was where Joanna came—when they were not within easy reach of Midhurst. Tuesdays and Fridays for dinner and to spend the night. "Be civilised, old boy; Victoria's been dead more than half a century." What was that Doutelle had said in his closing speech today? Some quotation: "Who shames a scribbler? break one cobweb through, He spins the slight, self-pleasing thread anew; Destroy his fib or sophistry—in vain, The creature's at his dirty work again." Perhaps the real disease of civilisation was civilisation. Men like Roger came to power and influence and fastened their standards on a world too sheep-like and dim-witted to question them. It was time someone questioned Roger.

The house was easy to pick out because the one nest door to it had been bombed and re-built. Don crossed the street and went up the steps. The door was shut and he pressed the bell over the visiting-card. There was a light on in the hall, and almost at once the door opened. It was Roger himself. He stared at Don as if he didn't know him.

Don's nerves bunched in the pit of his stomach. "I've come to talk to you."

"Oh," said Roger. "I was—just going out ... I—could you get me a taxi, Don?" His voice was hoarse.

Don said: "What the hell are you talking about!" He pushed Roger back and followed him into the hall.

In the light he could see that Roger had just been sick. There were stains down the front of his suit, and the smell. Roger said: "I can't talk now. I've just heard Michael's dead."

In the rain, as usual, there were no free taxis. They stood there on the pavement together not speaking. Roger had brought his umbrella but did not open it. The clammy darkness enveloped them both. Don remembered once when he had stood like this with his father when he was home from school during the blitz, and someone stopped a car nearby and said to them: "They've dropped a stick in Baker Street, there's a score of people buried." Then the man had driven off, and one of his tyres was on the rim and he didn't seem even to notice.

Roger raised his umbrella and a taxi stopped. Don said: "I'll come with you."

They got in. It was no distance; they could have walked. Lights and shadows moved constantly across them in the taxi like accelerated seasons of day and night.

Roger said: "I don't understand—what I could have done."

"What?"

"One tries ... I should have been able to prevent it. I—gave him too much rope too young."

Don stared out of the window. For him there was only silence in this moment, neither sympathy nor reproaches were in order. Death was an event, a road-block, that got in your way. For the moment you could only acknowledge it, not feel it or understand.

But Roger was talking. Sentences kept coming through a sort of protective filter that Don's mind had put up. Roger was talking as if he'd forgotten there was any wrong between them. Whatever touched his own life at the moment was what mattered; even the tragedy of Michael had to be related to himself; the personal pronoun kept repeating. It was not until they were near the hospital that Don realised Roger was talking only because he couldn't make do with silence, because he was on the verge of some sort of break-up Thoughts were scurrying in his head like rats in a burning barn; they'd get half out, then be pushed on, all hurried panic.

Someone had left an evening paper in the car. "Jury Retires", said one headline. "Judge Sums Up in Marlowe Case". The taxi came out the wrong way, and it had to make a complete circle of Hyde Bark Corner. Before it stopped Roger was fumbling with the door.

They got out and Don paid. Roger stumbled over the step and a porter caught his arm.

"I've come to see my son."

"Yes, sir, if you'll ask at the desk."

"He's—dead. Shorn is the name."

"Oh, yes, sir. . . . Would you wait here a moment, sir? I believe there's a young lady still here, in the waiting-room."

Don came up behind Roger and saw him for the first time in a good light. Roger smiled. It was a sick sweaty smile that left Don unarmed.

Bennie came down the passage. Her eyes were enormous. Her skirt and stockings were stained with blood and there was a smear of it on her cheek. A nurse was with her.

She said: "I'm glad you've come."

"Where is he?" Roger said.

"If you'll follow me, sir," said the porter.

Don put his arm round Bennie. She laid her face against his coat.

Roger said: "Were you with him all the time?"

"No."

"I went round to see him last week, asked him. . . . I thought he looked ill but. . . ."

"He wouldn't go to hospital before because he was afraid of getting into the hands of the police."

Roger leaned on his umbrella. "The police. . . . He should have told me."

The porter was waiting. Roger seemed unable to move, as if Michael's death was still a premise in his mind and not an acknowledged fact.

"You'll be all right now, miss?" said the nurse.

"Yes, thank you."

The nurse smiled at Don with professional sympathy. "I gave her a cup of tea. She should go home, get those things off, go to bed with a hot-water bottle."

"I'll see she does," said Don.

"No," said Roger. "I'd—like her to come with me if she can—if she will."

"Should she?"

"I'll go, Don. I don't mind."

"Then I'll come too."

They followed the porter down passages to the mortuary chapel. Michael was lying on a trestle table covered by a sheet. The porter stood by the door. Don and Beanie followed Roger about half-way and then let him go up to the body alone.

He pulled the sheet back. Michael looked deader than any man Don had seen before. In the faintly-coloured chapel with its window and its cloths his face had a grey pallor that was luminous. He didn't even look young. Already he was beyond time.

For a moment it was as if they were all three in sudden personal contact with the central reality and paradox of life, at once dignified and derisory, around which all human activity circles and eventually stops short.

Roger stared at his son. Somewhere a dock was chiming again. Roger took out a handkerchief and gently brushed a smear of dirt off Michael's face. Then he smoothed Michael's hair away from his forehead. After a time he put back the sheet and lifted the handkerchief to his own eyes.

Don took Bennie home in a taxi. She was calm enough. Before they left she told Roger and two hospital officials all she knew, and she gave them the money in her bag. In the cab she asked about the libel verdict, whether on the whole he was satisfied. Don said, yes, he was satisfied.

When they got to her flat Pat Wilenski wasn't in, and Don said, "Why don't you come home with me?"

Bennie said, "No, I'd rather stay in my own place. Really."

Then when they got upstairs she suddenly began to shiver. Don went into her bedroom and lit the gas fire and came back to find her in an armchair with her head in her hands trying to keep still. There was no whisky in the house so he gave her gin almost neat. The shivering seemed to stop for a bit, then she began again, like someone with malaria. Don filled a hot-water bottle and put it in her bed. When she still sat there he picked her up and carried her into the bedroom. She sat on the bed and he began to undress her.

When he was unfastening her suspenders she said: "Don, I can't let you——"

"Dear Bennie, don't be a fool."

Somehow be got the sticky frock off. One knee and leg was stained right up to the thigh, but he rubbed her gently with a towel. Her skin gleamed palely as he managed to get her nightdress over her head while she slid out of her girdle. He got her in bed with the bedclothes tucked in round her chin, and she looked at him with enormous eyes and half smiled and tried to stop her teeth from chattering.

He went into Pat's bedroom for aspirin and when she had taken some of these she quieted down a bit. He sat beside the bed and held her hand.

He said: "Relax."

"Uh-huh. D'you want to go?"

"No, of course not."

Silence fell. He could tell by her hand how she was going on. For a rime it would be quiet, and then it would grip his again. The last time he had held her hand was when she was about eleven. It still felt the same.

They had left Roger at the hospital with the casualty officer. After seeing Michael, Roger had pulled himself together. There would be bad moments later, but he had somehow got round the worst moment of all.

Before they left Don was alone with him for a few moments and Roger for the first time seemed to realise exactly who he was. "You—were coming to see me?"

"Yes."

"Was it about Joanna?"

Don shrugged. There wasn't anything to say now.

"Are you ... breaking up?" Roger said.

"Yes."

Roger made movements of the mouth before speaking. His face was ugly with fatigue.

"If you're going to try and destroy her for the sake of your own pride, that's all that's necessary, isn't it, to—to fill in the last square?"

A nurse pushed a trolley between them.

Roger said, speaking almost to himself: "Yes, that about ills in the last square."

The others had come back then. As he sat in Bennie's bedroom Don thought over it again. Was it true, what Roger said? Or if monstrously untrue, was there even a worm of reason? Was he in any way, even in the smallest way, throwing up his marriage because of his pride?

No, not so. His marriage was a write-off before ever Joanna came back tonight. It was over before he even came home from Canada. Perhaps it was lost before it began. Roger and Joanna had been together before he knew them. That sort of link didn't break; it was a trip-wire; an outsider only sprawled in the mud.

"I led Kenny to Michael, Don. That's what I can't forget. I led him there. I——"

"Don't think of it now."

"But if I hadn't gone. ..."

"Thinking of it doesn't do any good, Bennie. You——"

"You see, in essence, it all comes back to me. He was doing it for me. If I had acted differently I could have stopped him, because he wouldn't have had the need. . . ."

There was music in the flat opposite. Someone was having fun. There were men's voices and a woman's high giggle. Don wondered where Joanna was now. She would have left their house, probably be at a hotel. Unless, not knowing of Michael, she had gone straight to Roger. Maybe she would be able to comfort him. 'Roger was the man before we married. I thought I'd got him out of my system. I hadn't. I have now.'

I have now. So she said. I didn't want to go to him. I don't want to go to him. . . . The last square. That fills in the last square.

His hand moved in Bennie's.

"What is it?" she asked.

"I—thought I heard someone come in."

"Pat always whistles."

Time passed. A car stopped opposite and its door was slammed tinnily. Somebody shouted: "Well, if it isn't Oscar and Pam!" Don looked at his watch. Only ten-thirty. Since ten-thirty this morning was a year. He had lived through fevers of pain and anger and murdered love. In Bennie's bedroom stockings were hung on a piece of string by the window; the sleeve of a brightly-coloured blouse showed through a slit in the wardrobe door. French magazines on top of a B.E.A. bag. She too had her day.

Perhaps the commonest failure of human-kind was lack of imagination. How often in two years had he thought of his sister in terms of her own personal life? How often did anyone make the effort? If that was true between him and Joanna, then it was inexcusable. But it could not be true, it wasn't true. It certainly wasn't true.

Bennie said: "Why don't you ring Joanna?"

He started. "What d'you mean?"

"Well, won't she wonder where you are?"

"No. No, it's, all right."

She moved her hand free of his. "Darling, I think you must go."

"Why?"

"Well, in the end, sometime, I've got to face this alone."

"It need not be tonight."

"It's queer," she said. "When I first met Michael it didn't mean much to me. It did to him; but not to me. Now, in a few months. . . . Now even the word 'alone' means something different from what it has ever done before."

Chapter Thirty-Nine

Pat came in at eleven and Don left soon after. It was not very far, and he walked. The fine drizzling rain wet his hair once again, cooled the heat of his face. There was still a fair buzz of traffic. As he turned in by Harrods he realised perhaps for the first time what "alone" was going to mean to him.

Trevor Square was quiet and damp, and the gas lamps flickered over the railings and the parked cars. He went up the steps and let himself in before he saw a light in the bedroom. He stopped in the hall. His heart thumped once, and then he thought, she forgot to switch it off when she left.

Even this typical absent-mindedness struck at him. She would be adding needlessly to his electricity bill for the last time

He went upstairs. Joanna was standing by the bed fastening a small suitcase. Her delicately strong face looked paler than usual; otherwise it might have been any other evening.

She looked at him, jerked her head back to clear her hair from her forehead.

"You've missed your train."

"What train?"

"For Edinburgh."

The concert tomorrow. "Oh God," he said, dropping his hands. "It never entered my head."

"It's too late now. You couldn't get to the station in ten minutes."

"It can't be helped. There'll be an almighty fuss but it can't be helped. . . ." His sensations at finding her here had frozen on finding her here. "I thought you would be gone by now."

"I went. I got a room at the Hyde Park Hotel. Then I came back."

"Why?"

"Don't worry—not for long. I've just put some things in your bag."

"Kind of you," he said coldly.

"Wasn't it? I thought you'd be sure to remember the concert."

"No. . . . Even music takes second place sometimes."

"There's another train at eleven-fifty-five. You've missed your sleeper, but you could get there in time for rehearsal."

"How do you know?"

"I phoned just now."

He stood there trying to weigh up the cool unfriendly look of her, trying to beat his brain into some sort of decision. He felt as if all love and hope and faith had been squandered today and nothing was left but the atheism of staying alive.

He said: "Michael's been killed."

"*Michael*! How?"

He told her in a few sentences.

"Poor Bennie!"

"Yes. That's where I've been."

They talked warily for half a minute.

"I'll go and see her in the morning. . . . Such a pointless—futile thing to happen."

"Most things are."

Another silence.

She checked the other lock of the suitcase. "You've forty minutes to catch your train. I think I've packed everything you need."

Don put a hand down the damp front of his jacket. "You've put in a suit?"

"Yes."

"Thanks."

She moved to go past him. This was the last moment. If he didn't speak now the line didn't go any further. "Joanna, in what way did I most fail you?"

She smiled coldly, wearily. "Darling, I shall think you're being mock-humble, putting it that way round."

"I'm not being mock-humble, I'm trying to rationalise what otherwise makes nonsense of life altogether."

Her eyelids flickered. "You can't rationalise, Don. That's the first mistake. Life isn't rational. At least, mine isn't. Women—don't make patterns—we—we cross the road on impulse, without looking both ways. . . ."

"Yet I *have* failed you," he said. "I suppose I've missed the mark by letting other things sometimes take first place."

She said: "You've missed the mark in one thing only—in expecting too much from me. I warned you of that."

"You did. More than once. I suppose I didn't realise it was on quite such basic points. . . ."

She rubbed her cheek. Feeling was coming back to him. Looking at her face and lips and body so close to him, he knew that he still loved her so much that if he didn't get out of her sight he would hate her again. He went to the suitcase, unclicked it, stared at the things she had packed.

She said: "D'you remember once we were talking, and you asked me if I didn't think your love was equal to the strain of discovering things about me? I said perhaps it would be if you remembered I was your woman, not just your wife."

"What's that intended to mean?"

"Just what it does mean."

He said: "I think we're out of the stage where one can treat morals with a meat axe."

"Maybe that's a pity."

A towel was on the floor and he picked it up, put it on a chair. One of the drawers of the dressing-table was open and he tried to close it. He saw that it was nearly empty. The novel she had been reading this week was on the bedside table, a letter in it as book-mark. The photo he'd intended having framed was gone.

"Don't you want your lipstick?"

"Oh . . . well, if s nearly done."

He had forgotten what he was playing tomorrow, couldn't think. Something of Beethoven, Weber. . . .

"The programme's in the back pocket," she said.

He took it out, stared at it. "Tell me what you mean, Joanna, in plain language. So that a child could understand. I need it that way."

Only her hands showed her nerves: they fluttered up to her hair, pushed it away from her face again. "It's all in what I said before. But what I said before was meant to *explain*, not to excuse."

"If I've failed you, there's no need for excuse."

She said: "You want an honourable woman for your wife, that's it, isn't it? It's not a big thing to ask. Well, I'm not an honourable woman. What more is there to say?"

"A lot, I should have thought." He tried to collect his feelings, see them as if they belonged to someone else. "I'm not interested in 'honourable' women. I'm interested in *you*. You—my marriage has meant so much to me that nothing second best by a degree can possibly do. If you are going to go with another man it's something I can't stomach for a second, not because of honour or high-sounding things but because of the *ordinary* things: sex, possession, jealousy and. . . ." He tailed off. "They don't sound engaging when you list them but that's what they are. If you are going to be like that, this is the end, this moment; we go out of the house and go different ways. . . ." He put the programme back, fumbled the case shut. "But my marriage has meant so much to me—I can only speak for myself, I can't speak for you—that nothing about it ought to be allowed to go by default. Nothing that can be said should be left out for reasons of anger, pride—yours or mine—or false ideas of dignity or prudery or—or giving pain."

A dock chimed. Joanna moistened her lips. "If we talk any more now you'll miss your train."

"Let it go."

"You made me do my job today. Yours—tomorrow—is much more important."

"To hell with—with the train. To hell with my music, if that has in any way been the cause. I'd better have been a navvy."

"Don, let me come with you to the station."

"Answer me, and then we'll see."

"What do you want me to say?"

"Why did you come back tonight?"

"I've told you."

"It isn't true."

She turned, her face suddenly seeming to break up. "No, it isn't true. . . . I'll get the car." She went from the room.

He followed her half-blindly down the stairs. By the time he had taken two mackintoshes out of the cupboard she had started the engine. He threw his case on the back seat and got in at the wheel as she slid over. Her eyes were glassy with tears that didn't come.

They turned out into Knightsbridge. The traffic was sparse and only knotted at the lights. He drove to Hyde Park Corner and up Park Lane. For a time they didn't speak at all. The break in her self-possession had left him suddenly with no escape from feeling again. It was there in his stomach like a raw wound. He was caught up with a sense of self-blame, and also, perhaps illogically, with a sensation of pity and sadness, not alone for the woman sitting beside him but for all that had been lost today: their marriage, Michael's life, Bennie's love, even a little for Roger's twisted hopes. He seemed to see then and understand that the compulsions of life existed as elements too strong for the frail human beings that gave them existence. Like electrical forces they exerted sudden movements of attraction or repulsion, and the men and women in whom they moved were the victims of this force, not its masters. It was a new kind of pain that came to him then, a pain at once of compassion and contrition, as if he could suffer for them all.

They went right along Oxford Street and up Tottenham Court Road. He began to slow down.

"I can't *go*. How can you expect me to? I tell you I *can't* go now."

She said: "You're much better to have done with me. You need someone quite different, able to see things in quite a different way."

"Why did you come back?"

"I'm vain—and temperamental—and even now there's some sort

of—of . . . I can't invent or pretend the—the little excuses. Don't stop."

They turned into Euston Road and drove some way.

She said: "Of course I'm *sorry* it ever happened, but you may say it's easy to be sorry for something that's over. And I'm *sorry, sorry* that I've hurt you. But that wasn't why I came back. I came because . . . well, with you is where I belong. I thought even if this thing is too big between us now we might—well, after a time I thought. . . . You see, Don, I love you. That may sound pretty unbelievable after all the rest you've heard about me today, but it happens to be true."

He stopped the car.

"Turn in here," she said.

"I'm turning round."

"No. I'll come to Edinburgh with you if you like."

"To Edinburgh?"

"Yes."

"That's nonsense."

"It isn't nonsense. We can—talk it out on the train."

"I don't *want* to go!"

"Don, don't you see, if there's to be anything between us at all, that you *must*? That's the first condition."

"What's it to do with us tonight!"

"Everything."

They parked the car, and reluctantly he went up the steps. The station was dark and nearly empty. The clock said ten to twelve. A string of attached wagons piled with tomorrow's newspapers rumbled past them. Two soldiers were sitting asleep on a form. An elderly man in a tweed suit was weaving his way drunkenly in the wake of a porter.

"You can't come," Don said. "You've nothing with you."

"That doesn't matter."

Don didn't speak.

They went towards the booking office. Joanna said: "You'll have to sit up. We'll both have to sit up. We can talk then—if there's any more to say. At least—maybe I can. . . . By morning we shall know. If we still can't see it right then I'll—drop out of the game."

Don went to the window. "I want two tickets to Edinburgh, please." He began to count the notes.

"Single or return, sir?" said the clerk.

Don looked at his wife. A stray breeze was blowing her hair. She looked back at him with glittering embarrassed eyes.

"Return." he said.

THE END

Lightning Source UK Ltd.
Milton Keynes UK
UKHW01f0423080518

322257UK00002B/95/P